"EIRRIEL, LOOK AT ME....

"You must believe me when I tell you no harm will come to you here. The data you have given me will be relayed to our Main Terminal on Hakon. With their help we will find Dianthia. And then I will see you safely home and your people freed from the Blagdenian scum who hold them."

Eirriel gasped. "You would do this for me?"

"Yes." *And for myself*, Aubin added.

"Thank you!" Eirriel cried, her voice filled with an exuberance that warmed Aubin's heart. Her eyes alight with happiness, and a wide smile brightening her face, Eirriel ran to Aubin. Shyly, she leaned into him and planted a small kiss on his lean cheek. "Thank you."

Aubin's eyes darkened at the contact. Without thinking, he reached out and pulled her close. Laughter fled as she felt his arms close about her. Raising her face to his, she felt his lips brush hers. At his touch, a warmth coursed through her body and when he again brought his mouth to hers, she parted her lips and met his rising passion with her own.

Other *Leisure* books by Patricia Roenbeck:
GOLDEN CONQUEST

Golden Temptress

PATRICIA ROENBECK

LOVE SPELL NEW YORK CITY

LOVE SPELL®
May 1997
Published by

Dorchester Publishing Co., Inc.
276 Fifth Avenue
New York, NY 10001

The name "Love Spell" and its logo are trademarks of Dorchester Publishing Co., Inc.

Printed in the United States of America.

Chapter One

The massive estalon snorted and strained anxiously at his bit. Leaning forward, his rider ran her hand down his long sinewy neck.

"Patience, Onyx," Eirriel said softly. "Our time is almost at hand." In response the reins grew slack, the gait smooth. "That's it, my handsome one. Hold back just a little longer."

"Just a little longer! Patience!" Eirriel's green eyes glittered dangerously. How she hated those words! Words that had reached her ears too often in the last weeks. And for what? More than two months had passed since the Oldens' cryptic warning and nothing had happened. *Well, let them continue their senseless vigil*, she thought rebelliously. *I, for one, have waited long enough!*

"Timos!" she cried suddenly, startling her unsuspecting companion. "I think we're being followed."

With an oath Timos reined in his horse. "Where?"

"There. Beyond the bluff."

"Stay where you are!" Timos yelled over his shoulder as he spurred his horse toward the bluff. "I'll be back soon."

Stay indeed! Eirriel's eyes sparkled mischieviously. That

wasn't exactly what she had in mind. Dismounting, she drew the reins over the estalon's head and dropped them carelessly to the ground. Then laughing with anticipation, Eirriel leaped onto Onyx's back.

"Now, Onyx! Now!"

Onyx threw back his head, shook his long lustrious mane and lunged forward. No longer restrained, his strong muscular legs tore at the ground as he galloped faster and faster. With a final burst of speed, he spread his great blue-black wings and leaped swiftly into the calm pink sky of Dianthia.

Eyes glimmering like green jewels, Eirriel grasped Onyx's mane in one hand and reached up to pull the hark-bone clasp from her hair. A quick shake of her head and her waist-length tresses tumbled free to be captured by the wind and stream like a golden banner behind her. Closing her eyes, she breathed deeply, the brisk fresh fragrance of the air filling her lungs refreshing her. How she loved it up there— the beauty of the view; the cool crisp bite of the wind; the peaceful solitude; and, most of all, the feeling of total freedom she found nowhere else.

Unaware of Eirriel's deception, Timos scanned the horizon for some sign of their unwanted visitors. Seeing none, he swung his horse around and tore down the hill. Eirriel would have to show him exactly where she had seen the riders. Reaching the bottom of the slope, Timos drew Ertan to an abrupt halt.

"Eirriel!"

His frustrated shout echoed across the meadow. Where did the little minx go off to? A golden glimmer caught his eye and he groaned. It couldn't be! But even as the denial formed in his mind, he bent and retrieved Onyx's castoff reins from the thick purple grass. Damn it! She couldn't be trusted! The minute his back was turned she and that unruly estalon of hers were into some kind of mischief. His eyes shot open and his face paled. Her estalon. No. She wouldn't. Quickly, he scanned the sky. Yes, he nodded bleakly. She would and she had.

"That deceitful little . . . 'Someone is following us,'" he muttered, shaking his head in disgust. She knew he'd never have allowed her to take to the sky. Not now. Not when the threat of danger was so real.

Scowling, his blue eyes dark with anger, he looked skyward. Would she never do as she was told? He laughed in answer, the bittersweet sound evidence of his warring emotions. No, she would not. If she did, she would not be the Eirriel he loved. And, he added with resignation, if he didn't go up after her, she'd stay there for hours. He began to give his steed the command to follow her but stopped with a snort of self-contempt. Go after her! How? Ertan was no estalon.

Damn! Would he never learn? How well she had planned this little exploit, he thought sardonically, telling him that Onyx's mate was sick.

He could still see her staring up at him, all innocence and concern, explaining Scytiella's illness, then adding sweetly that he could either come with her or stay at home, the choice was his. She was going riding.

"Sick indeed," he growled. "Wait until I get my hands on her . . ."

The threat hanging in the air, Timos spurred his much begrudged mount into a gallop and followed Eirriel as best he could.

Increduously Eirriel watched Timos's valiant struggle to keep up with them. Did he forget that Onyx on land was unbeatable and in the air . . .Why it was unthinkable that he even try! She leaned forward and fondly stroked Onyx's neck, remembering her fifth life celebration.

Although her father had promised her something special, she had never expected it to be one of the rare winged horses. Unaware that when the estalon reached full maturity his color would deepen to a dark blue-black, Eirriel had named the glossy black creature Onyx. From the first, the two were constant companions, and a strong emotional bond developed between the young estalon and his mistress, which now, fifteen years later, was unbreakable.

Her reminiscing ended, Eirriel's bubbling laughter floated downward as she spied Timos wildly flailing his arms.

"Poor Timos, he looks upset. I'm afraid it's time we ended our ride," she said to Onyx regretfully.

Needing no more of a command than those softly spoken words, the graceful purebred carried his mistress swiftly to the ground and landed gently on the hill just in front of Timos. Eirriel slipped from Onyx's back and stood meekly before the irate Olden.

Eyes dark with fury, an angry frown marring his handsome face, Timos railed at her. "So you finally decided to come down." He grabbed her shoulders firmly. "What imp of mischief possessed you to fly Onyx? You've been warned of the danger!"

She pulled away from him. "Danger," she scoffed. "What danger? Where are your so-called invaders?"

"They are there."

Timos looked so solemm that Eirriel couldn't resist the urge to tease him. "Tsch! So cross. Could it be that you're jealous because I dared what you would not?"

His scowl deepened. "This is no laughing matter, Eirriel. Your fun was not lightly forbidden." His usual light tone was undermined by a desperate urgency as he added, "The danger is greater than you were told."

Eirriel arched her brow in question. "Tell me, Timos. Who is it who causes the Oldens such fear?" One look at his stern visage and Eirriel knew she could expect no answer, nor did she receive one. Instead Timos extracted her promise to remain grounded, threatening to inform her father if she did not.

At his words, the image of Alaric sprang to her mind and she groaned. When would she learn to think before she acted? She winced. As Primary Olden her father had enough burdens without her rash and reckless behavior adding to them. She met Timos's angry glare with large pleading eyes.

"You won't tell Father this time, will you, Timos? He'll keep me from Onyx."

"It would be no more than you deserve," he rebuked sternly. But looking into her brillant eyes, Timos knew he would keep silent. "Do I ever do what I know to be right where you are concerned?" he muttered. "No, I won't tell."

Eirriel rewarded him with a dazzling smile. "Thank you, Timos." She leaned over and kissed him on his smooth cheek. "I'm sorry I deceived you, but I knew you'd never let me fly."

"You're right about that," he muttered.

"But it was so much fun," she said wistfully. "And it has been so long."

Timos glanced at her warily, grimly realizing that she'd do it again without a moment's hesitation. Making a mental note to see that that opportunity never arose, he added gruffly, "It is done and cannot be changed. Now let's forget it."

Bristling under his harsh tone Eirriel prepared a scathing retort then thought better of it. The day was much too glorious to be wasted arguing. Smiling sweetly, she nodded her agreement then brushed past him. An impish spark lit her eyes.

"I'll race you to the bottom," she threw over her shoulder.

With a hearty chuckle, Timos answered her challenge. His long legs carried him to the base of the gently sloping hill before Eirriel had even covered half the distance. Waiting patiently, Timos took advantage of his easy victory and studied Eirriel's graceful form.

The ankle-length black skirt clenched tightly in her hands, Eirriel was innocently unaware that much of her long slender legs were revealed to his eager gaze. His heart pounded fiercely in anticipation as the low off-the-shoulder neckline of her full-sleeved blouse threatened to fall even lower with every step she took.

By the gods, she was a beauty! he thought with pride. And she was his. Or would be, he ammended confidently, just as soon as he talked with Alaric. Timos was startled from his thoughts as Eirriel, tears of laughter streaming from her eyes, stumbled down the last few feet of the hill and collapsed at his feet. He reached down and pulled her to her feet. Catching her up in his arms, he spun her around. Eirriel giggled as she pushed against his shoulders in a halfhearted attempt to free herself.

"Put me down," she demanded in what she hoped was her most commanding voice.

"No. I won and you are my prize," Timos replied with a forced casualness. Feeling the rapid beating of her heart as he clutched her tightly to his chest and inhaling her fresh earthy fragrance, his eyes darkened. "And a more enchanting prize I have never seen," he said huskily.

Laughing gaily, she reprimanded him lightly. "Don't tease. Enchanting indeed. Next you'll be saying I've bewitched you and you can't live without me. As for your prize, I'm afraid this will have to do." She kissed his forehead fondly. "Now won't you please put me down?"

Timos set her on her feet, his brow creasing. Was she so insensitive that she could laugh at his feelings or was it that she was truly unaware of her beauty and the affect it had on him? Did she have no idea how strongly he felt about her? That he loved her? Before he could ponder further, Eirriel was pulling on his arm and telling him that she needed to rest and perhaps a quiet spot could be found nearby.

Timos's good humor quickly returned under Eirriel's lighthearted chatter. Hand in hand, they walked leisurely, laughing and talking, their two mounts following slowly behind. Reaching a small secluded pond, they readily agreed that it was the perfect spot.

Tall czima trees had long since interlocked, their sturdy branches forming a natural shelter. The glow from Dianthia's dual suns slowly filtered through, creating a warm lazy atmophere. A cooling breeze, heavy with the scent of rhea berries, gently rustled the long deep purple leaves of the willowy lova trees.

With a sigh of pleasure, Eirriel dropped to the spongy grass and dangled her feet in the cool pink water. Lying on her back, she closed her eyes and listened to the hushed melodies of the tiny zelma birds. Timos joined her, his deep blue eyes greedily drinking in the exquisite beauty of the female lying next to him. Her thick hair had fallen around her like a silken pillow, revealing the flawless complexion of her oval face. Long lush lashes resembled a fan covering her large green eyes. Eyes unlike any he had ever seen—their coloring unique, their depths penetrating. Her full sensuous mouth, drawn up in a contented half-smile, made him ache to kiss it, and the rise and fall of her well-rounded breasts caused him to groan silently.

"Eirriel, listen to me." His carefree voice sounded

strained. "You said before that I teased you. I did not then, and I do not now. In the two years I've been away you have turned into a very beautiful young woman. You were an adorable, impestuous child when I left to study with the Oldens. You have grown much in mind and body. Too beautiful! Soon you will be of age and your father will allow many to pay court to you."

A hint of urgency crept into his voice. "With your passionate nature and a body that already cries out for love you would be an easy prey for those who would do you harm. In your innocence you would not understand. Let me be the one to protect you, to teach you. Let me love you. Tomorrow, I will go to your father and ask his permission to take you as my mate."

Timos's impassioned plea brought an embarrassed flush to Eirriel's face. Looking into his intense eyes, she experienced none of the joy she knew would have touched the heart of any other maiden in Edlyn. His fine brown hair, fair delicate features, and tall slim physique made him one of the handsomest men in Edlyn, if not all of Kinara.

Forced by the tragic deaths of his parents to devote all of his spare time to his land, Timos was the owner of the richest, largest acreage on Kinara. Wealth aside, his future had been ensured two years earlier when, at the uncommonly early life span of twenty-four, the Oldens had called for him to begin his studies with them. And yet Eirriel did not want him.

She knew whatever she said would hurt him, and she could only hope he would understand someday.

"Dear, Timos," she said softly. "I treasure your companionship. Our times together are always times of joy for me. We have many shared interests and ideals, but I could never be your mate."

"But why?" demanded a shocked Timos. Never had he considered her turning down his suit. "You've said you love me often enough."

"And I do. But I love you as a friend, as the brother I never had. I thought you felt the same as I, that the special feelings we have for each other are those of close friends. Nothing more."

"You don't know what you are saying! You can't," he said desperately. "You love me as a friend you say. I loved you that way. I still do. But my love has evolved. If you give yourself time, I know your love will change as mine did. You will come to love me as deeply as I love you."

Sitting up, Eirriel looked at him regretfully. "It can never be as you wish, Timos. All I can offer you is my friendship."

Timos studied the face of the woman he loved and for the first time let himself see the truth. A truth that ripped through his heart to drive the light from his soul.

"How, Eirriel? How can I be satisfied with friendship? I love you! I've always loved you!"

His tortured whisper brought tears to Eirriel's eyes as she watched Timos stand and walk away. Frantically, she searched for a way to ease the pain she had unwittingly inflicted on him, but could find none.

Slowly, Eirriel got to her feet and crossed to Timos's side. He flinched when she touched his shoulder and quickly withdrew her hand.

"I've hurt you. I . . . I'm sorry. I never meant for that to happen."

"The suns have almost set, Eirriel," Timos said coldly. "Your father will be waiting. Tell him . . . tell him I need some time alone. I'll return when I can."

"Timos, please . . ."

Eirriel was stunned by the unusual moistness in his eyes and the raspy huskiness in his voice when he turned to her.

"Enough, Eirriel. If you care for me at all, say no more. Just go."

Knowing her presence would only exacerbate his pain, Eirriel nodded and slowly walked away. Onyx, feasting contentedly on the sweet grass, raised his head as his mistress approached. He trotted to her side and gently nuzzled her face. He whinnied softly as she reached up and briefly stroked his long snout.

She looked back at Timos before she mounted. He was as before. Sighing dejectedly, she agilely sprang to Onyx's back. Not waiting for her command, the estalon broke into a gallop.

Timos looked up as the estalon spread his wings and

swiftly climbed into the rapidly darkening sky. He experienced a twinge of worry at the thought of her flying. Onyx's dark shape would be easily silhouetted against Dianthia's four moons, but as he looked up his fears were quickly allayed. Thick murky clouds obscured the sky. She would be safe.

Would he be all right? Eirriel wondered as she looked down on Timos's dwindling form. If the invaders were real as the Oldens claimed. . . . No, she shook her head. She hadn't believed the Oldens before, she would not start now just because Timos was alone. She looked down again but could not see him. How long would he stay away? Before she could answer, Onyx's soft whinny told Eirriel she was home.

She dismounted. Onyx nudged her gently, then trotted off to the stables.

Eirriel climbed through the casement and dropped softly onto the lush mauve floor covering. Walking stealthily to the door, she felt for the bolt and slid it silently into place. Moving her hand down the wall, she touched a switch and the chamber was illuminated with a muted pink glow.

In the revealing light it was easy to see that the large chamber was actually divided into two smaller sections. A partial wall to the left of the door allowed Eirriel privacy while using the cleanser. Just beyond the cleansing area was a large floor-to-ceiling reflector and a dressing table. Against the wall across from the door was a massive sleeper, surrounded by sheer mauve coverings. These coverings, draping from intricately carved golden ceiling bars, were raised during the day and lowered at night to form a protective screening. To the right of the door an enormous wooden wardrobe was filled to bursting with every article of clothing a young woman could desire.

Eirriel stepped into the cleansing area and turned on the water, silently thanking her father for constructing the private family chambers out of soundproof sonise stone. Eagerly, she shed her clothes and stepped into the hot soothing water. She leaned back and closed her eyes.

What would she say to her father when he learned she came back alone and why? Would he understand that she had no choice? That she could not take Timos as her mate?

Would Timos ever forgive her?

Exhausted from the intense emotional strain, Eirriel dragged herself from the cleanser and to the sleeper. A quick tug on the long cord that dangled from the ceiling dropped the protective screening into place. Snuggling under the cool silky quilting, Eirriel drifted off to sleep, dreading the morning, never suspecting for a moment there would be little need for explanations.

It was late the next day when Eirriel finally woke, refreshed from her dreamless slumber. Noting the lateness of the hour, she wondered why she had not been awakened. Moriah should have been bustling about by now, chiding her for oversleeping. Smiling to herself, Eirriel thought of how she had come to love Moriah, turning to her as she would have turned to Sidra had she lived.

Sidra, Eirriel's beautiful blonde-haired, green-eyed mother, had succumbed to the Zxyon plague shortly after Eirriel's birth. Left alone to handle his grief as well as his infant daughter, Alaric soon despaired. When one of the Oldens told him of Moriah, a village woman who had lost both her mate and infant sons to the last plague, Alaric had immediately sought her out. Moriah fell in love with the little Eirriel at first sight, and Alaric had never once regretted taking Moriah in.

Eirriel took another look at the suns and sighed. She dreaded the upcoming conversation with her father because she knew he was hoping she and Timos would find the love he'd had with his beloved Sidra and would be greatly disappointed to learn that was not to be. Sighing again, she sat up and pulled the covers back. Perhaps her father wouldn't be as surprised as she thought. Well, there was only one way to find out.

Her mind made up, Eirriel dressed quickly and went in search of her father.

Deep laughter drifted from the front of the dwelling. Eirriel followed the sound, stopping immediately outside her father's conference chamber. Puzzled by the unnaturally boisterous noises coming from behind the closed door, she paused before entering. Listening intently, she tried to isolate a familiar sound from the resonant din, but failed.

Shrugging off her concern to an overworked imagination, Eirriel opened the heavy door.

"Father, please excuse the interruption, but I must—" The words caught in her throat and all color drained from Eirriel's face. The chamber was filled with fierce-looking strangers, their small pinched faces registering shock at her sudden appearance.

"Well, now, what have we here, Commodore?" a voice sneered in a dialect Eirriel did not recognize. "Entertainment already?"

Drawn by his mocking tone, Eirriel was appalled at the raw hatred so evident on his face.

If Eirriel was appalled, the commodore was not. Rage burned through him as he cursed the incompetence of his staff, an incompetence that had left him open to Lieutenant Harlan's snide comments. The blundering fool of a wyman who reported the structure secure would forfeit his life— and not pleasantly! Secure! he fumed. Secure enough that a mere female obtained access to their parley without the least bit of interference! Catching Lieutenant Harlan's insolent smirk and damning stare, the commodore bristled. Soon, very soon, Harlan would push him too far. Then he would forget that Harlan was his sister's son.

His thoughts were interrupted by Eirriel's cold demanding voice. "Who are you? What are you doing here? What do you want?"

The stranger sitting behind her father's desk rose, dwarfing most of those around him. Eirriel stared at him, overwhelmed by his dark handsomeness so unlike the usual pale Dianthian coloring. As he walked toward her, Eirriel again noticed a difference. Tradition demanded that all men wear long, wide-sleeved, full caftans, yet this man was garbed in a very modified version of the ridding caftan. The full sleeves ended snugly around his wrists and the black shirt tapered in at the waist and was joined by close fitting material that covered his long legs. A quick glance showed her that the others were dressed the same, with the exception of the knee-length silver cape that draped from his shoulders.

With measured strides he crossed the chamber and stood

before Eirriel. After a short bow, he faced her, his slanted eyes with their chilling black color boring into her.

"Allow me to introduce myself. I am Kedar, Commodore of the Blagdenian Invasion Force." His voice, reeking of arrogance, spoke the Dianthian tongue as well as any native. "Alaric is, shall we say, otherwise occupied. I am here because this structure, pardon me, dwelling is now my command station and we want, well, we want only what is ours by right of conquest. I believe that answers all your questions. Now if you please," he motioned to an empty chair near the large desk. Without waiting for an answer, Kedar strode back across the chamber and resumed his seat.

Eirriel blanched as the meaning of the stranger's words became obvious. Invasion force! The very sound of those words sent waves of apprehension coursing through her. How had this happened? When? Where were her father and Moriah? Were they hurt when they resisted the attack or did they follow their teachings and fight with words rather than weapons?

"My dear," the icy steel of his voice jerked Eirriel's thoughts back to the immediate problem, "I said come in and sit down."

Eirriel stood defiantly in the doorway, knowing that if she obeyed him, she would forfeit any hope of escape. And escape she must. Someone had to be free if there was to be any hope for her people. She would show these strangers that all Dianthians were not tamed animals!

With a strong quick movement she slipped out the door and jerked it shut. She grabbed one of the chairs lining the long hallway, wedged it under the handle and bolted down the corridor to the main door. She knew if she could only make it to the stable, to Onyx, she would be free. Reaching the door without any interference, she pulled it open and stuck her head out. Seeing the yard empty, she ran with all the speed her shaky legs would allow toward the open stable door. With a burst of speed, Eirriel dashed in, not seeing the dark hulking shape that loomed in the darkness until it was too late. She bounced back, the force of the collision slamming her against the wall. White-hot pain burst inside her head, robbing her of her breath and her strength.

"No!" she gasped as blackness descended and she crumpled to the ground unconscious.

Chapter Two

In Alaric's dwelling the Blagdenians sat stunned. The other captives had offered no defense and they had hardly expected defiance from a lone female.

"Dolts! Fools!" Kedar yelled. "Don't just sit there, go after her!"

Seeing the puzzled looks on all except Lieutenant Harlan's face, Kedar swore to himself then repeated the words in the coarse, guttural words of the Blagdenian language. In unison, as if someone pushed a button releasing them, they sprang from their chairs and rushed to the door.

"It's barred, Commodore," said one of the wyman stating the obvious.

"Fools! Of course it is. Did you expect otherwise?" Seeing their befuddled stares, he roared in frustration, "Must I tell you everything? Break it down!"

Two of the protectors, unusually large wymen bred especially for the protection force, threw their huge shoulders against the door, splintering it on their second try.

"Split up. Lieutenant Harlan, take half the men and search this structure. The rest of you come with me," Kedar ordered. "Keep your sonulators on low. I want her alive."

Leading his group outside, Kedar halted. "Smol, search the foregrounds. Zorcan, the animal structure. Report back to me in fifteen minutes. I'll be searching the rear grounds. Now move it!"

Zorcan ran swiftly to the animal structure and was greeted with a surprise. Menox, the protector assigned to the foregrounds, was walking toward him, carrying the crumpled form of the female in his huge arms.

"Is she alive?" he called out.

"I think so. She came dashing through the threshold as I was leaving. She flew back and hit her head on the wall."

Zorcan looked up at the muscular giant. "You better hope she's all right. Kedar wants her alive. I think he has plans for her." The two snickered. "I'd better call the commodore and let him know we found his new pet." He pressed a knob on his belt. "Commodore, this is Zorcan."

"Did you find her?"

"Yes, sir. She appears to be unconscious, but otherwise unharmed."

"Good. Bring her back to the parley quarters. I'll meet you there."

"Right away, sir." Zorcan motioned Menox to follow. "Put her on the couch," he directed as they entered the quarters. "And for Sharzyx's sake, be careful with her!"

A dour-looking wyman strode into the quarters. Extending his left arm upward in a salute, he demanded to see Kedar. When Zorcan informed him that the commodore was on his way, the wyman handed Zorcan a report.

"When he arrives, see to it that he reads this immediately. It is a directive from the prime station on Blagden." The wyman saluted and left.

Zorcan glanced quickly over the message and smirked. When Kedar entered, he saluted and handed him the directive.

"This just came in, Commodore," he said gruffly, carefully concealing his gloating thoughts.

Kedar scanned the paper, crumpled it and threw it to the floor, his fierce face frowning. Zorcan, anxious to flee his ill-tempered commodore, quickly gave his report. With a curt nod, Kedar dismissed them. "That's all for now. Find

Lieutenant Harlan and fill him in. He'll have further orders for you."

The two wymen saluted and left, halting in their tracks as Kedar bellowed, "Close the door behind you!" Menox quickly ran back and pulled it shut.

"He's sure in a foul mood," Menox remarked. "I would have thought he'd be pleased with the swift victory."

"Normally he would be, but, as I said, our commodore had plans for the female. Plans that would have made her his personal slave, if he followed his usual method of operations, that is."

Menox raised his thick, dark eyebrows questioningly.

"That directive was from our great leader, Tozgor, himself. It seems that Tozgor has taken a special interest in this campaign. Interest in what he can drain from this small world, that is. Our good leader is demanding prompt payment of an unusually large and very specific tribute. If Kedar wishes to continue as Supreme Commander of this wretched little world, though Sharzyx only knows why, he must immediately launch a ship filled with the rarest ores, the most priceless jewels and—"

"Wait, let me guess," Menox interrupted. "With the loveliest females," he finished with a knowing smirk.

"Yes, and unless I miss my guess, Kedar will try and cheat our noble leader out of a certain young female."

"He would sample the goods first, eh?" Menox said, nudging Zorcan roughly in the ribs.

Their grating laughter echoed throughout the structure as they went in search of Lieutenant Harlan.

Kedar walked slowly to where the unconscious Eirriel lay. He gazed down on her, his hard, black eyes glinting with pleasure, and silently compared her to the female waiting faithfully for his return to Blagden. She was the complete antithesis of Tova. The Dianthian was fair-skinned, Tova dark. Her thick curly, golden hair tumbled haphazardly to her waist while Tova's thin, straight, black hair was, as with all Blagdenian females, cut close to the scalp and combed to a point at her neck and forehead. This one was tall, slender, and comely; Tova was short, thin, and flat.

Eirriel moaned, her lashes fluttering as she raised her hand to her head, her face etched with pain.

"Alaric?" she asked groggily, her blurred eyes staring at the shadowy bulk standing over her. She closed her eyes and tried to remember, tried to understand why her head hurt so much. She felt two strong arms under her then lift her easily from the couch.

"Timos, is that you?" she mumbled.

Kedar said nothing as he easily carried her to the rear chamber he had decided, by the soothing warmth of its decor, belonged to her. He laid her carefully on the sleeper, gently removed her bulky outer garment, then pulled the silky covering over her. After reassuring himself that she was as comfortable as possible, he quietly left the chamber.

"Wyman, inform the piecer that his presence is requested at once."

Saluting, the wyman left. He returned shortly to inform Kedar that the piecer was on his way.

"Have him meet me in the Dianthian's quarters." With a nod of dismissal, Kedar returned to Eirriel. He pulled a chair over to the sleeper and sat down. How delicious she looked, he thought as he leered down at her. Impatient to sample his newly acquired morsel, he added, she must wake soon!

"Where is that blasted piecer?" Bellowing for the wyman, he stormed to the door. Jerking it open, Kedar found himself face to face with a very startled piecer.

"You . . . you wanted to see me, Commodore?" the small, thin man asked nervously.

"The female hit her head and has been unconscious for quite some time. See to her!"

Walking to the sleeper, the piecer stared down at his intended patient. "But she's a Dianthian!"

"What else would she be, fool? Unless . . ." Kedar looked at him slyly. "Unless you brought someone with you on this mission and neglected to inform me."

The piecer blanched. "I didn't! I wouldn't!"

Kedar shook his head as he saw the piecer quail. Would he never be assigned men with backbone? he thought in disgust. But then again, puppets always were spineless. "No,

I thought not. Now if you've no other brilliant observations, I would like to continue. This one is to be part of the tribute that leaves on the next ship to Blagden. She is meant for our noble leader. Would you have me send him damaged goods?"

"No, but—"

"As I thought. Then see to her."

"That's impossible!" Realizing that he had just said no to Kedar, of all people, the petrified Blagdenian hastened to explain. "I know nothing of their functions. I haven't even begun testing the sample prisoners. I may do her harm in my ignorance."

"She must be well!" Kedar roared, his black eyes gleaming with cold fury.

"But—but I can do nothing! It is as I explained, I—"

"Bah! Enough of your explanations! I want her well! If you can offer her no help, then remove your useless self from my presence!"

"I—I do have a suggestion."

Kedar arched his brow in mock surprise. "Really?"

"These Dianthians, they must get injured or fall ill at some time. Even these barbarians must have their own piecer. Call him."

With a wave of his hand, Kedar dismissed the bumbling piecer, and bellowed for the wyman.

"Yes, sir?"

"Bring the Dianthian piecer to me at once!"

"A Dianthian piecer?" the young wyman looked startled, unaware that he gave voice to his confusion. "But why?"

"Are you questioning my orders?"

"Yes, sir . . . I mean no, sir! I mean right away, sir!" Turning on his heels, the wyman tore down the hall.

"Fools! I am beset by stammering, ignorant fools!" Kedar swore under his breath. "And as for you," he said, turning his thought once again to his beautiful captive. "Tribute indeed. I have no intentions of giving you to my illustrious leader. With all the other tidbits he is to receive, he'll never miss one. No, my sweet. You aren't going anywhere. You are mine!"

In no time at all, the wyman returned, ushering a very

reluctant Dianthian before him.

"I was brought here against my will!" the tall, slender man objected vehemently. "I will not treat a Blagdenian!"

"I assure you piecer," Kedar sneered, once again reverting to the Dianthian tongue. "I—"

"I am a healer, not a . . . a piecer!" He spoke the word as if it were a loathsome disease that could be caught merely by saying it. "I do not . . ." The words caught in his throat as he noticed Kedar's icy stare.

"Piecer, healer, whatever you call yourself. You would be wise not to interrupt me again." The deadly calm in Kedar's voice implied that no further argument would be tolerated. "Now, as I was saying, piecer, pardon me, *healer*, given the choice I would not trust you with the lowliest member of my force. You are such a backward race that whatever pittling amount of knowledge you possess would more than likely hinder not help. But since my piecer is unfamiliar with the ah . . . illness, I find I have little choice but to rely on your barbaric skills."

Kedar paused, smiling to himself. He loved toying with these simple-minded idiots. They were so trusting, so easily misled. The cretin actually believed that he was being ordered to treat one of his men! Kedar allowed the Dianthian to work himself up into an honorable rage, then stepped away from the sleeper.

"Here is your patient," he said quietly, anticipating the Dianthian's reaction with relish. And he was not disappointed.

"Eirriel!" The healer gave a small cry of despair and his regal bearing melted before Kedar's watchful eyes as the Dianthian recognized her. How could this be? he thought desperately. Alaric had told them Eirriel was with Timos when the invasion started. If she was a prisoner, then they had captured Timos as well. He would never have let them touch her, not while he lived. The healer blanched. Imprisoned or dead, it was all the same. No one was left to lead the few who would fight. All hope was gone. They were truly defeated.

"How did she get here?" he asked hoarsely. "What happened to—" The healer caught himself before he mentioned Timos by name. If, by some miracle, he were alive and free, his name might mean questions and a search. ". . . to her?"

"She blundered into our meeting earlier and met with a little surprise." Maliciously Kedar elaborated on Tozgor's demands, deliberately neglecting to mention his own plan.

"Tribute!" the Dianthian exclaimed, all manner of defeat vanquished by the shocking information. "You overrun our lands, deny us our freedom and now you would have tribute? You may steal our ores, our jewels. But our women?" Blue fire danced in his eyes as he ground out fiercely, "Never!"

"Never?" Kedar repeated smoothly. "Oh, I think it will be much sooner than never. Unless, of course, you plan to stop me."

The healer gritted his teeth in frustrated rage. The women were doomed and he was powerless to prevent it. His eyes flickered briefly to Eirriel. But he could save one of them! Defiantly he stared at Kedar. "This is one maiden who will not fall into your hands. I will not help you."

"She will die," Kedar threatened.

"Better that than be owned and debauched by your kind."

"I've had enough of the lot of you!" Kedar roared. "You are a race of mad cowards. Every time your precious honor is offended you choose the easy way out, death, rather than fight."

"To you, we are cowards. To us, we are the braver of our two people. Tell me, Commodore, which is the more courageous. To willingly sacrifice for one's ideals that which is most precious of all, life, or to direct a battle safe inside a warship?"

Kedar bristled. "Why you! I've no time or patience to listen to your trite teachings on your ridiculous Dianthian edicts. I repeat. Will you help her?"

"I repeat also. No, I will not," the healer answered with quiet dignity. "It would be better for her to die blissfully unaware of your designs than to wake and find herself at the mercy of you or your depraved leader. As for myself, I would rather die than render any aid to you in your foul plans."

"Wyman, you heard his request. Take him outside and fulfill it," Kedar said between clenched teeth, his voice edged with steel.

The healer gave Kedar a short, cursory bow and walked from the chamber, his proud demeanor and haughty expression conveying his contempt more eloquently than words ever could.

Kedar stormed around his chamber blinded by rage. Safe inside a warship! That ignorant buffoon! Did he think all there was to commanding an invasion force was the simple issuing of orders? Not all races had given up the way these cowards had. Many times the conquests had lasted years. But what did the Dianthians know of courage? He knew their kind, had met them often enough. They did nothing more than tend their rylans and hold numerous meetings in which they defined the senseless meaning of morality. They were a faint-hearted breed without the stamina to wait out a long seige.

Eirriel moaned softly, but it was enough to draw Kedar's attention. Walking to the sleeper, he marveled at the difference between her and the other Dianthians. Not just in her coloring, but her spirit. Perhaps that was what was so compelling about her. He had only seen her for a few moments before she had fled from her father's chamber, but as she stood there petrified, yet determined not to show it, there had been a vitality, a passion for life, for freedom that seemed to radiate through her. He had fully expected her to react in some manner to the things he had said. And she had for she was of that certain breed of humanity who never passively accepted fate.

"Timos, is that you?" Eirriel asked the dark unfocused figure bending over her.

Kedar's eyes narrowed. Who was this Timos she kept mentioning? Her lover, perhaps? No matter, he'd find out in time and then he'd see that the man was no longer around to plague her thoughts.

Timos? No, even with her mind groggy she knew it wasn't Timos. It couldn't be. Timos was some place safe. He hadn't come back with her. She'd upset him, she remembered painfully. Then she remembered more and thought he might thank her for keeping him away, if she ever saw him again. But who was it?

"Who are you? Where am I?" Slowly her eyes focused and she took in her surroundings and the shape above her. "You!" The fierceness in her voice matched the hatred on her face. "What are you doing in my private chambers? Get out at once!"

"Surely you remember now, my dear? I explained earlier. This dwelling is my station. These chambers mine as well. All Dianthians have been removed and sheltered elsewhere."

Dianthians removed and sheltered elsewhere? Her father would not allow. . . . Eirriel sat up suddenly. "My father!" She closed her eyes against the dizziness brought on by the sudden movement. "Where is he?"

Kedar watched Eirriel fight the weakness he knew she was experiencing and again felt an admiration for her strength of will.

"What have you done to him?"

"I have done nothing to him." Yet, he added to himself. "He is merely . . . waiting with the others."

"If you'll show me where that is, I'll join him. I have no desire to remain in Bla . . . Blag . . ."

"Blagdenian," Kedar supplied helpfully.

"*Your* chambers!" she snapped, refusing his help.

Eirriel rose from the sleeper, then gasped when she realized she wore only her abbreviated undergown. Spying her garment on the floor, she stooped to retrieve it. The moment she straightened, the chamber started to spin. Her hands flailed the air for something to grasp as her knees buckled.

Kedar caught her before she touched the floor. With one smooth movement, he lifted her and placed her gently back on the sleeper.

"You've been unconscious for several hours. You can hardly expect to stand and walk just like that. These things take time. I'm afraid you'll be confined to this chamber until your strength returns." Seeing her glance at her garment, Kedar answered the unspoken question. "I removed your gown before I placed you on the sleeper." He paused, giving her a long, lingering look. "And I must say, I enjoyed the task immensely. Such lovely legs."

A bright stain appeared on her pale cheeks. The thought of his dark hands touching her made her shudder in revulsion. "How dare you!" she demanded in righteous indignation.

"I dare, my sweet, because I am commodore here. I dare because, as such, I own everything on this miserable little world. Everything! You'd do best to remember that," he warned.

"Not everything!" she retorted, her green eyes blazing defiantly.

"Oh, but I do," he said quietly.

"No, you don't. You can never truly own people. And if we're such a 'miserable, little world,' why do you bother with us at all?"

"I have my reasons, my dear. Reasons you needn't concern yourself with. Enough of this chatter," he said impatiently. "Believe what you will, you'll soon see that what I say is true." Eirriel opened her mouth in denial only to be silenced by Kedar's glaring black look. "I said enough! Now lie back and rest. I want to leave in the morning."

"Don't let me stop you," she murmured sweetly. "I'd never be able to rest knowing I caused you to alter your plans."

"Oh, but you would, my sweet. You see, you are my plans."

"What?"

"You're coming with me."

"Going with you!" She looked at him, her eyes clearly showing her loathing and her perfectly shaped mouth twisted in contempt. "I wouldn't go with you if you were the last man in existence. You come here from your godforsaken world and turn my life upside down! You send my father who knows where. You overrun my dwelling with your slimy Blagdenians. You ruin my life completely and you expect me to go with you? No, I won't go! And if you force me, I swear to you, I'll fight you at every turn. You won't find me a willing captive," she promised.

"You forget yourself, woman!" Kedar raged, his black eyes snapping with fury. "You are my captive. I do with you as I will. You no longer have a choice about anything. You will obey me! You will carry out my every desire, no matter how minor. You are mine, my sweet Eirriel. Mine!"

"I belong to no man! Not Timos! Not you, especially not you!" she raved, the intense hatred of her feelings making her voice hard, callous. "You are contemptible! You are the lowest form of life! Crawl back into the slime you slithered from and—"

Kedar grasped her by the shoulders and jerked her to a sitting position. His voice was low and cold as ice. "Don't ever talk to me like that again, do you hear me?" She tried to pull from him, but his grip tightened with her every movement. Tears of pain welled in her eyes. "You are my slave. I own you. You will obey!"

Looking through her tears, she said faintly, but vehemently, "Never! I'll kill myself before—"

Kedar shoved her back, stopping her in midsentence. His hand shot up and struck her forcefully, knocking her to the other side of the sleeper. He struck her again, buffeting her back as easily as if she were a child. Seeing his face descending toward her, she spit at him. A black look of uncontrollable fury deformed his features. In one vicious motion, he wiped the spittle from his face and backhanded her across hers. Again he tried to kiss her, but this time she twisted away. Snarling, he seized her hair savagely and forced her mouth to his. With the ease of a man well practiced in the art of rape, he freed himself, drove his knee between her legs and rolled on top of her.

His crushing weight acted as a catalyst, waking Eirriel's pain-dulled mind.

"No!" she screamed painfully, as if her soul were being wrenched from her body. With strength born from desperation, she pushed him off her and sprang from the sleeper. She looked about frantically, not even sure what she searched for until her eyes rested on Kedar's sonulator on the dressing table. Without knowing why, she knew what it was and how to use it. She grabbed it and aimed it at Kedar.

"I . . . am . . . not . . . yours!" she hissed, gasping for breath. "What I have no man may take!"

Seeing him lunge at her, she pressed the activator. Her

aim was true and the sonic wave struck him forcibly on the chest. Kedar reeled backwards, stunned. But the exertion proved too much for Eirriel. Her heart pounded in her chest and a sharp pain seared through her head. With a cry, her hands shot to her head, the weapon dropping harmlessly to the floor. Blackness engulfed her and she sank to the floor.

Moments later, his head throbbing painfully, Kedar staggered to his feet. Luckily for him, the sonulator had been set on low, he thought grimly as he adjusted his clothing. But she'd pay dearly for that little mistake. Jerking the door open, he roared for the wyman.

"Yes, Commodore?"

"Find Lieutenant Harlan and bring him to me now!"

The wyman saluted and gladly left to search for the lieutenant. Something had happened between the commodore and his pet and he had the distinct impression it hadn't gone quite the way Kedar had planned.

Kedar paced from one end of the chamber to the other, his eyes fixed on Eirriel. He seethed as her words raced through his mind. She was too good for him, would rather die than belong to him. Well, death was too good for her. She needed a lesson and he knew just the person to give it to her.

Lieutenant Harlan strode into the chamber, his discerning gaze sweeping over Eirriel's inert form. "Trouble, Kedar?" he asked snidely.

Kedar chose, for the moment, to ignore Harlan's blatant disrespect. "This female volunteered to take a trip to Blagden. I want her sent with the others."

"It's a little too late to change your mind, I'm afraid." The lieutenant's smug grin left little doubt that he had guessed the reason behind Kedar's abrupt change of heart. "The tribute ship has already left and per his orders, Tozgor was informed of its departure time. I understand he is anxiously awaiting its arrival. To recall it now would necessitate an investigation." He paused, then added, "Of course, if you still wish it, the delay might not be too substantial." His voice threatened otherwise.

Kedar decided to call his bluff. "She is to be sent as tribute to Tozgor," he growled. "Those are your orders.

How you go about them is no concern of mine."

Harlan swore under his breath. If only the tribute ship were still within communication range, and he had delayed it, then he'd see how long the great Kedar retained his favor! Bitterly, he crossed to Eirriel.

As Harlan stooped over the unconscious Dianthian, Kedar said quietly, "Think what you will, my sister's son, but hear me well. Unless you wish to take the female's place, I suggest you devise a plan for her immediate departure. And quickly. I want her out of my sight!"

Harlan's dark face paled. The arrogant bastard had made no idle threat. It was common knowledge throughout the ranks that Tozgor cared little who or what his companion was as long as his perverted needs were seen to. With a blank look carefully concealing the hate and fury raging through him, Harlan lifted Eirriel from the floor and carried her from the chamber, his mind filled with vows of vengeance.

Kedar's eyes glittered with anticipation. A brief time in Tozgor's gentle care and the fire would be out of that one. He shook his head sadly. It was a pity he couldn't be there to watch.

With a look that caused fear to prick the hearts of the staunchest men, Kedar threw back his head and laughed, the harsh, evil sound resounding throughout the dwelling.

Chapter Three

He resembled a magnificent bronze statue lying on the restorer. Black pants taut against sinewy thighs. Powerful arms crossed behind his head, hands hidden by a mass of golden curls. Golden eyes stared unseeing at the pale green ceiling. Only the rise and fall of his lean muscular chest was testimony to his humanity.

Somewhere inside the cavernous depths of his mind, a frustrated Aubin waged a losing battle against the darker aspects of his nature—his insatiable appetite for action and his compulsive need for adventure.

The past month had seen little variance in his daily routine and instead of savoring each quiet moment, storing it in his memory for a time when solitude would be beyond his grasp, Aubin looked upon its continuance with dread.

It had been this side of him that had caused the one and only argument with his father when Aubin was only fifteen.

Lord Kiernan had been unable to understand the overwhelming suffocation Aubin experienced even then when he thought of his future, of the time when he would have to live his life according to protocol. When he would be unable to disappear, on a whim and alone, for a week, a day, or an hour. When he would control the fate of millions. When Aubin would become the Lord Director of Rhianon.

In a desperate bid for freedom, Aubin had promised to return to Rhianon at his father's request and then never leave again. Lord Kiernan had reluctantly acquiesced to Aubin's terms.

Aubin then attended the Academy of Cosmic Sciences and now, ten years later, he was aboard the fleetship, *Celestial*, patrolling the vast reaches of space for the Empyreal Protectorate.

But when his father had summoned him home, tragic circumstances had delayed Aubin's return to Rhianon and part of his unrest could be blamed on that.

The shrill whistle of the intercom pierced the silence of the cubicle and pulled Aubin from his thoughts.

"Com-center to Captain Aubin."

Springing from the restorer with an agility unexpected in a man of his height, Aubin walked quickly to the intercom.

"Yes, Garreth?"

"Captain, the questors are picking up an unidentified vessel moving randomly through Sector 3-E," reported the *Celestial's* second-in-command.

"Place the ship on caution watch," Aubin ordered as he pulled on his knee-length black boots. "Have Theron set the viewing screen to mag 5. I'm on my way."

Aubin swept up his uniform top and eased it over his broad shoulders as he left the cubicle. The long-sleeved white shirt had a collarless neckline that dipped to a point midway between his neck and waist revealing much of his brawny, golden-haired chest. As with each member of the fleetship, the conversor, a small, black, circular patch over the right breast, was worn at all times, and on the outside right shoulder a vee-shaped emblem identified in words the assigned fleetship and in color the bearer's rank. In Aubin's case, it was the brilliant gold of a fleetship captain.

The portals of the restricted fore conveyor whooshed open and Aubin stepped inside. He smiled proudly as he thought of the hurried, but disciplined, activity that would greet him when he reached the com-center. Each member of the extensively trained com-crew, with the exception of Ceara, had been painstakingly selected by Aubin himself at the time he assumed command two years earlier.

Highly skilled in computer sciences, Garreth carried the bronze badge of second-in-command with casual ease. Repeatedly offered a command of his own, the easy going Rhianonian consistently refused, cheerfully leaving the responsibility and demands of that position to his best friend, Aubin.

Theron, the *Celestial's* chief of navigation and third-in-command, was from the planet Strato, a world enveloped by dense heavy clouds. Living in the thick, almost opaque atmosphere, the Stratons had evolved into a small emaciated-looking people with white hair and skin, and large, bulging, pale pink eyes. Accustomed to the strain of seeing in the limited light of Strato, their highly sensitive eyes had to be protected by dark visors when away from their home world. Like all Stratons, Theron possessed the uncanny ability to navigate anywhere without consulting the star charts, almost as if he could sense their location. It was with great pride that Theron wore the brown badge of navigation.

A lion man from Xerth sported the yellow emblem of communications officer. As head of his department, Jarce prided himself on his small staff who, between them, could interpret almost any dialect they encountered.

Ceara's black hair, parted on the side and curling gently to her shoulders, her flawless skin with a yellow hue, her oval-shaped black eyes and her petite frame gave testimony to her Thyrian ancestry. The purple-badged chief of engineering was the only one of the com-crew not with the *Celestial* from her maiden voyage. Belonging to a race of highly advanced female technicians, Ceara met Aubin when the *Celestial*—which had just lost her chief engineer in a freak accident—along with several other fleetships had evacuated the tiny planet of Thyra whose sun was going to nova. Ceara's unlimited knowledge of machinery had so impressed Aubin that he had engaged her even before they had reached the Main Terminal on Hakon. And she had

made certain that Aubin would never regret his spontane-
ous decision to have her as a member of his crew.

Stepping from the conveyor, Aubin's long strides carried
him quickly across the passageway to the com-center.
Issuing short abrupt orders, he strode toward Garreth
whose tall lean form was bent over a panel of blinking lights.

"Garreth, can you identify that vessel?"

Pressing several buttons, the bearded Rhianonian replied, "Questors show it to be a small antiquated vessel of
unfamiliar origin. Apparently it's been heavily damaged.
The readout shows no drive power and very little internal
power."

"Scan it for life-readings. Jarce, open up inter-ship communications," Aubin ordered as he assumed his place at the
com-console.

"This is the E.P.F. *Celestial*. Identify yourself." After a
few moments of silence, Aubin turned to his chief of
communications. "Jarce, is it possible they're not receiving
us?"

The Xerthian's hairy limbs flew over his communications
board checking and rechecking the signal.

"I'm transmitting on standard inter-ship frequency, Captain. If their system is functioning, they're receiving us."

"Keep trying to raise her," Aubin ordered.

"We're picking her up on visual now, Captain," Theron
reported.

All eyes raised to the viewing screen as the tiny vessel
drifted into view, its front end a yawing mass of twisted
metal.

"No wonder there's been no response," Jarce's gruff,
gravelly voice broke the silence. "Nobody could have
survived that."

"It does explain why the ship has no functioning drive
power," remarked Ceara. "That hole is all that remains of
their, shall we say, com-center. The engines must be located
elsewhere or the explosion would have torn the ship asunder." Her eyes narrowed in speculation. "If we could locate
the bypass system, and if it's still accessible, I'm sure the
engines could be reactivated."

Aubin sat away from the com-console, his brow furrowed. From the ship's appearance, he would have to agree with Jarce. Yet there was something about the vessel, a nagging belief that there was someone or something alive onboard. And the ship itself. As impossible as it seemed, it looked familiar. He searched his mind for where or when he could have seen it, but the memory eluded him.

"Has anything visualized on the scan, Garreth?"

Garreth ran his hand through his golden, collar-length hair, a look of consternation on his face. "Our questors are affected by the unusual alloy used in the ship's metal construction, Captain. The beams are hardly penetrating and the slight reading I'm getting is very vague."

"Continue anyway." Aubin's deep voice hinted at urgency. And if anyone thought it odd that they persist at the seemingly hopeless search, no one said a word. Their captain's hunches had been proven correct too many times to be taken lightly. Aubin pushed a button on the console.

"Com-center to med-unit."

"Cian here," said a gentle male voice.

"Cian, meet me in the teleport. We may have need of your services."

"What seems to be the problem?"

"We're approaching a heavily damaged vessel. At this point the number of survivors, if any, are unknown."

"What people are they?"

"Also unknown. The computer has no data on the ship or its people. I hope to have more information to give you by the time we reach the teleport."

"Right. Cian, out."

Aubin glanced at Garreth who was studying the questor readout intently. "Garreth?"

He stroked his beard. "If there's life on that ship, it's got to be on the ship's lower level. There appears to be a slight variance at one point, but with the way the questors are registering I can't be sure what it is."

"Theron." Aubin addressed his chief navigator. "Take command. Garreth, relay those lower level lat-logs to the teleport, then meet me there. Jarce, call Balthasar. Have him report to the teleport at once."

Aubin rose from his seat and strode from the com-center. There was something alive on that vessel, he thought excitedly. Something alive and alone. And afraid. Aubin stopped in mid-stride, his brow furrowing. Afraid? He shook his head. The monotony of their mission certainly hadn't affected his imagination! Not only had he convinced himself that there was a lone survivor, but that he or she was afraid as well. His mocking laughter rang through the passageway as he continued toward the teleport. But deep inside he was unable to shake the premonition that somehow, someway the next few hours would have a profound effect on his life.

Cian was already in the teleport when Aubin arrived. "Can you fill me in?"

Aubin gave him a quick rundown, noting while he spoke that Cian had slipped into a trance.

Cian belonged to an ancient civilization whose roots began in some distant unnamed galaxy. For reasons known only to themselves, the Drocots had migrated across the vast reaches of space to appear suddenly on a variety of different worlds.

Small in stature, the blue-skinned Drocots were often mistaken for untried youths. But as they spoke in their soft courteous voices, their immense age immediately became apparent, for their sensitive tones resounded with all the joys and sorrows of countless civilizations since the beginning of time.

Aubin watched the Drocot, knowing that his patience would pay off. As Cian demonstrated now, when in a quandry, all Drocots slipped into a trance, inwardly searching through the ages to find a solution. All problems were treated in the same manner, with time as the only variable. In trivial matters, they lapsed in and out in the blink of an eye; in grave situations, they stayed inside themselves for hours. In all cases, they reverted to their normal state, fully conscious of any and all action that may have occurred around them. Since they were aware of their surroundings, any threat to their physical being while they were in the trance brought them to immediate and full alertness.

The rarest quality they possessed was the sense of well-being and trust that emanated from them just as heat radiated from a sun. All it took was a look, a word and the worst fears were dispelled. Because of these gifts, the Drocots had soon become the most sought-after medics in the galaxies, and Aubin was grateful to have Cian as part of his crew.

"Since we're unsure as to what we'll encounter," Cian's voice was hollow as he came out of his trance, "I'll keep a med-team on stand-by here in the teleport and I myself will accompany you. If further help is needed, my team can be at the scene almost immediately."

Cian was giving his staff orders via the intercom when Garreth and the thin pale safeguard officer arrived.

"I briefed Balthasar on the way, Aubin," Garreth explained. "The teleport is programmed and ready whenever we are."

"Set neutralizers on low," Aubin ordered. A quick glance at the others assured him that all was ready. "Let's go."

As the four crossed into the inner chamber, a glaring beacon of light switched on automatically. Encasing them, it conveyed them across space as particles of the light ray. A silent, but brilliant, flash of light appeared on the lower level of the alien vessel as Aubin, Garreth, Cian and Balthasar arrived at their destination and materialized.

The small gray cubicle appeared to be a storage area. Three of the four walls were lined with empty shelves, their contents broken and scattered across the floor. The fourth wall opened to a long passageway. Garreth bent down and picked up several broken containers.

"This vessel is more outdated than I thought," he said, studying the article intently. "This is apparently where the food supplies are kept. Unlike the automatic nourishment systems we use, these aliens must manually prepare theirs."

While Garreth dug through the debris, Balthasar stood by the portal and mentally sought signs of life.

Balthasar was a mutant from Tri-III, the end result of illegal scientific experiments on mind control. Experiments that left him with a deathlike pallor to his skin, a clammy chill to his hands and a dingy gray to his hair. Experiments that created in him a powerful weapon for someone with foresight to channel. Aubin had found him wandering from planet to planet with the Arvads, a nomadic troupe of space gypsies, a bitter exile totally dejected with life. He was an entertainer, if a hostile man can be called that, reading the minds of his audience for a reward, which was really a pittance for very few would pay him after hearing his caustic remarks. Aubin had at once recognized that Balthasar's telepathic powers would make him the perfect choice to head the *Celestial's* safeguard unit. Aubin knew that to this day Balthasar wore the black emblem denoting his position with an overpowering pride, as if by its mere presence he had had his revenge on a universe that had long ago denied him a place.

"I can pick up no thought patterns on this or any level, Captain," Balthasar reported in his flat voice.

Puzzled, Aubin turned to Garreth. "Where did that reading originate?"

Garreth pointed to the far end of the passageway.

"Cian, Garreth, check the cubicles on the other side. Start directly opposite this one. Balthasar and I will check this side. I want one of us to remain in the passageway at all times."

Stepping over the wreckage, they entered the passageway. Splitting up into their assigned teams, the four systematically investigated all cubicles and found each in the same ruinous condition as the first.

"Captain!" Garreth called excitedly from the last cubicle. "In here!"

They ran to him, their faces registering hope. Unlike the previous cubicles, this one was clean and orderly. From the furnishings it appeared to have been used primarily for sleeping. Garreth pointed to the table in the corner. It was set for one, with a partially consumed nourishment platter and a half-filled beaker. The seat lay backwards, as if its occupant had abandoned it quickly. Cian walked to the table and touched the food.

"It's still heated," he observed quietly.

Heated! Then there was a survivor! Aubin's penetrating gaze swept the obviously empty cubicle. The question now was where?

Chapter Four

Mechanically Eirriel reached for the carafe of Dianthia Rhea Extract and filled her goblet. Her delicate features were marred by the numbing black fury of her thoughts as she raised the goblet high above her head. In a voice saturated with hate, she pledged Kedar's destruction. "We will meet again, my good Lord Kedar. And when we do, you will have cause to rue the day you first set foot upon my world!"

She laughed, the bitter sound transforming into a hideous caricature as it echoed hollowly throughout the sparsely furnished chamber. With only enough provisions for three more days, she was making plans for her future!

Even Kedar's demonic genius could never have envisioned Eirriel's fate when he issued Lieutenant Harlan his orders.

The small vessel, with only three inexperienced wymen to maneuver it, had been unable to avoid the severe meteor storm that had crossed its path four weeks after leaving Dianthia. Protected by an ancient environmental suit, Eirriel had crouched in her lower level chamber until the pounding had stopped and the ship had stabilized.

Expectantly she had waited for one of the wymen to check on the safety of their valuable cargo, but no one came. The unwieldly suit had made walking almost impossible. But Eirriel had persisted and eventually had made her way to the far end of the long passageway only to find it barred by the automatic safety system. Once activated, the system sealed off all damaged areas restoring the artificial environment. It had been a grim Eirriel who had returned to her chamber, numbed by the realization that the wymen had been destroyed and with them her only chance for survival.

A quick check on supplies had given her a little hope but the hope was gone now.

Her green eyes frozen with hatred, Eirriel's fingers tightened around the goblet. "Damn you, Kedar! Damn you to a living hell!" She hurled the fragile container across the chamber and watched it shatter against the wall.

Her rage spent, for the moment, Eirriel slumped back in the chair. Anger now gave way to tears and they streamed from her eyes. She was so afraid. Afraid of dying, but more afraid of not. It had been three long months since she'd heard any voice beside her own, any sound besides the ones she created. She hated the monotony, the emptiness, the isolation. And the ever-present threat of death.

Pushing herself violently from the table, the chair tumbling backwards, she flung herself on the sleeper. Tired of waiting for death, she sobbed and begged for death which shadowed her to take her and end the misery and the waiting. Her lithe body wracking with sobs, she gave vent to all the emotions she had stoically stored inside her these past months and cried herself into an exhausted slumber.

A strange prickling inside her head roused Eirriel from her sleep. Groggily she raised her hands and pressed her long fingers against her temples. Whether the pressure helped or not she wasn't sure, but the annoying sensation vanished as suddenly as it had started.

Before she could ponder on the curious episode, a muffled sound caught her attention. Raising herself on one elbow, she peered toward the door. She listened intently, but all she heard was the all-too-familiar silence. A grin broke out on her face and she shook her head in amused disgust. How vivid her dreams appeared at times!

The gnawing of her empty stomach reminded Eirriel that she had not eaten for quite some time. Dragging herself from the sleeper, she crossed to the small warmer and removed her sparse fare. Placing the platter on the table, she bent to retrieve the chair when her ears again picked up a muted sound.

And again.

And again.

There could be no mistake this time. She had heard the sound! She wasn't dreaming! For the first time in months her eyes sparkled with excitement. Her people had finally found her! But as quickly as it had begun, the tiny spark of hope died. Dianthians had neither the technological knowledge nor the emotional character to attempt a rescue. To them, she had ceased to exist, a casualty in the pursuit of peace.

She heard the sound again. This time the nearness of it sent waves of apprehension coursing through her. Who or what was out there? As she had done so often since her misadventure began, she cursed the Oldens for restricting the scope of education to within the limited boundaries of their small world. The only people she had had contact with from outside her private world, the Blagdenians, had not come in peace. Were all but Dianthians hostile?

Momentary panic reflected itself in her eyes before they turned fiery with determination. She would not be waiting helplessly when her unknown visitors finally chose to enter. Looking about for someplace to hide she remembered the dressing compartment. With a bound she was inside, doors closed. Crouching in the darkness, she held her breath and waited.

Aubin's mind was racing. Something very strange was occurring. Appearances forced him to the conclusion that the vessel was indeed occupied. In fact, logic demanded its occupant be in this very cubicle. But if that were true, why hadn't Balthasar given them some kind of warning? The captain glanced at his safeguard officer seeking an answer and instead found a bemused frown creasing his brow.

Balthasar frowned. If their assumption was correct, why hadn't he picked up any unusual thought patterns? Closing his eyes he let his mind slowly expand and searched again for the absent alien.

In her dark refuge, Eirriel strained to hear something that would reveal the identity of the intruders. As she did, she became aware of an intangible uneasiness inside her head.

Reflexively, her hands shot up and pushed against the empty air in front of her face as if warding off a physical blow instead of the abstract probing sensation. The disturbance abated for an instant, then returned, stronger and more persistent.

Instinctively Eirriel reacted to the threat. Her eyes snapped shut. She felt herself drift up and away, leaving behind a lifeless shell and a blank mind. Time became irrelevant as she floated in a hazy, shapeless netherworld.

Then it was over.

Spontaneously, effortlessly, Eirriel reunited with her body. She sagged against the cool metal wall, taking comfort in the solid security it offered. She raised her shaky hands to press against her forehead, then realized it was no longer necessary. The prickling consciousness was gone.

Her heart pounded in her chest as she fought against the rising panic. Had it happened? Had she really hovered in the air, free from her body? No! She was just frightened! It was her way of coping with her fear and her wish to run from the danger the unknown visitors represented. It was her imagination! What else could it be?

Yet, deep down in a secret corner of her being, she knew the truth—a truth she would one day have to face.

Nothing! Balthasar opened his eyes. The good Drocot was mistaken, he sneered silently. There was no one here. Glancing surreptitiously at Aubin, Balthasar shrugged his shoulders. As long as his captain was in no immediate danger, he need not concern himself with the faulty conclusions of fools.

Pretending to pick through the abandoned food, Garreth

studied Balthasar. What was running through that crafty mutant's mind? Why was he rejecting the existence of a survivor? Were his powers failing him? Or was it something more? Catching Balthasar's stolen glance, Garreth's suspicious mind clicked.

It was a setup! A brilliantly constructed plan to commandeer the *Celestial*. It wouldn't be the first time such an attempt had been made. There were many willing to pay an astronomical fee for the delivery of any fleetship and the *Celestial*, the best of her division, would be a prize.

But would Balthasar betray Aubin, the one man who had faith in him? Every man had his price, Garreth decided grimly. Believing his conjecture at least a plausible reason for the mutant's behavior, the Rhianonian officer moved between his captain and the safeguard officer.

No!

The word seared Garreth's consciousness so ferociously that he jumped back, startled.

No! I am not a traitor!

In his fury Balthasar unintentionally broadcasted his thoughts to all three men.

"What do you mean?" Aubin demanded. "I heard no one accuse you." Aubin looked at Balthasar, concern etched on his handsome face. Nervously he recalled the day he had first presented the mutant to the *Celestial's* crew. A feverish air of anxiety had settled over them as the awareness of what Balthasar was and what he could do had been perceived. To assuage their doubts, Balthasar had vowed to use telepathy only when combating adversaries of the Protectorate, or face expulsion and/or punishment if he did not.

"There are instances when emotions or thoughts are so powerful that they invade my mind," Balthasar drawled. "I do not need to seek them out."

Garreth bristled at Balthasar's overbearing attitude. "Then why haven't you confirmed what we know to be a fact?" he demanded.

"And what is that?"

"That this cubicle is occupied!"

"You jump to conclusions," Balthasar scoffed.

Garreth stepped toward him, clenching and unclenching

his fists. "Why you no good, lousy—"

"My friends, please!" Cian placed himself between his two warring companions. "Remember why we are here. We can discuss your problem later. If the need still exists," he added. "For now, let us continue our search."

Oblivious to the discourse around him, Aubin walked slowly toward the cabinet at the far end of the cubicle, led by the same inner compulsion he had experienced on the *Celestial*.

Catching his captain's movements out of the corner of his eye, Balthasar bit back a reply and took his place at Aubin's side.

"Captain?" Garreth queried as Aubin pushed between him and Cian.

The Drocot reached out a small blue hand. "What do you see?"

At Cian's touch Aubin stopped abruptly. His golden eyes searching the rectangular cabinet, he shook his head.

"I don't know," he said distractedly. Whatever he had sensed about the cabinet was gone.

"It was the cabinet, wasn't it?" Garreth asked, following Aubin's perplexed stare.

Aubin nodded.

"You know, you might have something!" Garreth said excitedly, his eyes flashing with enthusiasm. "I seem to remember reading somewhere that many of the first interplanetary vehicles often had large storage units built between the walls. They were used to hide valuables from space pirates. Maybe there's a similar compartment here."

Garreth knelt and opened the smaller lower portals. Reaching inside, he felt along the upper edge until he heard a click. He rose and waited for Aubin's order before he completed the procedure. Aubin silently motioned Balthasar and Cian to cover the cabinet from each side. Once they were in position, he nodded to Garreth. Pressing a small knob, Garreth gave a quick push with his hands and jumped back to stand at Aubin's side, aiming his neutralizer, like the others, at the middle of the opening.

A few moments of stagnant silence passed before they heard a muffled sob. Aubin stepped forward.

"We are armed, but here in friendship. Come out slowly and identify yourself."

There was a subtle movement and a dark shape rose and stepped forward, successfully remaining in obscurity. Aggravated and disconcerted at having been proven wrong, Balthasar bolted rashly to the cabinet. Before Aubin or the others could protest, he reached inside and seized the shadowy form.

"I believe you were asked to come out," he said between clenched teeth, dragging a trembling Eirriel from the security of her compartment, his body situated so that she was still hidden from the others.

Looking into the steely-gray eyes of the thin man holding her, Eirriel knew he was the source of the strange vibrations. Face to face his thoughts were overpowering. She felt smothered. But before she could react, Balthasar withdrew from her mind, dropped her arm and stepped back, his expression a mixture of surprise, confusion, and envy.

With an oath Garreth moved forward, shoving Balthasar roughly aside. He stopped abruptly. There before him were the brightest, loveliest pair of green eyes he had ever seen. Framed by long dark lashes, they gave their owner the wide-eyed look of an innocent. A fair-skinned oval face, delicate nose and full red lips further enhanced the illusion. Never in all his travels had he seen such beauty. Surely one such as this could mean no harm.

"Don't be frightened," he said gently. The language transmittor attached to his wrist automatically translated his words from Hakonese, the universal language of the Protectorate, to words the alien female could understand and projected them telepathically to her.

"We mean you no harm. We are here to help," he explained, wanting to remove the fear from her eyes.

Eirriel stood paralyzed with fear. Who was this tall bronze stranger whose language she could somehow understand? Could she believe what he said? Her glance swung to the shorter, pallid man. Friendship was certainly the last thing he had in mind! She shuddered inwardly as she remembered the deathly cold of his hands and the chilling blackness of his thoughts.

"I am Aubin, Captain of the E.P.F. *Celestial*."

Erriel was so embroiled in her thoughts that she had not seen Aubin's approach. At the sound of his rich, deep voice she jumped, her mind drawn back to the present.

"We were passing through this sector when we spied your damaged ship. Our design was, and still is, to render assistance not destruction."

Intent green eyes scanned the men before resting damningly on Balthasar.

"It would seem, Captain," Eirriel said softly, "that your noble plans differ considerably with those of your companion."

Her low melodious voice sent shock waves through Garreth, increasing the urge to throttle Balthasar for threatening such an innocent creature.

"I apologize for my safeguard officer's abrupt behavior. He tends to be overzealous at times," Aubin explained, smoothly covering up his consternation. There was obviously more to her statement than Balthasar's unnecessary roughness. Again Aubin found cause to worry about him.

"Come with me, my dear," Cian said quietly, offering her his hand.

Looking down on the Drocot's upturned face, her gaze drawn like a magnet to his round blue eyes, Eirriel felt her taut nerves relax and her deepest fears flee. She knew that the small frail man with the thinning, dark blue hair draping below his shoulders, droopy mustache and long trailing beard would keep her safe. Warm and secure for the first time in months, she slowly reached out and placed her hand in his.

Cian nodded toward the upended chair and Garreth quickly righted it. Slipping his other arm reassuringly around her waist, Cian led her to the chair.

Balthasar observed his companions reactions to the female. Garreth, as expected, was enchanted by her beauty, Cian was deceived by her innocent appearance, and Aubin, well, he wasn't too sure about him. His expression was blank, his mind tightly closed. It was obvious, however, that none of them had any idea of what she really was.

Sweat beaded on his brow as he remembered the tremendous power he had glimpsed when he dragged her from the closet. He now realized why he had been unable to detect her presence. To be unhampered by physical boundaries! To become pure mental energy! The thought was overwhelming. With power like hers he would be untouchable. Whole worlds would be at his command. Nothing could stop him!

As Balthasar stood apart relishing the feel of the power he would soon siphon, Garreth questioned Eirriel.

"What are you called?"

"Eirriel," she said proudly.

"Your comrades, Eirriel, are they all dead?" Cian asked the question uppermost in all save Balthasar's mind and was taken aback by her fiery response.

"Comrades!" Eirriel spat out, hatred blazing in her eyes. "Does cargo, even valuable cargo, have comrades?" she demanded bitterly.

"Cargo!" Garreth and Cian exclaimed in unison. Even Aubin appeared startled.

Balthasar scowled cynically. With her power she claimed to be the vessel's cargo? Impossible! Unless, his lifeless eyes narrowed, unless she had not fully learned to control her ability. He had to know more! Determinedly, he strode across the cubicle.

"How was it that your people allowed you to be taken?" he asked, then added slyly, "or could it be you were sent from them?"

Her face flushed with anger, her jaw thrust forward in defiance, Eirriel glared at him, refusing to answer his absurd insinuation.

"Answer me, girl! Where are you from? What was your destination?" Furious at her continued silence, Balthasar grabbed her arm and shook her. "What kind of people are you?"

"That's what I like about you, Balthasar, old boy," Garreth interrupted dryly. "You never seem to lose control."

Balthasar threw him a look of pure unadulterated hatred. "I need answers!"

"I must remember your approach since it brings such immediate results," the Rhiamonian drawled. "Let me see if

I have it right. First you mentally abuse your victims, I mean subjects, and if that doesn't work, you throw them around." He paused, then added very quietly, "Tell me, Balthasar. What is it you fear?"

"You . . . you . . ." Balthasar sputtered. "First you accuse me of being a traitor, now a coward! Is there no end to your petty name-calling?"

Garreth choked back a laugh. He'd succeeded in distracting the poor devil. There was no need to torment him further. Giving the mutant a short cursory bow, he stepped away and made a sweeping gesture toward Eirriel.

"Captain," Cian cut in before Balthasar could voice his next question, "is this really necessary? Can't it wait until I've examined her?"

Aubin's intent glare swept over the men, rested momentarily on Eirriel, then focused on Balthasar. It was obvious the girl unsettled the telepath more than a little. Aubin decided to allow him free rein to see what developed.

"Answer his questions," Aubin ordered coldly, studying her reaction for some clue to Balthasar's bizarre behavior.

Eirriel met Aubin's piercing stare. Begrudgingly she said, "I am from Dianthia." She threw Balthasar a meaningful look. "Against my will *and* the will of my people I was sent from my home."

"And your destination?" coaxed Cian.

"Blagden."

"Blagden!" Aubin spat the name. Eirriel pulled back in fear as he stepped closer, his eyes dark with intense emotion and a fierce scowl on his face. "Who? Who sent you?"

"Kedar."

Aubin's gut twisted and a red mist descended over his eyes as he heard the name of his sister's murderer. Of their own accord his hands reached up and grabbed Eirriel's shoulders. He yanked her to her feet.

"Where is he?" he snarled. "Where is that murdering bastard?"

"I don't know!"

"Tell me, damn you!"

"Please! You're hurting me!"

Garreth stepped forward and placed a hand on Aubin's

shoulder. "She's his victim, Captain, not his compatriot."

Garreth's quiet rebuke penetrated Aubin's rage. He released her abruptly and stepped back, his hands tightening into white-knuckled fists. Cian and Garreth exchanged worried glances and Eirriel watched apprehensively as Aubin turned and walked away. Balthasar merely smiled smugly and prepared to make his move.

Cian turned to Garreth. "So, he is alive. I had hoped—"

"She's lying," Balthasar cut in as he stepped close to Eirriel.

Panicked green eyes flew to Balthasar. "I've never been off-world before. I didn't even know it could be done!"

"You're lying."

"No!" She turned to Garreth. "Please! You must believe me!"

Garreth gave her a reassuring smile before favoring Balthasar with an icy golden stare. "You *know* she's lying?"

"No, but . . .".

"Then leave her alone!"

"You are interfering with my job, Garreth. As safeguard officer I must determine whether she is to be secured in a restraining cubicle. That requires answers now, not at *her* convenience."

"She doesn't need to be badgered. She needs—"

"Enough."

Aubin's quiet order drew everyone's gaze. He was glaring at them with eyes that hinted at a rage barely leashed and a stance that spoke of rigid control.

"We know all we need to know, for now. She was in the care of Blagdenians," Aubin uttered the name as if it were a dreaded disease. "They are not known for their gentle ways. Cian should examine her before we continue." Aubin was rewarded for his consideration by Eirriel's small tremulous smile. "As to where she should be quartered"—he looked sternly at Balthasar—"I believe I am still captain."

There was no need to say more. Balthasar's expression left no doubt the message had been received. The safeguard officer stepped away. He would wait until he was alone with the Dianthian, and then he would have his answers!

Assured by Eirriel that she was indeed the ship's only

survivor, Aubin pressed the conversor.

"Captain Aubin to the *Celestial*."

"Theron here, Captain," came the instantaneous reply.

"Theron, have the teleport tech prepare to transport five on my signal."

"Will do, Captain."

Standing between Garreth and Cian, Eirriel took one last look around the chamber that had been her whole world for the past few months. She had hated its lifeless, cramped confines. But more than that she had hated what it represented: the means of carrying her far from all she knew and loved. Now she was on her way to an equally unknown destination. Would fate treat her as unkindly as before? She glanced at her four rescuers. Two she knew to be friends, one an enemy. As for their tall bronzed leader, she was certain only that all too soon she would learn which he would be.

Her green eyes mirroring her apprehension, yet her proud stance unwavering, Eirriel stared into Aubin's searching golden eyes. Taking a deep breath, she nodded in answer to his question. Yes, she was ready.

The bland gray walls of the cubicle were illuminated by a brilliant flash of light and Eirriel and her new companions teleported to the *Celestial*.

Chapter Five

"Garreth, activate the grapple beam," Aubin ordered, once again in his seat at the com-console. "I want that vessel secured in docking bay four."

The Rhianonian reached up and flipped a switch. "Grapple beam activated, Captain."

"Jarce, maintain caution watch. The possibility that she could be an unwitting decoy cannot be discounted. Theron, plot a course to the nearest terminal and proceed at vel 3."

"Caution watch maintained, sir," Jarce reported.

Theron pressed several studs on his panel. "Course plotted and"—he raised the control bar slowly—"speed increased to vel 3."

"Balthasar, Ceara," Aubin continued, "I want each of you to assign one member of your staff to that alien vessel. I want it searched from top to bottom, inside and out. I want to know everything about that ship. There has to be a clue somewhere aboard that will give us the location of Dianthia since the girl cannot help us."

The last statement caused Balthasar to mutter under his breath, and Aubin quirked an eyebrow. "Do you have something to report, Balthasar?"

The officer shook his head.

"Fine. You have your assignments. Begin at once. It was Blagden that invaded her planet. If we can quickly locate Dianthia, we might be able to save some of her people. You're dismissed."

As they left the com-center, Aubin turned to his Xerthian communications officer.

"Jarce, send the following message to Main Terminal: Chronicle 27X12, d27-8M. Have rescued one female survivor, Eirriel of Dianthia, from damaged alien vessel. Although used as a Blagdenian transport, the ship was not of their usual design. The vessel is secured onboard and a detailed search of its structure is underway. The Dianthian is under close observation in the med-unit. Will relay additional information as it becomes available. Aubin, Captain E.P.F. *Celestial*."

Having completed the necessary duties, Aubin absently studied the console before him, his thoughts reviewing the events of the past hour. After their arrival aboard the ship, Cian had protectively rushed Eirriel off to the med-unit, preventing further questioning until he examined her. Balthasar and Garreth had accompanied Aubin to the deliberation cubicle and a heated argument had ensued: Garreth accusing Balthasar of witholding information, Balthasar adamantly denying that he did.

Aubin himself was quite puzzled over the entire situation. He had complete trust in Balthasar to perform his duties, which would have compelled him to tell Aubin of Eirriel's existence. Yet he had not. The issue was further complicated by Balthasar's uncharacteristic behavior. A harsh, relentless, unsympathetic inquisitor when the need arose, he had always maintained a cool exterior. Yet today he had acted hastily, uncautiously and almost violently. Was it as Garreth had claimed? Had Balthasar been forewarned of Eirriel's presence and location on the ship? Was his conduct merely a cover-up? Then why had he looked so completely mystified when he saw Eirriel? Mystified and pained. But why the pain? Or had it been guilt?

And what about Garreth? Was his mind so clouded by

pity that he was harsh and accusative to Balthasar in order to protect Eirriel? Again uncharacteristic behavior. Garreth was a professional in every sense of the word. He had never let his inner feelings interfere with his judgment and Aubin couldn't believe he would begin to now.

Whatever the two men's reasons, they had reached an impasse, neither one relenting. Reminding them that they were officers of the Protectorate and were expected to be at their best deportment, Aubin had dismissed them.

How quickly the Dianthian managed to get under their skin, the girl with the haunting green eyes. There was something about her, something indefinable. Something. . . . His thoughts were interrupted by Jarce's gruff voice.

"I just received the reply from Main Terminal, Captain. 'Message received. Proceed to Xandor III. Have no data on planet Dianthia. Question the Dianthian as soon as the Drocot stabilizes her. Inform us of your progress. Shand, Supreme Commander, Exploration Division, Main Terminal, Hakon.'"

"Thank you, Jarce. Garreth, at our present speed how long before we arrive at Xandor III?"

"Twenty-three days, nine hours."

"Very good. Theron, Jarce, once your reliefs have finished receiving their briefing you may retire. As always you did a fine job. Thank you. Garreth, I'd like a word with you before you turn in. Would you wait for me in my cubicle?"

The Rhianonian nodded his head and then left the com-center. His report given and the night crew at their stations, Aubin took one last sweeping glance around. Reassured that all was secure, he bid his crew good night and left to join Garreth.

"A beaker of brew?" Aubin offered as he poured one for himself.

"Have you ever known me to turn down Melonnian sweet and sour?"

Aubin chuckled. "Now that I think of it, no."

The two friends raised their beakers high in silent toast then downed the icy liquid in one long swallow.

"You wished a word with me?" Garreth questioned,

refilling his beaker. He offered some to Aubin, but the captain shook his head.

"Yes, Garreth. I'd like you and Raissa to meet me here in the morning. I have a proposition to discuss with both of you, Raissa in particular, before I mention it to the Dianthian."

Garreth quirked a brow. Raissa? What did she have to do with Eirriel? He peered over the rim of his beaker and waited for Aubin to continue. Much to Garreth's chagrin, Aubin offered no further information. Garreth replaced the beaker on its tray and ran a hand through his hair. Well, whatever the captain had in mind he certainly wouldn't find out till morning. Shrugging his shoulders, he said good night and left to find Raissa.

"What you need is some nourishment." Cian's deep blue eyes crinkled and his small mouth turned up in the corners. "I seem to remember yours being rudely interrupted."

"That would be nice. I must admit I'm starving." Eirriel's eyes smiled back at him.

"Why don't you go into the other cubicle and relax?" Cian pointed to one of the many cubicles lining the far wall of the large med-unit. "In the meantime I'll try to find you something to eat."

Eirriel stepped inside the chamber and a small gasp of surprise escaped as the darkened chamber automatically illuminated. Was there no end to the skills these people possessed? As she looked around, she noted that the bright yellow cubicle held only a small restorer which extended from one wall and was anchored by a heavy chain at both ends.

"This will have to do for now," Cian said apologetically as he joined her, carrying a tray and a long green cloth. "I thought you might like to use the vitalizer after your nourishment." He handed her the cloth. "It's not much, but it's the only thing I have that will come anywhere near fitting you. Tomorrow we can order you something from the dispensary."

He crossed to the wall opposite the portal and pressed a button. Instantly the restorer was raised to the ceiling.

Simultaneously the wall next to Cian opened. Eirriel's eyes widened with wonder as a table and chair unit extended and unfolded.

"This place is truly marvelous!" she exclaimed breathlessly.

"You'll get used to it soon enough," Cian chuckled. "Now," he guided her into the chair, "I'll leave you alone to take nourishment. When you're finished, I'll show you how to use the vitalizer."

"Wait! Please don't go! I . . . I mean . . ." Lowering her eyes, she flushed with embarrassment. "I've been alone for so long. I was hoping you might stay. Unless," she added in a small voice, "you have to be elsewhere."

"I don't have to be anywhere. In fact, I was hoping you'd ask me to stay. You have been through an ordeal and sharing it often helps. I'd be willing to listen."

Hesitant at first, Eirriel soon relaxed under the Drocot's gentle coaxing. Between mouthfuls of food she spoke of Dianthia and her life before the invasion, of the frustration she felt when she learned her people were the captives of the Blagdenians and there was nothing she could do to help them. Of her fear for her father's safety. Of the terror she felt upon waking up far from home and among strangers on her way to Blagden.

Cian sat and listened as was his way, never saying a word, offering comfort by his presence alone. When she grew quiet and fearful, Cian gave her time to gather her fears into words.

"It was days before I learned where I was going and that I was being sent to Tozgor, the Blagdenian leader, as a tribute. And then after a month aboard the ship the meteor storm struck. At first all I felt was relief, then when I was able to get around and saw the extent of my supplies I grew worried. As time passed I grew afraid. I knew I was going to die, it was only a matter of time. Today I had given up. I'd actually begged death to come and get me. I was so tired of being afraid of dying for the past three months. I wanted to get it over with." She fell silent. When she spoke again, her voice was an embarrassed whisper. "I know it was cowardly of me."

"Cowardly! You have more courage, my child, than many aboard the *Celestial*, and a strength of will that is truly remarkable."

Eirriel flushed with pride at his words and murmured her thanks. She lowered her gaze to her hands. Cian watched as she twisted them in worry. After all she had told him, he wondered, how could she be afraid to reveal more? He gave her a few moments to work through her fears and was pleased when she once again raised her eyes to him.

"Cian, I . . . I was wondering . . ." She took a deep breath. "Your captain hates Kedar. Please, I need to know. Will he turn that hatred on me?"

Although he was stunned by the turn of her thoughts, Cian was quick to reassure her. "No. His pledge of loyalty to the Protectorate and his honor as a Rhianonian prevents that."

"What did Kedar do to him?"

Cian looked into the eyes of the young woman so new to all of them and made a decision he was certain his captain would greatly resent. But he was just as certain the time would come when she would play an important role in the life of his Rhianonian friend.

"Three years ago, Kedar lead a raid against a distant colony of the Protectorate. Aubin's twin sister died during that raid, and the captain holds Kedar directly responsible for her death. When he brought Liann's body home, he swore on her essence he would not return to Rhianon until he had avenged her murder.

"Aubin holds his word sacred. Liann's death forced him to foreswear an oath to his father."

"What oath?"

Cian sighed. He had hoped she wouldn't ask. Aubin was not going to be happy with his interference.

"When his lifespan reached thirty, he was to surrender his post with the Protectorate and return to Rhianon. The captain is two and thirty. Every day he cannot return home feeds his rage against Kedar."

"I can well understand that rage," Eirriel said, fierce lights burning in her eyes. "And now my world is at the mercy of that depraved beast!" Eirriel jumped to her feet. "I cannot stay! I must go to my people, my father. I cannot let them be destroyed!"

"And just how do you expect to prevent that from happening?"

Eirriel and Cian looked up to see Aubin leaning arrogantly against the portal frame. Having decided to check on Eirriel before he retired, he'd arrived just in time to hear her desperate cry.

"Do you plan to climb upon your golden stallant and ride to their rescue like the warriors of old?"

"I know nothing of your warriors, but yes. Somehow I will save my father and my people!" she declared fiercely.

"I can just see it," Aubin chuckled. "It will be at day's end, of course, and you will—"

"Don't you laugh at me." Eirriel rushed toward him, her green eyes spitting fire, her face flushed with anger. She glowered into his laughing golden eyes. "You, of all here, should know how I feel." The smile vanished from Aubin's face. "What do you care that a world filled with people you don't know faces destruction! How soon we forget those who have died!"

His eyes glittering like ice, Aubin glared at Cian who merely raised his hands in a gesture of what-can-I-say-I-did-what-I-felt-was-necessary, then turned to Eirriel. "Listen, you little hellion, I don't have to explain my actions to you or anyone. As for this little rescue expedition, when would you like to leave?"

"The sooner the better!"

"Well, then, come with me."

Dragging her by the arm, he stormed into the outer cubicle. Releasing her abruptly, he walked to one of the walls and pushed a button. The wall slid open, exposing a small screen. He pushed another button and the screen lit up displaying blackness and a myriad of stars.

"Tell me, spitfire, where would you go?" At her blank stare, he explained laconically, "If you were to leave right now, that's where the teleport would deposit you. Right in the middle of nothing. Hardly conducive to life is it?" he sneered.

"My people, my father . . ." Her eyes bright with unshed

tears and her heart crying out with a need to get home, Eirriel stared at the screen.

"And what were you going to do once you got to your world?" Aubin demanded, knowing he had made his point, but wanting, for some perverse reason, to continue. "Kedar doesn't do anything unless he gets something out of it. What could you possibly offer him in exchange for the safety of your people? You have nothing to bargain with."

She looked at him. "I have myself," she said softly, then walked slowly to her cubicle.

Cian shook his head in disgust. "Was that really necessary? She had to realize she could not leave, but did you have to be so harsh?" Cian paused as the air was filled with the loud clatter of falling dishes and the sudden onset of soul-rending cries. He tugged at his beard and his dark blue eyes were filled with reproach. "You have never done anything without a reason, Captain. Until now," he added.

"Where do you think you're going?" Cian demanded when Aubin started toward the little cubicle.

"To Eirriel."

"You've done enough for one day's end, Captain. Leave her be."

Aubin drew himself up to his full height. "Do you forget who you're talking to? I'm captain here! I go where I will!"

"You may be captain, but I am the medic," he reminded Aubin firmly. "And I have the final say over those in my care. That little hellion, as you so gently put it, has had more traumatic experiences in her short life than you will ever see in yours."

Cian gave Aubin a blistering account of all that Eirriel had endured. "Not many would have survived what she did and remained mentally intact. She has an inner strength that is remarkable. And now, just listen to her. After all she has been through, it's you who proved too much for her. Tells you something if you care to hear it."

Aubin stared after Cian as the irritated Drocot headed toward his charge, then Aubin stormed from the med-unit.

"Why did he have to be so cruel?" Eirriel sobbed. "I just wanted to go to Dianthia. They need me."

Cian stroked her head tenderly. "And you need rest. Come, I'll give you something to calm your nerves and help you sleep. It will do you good."

Eirriel stood away from the table/chair as it closed and went back into the wall.

"Lie down on the restorer," Cian directed as it lowered from the ceiling.

Eirriel slipped under the covers, drawing them up under her chin. She looked at Cian apprehensively when she saw the small tube he carried.

"It won't hurt, child. Trust me." He placed the tube next to her temple. His voice was soft, hypnotic. "Sleep, Eirriel, sleep. You'll feel better when you wake. Sleep."

Stepping out of the cubicle, Cian touched a switch and the cubicle plunged into darkness.

Aubin paced in his cubicle. Cian was right. He'd no reason to be so harsh with her. Well, he hadn't planned it that way, he defended himself. It wasn't until she referred to Liann that he lost his temper.

"Damn you, Cian! There was no need to tell her about Liann!" he swore outloud.

He poured himself a beaker of brew. No, he thought grimly, Cian did have a reason. Him. Damning his volatile nature, Aubin stripped off his uniform and flung himself on the restorer. His arms folded behind his head, he pictured Eirriel. What a feisty little warrior she was, fighting him the entire time, her beautiful eyes sending fiery daggers straight to his heart. She was proud and lovely. Even as he'd taunted her with her lack of bargaining power, she'd stood up to him.

"I have myself."

He could still hear her words and the quiet dignity in her voice. They weren't empty words, and it bothered him to know that. She was well aware of what Kedar would have demanded, yet for her people and her father she would have willingly given herself to him. Something inside him twisted painfully at the thought of her lying in Kedar's arms, of the Blagdenian bastard running his cruel hands over her smooth white skin.

"What's wrong with me?" he muttered disgustedly. "I hardly know her yet the thought of anyone, let alone that murdering whoreson Kedar touching her, makes my skin crawl. What spell has she cast over me with those haunting green eyes?"

Chapter Six

The next morning a sharp rap on the portal roused Aubin.

"Yes, who is it?" he asked sleepily.

"Garreth."

"Enter."

Aubin reached for his pants and slipped them on as his friend entered carrying a tray with three steaming mugs. Garreth placed the tray on the table.

"Raissa will be by shortly," Garreth said, handing Aubin a mug which he accepted gratefully.

"Before she comes, tell me, do I offer my congratulations?" Aubin asked.

"No," came the grim reply. "She refused me again."

"Did she at least tell you why?"

"She needs more time."

"It's been nearly two years, Garreth. That's not enough time?"

"Obviously not," Garreth replied, offhand.

Aubin was not fooled by his friend's casual manner. Garreth was far from unaffected by Raissa's continued refusal to become his life mate. The tall Rhianonian loved Raissa with a passion few people experience in their lifetime and, in spite of indications to the contrary, he knew Raissa felt the same way. Aubin frowned. There had to be a reason she rejected all of Garreth's attempts to formalize their relationship. Perhaps it was something in her past not mentioned in her personnel files.

Before Aubin could voice his idea, Garreth looked at him and Aubin was stunned by the intense emotion burning in his eyes.

"She's afraid, Aubin, that I'll die and leave her. She loved someone, deeply I think. He died. I'm not sure how or when it happened. But I do know it affected her in a way she's not even aware of."

"Have you asked her about him?"

"I can't."

"Why not? If it prevents your life-bonding, I would think you have a right to know the details."

Garreth sighed. "She doesn't know I know. After the Hundar Expedition she woke up screaming his name. I held her as she sobbed and pleaded with him not to die, not to leave her."

Aubin was stunned. "I had no idea."

"For whatever reason it's a well kept secret."

"What do you plan to do now?"

"The only thing I can do. Give her all the love and support she needs."

"Will you ask her again?"

"Wouldn't you?"

Aubin smiled. "Yes."

There was another rap on the portal.

"Come in, Raissa," Aubin called out.

Raissa, tall and shapely, with finely chiseled features enhanced by warm russet-colored, oval-shaped eyes and fine straight black hair that reached well below her waist, stepped into the cubicle. Garreth quickly greeted her.

"Good morn, love."

His kiss brought a peachy flush to her usually light cream complexion and her eyes darkened to a rich brown. She flashed him a radiant smile before turning to Aubin.

"You wanted to see me, Captain?" Her voice was light, melodious.

"Yes, Rai." He motioned to the couch at the far side of

the cubicle. "Please sit down."

She did and Garreth joined her, handing her the mug of now cool liquid.

"If you've no objections, I'd like to assign someone to share your cubicle. In view of your position as chief culturist, I think you should be quite pleased. I have in mind the Dianthian."

"Dianthian? I don't believe I've ever encountered a Dianthian before."

"No doubt you haven't. She's from a planet even the Protectorate seems to have no data on. So as well as the possibility of friendship, there's also the professional aspect to consider."

"If you don't mind, Captain, I prefer to reserve judgment until after I've met her. That is my right by my position, is it not?"

Aubin nodded. "Yes, it is, and I fully understand why you have reservations. The petty jealousy Tira had toward you did not escape my notice. Although there was nothing I could do about it at the time," he added.

Tira, a culturist who had worked and lived with Raissa, had made no secret that she felt she had deserved the promotion to chief culturist, not her cubiclemate. Aubin had arranged for her transfer at the first possible opening, but still Raissa had had to endure several months of snide remarks and unfounded accusations.

"I don't think you'll have any problem this time, but as you said, the decision is totally yours. Now, if you don't mind, I'd like to talk to Eirriel first since I still need answers. Why don't you plan on meeting me in the med-unit at, say, 1900 hours?"

Raissa nodded in agreement. The three of them crossed to the fore conveyor. As they entered, Garreth turned to Aubin.

"Captain, if you've no objections before I report to the com-center I would like to glance through our planet classifications to see if I can find any data on Eirriel's world or a world with similar qualifications. I realize we have little to go on and that Main Terminal couldn't locate anything, but you know as well as I, how haphazard they can be at times. I'd like to give it a try."

Aubin nodded and when the portal opened, Garreth and Raissa, who had offered to help, headed for the file cubicle.

Eirriel laughed with pleasure as the water from the vitalizer sprayed over her. Cian had explained that each private cubicle was equipped with a vitalizer similar to the Dianthian cleansers, but since there space was limited in the med-unit these vitalizers were used while standing. It reminded her of a waterfall except that the water was warmer and made her skin tingle with its gentle pulsating action.

She stepped out and reached for the long robe Cian had loaned her. Slipping it on, she found it wasn't nearly as long as she first thought.

The full sleeves ended midway between her wrists and elbow, and the length reached mid-thigh. Luckily, it was loose and the braided belt was long enough for her to fasten it around her slim waist.

Back in her cubicle, she sat on the restorer and combed her hair. Having slept through the night and well into the afternoon, she was relaxed and refreshed and she let her mind wander. Why did she feel so safe and secure here, especially when the captain treated her so horribly? What did she know about these people? Though they appeared friendly, with the exception of the pale-skinned one, she knew she should not trust them so easily. What if they proved hostile? She was at their mercy with no hope of escape.

She used the small metal clasps Cian had so thoughtfully found for her and pulled her hair up and back to the top of her head. Parting it, she made two long plaits and coiled them about her head. What did the captain plan to do with her, that bronze giant whose searching eyes seem to pierce through all her defenses? Did he plan to send her to his superior, as Kedar did, or would he keep her for himself?

The day was nearly spent with no sign of Aubin, and Eirriel started pacing in frustration.

Enough of this! she railed inwardly. She was tired of not knowing her future. She had existed these past months with no control over her fate, but no longer! If he wouldn't come to her, she would go to him and the consequences be damned! She wanted to know what he planned to do with her and she wanted to know now!

The outer portal swooshed open and Eirriel called out, "Cian, I must see your captain. Please take me to him."

"There's no need for that, Eirriel," Aubin said softly as his burning gaze swept over her approvingly. "I'm here."

Unflinching under his warm perusal, her eyes blazed with anger. "So, you finally return. Are you here to taunt me further?" she demanded, forgetting that scant moments earlier she had been about to seek him out. "Or did you think you kept me waiting long enough and I would be cringing in a corner anxiously awaiting my fate? Well, no matter how long you keep me waiting, you won't find me cowering like the rest of my people! I'll stand up to you like I stood up to Kedar!"

Damn the little minx! Aubin fumed as she continued to berate him. Must she always provoke him? He grabbed her shoulders to stop the barrage.

"Now you listen to me!" he ordered, his deep voice edged with steel. "There are a few matters we need to get straight here and now! I am the captain of this ship and contrary to your belief, you aren't the most important matter that needs my attention!" Eirriel opened her mouth, but the words stuck in her throat after one glimpse of the deadly fury in his eyes. "As captain of this ship, my word is law. You have no alternative, but to do exactly as I say." He paused, "Unless, of course, you plan to leave and I believe you already know just how far you'd get. As for keeping you waiting all day, believe it or not, I am sorry.

"Now"—he released his hold on her—"before I can decide your fate, as you so aptly put it, I need answers."

Knowing she had little choice but to give him the information he demanded, she nodded.

"Good, if you'll have a seat we can get started."

Aubin couldn't help the slight smile that curved his lips as he watched her carefully walk across the cubicle, sit on the very edge of the chair, and attempt to pull the robe's very short hemline down. Wisely, he refrained from pointing out the futility of her efforts.

"My investigation of your world has come up negative. If you can give me more than its name, it would be helpful. Size, climate, topography, anything we can use as a cross reference."

"Dianthia consists of two land masses," she began in a cool, indifferent voice, "surrounded by lots of water. Our climate is ideal and since I have nothing to compare it to I can't tell you about size."

Aubin shook his head. Why had he thought this was going to be easy? "Do you want to go home?"

This brought Eirriel's head up quickly. "Home? Of course I do."

"That cannot happen unless I know where home is. In order to know where it is, I have to know as much as I can about it. Is it pretty?" he coaxed.

Her eyes lit up. "Dianthia is beautiful. The sky is pink, the mountains blue and the grasslands, purple. My people live on Kinara, the largest of the two land masses. Father said it's centrally located." She frowned. "How would he know that?"

"Didn't you explore your world?"

"Me? No, although I did see more of it than most of my people."

"Oh, how was that?"

She smiled, a warm radiant smile and Aubin felt himself blinded by the beauty of it. "I had Onyx, my estalon. From his back I could see the mountains, valleys and flatlands of Kinara."

"An estalon? I don't believe I've ever heard of a creature by that name?"

Eirriel quickly explained what Onyx was and Aubin nodded. "I had heard rumors that they existed. You refer to Dianthians as your people?"

"Dianthia is ruled by Oldens and my father is the Primary Olden. They are my people."

Aubin asked her questions about her town and the crops. In answer she explained that she lived in Edlyn, the largest town of Kinara, built at the junctions of the three main rivers. Because of its ideal location, Kinara had plenty of sunshine and enough rain to keep the crops well watered.

The other land mass, Rimeland, located at the southern-most point of the planet, was a bleak frozen wasteland.

As Eirriel spoke, her eyes glowed with a hidden warmth and her face gentled. Aubin listened intently, his fierce anger melting under her soft caring tones. Seeing her for the first time without her cold defensive manner, he thought her an exquisitely complex creature.

"And your people? You said they cowered when Kedar came."

"I . . . I wasn't there when he arrived, but I know they wouldn't have stood up to them. You have to understand," she said defensively, "we are a gentle people. Much of our time is spent tending the large areas of land, we call them rylans, used solely for growing the provisions we need. We have no machinery and no weapons. We are easy prey for an invader."

"If you weren't there when Kedar landed, how was it you were taken? Was there no one to see to your safety?"

"I had been with a friend, Timos. He would have been all alone when the Blagdenians found him." Her voice lowered to a pained whisper. "He could be dead now and it would be my fault!"

Her torment made Aubin want to comfort her and at the same time he wanted to throttle the man who had such control over her emotions.

"You are only one person, Eirriel, you couldn't have stopped them."

"If I had been with Timos, Onyx would have carried us to safety. Don't you see, I left him landbound!"

Eirriel raised luminous green eyes to Aubin. The sight of her tears proved too much for him and Aubin moved toward her. Raissa's voice calling from the outer cubicle stopped him. With a start, he realized he had been about to take Eirriel in his arms and calm her fears. Even while damning Raissa for her interference, he thanked her.

He had no doubt that once he had Eirriel in his arms he would be hard pressed not to do more than just reassure her. He wanted her, wanted her badly ever since he had first seen her on the alien vessel. But now was not the time. It would never be the time for someone like Eirriel. She would require more from him than a passing dalliance and he had neither the time nor the desire to offer more, no matter how pleasing the end result might be.

"Eirriel, look at me."

The husky timbre of his voice drew Eirriel and she raised her eyes. A shock traveled through her body as their gazes met. *What beautiful eyes he has*, she thought, *when the piercing ice is replaced by a warm golden glow.*

"You must believe me when I tell you no harm will come to you here. The data you have given me will be relayed to our Main Terminal on Hakon. With their help we will find Dianthia. And then I will see you safely home and your people freed from the Blagdenian scum who hold them."

Eirriel gasped. "You would do this for me?"

"Yes." *And for myself*, Aubin added.

"Thank you!" Eirriel cried, her voice filled with an exuberance that warmed Aubin's heart. Her eyes alight with happiness, and a wide smile brightening her face, Eirriel ran to Aubin. Shyly, she leaned into him and planted a small kiss on his lean cheek. "Thank you."

Aubin's eyes darkened at the contact. Without thinking, he reached out and pulled her close. Laughter fled as she felt his arms close about her. Raising her face to his, she felt his lips brush hers. At his touch, a warmth coursed through her body and when he again brought his mouth to hers, she parted her lips and met his rising passion with her own.

Raissa called again and Eirriel flung herself from Aubin. Staring up at him, she raised a trembling hand to her lips. Aubin swore softly. What kind of a man was he to take advantage of her naive show of happiness?

"Eirriel?" he said huskily, fighting the urge to take her in his arms again. "I'm sorry. I shouldn't have let that happen."

Embarrassed by her actions, Eirriel turned her back to him and tried to understand the new sensations assaulting her. Why had she allowed him such liberties? What would he think of her? She felt Aubin's hand on her shoulder and pulled away, unable to control the trembling that overcame her at his searing touch.

Watching Eirriel wrench away from him as if his touch

caused her pain, Aubin cursed. "Eirriel, you don't have to be afraid. I won't touch you again."

He took a deep breath and when he spoke, Eirriel was disappointed to hear him sound once again like the cool captain she had feared.

"There is someone I'd like you to meet. I'll bring her in."

She waited until Aubin left then turned toward the portal. She couldn't understand why, but she felt she belonged in his arms. She frowned. But how could that be? They had just met, how could she know where she belonged? Yet, deep in the very depths of her soul, there was a certainty she could not shake.

Eirriel remembered Aubin mentioning her meeting some-one and hastily ran a hand over her hair, tugged at her belt, took a deep breath and waited. She met Aubin's worried gaze as he reentered and smiled at him, wordlessly reassur-ing him that all was well with her before shifting her eyes to the woman at his side.

She was dressed in a uniform much like Aubin's, with a high narrow heel to her boot. On her shoulder of her fitted top was a blue emblem that Eirriel would later learn labeled her a member of the elite science unit. Her hair was pulled back to the top of her head and clasped with a small golden cylinder.

"Eirriel, this is Raissa. Raissa, Eirriel."

Raissa clasped Eirriel's shoulders and pressed her lips first to one cheek then the other. Releasing her, Raissa stepped back. "One of life's many blessings is the making of new friends. It is my hope we may be so blessed."

"That's the traditional Melonnian welcome," Aubin ex-plained. "I've asked Raissa to share her cubicle with you, Eirriel."

"Are you sure you don't mind?" Eirriel asked.

Raissa smiled warmly. "Not at all."

"Of course, the situation could change," Aubin said with a smile. "Raissa may say yes to Garreth and . . ."

"Captain, you promised you wouldn't get involved," Raissa reminded him sternly, then ruined the effect by laughing.

Eirriel looked at the two of them and felt a sudden ache

for home, for her father, and for Timos. Raissa saw her sad look and quickly reached out to her.

"I'm glad you're here. It'll be nice having someone to talk things over with."

Aubin smiled, pleased by the indications that the two women would do well together. Raissa had always been one of his favorites with her quick mind and gentle wit. She would help take some of the strangeness out of the circumstances for Eirriel, and perhaps some of the sadness as well. A friend, confidante might be what both women needed.

"Raissa, why don't you take Eirriel to your cubicle and then consider your shift ended. I'll see both of you tomorrow." With a wave of his hand Aubin left only to stick his head back in a few moments later. "Oh, Raissa, might think about a uniform for Eirriel. Although I find the way she's attired ravishing, I don't think it's quite right for daily wear."

Eirriel felt her cheeks grow warm under Aubin's heated stare and Raissa's low chuckle. "I guess there is a bit more of me showing then is proper," she admitted sheepishly, then mixed her lilting laugh with Raissa's.

Raissa led Eirriel out of the med-unit and down the passageway, giving her a brief tour as they walked.

"Down there, at the far end is one of the engine cubicles. That area is off limits to all personnel except those in engineering. Ceara, the chief engineer, can show you around at some future time, if you're interested. In between there and here are the science labs and the teleport. Across from the med-unit is the computer cubicle where the main computer is located. From there you have access to all data stored in the individual unit computers."

Eirriel halted in mid-stride. "Com–pu–ter? What is computer? This machine"—she pointed to the language translator strapped to her wrist—"doesn't have a word for it that I can understand."

Raissa laughed. "You really do have a lot to learn! For now let's say that a computer is like a large brain. Information is relayed to the brain where it is stored forever in its memory. When someone needs the information, he or she merely asks and the computer answers, providing, of

course, that the required data has been keyed into its
memory banks. If you really want to understand computers,
ask Garreth, they're his specialty."

"Perhaps I will. I want to learn everything," Eirriel
replied earnestly.

"I'm afraid that will take forever." Raissa smiled. There
was something about Eirriel that reminded Raissa of herself
when she first entered the Academy. She, too, had wanted to
learn everything. All too soon she realized the impossibility
of her desires.

"Listen, Eirriel," she said seriously, "don't feel you have
to learn everything. Even Captain Aubin doesn't know all
there is to know about running the *Celestial*. Give yourself
time to get adjusted to your new surroundings. Start at the
beginning. The first thing you have to learn is our language.
Now let's go to our cubicle."

Raissa continued the tour. "We're now on the lower level.
This is where the com-center is located, the labs, and the file
cubicles, everything needed to run the ship. The three upper
levels are for the crew's private cubicles. The nourishment
center as well as the uniform and clothing dispensaries and
the rec-cubicles are directly below them. In between are the
storage cubicles, the safeguard unit and other units equally
important to the smooth running of the ship. This way."

Raissa guided Eirriel into the conveyor. The portals
closed, only to open scant moments later revealing the
crisscrossing passageways of the upper level. Eirriel stared
about her. Gone were the stark white walls, and in their
place were walls painted in pretty soft shades.

"But how? What? How?" Eirriel stammered. "We walk
into one door, er, portal . . ." She glanced at Raissa to make
sure she had used the correct word. Raissa nodded and she
continued, "And we step out in a completely different
place."

"That was one of seven conveyors used to transport
personnel. This one and two others on this side and the
three on the other side are used by all personnel. The
seventh is for the com-crew only. Located in their private
section, between the captain's and Garreth's cubicles, it
opens directly across from the com-center."

Raissa explained how the conveyor worked as they continued down the passageway to the cubicles near the front of the ship. Stopping at the last portal of the middle section, she said lightly, "Well, here we are. Home for however long you are with us. By the way, this cubicle is 8-1 of the blue section, named after the color of the wall. Remember that. It is important in case of attack."

The Melonnian pressed a switch and the portal slid open. "There are a few things you must know about these cubicles. First, this switch"—she pointed to the last switch on the panel just inside the portal—"is the lock. Normally we don't need it, but it does come in handy at certain times. The middle switch opens the rear portal and the top one this one." Then she walked to a storage unit next to the rear portal and opened it. Taking out two small cylinders she continued, "Second, in here are the emergency oxygen supplies. If, when under attack, the shield doesn't hold and the hull is ruptured, this may be your only supply of breathable air until repairs are completed. And last, that" —she pointed to the restorer next to the rear portal—"is yours. Now I, for one, have had a busy day and I think you have had enough excitement. So why don't we turn the lights off and take our well-deserved rest."

Raissa reached into the storage unit next to her restorer and drew out a long robe. "Don't wait for me. These old bones need a soaking. See you in the morning."

Eirriel studied her new surroundings carefully. According to Raissa the rear portal, her tongue stumbled over the strange word, was kept locked at all times. When the ship was under attack that portal, as well as the one they entered through, automatically unlocked providing easy access to the main passageways. It also served to divide the cubicle into two sections. To the left of the portal were two sleepers—restorers, she corrected herself—each with its own storage unit for private use. To the right, a small section with a relaxer, table and chairs and the portal Raissa had disappeared through.

Eirriel quickly pulled back the silky coverings and slipped into the restorer. As she snuggled under the coverings, she thought of the people she had met who, except for Balthasar, had done their best to make her feel at ease. It would take time but she vowed she would soon take an active part in the running of the *Celestial* for she believed that her destiny was here among these people. That thought in mind, she succumbed to the exhaustion that had been creeping up on her and drifted into restful slumber.

Chapter Seven

Reluctantly, Eirriel stretched and opened her eyes. Glancing at the nearby restorer, she was disappointed to see it empty. Hopefully, she called Raissa's name, grimacing when there was no reply.

It must be late, she thought as she sat up and swung her long legs to the floor. Raissa had mentioned she was on early-morning duty but had promised to return as soon as it ended. Anxious to see more of her new surroundings, Eirriel decided to use the vitalizer now so that she would be ready when Raissa returned.

Walking past the couch, she saw a uniform laid out neatly on its large round cushions. Before she had time to wonder about it, out of the corner of her eyes she spied a small object sitting in the middle of the short cylindrical table. Intrigued by its bright color and unusual design, she picked it up. To her dismay, the multicolored oval on its top started flashing.

"What have I done?" she groaned, frantically searching for whatever it was that triggered the light. Unable to locate it, she gingerly placed the box back on the table, hoping that it had been activated by her touch.

"Why does it keep blinking!" she cried in exasperation. Furious with herself for touching the strange box, she threw it one last angry glare and entered the vitalizer.

Casting aside thought of the blinking light along with her robe, Eirriel stepped into the quickly filling vitalizer. Sinking into the warm soothing water, she unwittingly compared it to her private cleanser which sparked memories of Dianthia. She closed her eyes and laid back as a great sadness washed over her.

Unbidden, thoughts of her father crept into her mind. Alaric, Primary Olden of Dianthia, tall, stately, and proud. Brown of hair, blue of eyes, always ready with tender words or unasked for trinkets. *Alaric, my father, how do you fare?* Eirriel asked him silently, imagining his bitter laugh and answer.

"Invaders overrun my dwelling, unfeelingly murder my people and send my daughter away from me and you would know how I fare? Not well, my little Eirriel, not well."

"Do not despair," she cried to the distant Alaric. "Do not give up, my father. Stay well, please stay well. I will return and not alone. I will bring men the likes of which you have never seen. And, oh, the devices they have! You will see. Together we will rout our enemies and you will once again be Primary Olden. Life will be as it was."

"Nay, my child, it can never be."

Eirriel opened her eyes. They widened in wonder as she beheld a hazy Alaric before her, his voice strangely hollow.

"What was is dead. Too much unhappiness has passed. Nothing can be done to bring back the past. Life continues and so must you. Be well, seed of my Sidra, sprout and grow. Be happy. Know love. Grasp what joy you can find for when you return you'll know nothing but sorrow." Alaric faded from her sight and she heard his voice faintly for one last time. "Farewell, my daughter, we will not meet again. May my love join with Sidra's and protect you. Fare you well, my sweet Eirriel, fare you well."

"Father!" Eirriel called, but he did not answer.

Puzzled, she rose from the vitalizer. Grabbing a soft cloth, she dried herself and wrapped it snugly around her. It seemed so real! she thought and perhaps it was. She knew there were many skills learned by the Oldens. But if that were true, why had her father appeared now when she was safe and with friends and not when she was alone and afraid? Her breath caught in her throat as a chilling thought pierced her heart. He was dead! It was as the Oldens taught, that the essence of a person left the lifeless body and sought those left behind to offer words of comfort. *No! It can't be!* Her heart cried out the denial while her mind reasoned that it had to be. Why else would Alaric have appeared as he did?

Numb with grief, her heart heavy, she sank into the chair, her mind quietly addressing her father. *Alaric, you were all I had left. Why did you have to die? Your life span was still young. There were dreams yet unfulfilled. Why? Why?*

Lost in her private grief, Eirriel did not hear the soft rap or the sound of the portal opening.

"What, still not dressed?" Aubin teased as he entered.

Eirriel raised her tear-strained face and shook her head mutely. Laughter caught in his throat as he saw the tears streaming from her eyes. He quickly crossed the cubicle and gathered her in his arms.

"What is wrong, Eirriel? Trust me, little one. Let me help."

A sob escaped her lips, and she threw her arms around him. "He is dead," she cried.

"Who, my love?"

In her sorrow she did not hear his question or the softly spoken endearment, nor was he aware that he spoke it. "Why, Aubin? Why did my father leave me? Why didn't he wait? Why did he have to die without loved ones to comfort him? Why?"

Knowing she expected no answer, he gave none. His heart twisting with pity, he held her tenderly as her body wracked with sobs. When he finally spoke, it was with deep tenderness. "I'm sorry for your loss. But, tell me, how do you know your father is dead?"

Haltingly she spoke of Alaric and the strangeness of his words. Once again tears spilled from her eyes.

"Come, little one, dry your eyes. Your father must have been greatly troubled as he watched his lands overrun and his people rendered helpless. He had to have been torn between his teachings and his desire for vengeance. Knowing Kedar as I do, he would have threatened your father with your people's destruction unless Alaric made himself his pawn. For someone whose beliefs were as deeply imbedded as Alaric's must have been, there would have been great turmoil raging inside of him. He could not be the cause of further harm to your people, but neither could he allow Kedar to use him to force their obedience. In his death, Alaric, or as you say, the essence that is Alaric, will know a peace he could never have known again in life. Surely you see this?"

Eirriel nodded, not trusting herself to speak.

"On Rhianon, my home planet," Aubin continued, "we believe that at the beginning of time the All-Powerful freed the root of humanity, the soul, and allowed it to inhabit a body of its own choosing wherever it chose. He then charged the soul to always remember its soulmate for only by finding each other would they truly be happy and at peace. Try to think of Alaric once again reunited with his beloved consort. I know it won't make the hurt any less, but it might make it a little more bearable.

"Come. Your father traveled a great distance to speak to you. The least you could do is listen. Make him proud of you! Stand tall. Life goes on and so must you. You have your whole life ahead of you!"

He searched desperately for something to bring the spark back into her eyes. "What about your people? Who is going to help them now?" Seeing her shrug her shoulders apathetically, Aubin stormed, "Don't tell me you don't care! Where's the little warrior that was going to singlehandedly wipe her enemies out of existence? Did she die with Alaric? If so, then his death was wasted and his people still doomed to eternal slavery." Aubin paused, noting with satisfaction a glimmer of defiance in her eyes. "Where is the innocent that would give herself to the enemy to save her people? Did she die, too? And what of the saucy wench who threw herself into my arms when I promised to rid her world of the invaders? Is she gone never to be seen again?" His eyes sparkling with golden lights, he added softly, savoring each word as if it were an exotic dish, "More's the pity for I looked forward to many such encounters with her."

"No, she is not dead!" Aubin's smug grin faded as Eirriel

pulled away from him. She stood up, facing him, her green eyes flashing brilliantly. "But neither is she a succulent morsel to be sampled at will!"

His eyes darkened with anger. Damn! Of all the things he said why did she have to grab onto that one? He stormed across the cubicle. Reaching the portal, he turned to her, his voice coolly arrogant. "If you'll excuse me, I have more important matters to attend to. I have done my duty here!" *All too well*, he thought bitterly as he stepped into the passageway. *All too well.*

Eirriel stared after him stung by his parting words. Duty, was it! she fumed. She stormed to Raissa's side of the cubicle, snatched up Raissa's brush and violently started to brush her hair.

"Duty! Well that's the last time he'll feel duty bound to help me. I don't need him!" she cried adamantly.

Where was Raissa anyway? Why hadn't she returned? Her glance wandered to the couch and she covertly eyed the uniform.

If Raissa wasn't coming back, then Eirriel was going to find her and she certainly couldn't do that dressed in a cloth. Hoping Raissa wouldn't be too angry, she scooped up the uniform and placed it on her restorer.

She dressed quickly, surprised at how well the uniform fit. Stepping in front of the imager, Eirriel was astonished by what she saw. Her hair, parted down the middle and fastened by the short tube clasps Cian had given her earlier, cascaded in long golden coils on either side of her head. The pants stretched like a layer of black skin across her slim hips and tiny waist. The long-sleeved white blouse fit snugly against her full round breasts. The sleek curves of her long legs were emphazied by narrow-heeled, knee-high, black boots.

Pleased with her appearance, Eirriel whirled before the imager. Never having worn pants before she felt wickedly free without the bulky excesses of her gown and reveled in the feel of the soft satiny material that caressed her legs as she walked.

She opened the portal and stepped hesitantly into the passageway. Looking down its long length, she saw that it was empty and breathed a sigh of relief. She wasn't ready to meet anyone new yet. Retracing her steps of yesterday, she found herself in front of the conveyor. Staring at the panel of four buttons, she paused. Now what was she to do? She hadn't paid attention to which one Raissa had pressed and after the episode with the nasty box that was still blinking faithfully, or rather faithlessly, away in her cubicle, she was leery of experimenting. Swearing at herself, she made a mental note to be more aware of what happened around her. If she was to be independent, she could not keep making mistakes nor could she constantly ask for help.

There was no escape. She must either chance that she would press the right button or she must retreat to her cubicle. Reaching tentatively to the top button, she heard a sound from behind the closed portal. Panicking, knowing she would never be able to make it back to her cubicle unseen, she looked for a place to hide. There was none. Caught, she stepped away from the conveyor as the portal swooshed open.

"Garreth!" she cried with relief as the tall Rhianonian stepped into the passageway. "It's you. I feared it would be a stranger."

"Eirriel?" Garreth blinked, unable to believe his eyes. "I hardly expected to meet you wandering around the passageways. I was on my way to make sure you were all right. Aubin told me what happened. I want you to know you have my deepest sympathy. If you need a shoulder, mine is available," he offered amicably.

"Thank you, but I'm fine now." She smiled at him. "But it's nice to know someone cares, just the same."

"We all care," Garreth said gently. "Cian, Raissa, myself. Even Aubin."

Two perfectly shaped eyebrows arched in surprise. "Does he now?"

"Sure. Why else would he have taken the time to comfort you?"

"Thank you, but his kind of comfort I don't need." Garreth's brow furrowed in confusion. "Did Aubin say that he did all he could to offer me support and reassurance?"

He nodded.

"Did he also tell you he did so because of his high sense of duty?" she snapped bitterly. Seeing Garreth's eyes darken in anger, she said, "I didn't think so. He wants you to think he was kind and gentle. And so he was until I was comforted, then he left me, as he so sweetly put it, to see to more important matters. Care indeed! If that's his way of caring, I don't want any of it!"

Garreth swore under his breath. What was wrong with Aubin? Didn't he realize the great strain Eirriel had been under? There was no telling how much more she could take, or for that matter, if she could take any more at all. Most of the females he knew would have cracked under such tremendous pressure a long time ago.

"I'm sorry, Eirriel. If I had any idea of the way Aubin treated you, I would have come sooner. I must admit I'm really surprised by his actions. I've always known him to be extremely compassionate when it's needed."

"Don't you see, it's bad enough that he feels duty bound to see that I'm kept well until he delivers me to his superiors. I won't have him be kind, compassionate for the same reason. If emotions are forced, they are truly worthless.

"Don't worry," she said softly. "As you can see, I suffer no ill effects from your captain's boorish behavior. He is uncouth and ill-bred. Honest emotion is beyond him." She reached up and gently ran her fingers across Garreth's frowning countenance. "Don't let it bother you. I've no desire to be the cause of trouble between you and your captain. I can see that you are close friends. Please, it is of no concern."

His brow burned from her brief touch. Looking into her soft pleading eyes, all he could do was nod.

"Good." She whirled around. "Tell me, am I not truly pleasing to look at?" she asked, casting him a coy look from over her shoulder.

Garreth stared at her. He had been so concerned with her emotional state that he had paid little attention to her clothing. Watching her as she pranced and posed, he felt his blood surge at her incredible beauty. He laughed, totally entranced by her innocence and childlike pride in her new clothes. What other female could gambol about and beg for a compliment yet not seem the least bit calculating?

"Yes," he said, mimicking her words, "you are truly pleasing to look at."

Her soft lilting laughter echoed in the passageway and Garreth could not remember ever hearing such a lovely sound.

"I must confess I spent some time in front of the imager staring at myself. I still can't believe it's me!" Her eyes clouded. "You don't think Raissa will be upset that I borrowed her clothes, do you?"

Garreth shook his head. "No, I don't think she will be too upset since they aren't her clothes to begin with. Didn't Raissa explain that she picked up that uniform from the dispensary before she went on duty?"

"No, she had already left when I woke. I waited for her to return and when she didn't, I put them on anyway."

"Then all is well. See, the emblem is gray not blue. These are yours."

"Mine!"

"Yes, yours. Now come, tell me, where were you off to before we met?"

"When Raissa didn't return, I decided to look for her. She told me her lab was down the passageway from the med-unit so I was going to meet her there. I got as far as the conveyor and didn't know which button to push."

Garreth roared with laughter. "Raissa will be busy most of the day, so I'm to be your instructor." Garreth placed his hands behind his back. Holding his face stern and keeping his voice gruff, he paced in front of the conveyor. "As your first lesson, I will attempt to explain the proper way to utilize the conveyor. As you can see, there are four buttons." He looked down at her, and frowned. "You can see that, can't you?"

Eirriel nodded, her eyes glowing brightly.

"Very good. Now the first button"—he reached up with a quick abrupt motion and tapped the button, then put his hand behind his back—"is used to bring the conveyor to you. The second"—again he pointed and hid his hand—"holds the portal open. The third"—gesturing as before—"

is the automatic override in case the conveyor malfunctions and the fourth is the intercom.

"Now if you'll step this way." He motioned for Eirriel to follow him into the conveyor but she was laughing so hard she couldn't move. "Come, come, my girl. This is hardly the time for frivolity! There are lessons to be learned!"

"Yes, sir. Right away, sir."

She scurried into the conveyor, looking so like a timid meek student that Garreth burst into laughter. As the portal closed, Garreth and Eirriel were both clasping their sides, tears streaming from their eyes.

Garreth gave her a tour of the ship, explaining the function of each department in the simplest terms possible. She listened intently, asking questions till she understood, then storing the information away until it was needed. Having vowed that she would one day become an active member of the crew, she attacked the task with fierce determination. Eirriel knew it would take a long time to learn all that was needed and time was one thing that was in short supply.

Before either of them realized, it was time for Garreth to return to the com-center. He walked Eirriel to her cubicle, promising to continue with his instructions each day. As the portal opened, Eirriel caught sight of the little box and its persistent light.

"Garreth, please, before Raissa returns." She dragged him into the cubicle. "I saw this wretched thing on the table and when I picked it up, it started doing that!" She waved a frenzied hand in its direction. "See if you can fix it. Please," she begged desperately.

Garreth groaned, his hands flying to grasp his head. "What have you done!" He crossed the cubicle and picked up the baneful object. With a quick twist of his hands, it stopped blinking.

Eirriel threw herself at him and hugged him. "Thank you, thank you!"

"It was nothing," he boasted, his golden eyes twinkling mysteriously.

"Nothing! You probably saved my life. Now Raissa will never know—"

She stopped in mid-sentence and wrenched herself from Garreth as she heard Raissa's voice drifting from inside the horrible little box. "Eirriel, you were sleeping so peacefully when it was time for me to report to the lab, I didn't have the heart to wake you. The uniform on the couch is yours. I hope it fits. Garreth will be by this morning to complete your tour. See you at the day's end."

"Why you . . . you . . . !" Eirriel picked up a small cushion and hurled it at Garreth. Garreth ducked and it sailed harmlessly over his head, smashed against the wall and fell to the ground with a thump.

"You! You!" she sputtered unable to say any more.

Garreth cast a bemused look at the cushion, flattened from the force at which it struck the wall, and rubbed his head.

"You really hurled that thing with a vengeance! I do believe you intended to do me harm." He laughed. "Sorry. I couldn't resist. You looked so forlornly desperate. As you heard, that thing is used to relay messages. It must have malfunctioned because the light should blink once the message has been stored thereby attracting your attention. Once you pick it up, the message is automatically played and the blinking ceases."

Eirriel walked away in a huff. She did not like being made to look like a fool.

Garreth dropped to bended knee. Raising his hands beseechingly toward her, his face the epitome of contriteness, he lowered his eyes to the ground.

"Sweet maiden, forgive your lowly servant," he implored her. "He meant no harm. It was but an innocent ploy to bring a smile to your fair lips. Please forgive me. Knowing I have caused you displeasure, I will throw myself into the jaws of the wildest beast. Of course, I must wait until we find a planet inhabited by wild beasts. But when we do, I vow to hurl myself into their fierce jaws to be torn asunder as punishment for this foul deed."

Garreth raised his eyes and stole a glance at Eirriel. She stood with her slender hands crossed over her mouth trying to keep the laughter from bubbling forth. He reached up, grabbed her hands and kissed them.

"Say you will forgive me, oh most beautiful one, and I will slink away into yon corner never to bother you again."

The picture of the tall Rhianonian slinking away proved too much for Eirriel's severely tested restraint and her merry laughter soon filled the air. Just as Garreth started to rise from the floor, pleased that his ploy had worked and that she was smiling once again, the portal opened and in walked Raissa followed by Aubin. Eirriel's and Garreth's smiles quickly transformed into embarrassed grimaces.

Raissa took one look at the scene before her and burst into laughter. Aubin, however, had quite a different reaction. His golden eyes darkened and a look of black fury flashed across his face before being replaced with a look of utter contempt. Garreth rose and placed a protective arm around Eirriel as Aubin addressed her.

"I came to ask you where you secreted my second-in-command and I find him here on bended knee. What was he doing, begging kisses from you?" he sneered.

Eirriel's face burned with anger. Secreted! Begging kisses!

Before she could give voice to her fury, Aubin had turned on Garreth. "Really, Garreth. A man of your age groveling on the floor. Besides," he added snidely, "you don't have to beg her kisses, she gives them freely."

Eirriel gasped and felt Garreth clench his hand in fury.

"You've no right to talk to her like that," he said, his voice deathly quiet.

"My, she certainly seems to have found a champion in you and in such a short time. Tell me, what did she offer in exchange for your protection? The same thing she offered Kedar?"

Eirriel blushed at his lewd suggestion. Garreth brought his fist up with every intention of striking Aubin, but she grabbed his hand.

"Garreth! No!"

Raissa rushed over to the man she loved and forced him to hear her. "What are you doing? You know it's an instant court martial to strike your superior."

"Garreth, it's all right. I want no harm to come to you on my account. Please, leave it be." Eirriel looked up into his eyes. "Go to your post. I'll be fine."

Garreth shook his head, his golden eyes sparking with anger, unwilling to leave Eirriel at the mercy of Aubin's biting tongue.

"For me, Garreth," she pleaded softly. "I cannot be the cause of you losing what you have worked your whole life for. Please go!" Garreth started to object, but she shook her head. "Say no more. Just leave."

Reluctantly, Garreth crossed to the portal.

Aubin laughed sardonically. "How easily you obey her."

Garreth turned, his handsome face contorted with rage, but catching Eirriel's round eyes silently entreating him, he left.

"Raissa, go after him. Talk to him. Make him understand," Eirriel begged.

Raissa nodded her head and grimly followed Garreth. No sooner had the portal closed than Eirriel whirled to face Aubin. Green fire flared in her eyes.

"Bastard! You are lower than a Blagdenian! He is your friend. How could you belittle him so? Did you want him to strike you? Is that why you continued to goad him? Would it ease your conscience to know that he could act as unthinkably as you? It didn't work, did it?" she taunted. "Garreth proved himself to be the gentleman his uncouth captain is not."

His eyes glinting with unreadable emotion, Aubin pulled her to him, his mouth crushing hers. She struggled against the overwhelming need rising in her to answer his passion with her own. Feeling herself on the brink of giving in to his searing kiss, she pushed herself from him and delivered a sound slap to his cheek.

"Bastard! Don't you ever touch me again! I loathe you!"

Aubin looked into her eyes and saw the virulence she professed all too evident. Needing to hurt her, he said bitterly, "I wouldn't touch you again if you were the last woman alive. Frankly, I don't understand what Garreth sees in you. Your lips are as cold as your heart. A kiss from you, my sweet, would freeze a man's blood in the middle of a burning desert!"

Eirriel attempted to strike him again, but he was ready and caught her wrist.

"You struck me once. Don't ever try it again!" His voice was chillingly quiet. "I've never struck a woman before, but there's always a first time so don't tempt me." He raked his eyes over her. "But then you aren't much of a woman."

She yanked her wrist from his hand and gave a sharp laugh. "It takes a man to know a woman. And you, my good captain, are nothing more than a half-grown youth caught up in a masquerade."

Coolly, she walked into the vitalizing area and closed the portal. Aubin threw an ominous glare at the offending portal, swore loudly, then hastened from the cubicle.

"Garreth, wait! I have to talk to you," Raissa called just as he was about to enter the fore conveyor.

Garreth turned impatiently, his eyes still dark with anger.

"Garreth, I . . ." Suddenly she didn't know what to say. Aubin's actions were inexcusable.

"Well, let's hear the excuses. That's why he sent you after me, isn't it?" he said bitterly. "Aubin always has someone make his excuses. He never could apologize. After all, that would mean that he had erred and we all know Aubin never makes mistakes. This time it won't work. I'm sick and tired of his temper," he stormed. "What the hell is wrong with him? He had no right to say the things he said!"

Raissa waited for Garreth to finish venting his anger then it was her turn. Red sparks danced furiously in her russet eyes as she railed, "You're just as bad as he is! You're jumping to conclusions. Aubin didn't send me after you, Eirriel did. And you're not thinking straight. You know Aubin always takes care of his own excuses and apologies. He always owns up to his mistakes. Now calm down and think. When have you ever known Aubin to fly into such a rage over such an innocent scene?"

Begrudgingly, Garreth said he didn't. "But that doesn't excuse him."

"Agreed. But I think you'll find Aubin is as disturbed as we are. From what I hear, the minute he saw that alien vessel he started acting strange, almost compulsive. And onboard the ship, you told me yourself, he knew exactly where she was hiding. He's been alternately kind and cutting, gentle and harsh. It's as if he can't quite decide whether to strangle her or to comfort her. And Eirriel's no better. She's sweet and friendly to us, but as soon as Aubin arrives, her defenses slam into place. There's something between the two of them, an attraction that goes far beyond the physical."

"You expect me to believe that Aubin, who thinks all women are cold-blooded bitches, is in love with a girl he just met?"

"Well, he doesn't know it's love and would laugh in my face if I were to tell him that, but, yes, he loves Eirriel and she loves him. Oh, they're fighting it, each for their own reason and I imagine they will continue to do so for quite some time. As for us, my love, we're caught in the middle and that's precisely where we've got to stay. It'll be hard but we can't choose sides."

"I can't let him walk all over her."

"You have to. Besides, I'd venture to say, they're evenly matched. This is something they have to work out for themselves. I don't think either of them would appreciate any true interference on our parts. Think about it. You'll see that I'm right."

"All right. I'll give it some thought and I'll keep my mouth shut—for now. But if I see he's abusing her, I'll open my mouth so loud that they'll hear me all the way back on Hakon! Fair enough?"

"Fair enough!"

Garreth pressed the button and the portal opened. He stepped inside the conveyor. Raissa watched the portals close, then left for her cubicle, fervently hoping Aubin had left.

Aubin arrived in the com-center shortly after Garreth and immediately approached his best friend. "Garreth, I'm sorry. I don't know what came over me," he said sheepishly. "I spoke in anger. I guess it just got to me. Hearing the two of you laughing all day when she hasn't a nice word to say to me, and then catching the two of you at play . . . Well, I got carried away."

Aubin extended his right hand and Garreth, remembering Raissa's words, clasped it soundly.

"Consider it forgotten."

"Thanks."

"Don't mention it. Besides," Garreth teased, "why bicker over one female when we have the whole universe at our disposal."

Eirriel was already settled in her restorer when Raissa entered their cubicle.

"Yes, I found Garreth," she replied, anticipating Eirriel's question. "And, yes, he's promised to forget it. The next time you see Aubin and Garreth they'll be the best of friends again."

"Thank you. I wouldn't be able to live with myself if I broke up their friendship. They've known each other a long time, haven't they?"

Raissa nodded. "Since the Academy. Although Garreth's three years older than Aubin, they were in the same level and, in fact, shared the same cubicle. They soon became good friends, but it wasn't until Aubin saved Garreth's life that Aubin was accepted by the rest of his older classmates."

"Saved Garreth's life! What happened?"

"It was during one of the practice runs in which they had to maneuver their mini-cruisers through an extremely difficult and dangerous training course. Garreth's controls malfunctioned and he was unable to steer his cruiser away from the largest asteroid in the course. He was headed straight for it and certain death. Aubin saw the danger to his friend and quickly plotted an intercept course. As he passed between the asteroid and Garreth, he activated the grapple beam and dragged the inoperable cruiser to safety. From what I know, Aubin had only one chance to grab onto Garreth's cruiser, and his course took him so close to the asteroid that a slight miscalculation on his part would have sealed Garreth's fate and his own. He pulled it off and to hear Garreth speak of it, he made it look easy."

"Garreth must be very grateful to him."

"Yes, but over the years he has returned the favor, as has Aubin. In fact, if I remember correctly Garreth's one up on Aubin."

"Is what they do that dangerous?"

"Very. I know it's hard for you to imagine because we seem so invincible to you, but while the *Celestial* is the best of her class of fleetships and has yet to be so badly damaged that her crew's safety is threatened, every time we engage an enemy, be they Blagdenians or someone else, we risk our lives. And those of us who form the landing crews are even more susceptible. We have no idea what or whom we'll encounter when we teleport down to a strange world. Aubin and Garreth are always the first ones down. In this, they flout Protectorate policies."

"How so?"

"Because one or the other should remain safely aboard the ship should something go awry. But Aubin will not send one of his crew into an unknown situation and Garreth wouldn't think of letting Aubin go alone. Both are confident that, should the need ever arise, Theron is more than capable of assuming command."

"How long have you been with the *Celestial*?"

"Since her maiden voyage and I've loved every minute of it. Now that I've satisfied your curiosity won't you do the same for me and tell me what happened after I left?"

Eirriel shook her head. "I'd rather not talk about it."

Tactfully Raissa ignored the tears in her friend's eyes and after changing into her sleeping robe, slipped into her restorer.

"Before I forget, Garreth, Cian and I have worked out covering our shifts so that we can each help you at different times of the day. Cian will be by early in the day to help you with our language."

"I'm grateful for all your help."

"We're glad to do it." Raissa reached up and pressed a switch above her head. "Sleep well, my Dianthian friend."

"You as well, Raissa."

Eirriel lay back on the small cushion and closed her eyes. Remembering that she had forgotten to thank Raissa for the uniform, she sat up again.

"Raissa, are you awake?" Hearing a mumbled reply, she thanked her and then settled back down.

Raissa turned to face Eirriel. "I'm glad you liked them.

They fit so well, but then Aubin always was a good judge of size."

In the dim light filtering from the passageway, Raissa saw Eirriel's eyes shoot open. A pleased look appeared on the Melonnian's face. *That will give her something to think about*, Raissa thought smugly, as she turned over and drifted off to sleep.

Chapter Eight

When Cian arrived the next morning, Eirriel was already dressed and waiting anxiously to start her lessons. After a light nourishment, they proceeded to the lower level computer cubicle. It was there that she would spend the first half of the next few days learning the Hakonese language.

Cian activated the computer's circuitry. Pulling a long wire from the translator Eirriel wore strapped to her wrist, he plugged it into the terminal. While he was doing that, he explained the background of Hakonese, the universal language of the Empyreal Protectorate.

Each member world had its own planetary language, time and culture, but because of the enormous differences between each planet, there had to be one language all could understand. It was decided that the language spoken on Hakon, the Main Terminal of the Protectorate, would be taught to every planet at the time they joined. They were also expected to adapt time measurements and the customs of the Hakonese.

Eirriel protested the unfairness of making members forfeit the uniqueness of their cultures in order to join the Protectorate. But Cian quickly reassured her. Each member retained its individual culture and only used Hakonese methods and language when dealing with the Empyreal Protectorate.

"Everything's set. Eirriel, say a word in Dianthian."

"Dwelling."

As soon as she said it, the viewing screen projected several images. As each image was displayed, the computer spoke its name. Thus she learned that dwelling was "haus" in Hakonese, "clan abode" in Rhianonian and "ham" in Melonnian.

Cian shook his head and punched several keys. He asked her to say another word and she said "sleeper." This time, however, only one image appeared and one word was spoken—"restorer."

"Much better. That blasted machine expects you to learn all member and ally languages as well as Hakonese. Now, any questions before we start?"

"Yes. Aubin told me the Protectorate knows nothing of Dianthia. If that's true, then how does this computer know my language?"

"It doesn't, my dear."

Eirriel frowned in confusion.

"Then how does it give you new words?"

She nodded.

"It's really very simple. Remember I told you the translator works telepathically?" Cian paused and again she nodded. "This works the same way. When you say a word in Dianthian, your subconscious forms an image of that word. It is the image, not the spoken word, that is relayed to the computer. It then connects the image with its equal, or its closest counterpart, in Hakonese and relays it to you. Understand?"

Cian read the understanding in her eyes, and said, "Good. We'll spend two hours on this and two hours on the written language. I can see you are anxious to begin, so start any time."

A wave of panic rushed over her. What made her think she could ever be part of these people? There was so much to learn. Customs. Rules. And the language. It was so different! So complicated! The enormity of the project struck her and her mind drew a blank. How was she to learn? What was she to say? She closed her eyes and took several deep breaths until she felt calm and ready to work.

Her jaw set with determination, her green eyes sparkling, she attacked her chore wholeheartedly. Methodically, she named one object in the cubicle, listened to the computer relay the Hakonese word, repeated it several times, then moved on to the next object. By the time Garreth arrived, she had memorized each item in the cubicle.

A pattern soon developed. Eirriel spent the early part of the day with Cian learning Hakonese, the later part with Garreth learning the basics of the ship and the evenings with Raissa learning the customs.

Eirriel and Raissa became inseparable, their friendship steadily increasing with each passing day. On her seventeenth day as they were beginning to retire, Eirriel told Raissa she was surprised that they had not seen more of the captain other than the brief encounters in the passageway.

"Not that I mind in the least," she said in fluent Hakonese, "it's just that I'm afraid he's still angry with me. He might send me away before I have a chance to prove myself capable of joining the crew."

"I see no reason for you to leave unless you choose to," Raissa quickly reassured her. "Captain Aubin has always chosen his own crew and the Protectorate has backed him. No matter what there is between the two of you that sets you at odds with each other, he is a professional. If he feels you would be an asset to the ship, he'll enlist you despite his personal views. As far as not seeing him, there are many times when several days pass in which I hardly . . . Eirriel, what's wrong?"

Eirriel pressed her hands to her head as if in great pain. Her eyes blurred.

"Eirriel!" Raissa waved her hand in front of her friend's eyes. No response!

"Eirriel!" she called again. This time Eirriel's eyes flickered, then focused. "What happened? Are you all right?"

"It's him." Eirriel lowered her hands as the pain vanished. In a voice that was lifeless and shallow, she said, "The man whose touch is as cold as ice and skin as pale as the dead."

"Balthasar?"

Eirriel nodded.

"What about him? Please tell me what's wrong? I want to help."

"He's inside my head! He's trying to . . ."

There was a rap on the portal, and Eirriel's eyes widened in fear. "It's him!" she cried. In her fright she lapsed into Dianthian.

"But how do you know?" Raissa asked, trying to make some sense out of her friend's peculiar behavior.

"I know."

There was another rap on the portal.

"Please don't leave me alone with him!" She clutched at Raissa's hands with ones that were frighteningly cold. "I'm not strong enough to keep him out of my mind at such a close distance!"

"Eirriel! You're not making any sense! Keep him out of your mind! How! What do you mean?" Raissa's voice was frantic with worry. Whatever was troubling her friend was no simple thing.

"I know you are in there, Dianthian. Let me in!"

Raissa glanced at Eirriel then bid him to enter.

"I'm sorry we took so long answering, your lordship, but I had to finish dressing," Raissa lied, her voice implying anything but regret.

"Well, now that you are finished, leave us," Balthasar ordered, ignoring her sarcastic address.

"This is my cubicle and you've no right to order me to leave. You old bully," she added under her breath.

"What was that, my dear?"

"Apparently you heard me!" Raissa retorted. "And I'm not your dear!"

"I'll report you to the captain."

"Go right ahead," she replied sweetly, calling his bluff. She had the distinct feeling that Aubin knew nothing of the scene that was about to unfold and would be furious when he found out.

Blast the interfering Melonnian! Balthasar seethed inwardly. He had wanted to interrogate Eirriel alone so that he could pressure her into revealing the source of her powers, but he hadn't been able to catch her alone. Now with only five days left until they reached Xandor III, he could wait no longer. And with the quick-witted Raissa present, he would have to try and pry it out of her with very subtle questions.

"I think I have given you ample time to recuperate from your emotionally draining experiences, Dianthian. I want answers and I want them now!"

"I spoke with Captain Aubin long ago," Eirriel answered in Dianthian. Only Raissa and Cian knew she had mastered Hakonese and for some reason Eirriel knew it would be deadly if Balthasar found out. "I don't know what more I could add."

"I believe you do. But go ahead, play the little innocent. This planet of yours, Dianthia I believe you call it, don't you find it odd that with all the methods at their disposal the Protectorate has been unable to discover a planet by that name?"

Raissa jumped to her feet. "Balthasar, you of all people should know that nonmember planets are not always classified by the same name they use themselves."

"I was not talking to you, Melonnian. Do not interrupt me again!"

Raissa favored him with a withering glare, then walked over to her dressing compartment. Pretending to search for something to wear, she switched on her portcorder, the mini-recorder she used to record her notes while on a planet's surface.

"Do you think I should wear the blue print or the pink?" she asked, grabbing the first two outfits her hands touched. At Balthasar's glare, she shoved them back in. "You're right, neither will do."

"Shut up and sit down!" Balthasar bellowed.

Raissa raised her head and with quiet dignity walked to the restorer, sitting down stiffly beside Eirriel.

"Now if you've no further objections?" Without waiting for her answer, he began drilling Eirriel. "What is the name of your planet?"

"Dianthia."

"It's true name!"

"Dianthia. I know no—"

"Where is it located?"

"I don't know!"

"Do you really expect me to believe that? Where is it?"

"I already told you!"

"You are a liar! Well, no matter. Is it true that your people possess great mental powers?"

Shocked by his abrupt and, to her mind, absurd accusation, Eirriel could only stare. As she did, she was taken aback by the wave of irrational fear he projected.

"Why are you afraid of me?" she asked in awe.

"I fear no one," he sneered. "Especially you. It is my duty to protect my captain from those who would do him harm."

"And you think I could hurt him?" Eirriel laughed. "You are not making any sense."

"There is a way and you know it!" Balthasar ground out fiercely.

A profound silence settled in the cubicle as the two stared into each other's eyes. Raissa would later recall that it looked like a battle of wills. Green eyes boring into gray, until the gray ones lowered.

"I said you were mistaken," Eirriel said very quietly.

"You lie!" Balthasar accused again.

Realizing that Balthasar would keep drilling Eirriel unless she put a stop to it, Raissa cut him off before he could speak. "I believe you heard her answer once, no twice. Do you need to hear it again? Perhaps you do. She said—"

"Bah! Enough of this!" His eyes darkened ominously. "I will be back, I promise you! And the next time you will be alone," he threatened, the sound of his voice causing Eirriel to blanch and Raissa to shudder.

Balthasar crossed to the portal, turned and faced Raissa. "You would be wise to forget your interfering ways and keep this to yourself."

"I promise I won't repeat a word." Raissa silenced Eirriel with a glance. She walked to the portal and pressed the switch. As it swooshed open she said, "Now if you'd be so kind."

In a huff Balthasar stormed from the cubicle, the portal closing automatically behind him.

Eirriel looked at Raissa, the tears she had struggled so
long to keep hidden streaming from her eyes. "I thought you
were my friend. Why won't you tell Aubin of this visit?"

"Do you plan to tell him?"

"Yes, but he might not believe me. If you're my witness,
he'll have to. He trusts you."

"I promised not to repeat a word and I won't." Raissa
walked over and retrieved the portcorder from its hiding
place. Laughing gleefully, she said, "I won't have to. Captain Aubin will hear it from none other than Balthasar
himself!"

Raissa told her to activate the electronic lock, then left in
search of Aubin. Both women were unaware that Balthasar
was skulking around the corner, a bright glint reaching his
eyes as he watched Raissa leave.

Raissa stormed into the med-unit. "Cian, I realize it's
late, but I have to talk with you and the captain. And it has
to be now!"

Bushy brows arched in silent question, but always sensitive to the moods of others, Cian crossed to the intercom.
"Med-unit to com-center."

"Aubin, here."

"Good, you're still there. Can you spare me a few
minutes before you retire?"

"Something wrong?"

"Possibly."

"Can you meet me here?"

Raissa shook her head emphatically.

"It would be better if you come here, Captain," Cian told
him.

"Very well, I'm on my way. Aubin out."

Raissa gestured frantically.

"What's that? Oh, all right. Er, Captain, would you bring
Garreth as well? Thanks, Cian out. This had better be
important, young lady," Cian rebuked sternly.

"It is, Cian," Raissa promised. "Something very strange
just happened. I'd rather explain it only once, if you don't
mind."

"Harumph! Wouldn't make any difference if I did, would

it?" he muttered. "Well, sit down and make yourself comfortable."

Eirriel tossed fitfully on the restorer, her much-needed rest plagued by nightmares. A smothered hiss escaped her tightly drawn lips, but to the young woman ensnared in the black depths of unreality, the cry was all too real. "Stay away! Don't touch me!"

She ran, lost in the murky world of shadows. Unusually large luminescent eyes lurked everywhere, their grotesque bodies hidden by the thick umbra. Clammy hands clutched at her, ripping pieces from her gown as she eluded their grasp. Unable to see, she stumbled over an object sprawled across her path. She gasped in horror as the somber half-light revealed it to be Timos, the back of his head a bloody pulp. Crawling over his lifeless form, she staggered to her feet. Looking wildly for someplace to hide, she found none.

Again, she felt the clutching hands. Again, silent screams issued forth. Again, she ran. And ran. And ran.

"Eirriel!"

She stopped abruptly. Her frantic eyes scanned the darkness and rested on a large hulk looming in the distance.

"Eirriel! Over here!"

She laughed with relief as she recognized Aubin's deep voice. She ran to him, and strong arms pulled her close. She buried her face in his shoulder. Lulled by the warmth of his embrace, and secure in the knowledge that he would keep her safe, she rested her head on his chest and closed her eyes. He reached up and tenderly ran his hand down the side of her face. Startled by the iciness of his touch, she looked up. Horror overcame her as the bright golden lights in his eyes dimmed and turned gray.

"Balthasar!"

"Yes, Balthasar," he sneered.

Repulsed by his nearness, she pushed against him and was surprised by the iron strength in his frail arms.

"Your struggles are useless, my dear. Here it is the mind that supplies strength, not muscle." He threw back his head and laughed triumphantly.

Icy fingers of fear traveled down her spine as Eirriel realized she was no longer dreaming. Ruthlessly, using his skills to pierce her defenses, he had pressed his advantage while she slept and entered her mind.

"What—what do you want?" she rasped.

"You know already."

"No! I don't!"

"Why do you insist on playing this little game?" he demanded. "You and I both know you possess great mental abilities."

"I don't know what you are talking about!"

"Then you are a fool!" he retorted scornfully. "Within you is a force so unlimited, so potent, that a mere thought could wrought untold destruction!"

"You're mad! If what you say is true, why am I so helpless now?"

"I must admit I haven't the answer to that—yet! But be warned. I will have it soon, but until I do . . ."

Balthasar dropped his arm. Freed, Eirriel turned to run, but found her feet unable to move. Her hands shot to her temples as a sharp pain seared through her head. Automatically her mind tried to flee and failed.

"You won't escape me this time," Balthasar said with menace. "I underestimated you once. That will not happen again."

His gray eyes bore into hers. A chilling numbness started in her toes and crept upward. Her breathing became strained as a great pressure settled on her chest. Gasping for breath, Eirriel screamed Aubin's name as a wave of icy blackness encompassed her.

Chapter Nine

"Now what is this all about?" Aubin asked as he and Garreth strode into the med-unit.

"I asked Cian to call you," Raissa said. "I didn't want it known that I was talking to you." Aubin arched a brow in question. "You'll understand soon enough. It concerns Eirriel. There's not much I can say at this time to back me up. In fact, I was going to wait until I had specific data to give you, but my hand has been forced prematurely." Deep russet eyes glanced over the men as she said intently, "Eirriel is not what she seems. Oh, I don't mean she's an enemy or a threat of any kind, or that she's lied in any way. I'm not even sure myself exactly what she is. But what I do know is that she's more than she claims to be." Raissa paused to give the three men time to absorb her startling opinion.

"There's something about the way she looks," she continued, "physically looks, that puts me in mind of something, someone. Then there's the incident with Balthasar when he first saw her. Why was he unable to sense her presence? Why was his behavior so erratic?

"No, Garreth," she said quickly, stopping his accusations before he voiced them. "It's not what you think. I honestly believe he was as surprised as any of you that she was on that ship. And what about you, Aubin? You told me yourself you knew before you set foot on that ship that there was a female, a very frightened female to be specific, on board. Even though you had never been on a vessel of that kind you knew exactly where she was hiding.

"Finally, there's this last episode." She told them of her conversation with Eirriel, of her fears of Balthasar, of the knowledge that he was outside the portal. "But most of all, it was what she said. 'I'm not strong enough to keep him out of my head at such close distance.' I don't even think she realized what she implied she was capable of when she said that. There's also Balthasar's strange questions and leading innuendoes, but above all else there's this. If he had such an obsessive need for answers, why didn't he just read her mind?"

Raissa explained how she turned on the portcorder and the trio listened to the strange conversation.

"Well, what do you think?" she asked after they had listened to it several times.

Cian was the first to speak. "I agree with Raissa. There is indeed something very different about our Eirriel. Besides everything already mentioned, she seems to have an uncanny knack for language. Are you aware, Aubin, how far she has progressed in only seventeen days? Remarkable! Like you, Rai, I am unaware of what or who she is, but I think we might find some clues in your reports. Somewhere you must have studied cultures that dabbled in mind-control experiments like those on Tri-III."

"There have been rumors of cultures where people are born with some degree of telepathic powers," Garreth offered. "But if her people are of that nature, why would they let Kedar walk right in?"

Aubin shook his head. "I don't think they are, Garreth. Eirriel was very candid with me about her people once I told her that the more I knew about them the better our chances were of finding her planet and getting her home." He dragged his hand through his hair. "Until we learn the reasons behind Balthasar's unsettling reaction to her, I don't want her left alone. We'll have to act as a buffer between the two of them. Raissa, if you can't be with her, call one of us."

"You don't think he'll hurt her, do you?" Garreth's tone implied his belief in the opposite.

"No," Aubin replied confidently. "He may push a little too hard for answers to whatever he's searching for, but I can't see him actually harming her in any way. If I did, he would be in a restraining cubicle."

"He better not." Garreth warned gravely.

"I don't want to see her hurt any more than you do, Garreth. In the meantime . . . Yes, Rai?"

Raissa looked at her captain as if he'd suddenly sprouted wings. "I didn't say anything."

Aubin frowned. "I thought I heard . . . Never mind," he said, brushing aside the disquieting feeling. "In the meantime, Cian, I want you to run some tests on her, ostensibly to study her Dianthian anatomy. Garreth, while Eirriel is with Cian, you help Raissa search her files." Aubin cocked his head and listened, sure he heard his name called. Again, he brushed aside the feeling. "Something about Eirriel nudged a memory in Raissa. I want to know what it is. Any questions?"

All three shook their heads.

"Good. Then I think you should get back to Eirriel, Rai. She's been alone long enough. Cian, continue as you were. Garreth, I'd like a word with you. Oh, one last thing. I don't want either Balthasar or Eirriel to think anything is wrong so be very discreet in your questioning."

Garreth accompanied Aubin to his cubicle. As soon as they entered, he turned to Aubin.

"Yes, I will keep a close surveillance on Balthasar. And, no, I won't let him know I'm doing it."

Aubin's deep laugh rang out. "Are you into mind-reading as well?" he teased, slapping Garreth playfully on the back. "Come share a drink with me before you retire."

The Rhianonian captain walked to a wall unit and pressed a button. A small section sprang open and a tray moved out. Knowing his friend's taste, he poured two beakers of the sweet and sour Melonnian brew. Handing one to Garreth, he quickly downed his.

In the middle of refilling his beaker, Aubin stopped abruptly. He looked at Garreth, his eyes squinting in concentration. The beaker crashed to the floor as he cried Eirriel's name. Grabbing the neutralizer from its clip on the wall, he tore from the cubicle. A very confused Garreth quickly followed suit.

Arriving at Eirriel's cubicle, Aubin found Raissa frantically pounding on the portal. Thrusting her aside, he raised his neutralizer and fired at the lock. The mechanism released its hold. Rushing in, Aubin glanced around, uncertain as to what he would find. His face blanched as he spied Eirriel lying on the restorer, her face contorted with fear, her body stiff. Aubin dashed to her side and scooped her up in his arms.

"Eirriel, little one, wake up."

He ran his hand gently down her hair. At her name, Eirriel's eyes sprang open, but there was no recognition in them as they stared straight ahead, unseeing.

"Garreth, get Cian!" Aubin ordered, his voice harsh with concern. "I can't wake her!"

Garreth quickly pressed the intercom and paged Cian.

Drawing her closer, Aubin rocked her, his softly spoken words of reassurance falling on unhearing ears.

Raissa's russet eyes deepened to a dark brown. "Balthasar!" She uttered the word with a quite vehemence, unknowingly voicing Garreth's suspicions. Garreth glanced at Aubin, who nodded grimly at his unvoiced question. Garreth tore out of the cubicle, almost knocking Cian off his feet as he arrived.

Deep blue eyes instantly turned inward as Cian evaluated Eirriel's condition and sought a remedy.

"Release her," he bid his captain scant moments after he entered the trance.

Reluctantly, Aubin lay her on the restorer and stepped away. Cian leaned over Eirriel and placed two fingers on each of her temples. Slowly applying pressure, he chanted softly.

Aubin studied the strange young woman. Her pale beauty

was whitened by fear, her animated green eyes unseeing, or perhaps all too seeing, her slender body tense as if warding off unseen blows. His heart ached at the thought that she might die. His golden eyes blazed with hatred. Why had Balthasar done this? How? Had he misjudged Balthasar's honor and his strength all along?

Cian straightened his small frame and turned to Aubin. "I've done all I can. We must wait."

"When will we know?"

"Not for several hours, I'm afraid."

"I must find Garreth. You'll call me if there's any change?"

Cian nodded. "Before you go, tell me, how did you know she was in danger?"

Aubin cast a haggard look in her direction. "I heard her call me. I mean, inside my head I heard her call!" He paled. "Do you hear what I am saying! What have I done?" He was silent for a moment then continued, his voice a hoarse, guilt-ridden whisper. "I heard my name called twice during our discussion. At first I thought it was you, Raissa, but when you said it wasn't I ignored it. I thought I was hearing things! If only I had paid more attention, maybe I could have reached her in time!"

"How were you to know it was she who called? Do not worry, my friend. Eirriel has a hidden strength or else she would have succumbed long ago." Cian spoke with a reassurance he far from felt.

"She will live?"

"Do not worry. Go. Find Balthasar before he does further harm."

Aubin took one long look at Eirriel, then left.

"What could have happened, Cian?" Raissa asked.

"I can only guess based on your report. I believe Balthasar took advantage of your absence and attacked Eirriel mentally. I fear Garreth may have been correct. Balthasar's mind may have snapped."

Raissa's eyes darkened with worry for her new friend and for her captain.

Aubin had dropped his guard when he had first seen the stricken Eirriel and Raissa had borne silent witness to the

deep feelings that had flickered across his handsome face.
His golden eyes, however briefly, had held the tortured look
of a man whose woman tottered precariously on the brink
of death. A feeling she herself was no stranger to.

Although he had been her brother and not her lover,
Dever's death had threatened Raissa's sanity. Holding him
as he lay dying after the fluke cruiser accident, she had
sworn to protect herself from the pain of loving and losing
someone by never letting her heart become involved again.
And she hadn't, she thought fiercely, denying her deep
feelings for Garreth, feelings she refused to admit rivaled
those she believed her captain had for her young friend.

Raissa turned her thoughts away from Dever and back to
Eirriel and Aubin and their love for each other that neither
would admit to.

Her eyes grew warm with remembrance as she recalled
the teachings of her world, so similar to those on Rhianon,
that ordained the unconscious quest of the soul for its mate.
The road was rocky, many fought the compulsion only to
surrender in the end to an all-consuming union. Others,
fearful of losing themselves, fled, forever denying themselves complete happiness. Raissa believed Aubin had
found his mate in Eirriel.

Though they continued to wage their separate wars,
denying to themselves their obsessive need for each other,
they would succumb. Their souls would unite and theirs
would be a love of such magnitude all else would pale before
it.

Even as Raissa continued to think about Aubin and
Eirriel and never once saw herself as one of those who
denied their love, Cian studied Eirriel.

For one of the few times in his life he felt unsure. If
Balthasar had physically injured Eirriel, no matter how
severely, he had no doubt that he could have helped her. But
this, he mused dispiritedly, stroking his beard. This was so
unique, so potentially lethal. He had no means to determine
the precise damage. The mind was such a complex, extremely sensitive organism. There were so many variables!

His hands behind his back, his shoulders bent, Cian
paced about the cubicle. If only he knew more about her.

Raissa's data prior to the vicious attack led him to hope he had acted correctly. The Turlian Chant should cause her mind to relax enough to conquer its fear and regain control of her will, thereby healing itself. It had to work!

The Drocot's steady pacing drew Raissa from her thoughts, and she shuddered to see how really worried he was.

"I should have been here when she needed me. Perhaps I could have prevented this."

Cian stopped his pacing. "You were correct warning us, Raissa. Precious time would have been lost trying to determine her ailment. Even if you had been here, you would have been unaware of her peril. Balthasar besieged her in a way none could have witnessed. I suspect he wasn't even in the cubicle."

"You're right. When I arrived, the portal was still secured. The captain had to use his neutralizer." An impish gleam appeared in her eyes. "Lurking in the shadows does seem to be Balthasar's style."

Cian nodded in agreement, smiling slightly before his face grew grim. "This only enforces the need to discover the true reason behind Eirriel's uniqueness. I know it's late, but—"

"Would I start looking now?" Raissa finished. "Gratefully. It'll give me something to do while we wait."

Raissa was on her way to the culture lab before Cian had time to turn back to his patient.

Aubin joined Garreth just as the safeguard team finished the search of the crew's quarters.

Garreth took one look at his friend's closed expression and knew Aubin didn't need to be reminded that this all could have been avoided if Balthasar had been restrained as Garreth had suggested. He also knew the mutant would have cause to regret touching Eirriel. Aubin would see to that.

"What's the status?" Aubin demanded in clipped tones.

"Balthasar was sighted near the rec-cubicles less than half an hour ago," Garreth reported.

"And the lower level?"

"We're just about to—"

Garreth was interrupted by the shrill whistle of the intercom.

"Com-center to Captain Aubin."

Aubin strode to the nearest intercom. "Aubin here."

"Captain, on-board computer indicates the dispatching of two mini-cruisers. Did you authorize any departures?" queried the nightshift navigator.

"No. Activate viewing screen full mag. Keep those cruisers in view at all times. Scan them for life-readings, though I'm sure you'll only find one of them manned. I'm on my way. Aubin out."

Aubin ordered the safeguard team on stand-by, then he and Garreth headed for the com-center.

"Did you locate the manned cruiser?" Aubin asked, assuming his place at the com-console.

Vanux, who was studying the questor readout, wore a puzzled look as she shook her head. "The questors seem to be malfunctioning. I'm receiving nothing but static."

"Thank you, Vanux, I'll take over now." Pressing the blinking buttons, Garreth swiftly confirmed her report. Bending down, he removed one of the panels. Checking the circuits, he replaced the panel and stood up. "This static is not caused by a malfunction, Captain. Something is interfering with the beam."

Aubin pressed the intercom. "Engineering?"

"Yes, Captain?"

"Ceara! I'm glad you're still on duty. Did you install any of the experimental scramblers today?"

"Yes, I did, Captain. Cruisers I and III. Why?"

Aubin quickly explained the problem.

"I'll be right there. Engineering out."

"Shalter, what's our status?"

"We're in the Olion IV star system, just entering Sector 5 traveling at vel 3."

"It seems he knew what he was doing," Garreth remarked dryly. "Not only did he utilize the only two cruisers with scramblers, he jumped ship in one of the most populated sectors of this star system. Olion IV consists of fifteen large planets, ten planetoids, and twenty-eight smaller satellites, not to mention the two asteroid belts. Total occupancy of

.seventy-seven percent."

Ceara rushed into the com-center in time to hear Shalter's report that the two mini-cruisers were passing out of visual range.

"I was staying late to hook this up, Captain." She indicated the tiny circuitry she held in the palm of her hand. Removing the top panel of Garreth's computer system, she quickly attached the unit to the questors. "There. All you have to do is activate the questors. The booster I added overrides the scrambler. After all," she added, her black eyes twinkling, "the reason for the scramblers is to confuse the enemy, not ourselves."

Garreth switched on the questors and swore. In the short time it had taken Ceara to connect the booster, the cruisers had passed out of range.

"We've lost them, Captain."

"Shalter, increase speed to vel 5. Compute the projected course of the mini-cruisers and alter our course accordingly. While he may outmaneuver us with his mini-cruiser, the unmanned craft is on automatic."

"Course plotted, Captain. Increasing speed to vel 5."

"Captain, you said he. You know who commandeered the mini-cruisers?" Vanux asked.

"Balthasar."

All faces, except Garreth's, turned toward him, stunned. Although few liked the safeguard officer, none thought he would desert.

"From all appearances Balthasar has turned renegade. He has used his powers to seriously injure the Dianthian. We've yet to discover his reasons since she's in no condition to talk. It may be that he is only off balance where she is concerned or he may be totally unstable. Whatever the case, I can't risk his being free. He must be captured. Vanux, inform Main Terminal of my suspicions. Tell them we are pursuing Balthasar with all due haste."

"Yes, Captain."

"Got him!" Garreth exclaimed. "Or rather I have one cruiser located just ahead and in one moment . . ." Pressing a series of switches, he adjusted the questor. "Damn! Unmanned!"

Now it was Aubin's turn to swear. "Shalter, activate the

grapple beam and bring it in."

"Grapple beam activated, sir."

Turning to Garreth, Aubin asked, "And the other?"

Garreth shook his head.

"Com-center to safeguard unit."

"Drex here, Captain," came the booming voice.

"Drex, we're bringing in the unmanned cruiser. I want a team to report to docking bay six immediately. I want a full report—where it was headed, when it was programmed, anything that might help us locate Balthasar. And I want it as soon as possible."

"Very good, Captain. Drex out."

"Aubin?" Cian's voice came over the intercom.

"Is she awake?" Aubin asked anxiously at the same time dreading the answer.

"Yes."

"We'll be right there." Uncontrolled relief flooded Aubin's features until he remembered where he was. Masking his emotions, his cool calm voice making a lie of the feelings bursting inside him, he told Vanux to replace Garreth at the questors. Ordering Shalter to reduce speed to vel 2 and to call him at once should there be any sign of the missing cruiser, Aubin left the com-center accompanied by Garreth.

"Do you think she'll be up to questioning?" Garreth asked.

His voice was so deep with concern that it drew Aubin's scowl. Was it his imagination or was Garreth overly concerned? Why? Did he foster a tendre for Eirriel? Aubin quickly forced aside that ludicrous thought with a disgusted shake of his head. Garreth's affections were very firmly settled on Raissa. Annoyed that Garreth's innocent friendship with Eirriel should bother him, Aubin snapped his reply. "She has no choice. I need answers."

Aubin's unfeeling response drew Garreth up short. What was that all about? After witnessing Aubin's reaction to Eirriel's condition, Garreth had thought, at the very least, Aubin would be anxious that she be spared further stress. Yet here he was, coldly stating that he didn't care how she felt, that he would have his damned answers. Shaking his head in disgust, Garreth wondered if he would ever understand Aubin's attitude toward Eirriel.

Entering her cubicle, they found a very alert Eirriel sitting up in her restorer, laughing at something Cian had said. Garreth walked over and placed a gentle kiss on her forehead.

"You hardly look like someone who was near death. The least you can do is look a little less appealing. We rush here expecting to find you lying pale and listless and instead you're sitting up, laughing with flushed cheeks. I think we've been rooked," Garreth teased lightly, though his relief at her condition was very evident in his golden eyes.

Eirriel reached for Garreth's hand. "You mean you've been concerned about little old me," she drawled coyly.

"Nope. You didn't have me bothered one bit. It was Aubin here." Garreth threw a glance back at his friend and continued, despite the darkening of Aubin's eyes and the furrowing of his brow, "Now he was worried. He's been surly and ill-tempered. Why you wouldn't believe—"

"That's quite enough, Garreth," Aubin warned. "How are you, Eirriel? You look well enough." Unlike Garreth, Aubin's profound relief was evidenced nowhere on his cool visage.

"I feel fine, Captain. There's no need to be concerned. Although"—she glanced at Garreth, her eyes twinkling—"I have a feeling Garreth overplayed his role."

"Me! Never!" Garreth said in mock protest. "Why you should have seen him!"

"Garreth!" Aubin said sternly. "If you don't mind."

With a mocking bow and a smug smile, Garreth stepped away. "By all means, Captain, business before pleasure."

Aubin favored him with a withering glare, then addressed Eirriel. "If you feel up to it and if Cian agrees, I'd like to ask you a few questions."

Cian nodded his assent.

"Was it Balthasar?"

Eirriel's face registered shock. "Yes, but how did you know?"

"I'll explain later. Was he actually in the cubicle?"

"No, his physical presence was not in the cubicle."

Aubin raised an eyebrow. "Physical presence? That's a strange way of putting it."

"Perhaps, but it's the only way it can be put." Her voice was deathly quiet as she briefly recounted her horrifying conflict with Balthasar and its abrupt change from dream to reality.

Aubin watched Eirriel's green eyes widen with mounting terror as she relived her experience, his rage mushrooming in direct proportion to her fear.

Her tale ended, Eirriel smiled up at Aubin. "Cian told me you called him, Captain. I'm deeply indebted to you. Once again you saved my life. I don't think I could have stood much more." She frowned. "But tell me, Captain, how did you know I was in danger?"

Not wanting to tell her he "heard" her call until he knew more of how she had called him, he lied, "I didn't. It was merely a case of being at the right place at the right time." Seeing her puzzled expression, he explained, "Raissa had just finished relating the details of Balthasar's impromptu visit. I felt it best to get your views on what happened before I took it up with him. When I arrived at your portal, I heard you cry out."

"Oh, I see," she said, hoping her disappointment couldn't be heard in her voice. *Fool!* She berated herself. *Did you actually think he sensed your danger and had come to rescue you?* Pretending indifference, she said coolly, "Then I should assume you wish to question me?"

"That was my original intent, yes," he replied warily, noticing her change in attitude and not liking what it forebode.

"I'm sorry you had to wait so long for your answers," she retorted sardonically. "By all means, ask your questions now."

Aubin bristled. Damn the woman! Why did she always think the worst of him? Making a concerted effort to hide his frustration, Aubin said, "It sounded like Balthasar was after something specific. Do you have any idea what he wants?"

"It's his belief that I have some strange power," she stated, her voice clearly implying her doubts as to

Balthasar's sanity.

Aubin appeared to contemplate the notion for a few moments. Although Balthasar may have been correct as far as Eirriel's strangeness was concerned, Aubin sincerely doubted that she was endowed with a "power." However, Aubin felt that this was the perfect time to find out the truth. If there was any truth to Balthasar's accusations, he felt certain it would be revealed in her enigmatic eyes.

Studying her from under his hooded brow, he asked nonchalantly, "And do you?"

Eirriel's eyes shot open as she said bitterly, "Don't you think I would have fought him if I had it in me to do so?"

Aubin passed over her remark. "Do you know why he thinks you possess such power?"

"No, Captain, I do not."

"I didn't think you would. It appears I'll have to wait until we find Balthasar to get the answers I need."

"Find him? You *knew* it was Balthasar! Why isn't he under guard?" she demanded, her voice shrill with fear. "Don't you understand? He tried to kill me!"

She sat up quickly and threw off the covers. Her green eyes, bright with panic, darted around the cubicle. "I've got to get out of here! I've got to hide!"

Her hand flew to her mouth as she realized her vulnerability. She slumped back to the cushions in defeat. There was no place to hide. He could reach her anywhere!

Chapter Ten

Garreth watched her thoughts wreak havoc on her face. "Relax," he soothed, leaning over and drawing the covers over her. "Balthasar took one of the mini-cruisers and escaped. We haven't located him yet, but we're searching every corner of this sector. We will find him and when we do——" He stopped leaving the unspoken threat hanging in the air.

"You would do this for me?" she asked increduously.

Aubin had used the time Garreth had taken to calm Eirriel to subdue his own blind rage that had threatened to overwhelm him as he witnessed Eirriel's all-consuming panic. His hands still itched to grab Balthasar's skinny neck and strangle the life from him after Aubin made him suffer greatly for the terror he had brought to Eirriel's beautiful eyes. But Aubin knew he would have to control himself until he had the bastard in his hands. His mind still on the torture he would ever-so-slowly inflict on the treacherous mutant, he mouthed the same answer he had given his crew to Eirriel, unaware of how distant and uncaring he sounded.

"He's a renegade and must be stopped at all cost. We

must defend the name of the Protectorate."

A pained look flickered across Eirriel's face before being replaced by one of disdain. When she spoke her voice was cool, haughty. "Captain, I apologize. I'm still somewhat unfamiliar with your methods. I didn't mean to imply your concern for my well-being would cause you to act other than you should."

Her snide remark pierced Aubin's thoughts and he glanced down at her. Why was she glaring at him? Before he could speak, Garreth cut in.

"Of course we're concerned about you, Eirriel. You're already a part of us. Everyone's been asking about you."

She looked up at Garreth, a forced smile on her face. "Thank you, Garreth. It's sweet of you to try to make me feel better, but we all know I'm an outsider. Now if you don't mind, I'd like to rest."

Bending over, Garreth placed a tender kiss on her lips. "I'll check on you first thing in the morning." Straightening his tall form, he turned to Aubin, his manner abrupt and formal. "Captain, unless you have further orders I'll stop by the com-center to see if there's any news of Balthasar, then I'll retire."

Aubin shook his head. Throwing one last angry scowl at Aubin, Garreth left, muttering under his breath.

"If you need me, my dear, I'll be in the med-unit. Just call," Cian said as he, too, turned to leave. "Coming, Captain?" he said quietly.

Not understanding why he bore the brunt of his two friends' disapproval, Aubin mistakenly surmised that it was Eirriel's attitude toward him that was responsible. He glowered at her, then spun on his heels and stormed past Cian.

"Don't worry, child," Cian said as the portal shut behind Aubin. "He'll come around." Cian smiled at her reassuringly before he too left.

Eirriel lay on the restorer, her eyes blazing with anger. How dare Aubin treat her like that! She wouldn't have been any trouble if his safeguard officer hadn't attacked her! Now she was in his debt. Again! Why couldn't Garreth have been the one to rescue her? Her features softened as she thought of the tall Rhianonian. His friendliness and caring manner was no act. He really did care what happened to her. So did Cian and Raissa. The only one that treated her so indifferently was Aubin. She gave a short bitter laugh. The one person out of all the others that she wanted to please, needed to please, viewed her as nothing more than an inconvenience.

If only she could take an active part as a member of the ship's crew, then she would prove to him that she wasn't an inconvenience. Her brow creased. But how was she to help? She thought for a few minutes, then brightened. She could help Raissa! After all, just the other day the Melonnian had complained that there was too much work for one person. Confident that Raissa would agree to her plan, Eirriel burrowed under the covers, a sleepy yawn escaping her lips. She would go to the lab first thing in the morning!

The next morning Aubin sat at his console, studying the night crew's reports when he was interrupted by the intercom.

"Culture lab to com-center."

"Yes, Raissa, what is it?" he asked wearily.

"Captain, if you've no objections, I would like Eirriel to assist me in the lab. Ever since my aide was transferred, I haven't been able to keep up with my work. It's just too much work for one person to handle."

Aubin frowned. After being on duty all night searching for Balthasar, he was hardly in the mood for petty problems.

"If she can be of any help to you, it's fine with me. But of what benefit a non-Hakonese speaking assistant can possibly be, I can't imagine." Aubin's overtaxed mind had momentarily forgotten Cian's report on Eirriel's amazing progress.

"For your information, Captain Aubin, my knowledge of Hakonese should be quite suffcient. I don't forsee any difficulties in performing my assigned duties."

Aubin's jaw dropped in surprise as he recognized Eirriel's voice, speaking impeccable Hakonese but he'd be damned before he'd let her know she'd caught him unaware.

"Then by all means proceed," he replied smoothly.

"With your permission, Captain?" she pressed.

"With my permission!" he nearly shouted. "Now if you don't mind I have business to attend to!"

"Not at all, Captain," Eirriel replied sweetly. "Carry on."

Before Aubin could reply, the connection was severed. Fuming, he slammed his fist down on the console. By all that was holy, she tried his patience! Each and every time he vowed to treat her gently, she baited him until he had no choice but to answer her in like manner. A reluctant smile crept over his lips. He had to admit she had him this time. He could have run into a fleet of Blagdenian warships orbiting Hakon and not have been more surprised! Her accent was so perfect that she could have been a Hakon native for all he could tell. How had she learned it so fast? A grimace passed over his face as he remembered Cian's observations from the previous day. He shook his head in disgust. He couldn't say he hadn't been warned!

His brows drew together in a frown. Cian had said it was remarkable and it was. How had she mastered it so quickly? His frown deepened and his eyes darkened as he heard Eirriel saying "He seems to think I have some strange power." Was it possible that Balthasar was not wrong?

"I would have loved to see his face when he heard your voice," Raissa laughed, her shoulders quaking. She could tell from Aubin's voice that he had forgotten Cian's comments. "I think you set him back on his heels."

Eirriel's eyes glowed. "Yes, I do believe I did. And I'm glad I was able to do it to him for a change!" She looked at her friend. "But seriously, Raissa, are you sure you don't mind me helping you?"

Raissa stared into her anxious eyes. After the near tragedy of yesterday, she was just grateful that Eirriel was alive and able to help.

"Don't be ridiculous, Eirriel. You know I can use your help. Especially now. On top of all my other projects I have to decipher all the data Garreth and I amassed on the XXliurew, program it into the computer banks and compare the shapeless XXliurew with other cultures for similarities in size, intelligence, breeding habits, and other data.

And all by the time we reach Xandor III."

"But the terminal is only five days away!"

"Precisely. I thought I had long days and sleepless nights ahead of me, but with your help we can have all the reports completed by then." Raissa handed her a stack of printouts. "Here, you start with these."

Raissa showed her how to translate the data from the sheets and feed it into the computer. Eirriel attacked her job the way a starving man attacked food. Too much time had gone by since she had done anything useful.

Raissa watched the Dianthian slyly from behind lowered lashes. Incredible! Eirriel was deciphering those data sheets with no difficulty whatsoever! Raissa had purposely chosen the most intricate, most minutely detailed records available to test Eirriel's use of Hakonese.

"Did you study much on Dianthia?" Raissa asked conversationally.

"Not formally. The Oldens didn't want us to know more than we could use and since I was a female I didn't need to know much. I always resented their highhanded attitude and would sneak into my father's conference chamber and read his books whenever he was away. Why do you ask?"

"It's my job to classify all unknown cultures, and you, my Dianthian friend, definitely fall into that category." *In more ways than one*, Raissa added to herself silently. "What about your language? Were you allowed to learn the different dialects?"

"What different dialects? We are a small people living in a small area on a small world. We all spoke the same language."

Raissa stared at her increduously. "You mean you never spoke anything except pure Dianthian!"

Eirriel shook her head. "No, not until I was well on my way to Blagden."

Raissa raised her eyebrows in astonishment.

"I had to have some way to communicate with my captors," Eirriel said defensively, attributing Raissa's startled expression to the fact that she spoke with the Blagdenians.

"You can speak Blagdenian?"

"A little," she admitted sheepishly.

"How did you learn their language?" Raissa asked in the coarse gutteral manner of the Blagdenians.

"By listening to the wymen on the ship," Eirriel answered in like manner.

For the next hour an amazed Raissa and a confused Eirriel carried on all conversation in Blagdenian.

It was just after midday when a sharp intake of breath drew Raissa's attention. She followed Eirriel's shocked stare to the portal. A very haggard Aubin stood before them, his uniform wrinkled and dark circles under his eyes.

"Aubin!" Eirriel, disturbed by his disheveled appearance, forgot her plans to treat him with disdain and ran to him. "You look terrible!"

"Are you all right? Is something wrong?" Raissa asked, her voice tight with concern.

Running a hand through his already rumpled hair, he gave them a tired smile. "Yes, I'm all right. Just a little tired. We spent all night and most of the day searching for Balthasar."

"Did—did you locate him?" Eirriel asked fearfully.

Aubin nodded and relief flooded Eirriel's features.

"The questor picked up an automatic distress beacon being transmitted from an outlying planet early this morning. We just now entered orbit and the questor has confirmed the signal to originate from a Protectorate minicruiser. A search team is already standing by in the teleport. I just stopped by to pick you up, Raissa."

Raissa's russet eyes gleamed with inner excitement. Not only would she be on hand when they captured Balthasar, but she could take the opportunity to gather further data on the Olion IV Star System.

"Just let me get my portcorder," she replied excitedly. "Damn! It's in our cubicle. Eirriel, you know where I keep it. Would you run and get it while I end this report? Thanks."

The portal had just swooshed closed behind Eirriel when Raissa quickly told Aubin about Eirriel's proficiency in Blagdenian.

"She has an aptitude for languages that makes Jarce

appear dimwitted. Almost perfect recall, I think, at least for languages. Tomorrow I'm very casually going to introduce her to Melonnian. I'm willing to risk my next bonus that by the time we reach Xandor III, she'll be speaking it as well as any native, myself included."

Aubin absorbed this new data into his weary brain. What manner of race was these Dianthians? Why had they never been heard of before? And why was Balthasar so interested in Eirriel? Because she was Dianthian or because she was Eirriel? Aubin shook his head to clear it. No time for abstract questions. In less than one hour he would have Balthasar in custody and safely aboard the *Celestial*. And then he would have his answers.

Eirriel arrived in the lab, her breathless state making it obvious she had run all the way. Handing the portcorder to Raissa, she turned to Aubin. "Captain, request permission to accompany the search team?"

Aubin gave a brief nod. It would be interesting to observe Balthasar's reaction to a very much alive Eirriel, he thought as the three of them left to join Garreth, Cian, and Drex, Balthasar's temporary replacement.

Unarmed, Eirriel took a position between Raissa and Garreth. Why had she asked to join them? The last thing she wanted to do was come face to face with the man who had almost destroyed her. Yet, here she was, a voluntary member of the search team that would find him and escort him back to the ship and imprisonment.

A brillant flash of light appeared briefly on the planet's surface depositing six human forms where none had been for countless centuries. His microcomp locked onto the distress signal, Garreth scanned the area. Swearing, he pointed toward the large cluster of very tall, very thick brush.

"About one hundred meters ahead, Captain. Behind that mass of foliage."

"So much for surprise," Raissa muttered.

"Garreth, you and Raissa take the east approach. Cian and Drex, the west," Aubin ordered. "Eirriel and I will come up dead center. All of you, keep alert."

Aubin waited until they were in position, then motioned

them forward. Swiftly the team crossed the smooth grassy terrain. Neutralizers ready, they cautiously struggled through the dense growth.

"By all the gods!" Drex's stunned exclamation broke the silence as he glimpsed the charred skeleton of the mini-cruiser.

Caution thrust aside, Aubin and the rest burst into the opening made by the downed cruiser. Cian raised his medicorder and perfunctorily scanned the wreckage. There was no doubt in his mind, or in the minds of the others, as they converged on the ruins, that Balthasar could not have survived the crash.

Unseen by her companions, an uneasy Eirriel moved slowly away from the cooled hulk. Her arms drawn tightly around her waist, she shivered, unable to shake the feeling of being watched. Hesitantly she glanced over her shoulder and saw her friends busily searching the area. A deep disquiet settled over her. All was not as it seemed!

She jumped as a hand touched her shoulder. Whirling, she turned to face a confident Aubin.

"There's nothing more to fear, Eirriel," he said firmly, reading the apprehension on her face. "He is dead."

Raising her eyes to his, she gave him a weak smile and nodded. He was dead. Balthasar was dead! Her green eyes darkened. Perhaps if she said it often enough she would believe it.

Chapter Eleven

"Come in." Aubin's deep voice rang from inside the vitalizer. "I'll be out shortly."

Raissa poured herself a beaker of brew and sat down. While she waited, she tried one last time to make some sense out of the jumble of clues that she believed explained Eirriel. If only she could connect them.

There was Aubin's strange knowledge of Eirriel's presence aboard the alien vessel and her location; the encounters between Eirriel and Balthasar, as well as his cryptic insinuations; Eirriel's uncanny ability to master any language and to operate the computer in an undeniably brief time; and finally, Eirriel's uneasy belief that Balthasar was still alive. Somehow, all these pieces fit into a puzzle, but for the life of her she had no idea how.

Aubin walked out of the vitalizer garbed only in his uniform pants.

"Oh, it's you, Rai. What brings you by so bright and early?" he asked as he slipped his shirt over his head.

"Eirriel."

Reaching for his boots, he paused. "Is something wrong?"

"Not really, Aubin. It's just that Cian and I have been running tests on her and we can't seem to reach any definite conclusions. You know, of course, that Cian's tests show extremely hyperactive brain functions."

Aubin nodded.

"Did you also know that she has mastered Melonnian?"

His jaw dropped in surprise. "In only four days?"

"That's right." Her russet eyes took on a brown hue as she stared at her captain. Her voice was pensive as she continued, "But what troubles me most is her nagging fear that Balthasar is still alive."

At her statement Aubin stopped what he was doing and stared at her. "Explain."

"It started the night after we found his wrecked mini-cruiser. I wouldn't have known anything about her fears except that she cried out in her sleep. Something about 'You can't be alive. They told me you were dead,' and then a little later she cried out his name. Every night since she has had the same recurring dream. Or at least it sounds the same to me."

Aubin's brow furrowed. "Could they just be night-mares?"

Raissa shook her head. "If they are, they're not the usual kind. I've tried to awaken her, but to no avail. And in the morning when I make a vague mention of her dreams, she has no memory of them. In fact, she claims to have had a wonderful night's sleep."

"That's not unusual."

"Maybe, but it bothers me just the same. I've mentioned it to Cian and he's going to do a sleep study on her tonight. There's one other thing. Have you noticed that when Balthasar's name is mentioned she grows quiet and anxious. I would expect a little hatred mixed with relief now that he's dead, but it's the haunted look in her eyes that disturbs me the most."

"I hadn't noticed," he admitted, "but then I haven't had much contact with her lately."

"There's a reason for that as well, Captain," Raissa said, a mischievous light in her eyes and a hint of a smile about her lips. Before Aubin could question her, she jumped from her chair and headed for the portal.

"Have a nice day, Captain," she said lightly, and was gone.

Aubin absorbed Raissa's news. He had been unaware of Eirriel's belief in Balthasar's survival or that she reacted so strongly when his name was mentioned. It was time they had a talk, he decided grimly. She had to stop denying the evidence they all saw on that deserted planet. Balthasar was dead! Now if she would just stay in one place long enough for him to talk to her! For the last four days she had actively been evading him. When he entered a cubicle, she left. When he stopped by her cubicle, she had just stepped into the vitalizer. He remembered Raissa's parting remark. What the devil did she mean? he mused as he finished pulling on his boots.

Eirriel stared at the ceiling, trying desperately to fall asleep. She just couldn't. She felt like a blasted computer, as she lay in the med-unit with all the terminals attached to her. Cian's experiment was slated for failure, she thought glumly.

It had been early in the day, just after she had arrived at the lab, when Cian had approached her. Tomorrow they would arrive at Xandor III and he needed one last bit of data to complete his files on dreams.

"All humanoids, no matter their origin, devote a certain period of their sleep to dreams. The sleep/dream ratio, or SDR as it is commonly called, is as unique to each race as a fingerprint is to an individual." After reassuring her that the procedure was completely painless, he explained how it would be done.

"When you're finished with your work and you're ready to retire, you'll report to me at the med-unit where you'll spend the night. I will attach eight tiny terminals to various sites on your head. While you sleep, the computer monitors and runs an analysis of your brain waves. By the time morning arrives, the computer will have finalized its interpretation of those waves and present me with your SDR."

So, after many hectic hours divided between her work in the lab and Raissa's and Garreth's last-minute questions,

Eirriel had dutifully reported to the med-unit, exhausted and ready for sleep. Cian had immediately led her to the little cubicle where she had spent her first night aboard the *Celestial*, placed the terminals on her head and bid her good night. That was two hours ago and she was still awake.

At first she had thought it was nervous anticipation of their arrival at Xandor III and the possibility of her being detained at the Terminal that had kept her awake, but she had quickly discarded that idea. With a certainty she could neither explain nor deny, she knew she would be back on board when the ship broke orbit.

Even if she could blame tonight on concern, what about last night? And the night before? And the night before? Her heart started to pound and her palms grew moist. Did she really want to know? Wasn't it bad enough that, without trying, she could sense the malevolent presence that hovered tenaciously at the edge of her consciousness? That she *knew* it waited for her to drop her guard and fall asleep? Did she have to know what it was? Shuddering violently, her mind repelled any further probing. She knew too much already!

Pressing her fingers to her temples, she forced her mind to relax. Maybe it would leave her alone tonight? Reluctantly yielding to her body's need for rest, she drifted into a fitful slumber.

Instantly she was assailed by visions of Balthasar standing over her as she lay bound and gagged on a stone altar. Her agonizing scream rent the air as she felt her mind enveloped by the corrosive malignancy called Balthasar.

Aubin entered the med-unit in time to hear her screams. The hair at his nape bristled. Never had he heard such a soul-piercing cry! Brushing past a startled Cian, he tore into the inner cubicle and gathered Eirriel into his arms. Feeling arms encircling her, she frantically fought for her freedom.

"Shh, little one, it's all right," Aubin whispered against her brow. "I'm here."

Recognizing his voice, she threw herself against him, startling him by the fierceness of her embrace. Silently he held her close, letting her draw courage from his strength, until her grip relaxed.

"Eirriel," he said softly, "tell me about your dream."

She shook her head, fear in her eyes. "It wasn't a dream."

He stared at her, his brow furrowed. "What do you mean?"

"It wasn't a dream!" she repeated emphatically, then would say no more.

Cian, joining them, heard her whispered denial. Aubin glanced at him questioningly. Cian shook his head and beckoned Aubin to the outer cubicle. Aubin started to pull his arms from Eirriel, but she tightened her grasp.

"Please stay," she begged, distraught. "He won't come if you are here."

Aubin longed to question her about "he," but did not. Instead he held her, murmuring reassuring words against her hair, until he heard the shallow rhythmic breathing of sleep. Placing a kiss on her forehead, he lowered her to the restorer. Pulling the silky coverings up to her neck, Aubin went to join Cian, anxious to hear his explanations.

Cian stood absently stroking his beard, his forehead creased. Staring at the computer printout, he muttered, "She's right, you know. She wasn't dreaming."

A few moments of heavy silence passed while Aubin waited impatiently for the Drocot to elaborate. When nothing more was said, Aubin prompted him. "If not dreams, what?"

Cian shook his head. "I'm not precisely sure. Look here." He pointed to the new readout being printed on the small screen. "See, this is dreaming. The peaks are low, far apart and being transmitted from the theta section of her brain as it should be. Now these . . ." He pushed a button and a set of sharp erratic lines flashed across the screen. "These are from the past episode. They are closer together and travel at a faster rate. But most of all, they did not originate in theta, but in the zed. She was not dreaming."

Aubin's brows drew together and his eyes sparked dangerously. "If she wasn't dreaming, then what, in the name of Dorga, *was* she doing?"

The medic shrugged his shoulders. "I'm afraid I don't know," he admitted quietly.

"What do you mean you don't know!" Aubin roared, his

concern for Eirriel overshadowing his calm reasoning. "You're the medic. It's your job to know!" He walked to the portal of Eirriel's cubicle as if to enter, then spun on his heels. Scowling, he faced Cian.

"Why don't you try your famous Drocot trance?" he sneered. "Maybe it will refresh your bewildered brain!"

Patient blue eyes stared into irate golden ones until the sparks died, the brow soothed and the sneer vanished. Crossing to Aubin, Cian placed a small hand on his friend's shoulder.

"You're exhausted and overwrought," he replied, ignoring Aubin's caustic remarks, not bothering to explain that he had gone into a trance, had searched for an answer, but to no avail. Eirriel was unique, and his experiences were of no help. "Go get some sleep, my friend. I doubt that she will experience any more of her 'dreams' tonight. I will watch over her. Do not worry."

Aubin entered Eirriel's cubicle and stood by her restorer. His eyes darkened as he studied her sleeping form, the peaceful smile that tugged at her lips such a contrast to the stark terror that had been reflected on her beautiful face a short time earlier.

"Do you think she will remember?"

"Not according to Raissa."

"How can that be? She was so terrified that her whole body trembled." Pain etched itself across his face. His voice was low, raw with emotion. "And her screams! I don't think I'll ever forget them!"

Cian fingered his beard. "Raissa never mentioned them and she would have if Eirriel had screamed. She did say that she couldn't waken her. Something you were able to do." He paused. "I don't think she would have responded to anyone but you, Aubin. Still, the pattern has changed."

"Then it's possible she may remember enough to give us some clue as to what she saw?"

"Perhaps."

The tall Rhianonian leaned over and placed a tender kiss on the young woman's lips. *Ahh, little one*, he mused, *why does the thought of you in pain wreak such havoc on my soul? We will have to spend more time. . . .* He stiffened as he suddenly remembered that she was to leave them tomorrow. His lips twisted bitterly. It was just as well. For a brief time he had forgotten the harsh lessons he had learned in the past. She was not for him.

Turning on his heel, Aubin bid Cian a curt good night, then left for his cubicle and the mind-numbing arms of sleep.

For the object of Aubin's bittersweet thoughts the rest of the night passed without mishap. The morning found Eirriel refreshed for, as always, once the episode passed, she fell into a deep exhausted slumber. When Cian asked her of her dreams, she could tell him nothing, for when they ended so too did the memory of them—until night came and the vague uneasiness returned. But as with Raissa, she said nothing of that to Cian.

The Drocot thanked her for her help and told her he would see her later. Smiling, Eirriel went to join Raissa, arriving at their cubicle just as the Melonnian was dressing.

"Before you report to the lab this morning," Raissa said with a forced cheerfulness, "the captain would like to see you in the com-center."

Eirriel's eyes sparkled at the thought of seeing Aubin, but as she saw Raissa's solemn face, she sobered. Walking toward her friend, she asked, "What's wrong, Rai? Why such gloom?"

"I know we've only known each other a short time, but . . ." A sob escaped Raissa and she turned away. "Well, anyway, it's been fun."

Eirriel placed her hand on Raissa's shoulder and turned her around. "Look at me, Rai." Tear-filled russet eyes were raised. "It has been fun and I love you as the sister-friend you've become, but why are you telling me this?"

"We arrive at Xandor III in less than one hour. Ohhh . . ." She flung her arms around Eirriel. "I'm going to miss you!"

Now Eirriel understood. Gently, but forcibly, she pulled herself from Raissa's embrace.

"Rai, I'm not going anywhere."

She spoke with such quiet conviction that the Melonnian stepped back.

"But—" Raissa began.

"Yes," Eirriel cut her off, "I know. We enter orbit in one hour. You told me already. Look"—Eirriel led Raissa to the couch—"I'm not worried, so why should you be? Oh, I know, they'll ask me all sorts of questions about Dianthia, the Blagdenians, Kedar in particular, and I guess even"—a haunted look flickered through her eyes—"Balthasar. But when they're through, I'll be back here with my friends. For good this time."

Raissa was astounded by the unmistakable confidence in Eirriel's voice. "How can you be so certain?"

"It's just a feeling I have," Eirriel responded lightly, reluctant to mention her own concern about her unshakable belief. "Now, don't worry. You won't be left without an assistant who can translate Dianthian."

Strangely reassured, Raissa laughed. "Yes, my friend, what would I do without a Dianthian translator, we come across it so often."

Eirriel's low laugh blended with Raissa's until Raissa glanced at the chronometer. "We better hurry or we'll be late."

Aubin sat at his console lost in silent recrimination. He should never have promised Eirriel that he would take her safely back to Dianthia. Not when the high commander could dismiss that promise with a wave of his hand. Would probably dismiss it and insist she stay on Xandor III until they knew all about her planet, her people, herself. How would she take it? He hoped she would understand why he was unable to keep his reckless promise.

"Raissa said you wanted to see me, Captain."

Drawn from his thoughts, Aubin forgot that he had never told her she might be staying on Xandor III, and, as a result, was taken aback by her radiant smile.

She's happy to be leaving us, he thought morosely, before replying in a voice he hoped belied his concern at the day's outcome. "Yes, I thought you might like to watch our approach."

"Thank you. I'd like that very much." Pleased that he thought enough of her to ask, her green eyes glimmered brightly. *Surely it must mean he cares about me*, she mused hopefully, her already brilliant smile widening.

Damn! Aubin muttered to himself. *I must have been insane to think she might be sorry to leave us.* He gave her a sidelong glance. *Look at her. Her eyes are dancing with excitement, her cheeks are flushed. She's so damned beautiful, and she can't wait to be free of our company.*

Eirriel stood next to Aubin's console and watched the viewing screen as the huge planet grew in size until all she could see was a small section of the planet's surface, its bright blues, greens and yellows revolving slowly into view.

As Eirriel absorbed the breathtaking sight, Aubin feasted on the one next to him, trying to make some sense out of the jumble of emotions assaulting him. Why, he groaned, did he wait until she was about to walk out of his life to realize that he wanted her in a way that he had never wanted another woman? The thought scared the hell out of him and he shied away from all it implied, concentrating instead on the business at hand.

"This is Captain Aubin. All personnel with business on Xandor III report to the teleport in full dress uniform. All crew members must be back aboard the *Celestial* and at their stations by 1800 hours, at which time we will break orbit. Aubin out."

Turning to Eirriel, his voice harsh in an attempt to conceal the conflicting emotions raging inside him, Aubin said, "We have a session with High Commander Lux in one hour. Will that give you enough time to prepare?"

Stung by his churlish manner, Eirriel retorted disdainfully, "More than enough time, Captain."

"Fine. I'll stop by your cubicle and pick you up."

"You needn't trouble yourself, Captain. I believe I know the way to the teleport by now. I'll meet you there."

His eyes glittered with barely suppressed rage. "I said I would pick you up."

"As you wish, Captain."

Eirriel haughtily departed the com-center.

"To think I had been anxious to see him this morning," she muttered under her breath as she entered her cubicle.

She yanked off her clothes and stomped into the vitalizer. She spent a few minutes under the relaxing, steaming water, then quickly dried herself and secured the large cloth around her.

When would she stop deluding herself? she demanded, pulling the clasp from her hair. She meant nothing to him. Nothing!

Eirriel snatched up the brush and ferociously vented her anger on her long tresses. A short time later, her temper finally under control, she placed the brush back on the table and reached for the uniform she had laid out earlier that morning. She had just finished dressing and was checking her appearance in the imager when she heard the sharp rap.

"Enter," she answered coolly.

Aubin did. Eirriel, catching his reflection in the imager, felt her heart quicken at the sight of his tall, muscular form garbed in its finery.

A gold stripe ran down the outer seams of his black pants that flared gently and ended just below the ankles. His usual low-necked shirt had been changed to a full-sleeved white shirt that fastened up the front to a folded collar about which was tied a thin, black, silk ribbon. Over this he sported a waisted jacket that had two golden stripes on each cuff and the *Celestial's* emblem emblazoned in gold on his right shoulder. Never had it been more obvious that he was in command.

While Eirriel discreetly studied him, Aubin blatantly stared at her reflection. He was pleased that her dress uniform, similar in design to his, had been tapered to follow the perfect curves of her slim figure and that the back slit of the knee length skirt afforded him tantalizing glimpses of her long, slender legs, but it was her hair that drew his attention. She had chosen to wear it loose and her savage brushing had made it shine like the brightest star.

Aubin stepped forward and gently ran his hand down her waist-length curls.

"I'd forgotten how dazzling it is, set free like this," he murmured softly. "You should wear it down more often."

Still hurt by his earlier arrogance, she whirled around fully intending to ask him how he expected her to work with her hair hanging in her face, but the retort stuck in her throat as she caught sight of his smoldering gaze.

"I just wanted to say good-bye," he said huskily, lowering his mouth to hers.

Caught off guard, her arms acted with a will of their own and encircled his neck. A burning glow began in the depths of her stomach and spread upward until her mind was aware of nothing but the warmth of the man holding her and her mouth parted under his slow kiss. Aubin felt her response and the taut rein he held on his desire snapped. His arms pulled her closer, molding her body to his and he lost himself in the sweet passion of her kiss.

A loud rap on the portal caused them to pull apart. Aubin's golden eyes burned into Eirriel's as he ran a finger gently down her face and across her lips, searing her skin with his touch.

"We will meet again, little one, I promise you. Then we will finish what was begun today."

She raised her eyes to his, eyes that danced for reasons known only to them. She laughed huskily. "Of that, my bronze giant, I've never had a doubt."

Aubin frowned. There was more behind her statement than the obvious. Before he could question her, another rap sounded.

"Eirriel, are you in there?" Garreth called from the passageway.

"Of course, she's in here," Aubin yelled, chafing at the intrusion.

"Come in, Garreth," Eirriel called gaily.

"You sure seem to be unaccountably cheerful," a somber Garreth muttered as he entered. "Are you that glad to be leaving us?"

"Are you anxious to be rid of me?" she countered.

"You know that's not true, Eirriel. It's just that knowing High Commander Lux's reputation, he'll be so enchanted with you that he'll insist on your remaining on Xandor III until they locate Dianthia, and it would suit him fine if they never found it."

Eirriel turned to Aubin for confirmation and did not need to hear it. One look at his scowling face gave credence to Garreth's statement. Still, Eirriel had no doubt that she would be safely ensconced on board by 1800 hours to-night.

"Let's get this over with," Aubin muttered, not the least bit eager to turn Eirriel over to Lux's lecherous hands.

Chapter Twelve

"Enter," a deep voice commanded from behind the double portals.

An awestruck Eirriel followed Aubin and Garreth into High Commander Lux's private sanctuary. Though the outer cubicle had appeared large and lush, Eirriel was totally unprepared for the opulence of the inner cubicle.

Thick red carpeting covered the floor and matching drapes concealed the floor-to-ceiling windows that spanned the entire far wall. Vivid graphics, depicting the dynamic history of the Protectorate, littered the side walls and emblazoned on the high ceiling was the golden seal of the Empyreal Protectorate. A long conference table with twenty chairs, set off to one side of the large cubicle, was made of ornately carved pieces of gilded wood.

Situated at the far end of the cubicle, on a raised platform, was a massive desk. Behind the desk, a large, powerfully built man sat sifting through a mountainous stack of papers. Finding what he needed, his sharp, black eyes traveled down the paper.

"Well, don't just stand there," he ordered, never bothering to raise his eyes from the report, "tell me what you want."

Aubin gave a short bow. "Captain Aubin of the E.P.F. *Celestial* reporting as ordered, sir."

High Commander Lux dropped the file, crossed his large hands, and gazed imperiously down at Aubin.

"So you're the young twit that caused such a ruckus at Main Terminal when you made captain," he snorted. "Not much to you is there? And him?" He flicked a finger toward Garreth.

"My second-in-command, Garreth."

"Another Rhianonian," Lux muttered. "Never did cotton much to Rhianonians." Abruptly his manner became businesslike. "I expected you earlier."

"As I mentioned in my report, High Commander, we ran into some difficulty."

"That's no ex . . . What's that hiding behind you?" Lux demanded, catching sight of a slight movement.

Eirriel stepped away from Aubin, her green eyes sparking dangerously, her jaw thrust forward defiantly.

"Well, now, what have we here?" the high commander questioned gleefully forgetting, for the moment, his impatience with Aubin.

"Not a what, but a whom!" Eirriel corrected haughtily.

The high commander's brow shot up in surprise. "Feisty little thing, aren't you? What's your name, girl? Where you from?"

"The name's Eirriel," she replied, mimicking his curt manner. "And I'm from Dianthia."

Her retort brought a roar of laughter from Lux. "Come here, girl. Let's have a look at you."

Eirriel refused to move, and Lux was too amused by her defiance to take offense. He leaned forward and squinted at her. "What's the matter, girl? Afraid?"

"Of you? Certainly not!"

"Well, then, prove it," he challenged, raising his hand and gesturing her closer.

Begrudingly, Eirriel did as he bid.

"Pretty little thing, aren't you?" He shifted his gaze to the others. "You may go."

"Requesting permission to stay, sir," Aubin said respectfully. The thought of leaving Eirriel alone with the old fool did not sit well with him at all.

"Permission denied."

Scowling, Aubin gave a short bow. "High Commander," he said, and turned to leave, adding to Eirriel as he paused, "we'll be waiting outside."

Eirriel flashed him a grateful smile.

"You have a mighty long wait ahead of you, Captain. I need quite a bit of information from the young lady before I decide what's to be done with her."

Aubin halted, his back to the high commander, and drew a deep breath. Turning, he said quietly, but firmly, "With all due respect, sir, Eirriel is now a member of the *Celestial's* crew and is required onboard by 1800 hours tonight."

"With all due respect," the high commander sneered, "I am in charge of this terminal, not you! And as high commander I'm telling you that it will be quite some time before I complete my evaluation of the Dianthian. Now unless you have something of value to report, you are dismissed!"

Striving to hold his temper in check, Aubin glared at Lux. "Requesting permission to maintain orbit until my crew member is free to join us?"

"Denied!" Lux bellowed. "Now for the last time, you are *dismissed!*"

Aubin spun on his heels and stormed from the cubicle, Garreth quickly following. As the double portals swung shut behind them, Aubin spewed forth a multitude of curses. Garreth, worried that his friend's anger might get the best of him, swiftly ordered the teleport activated. The sooner he had Aubin off Xandor III the better!

Eirriel stood staring at the high commander. His graying black hair, combed back from his face and worn short above his collar, drew attention to his well-lined face. Eirriel had decided that he was the epitome of arrogance and conceit as she listened to him address Aubin. *Why that old fool doesn't realize that Aubin is worth two of him! Or maybe he does*, she deduced wisely.

"I said, please sit down," Lux repeated, drawing Eirriel out of her musings. Once she was seated, he continued, "Now tell me about yourself. How did you come to drift across space in a damned Blagdenian vessel?"

"The vessel I was in was not Blagdenian," she corrected, "but rather an old relic they found hidden just beyond my father's land. I believe Captain Aubin explained as much in his reports."

Flustered at having been corrected by a young slip of a girl, Lux frowned. "Yes, of course. I was just verifying the details. Continue."

Eirriel began, repeating her story for what she hoped would be the last time. The high commander interrupted her several times and seemed particularly interested in Balthasar.

"Never did trust him. Seems to me Captain Aubin proved himself a poor judge of character when he enlisted that mutant. Said as much in my report. Hired himself a Staton as well, from what I hear. That Rhianonian's too careless to be in command of a fleetship."

Eirriel got to her feet, her eyes blazing with fury. "Why you blustering old fool! You don't know what you're talking about! What Balthasar did was of his own accord. Captain Aubin was in no way responsible for his actions. And as for Theron, he is well respected by his captain *and* his fellow crew members. His actions are impeccable. Maybe if you spent more time reading your reports than listening to prejudiced gossip you might learn something!"

Lux glared at Eirriel a few moments, then chuckled. "You know, girlie, you might have something there. I do seem to be a bit behind on my reports. Confounded things. Waste of time." Lux rose from his chair and crossed to Eirriel. "Now, my dear, how about some nourishment?"

Eirriel glanced at the chronometer. Only three hours left. "As long as I can be aboard the *Celestial* when she leaves, sir."

Lux frowned. "You, too? Didn't you hear me when I told that Rhianonian captain of yours that you would be here for some time? Now come, our nourishment awaits us."

He held out his hand, and Eirriel demurely placed her

hand in his and allowed him to lead her from the cubicle.
He stopped before an adjoining portal and told her to go in
and refresh herself.

"There's a wardrobe inside. If you look, I'm sure you'll
find something more appealing than your uniform. Beauty
like yours should be draped in a manner complementing it,
not hiding it." He turned toward the other portal. "Nourishment will be in one hour."

Anxious to be away from his leering black eyes, Eirriel
hurried into the other cubicle. Opening the wardrobe, she
glanced through it quickly. As she did, it became very
apparent that if nourishment was in one hour, she would be
dessert in two!

The audacity of that aged cretin! Did he think she would
fall into his arms just because he was the high commander?
Well, he had another thing coming to him! Eirriel was about
to storm from the cubicle and give the overbearing
Hakonese a piece of her mind when an idea flickered
through her brain. Of course! she thought gleefully. There
was a way to be on the ship at the appointed hour *and* set the
blustering fool back at the same time. Humming to herself,
Eirriel grabbed a long gown from the wardrobe.

"Are you ready, my dear?" Lux called at the end of an
hour. "Our nourishment awaits."

"I'll be right out," Eirriel replied sweetly.

Surveying herself in the imager, her green eyes glowed
wickedly. *This should give my Lord High Commander
something to dream about*, she gloated, *for a long, long time!*
Taking a deep breath, she opened the portal and stepped
into the larger cubicle.

The whispering rustle of her gown caught Lux's attention
and he turned toward her. She favored him with a slow,
seductive smile and his jaw sagged open. Lux could not
believe his good fortune as he watched Eirriel glide across
the cubicle.

She was dressed in a long, green sequined gown that clung
to her like a second skin. Long, tight sleeves ended in a
point just above her middle fingers. The back of the gown
scooped down, ending just above the gentle curve of her
buttocks, and the front veered sharply to her waist, reveal-

ing much of her full, round breasts to his heavy scrutiny.
Her hair was braided and twisted around her head forming
a golden coronet.

Her eyes smoldering, Eirriel stopped before Lux.

"Does my appearance please you, my Lord High Commander?"

"You are ravishing, my dear. Simply ravishing." He
pulled out the chair. "Please be seated."

She complied, gracefully lowering herself into the chair.
Lux bent and placed a wet kiss on the back of her neck and
it was all Eirriel could do not to shudder in revulsion. Lux
seated himself across from her.

"You tempt me greatly, sweet Eirriel. Perhaps we should
take nourishment later."

Eirriel panicked. Maybe she had overplayed her hand.
Collecting her wits, she gave a low laugh that sent warm
shivers down Lux's spine.

"My lord, I find I am much more amusing after my
appetite has been sated."

"Then by all means, eat up, my sweet, for I am most
anxious for dessert."

Eirriel poured two beakers of a sweet-smelling black
liquid and gracefully handed one to Lux.

"First a drink to new aquaintances," she breathed.

With relish Lux emptied his beaker. All through nourishment Eirriel kept his beaker full so that by the time he
suggested they retire to his private cubicle, he was quite
drunk.

When they entered his cubicle, Eirriel glanced nervously
at the chronometer. Only thirty minutes left! How was she
going to get Lux's permission in that brief time? Feeling his
black eyes boring into her, she slowly sauntered over to the
small corner desk where she spied a cruet. Filling two
beakers, she turned. Her sultry voice drifted across the
cubicle and burned its way into Lux's sodden brain.

"One last drink, my lord, and then . . ." She let her eyes
drift languidly over to the restorer.

Eagerly, Lux strode to her. In one great gulp he swallowed
the entire contents of the beaker then tossed it into a corner.
Eirriel placed her untouched beaker on the desk. Leaning

against him, she ran her hands up the front of his shirt. Looking deep into his eyes, she opened his shirt and drew small circles on his gray-haired chest. Her mouth forming a moué, she reached up and let one slim finger brush teasingly across his lips. He reached for her, but she backed away. A small sigh escaped her lips and she stared at him, a frown creasing her brow.

"What troubles you, lovely lady?" Lux asked, slipping his arm around her waist and pulling her to him.

Eirriel allowed him to press her close.

"Oh, nothing," she said wistfully.

"Come, my sweet. You can tell me," he cajoled. "It hurts me to think you are sad."

"I know it's silly, but all my life I've wanted to join a fleetship crew," she lied, gambling that he was too befuddled to remember that up until a couple of months ago she had never even heard of a fleetship. "And now I won't be able to," she pouted. "I'd do anything to be on the *Celestial* when she breaks orbit. Anything at all," she promised huskily.

Lux looked into her dazzling eyes and melted. He glanced at the chronometer, squinting in an attempt to stop the digits from swaying, and through hazy vision misread it. Believing the ship was well on her way by now, Lux craftily decided a small lie would help his cause greatly.

"I could assign you to the *Celestial*," he said charitably. "If it's what you really want," he added.

Eirriel threw her arms about him and pressed her body close. "I would be most grateful, my dear Lux. Most grateful indeed." She paused, then added doubtfully, "If it can be done."

"Of course it can be done!" he blustered. "Am I not High Commander?"

Grabbing a piece of paper, he quickly scrawled an order assigning one Eirriel of Dianthia to the fleetship, *Celestial*, under Captain Aubin for the term of one year. He signed it, pressed his official seal to it, and handed it to Eirriel.

She snatched it from him with eager hands and sauntered toward the portal, her hips swaying provocatively. Reaching the portal, she turned. "Why don't you make yourself comfortable, I'll be right back. Then I'll show you just how grateful I can be."

Blowing him a kiss, she stepped outside the cubicle. Quickly, she activated the electronic lock and bolted down the passageway to the changing cubicle. She glanced frantically at the chronometer. 1800. No time to change. She scooped up her uniform, pressed the conversor on her shirt and the teleport activated.

Eirriel scurried from the ship's teleport, anxious to change before anyone saw her, especially Aubin. That was not to be, for as she stepped into the passageway, she collided with Aubin, her bundle of clothes tumbling from her grasp.

Aubin automatically stooped to retrieve the fallen bundle and return it to its owner. Recognizing Eirriel, his jaw fell open in surprise. A broad smile sprang to his face.

"How did you make it in time? I was afraid you—"

He stopped in mid-sentence as he took in Eirriel's appearance. She started to explain, but he cut her off, a black scowl crossing his face and a scornful sneer curling his lips. "Don't bother to explain!" he snapped angrily. "I can see all too well how you managed it."

A warm flush crept over her face and she stepped back, frightened by the hatred burning in his eyes. "Nothing happened, Aubin. Nothing. We had nourishment—"

"Nourishment?" he scoffed. "If it was just nourishment, then I would say a certain green-eyed temptress was the main course! Did it serve your purpose?" he demanded maliciously.

With lightning swift reflexes he grabbed the piece of paper she tried to hide behind her back. He scanned the order, his sardonic laugh echoing throughout the passageway.

"I would say it did! Everything seems to be in perfect order. Considering how reluctant he was to part with you earlier, you must have pleaded your case well."

Eirriel had had enough. Burning from his lewd accusations, she snatched her clothes from his hands and stormed passed him into the conveyor. Before the portals closed, Aubin joined her. Fuming, she presented her back to him, not trusting herself to speak.

"What's wrong? Can't you face me?"

The portals opened. Eirriel swept past Aubin to her cubicle. Angrily she threw her clothes on the restorer. Tearing at the hated dress, she stripped it from her and yanked on her robe. She was standing before the imager taking her hair down when Aubin burst into the cubicle. She whirled around, her eyes blazing with fury.

"How dare you burst in here!" she cried. "This is Raissa's and my cubicle. You have no right in here! Get out!"

Aubin stood there, staring at her, condemning her with his eyes.

"Get out!" she screamed.

"Not until I have some answers!"

"You already have your answers. Or so you think. There's nothing more to discuss!"

She turned and started brushing her hair. With an oath, Aubin moved toward her. Grasping her arm with one hand, he spun her to him, while with the other, he wrenched the brush from her and hurled it across the cubicle.

"Look at me!" he demanded. When she didn't comply, he placed one hand under her chin and forcibly raised her head. "What do you take me for? A fool?" Pain-filled golden eyes stared into defiant green ones. "Did you think I wouldn't find out?" he paused, then added in an agonized voice, "did you think I wouldn't care?"

Eirriel twisted from his grasp. "Why you arrogant, simple-minded, bastard son-of-a-Blagdenian whore! What right have you to sit in judgment of my actions and then demand answers? And now you claim to care! No, Captain! You're not the fool. I am," she said bitterly. Weary from her battle of wits with the high commander and numb from Aubin's unexpected attack, she said dispiritedly, "Think what you like, Captain. I'll make no explanations."

"Because you have none," he accused.

Eirriel stared up at him, her eyes bright with unshed tears. Slowly she walked to the portal and pressed a switch. "I'll make no explanations," she said quietly, "because there's nothing to explain."

Seeing her standing by the open portal, her shoulders

sagging, silent tears streaming from her eyes, Aubin's anger fled. He crossed the floor to stand in front of her. Gently, he cupped her chin and raised her face to his. All too briefly he glimpsed her anguished green eyes before she turned her head away.

"I have nothing more to say to you," she said bitterly. "Please leave."

Damning himself and his temper, Aubin dropped his hand and left. Before the portal closed, he heard the sound of heartbroken sobs as Eirriel flung herself on the restorer.

Raissa joined Garreth and Cian for an early-morning nourishment.

"Good morning," she called cheerfully, her russet eyes sparkling excitedly.

Garreth looked at her glumly. "Don't know what's so good about it."

"Plenty," she quipped.

"Not from where I sit, there isn't," Garreth remarked. "Eirriel didn't make it back in time and Aubin's never been in a fouler mood."

"Well, there's nothing I can do about Aubin's black mood. From what I hear, he got what he deserved. But as for the other. Now that I think I can change."

Garreth and Cian raised their heads simultaneously.

"Take a look," she said, pointing over her shoulder.

"Eirriel!" Garreth jumped up. "You made it! When did you come aboard?"

Eirriel warmed under Garreth's exuberant welcome. "Just before you broke orbit."

"How did you escape the old lecher?" Garreth asked.

"It wasn't easy, I assure you."

"I can well imagine," he laughed. "Does Aubin know? If not, he will soon."

Raising a hand, Garreth beckoned to Aubin, who had just entered the nourishment center. In doing so, he missed the pained shadow that flickered across Eirriel's face.

"What's wrong, child?" Cian asked. "Are you ill?"

"Nothing's wrong, Cian. I'm fine. Really."

"You don't look fine," he insisted. "You look drained."

"It's nothing." She smiled tremulously, hoping to allay Cian's fears. "There's no need to worry about me."

Cian frowned. She was hurting. What could have happened down on Xandor III? He looked at her again. Or could it have happened after she returned to the ship? That would explain Aubin's mood.

Eirriel played with the food on her plate. How was she to face Aubin, knowing what he thought of her? From a distance she heard Aubin's deep voice extending a greeting to all. It was too much! Mumbling something about being behind in her work, Eirriel hurried from the center, leaving one scowling and three concerned faces staring after her.

When Raissa arrived in the lab a short time later, Eirriel was deeply immersed in her work.

"Are you all right?" Raissa asked, placing a reassuring hand on her friend's shoulder.

"I'm fine," came the forced reply.

Like hell you are! Raissa thought to herself. How much longer would Eirriel and Aubin tear at each other before they realized their true emotions?

Chapter Thirteen

Aubin stepped onto the com-center and took his seat.

"Garreth, any luck with the search?"

"No, Captain. The link with the computer on Xandor III was no help. Dianthia's location is still a mystery."

"What's the next system on the patrol schedule?"

"Quaxdl V, Captain," Theron reported. "Course plotted and awaiting orders.

"Proceed at vel 7."

Theron raised the control bar. "Proceeding at vel 7. Our arrival time at the Quaxdl V star system twelve days, four hours and twenty-seven minutes."

"Captain, there's an Arvadian vessel ahead," Jarce reported. "Her captain's requesting permission to come aboard."

"Whose ship?"

"Chalandra's."

Chalandra! Aubin's eyes sparked with anticipation. She was just what he needed to take his mind off Eirriel.

"Permission granted," Aubin replied cheerfully. "Garreth take command. I must greet our guest."

Garreth frowned. He'd never had much use for
Chalandra or her troupe of players. Suddenly he grinned.
Eirriel was not going to like this and if he knew her at all,
life for his friend was going to become quite complicated.
Maybe this was just what was needed to force Aubin to
commit himself to Eirriel.

Aubin entered the teleport as it deactivated. A petite
purple-skinned beauty cried out and threw herself into his
arms. Aubin lowered his mouth to hers and kissed her
soundly and deeply.

"You miss Chalandra, yes?" the new arrival said softly,
her sultry voice echoing through the empty chamber.

Aubin glanced about questioningly. She laughed a low
husky laugh. "I come by myself. I think it's been a long time
since I see Aubin. Maybe he not want to see me. But now I
know. You want to see me very much, yes?"

"I want to see you very much, yes." Aubin laughed, his
golden eyes raking over the voluptuous form before him.

Chalandra was a gypsy, traveling through space with her
troupe of Arvadians, entertaining in their age-long tradition. Tiny of frame, coming no higher than Aubin's chest,
she was by no means small elsewhere. Chalandra was the
epitome of the sensual female.

She reached up and encircled his neck. "Good. Give
Chalandra one more kiss and she will go away and plan a big
surprise for tonight."

Aubin quickly complied with her request and Chalandra
stepped back into the teleport. Blowing him a kiss, she said
huskily, "Until tonight, lover," then she was gone.

The day sped by quickly. The whole crew was excited by
the prospect of a show. They knew from the past,
Chalandra's troupe was the best in the galaxies and they had
excitedly told Eirriel all the details of the different shows
they had seen.

Now Eirriel eagerly looked forward to the night's entertainment.

"You go ahead, Rai. I'll meet you later," Eirriel called
from the vitalizer. "I wouldn't want you to miss the
beginning."

"I don't mind waiting. Really," Raissa replied. There was no way she was going to let Eirriel encounter Chalandra by herself.

Eirriel came out of the smaller cubicle drying her hair. "Look, Raissa. I know why you're acting this way. I've heard all about Chalandra. She's on the lips of the entire crew. I don't care if she used to be Aubin's lover. I don't care if she still is, for that matter. What Aubin does is his business, not mine."

Raissa glanced at her friend. Her speech sounded a little bit too hollow for Raissa's liking. "I've seen her performances so many times they're boring."

"Then you must be the only one in the entire galaxy who thinks that way," Eirriel remarked dryly. She nudged Raissa toward the portal. "Will you please go? Contrary to what you say, I know you're as excited as everyone else."

Opening the portal, Eirriel gave Raissa a gentle, but firm, push. The portal swooshed shut before the startled Melonnian could object. Activating the electronic bolt, Eirriel left Raissa staring helplessly at the portal. Knowing she had no other choice, Raissa made her way to the show.

Finally dressed, Eirriel unlocked the portal and stepped into the passageway. Loud clapping to fast-paced music drifted to her ears. Leaning against the closed portal, Eirriel felt her determination slip away. *I can't do it*, she thought frantically. *I can't face Aubin's mistress knowing she has what I so desperately want and there's nothing I can do about it.*

The clapping stopped and a low instrument began to play a slow sultry rhythm. In spite of her reservations, Eirriel was drawn by the haunting melody. Entering the dimmed, fully opened rec-cubicles, she strained to find Aubin's large form. Where else would he be? she laughed bitterly as she spied him sitting slightly off to the side but very much in the front of the chamber near the musicians.

The low tune grew slightly louder and a faint musky scent permeated the air. Chalandra appeared suddenly from behind one of the curtains that had been suspended from the ceiling. Riding low over her rounded hips and connected only by thin silver chains were two panels of sparkling silver cloth. A tiny piece of matching material

barely concealed her large, full breasts. Over that, the
Arvadian had draped shimmery, transparent wisps of gos-
samer. As she danced, she brought her slender arms slowly
up her bared thighs and across her breasts. Provocatively
she slipped the pieces of material off one by one until all
that remained was the silver cloth and one wisp covering
her face and hair. The music grew louder, the rhythm
increased. Chalandra whirled faster and faster. Reaching
up, she grasped the covering and tossed it to the ground. A
gasp sounded throughout her audience as Chalandra's silver
hair tumbled to her knees.

Eirriel's mouth sagged as she stared at the petite form
writhing so seductively to the music. She had never seen
anyone so breathtakingly beautiful in her life. Next to
Chalandra's small, well-curved form, Eirriel felt very tall,
skinny and ungainly.

Swaying with the music, Chalandra beckoned outward
with her hands. Her slanted silver eyes were glazed as if with
desire. Her tongue flicked over her full lips. "Come, be my
lover," her eyes pleaded. "Together we will travel to the
heady summit of pleasure," her body promised.

Faster and faster the music played and faster and faster
Chalandra twirled. The air pulsated with excitement. Looks
of rapture appeared on the faces of her audience. A husky
triumphant laugh floated over them as she taunted them.
She drew her hands through her hair and tossed her curls
high into the air. She whirled across the cubicle her head
thrown back, her lips parted. Abruptly the music ceased
and the lights went out. When they came back on,
Chalandra was locked in Aubin's embrace, their mouths
tasting greedily of each other.

Eirriel watched with outraged eyes as Chalandra pressed
ever closer, molding her body into Aubin's. Hurt, angry, not
wanting to see Aubin make a further spectacle of himself,
Eirriel made her way to her cubicle where she could vent her
wrath unseen.

While Eirriel was seething in the security of her cubicle,
Chalandra was busy completing her performance. She
pulled from Aubin, who very reluctantly released her.
Spinning and twirling taunting and teasing, she repeated the

last few minutes of her performance. At her signal, the cubicle was again plunged into darkness, but this time when the lights came back on Aubin and Chalandra were conspicuously missing.

"Raissa, are you in there?" Chalandra's sultry tones drifted in from the passageway.

Muttering under her breath, Raissa purposely ignored the question and continued on with her work.

"Raissa?" Chalandra called again as she entered the lab. Her eyes widened momentarily as she spied the Melonnian. "Oh, you are here."

Not bothering to raise her eyes from a report, Raissa replied sarcastically, "Now where else would I be at this time of the day?"

Silver eyes narrowed. "Pleasant as always, Raissa."

"It must be the company I keep," she said dryly.

Chalandra reached over and patted Raissa's hand sympathetically. "Yes, I imagine it must wear on your nerves, sharing your cubicle with that homeless, underprivileged child. If there's anything I can do to make it easier, feel free to ask."

Raissa gritted her teeth to keep from telling Chalandra what she could really do. Instead, she replied politely, "Thanks for the offer, but I think I can manage. Besides, aren't you leaving today?"

"No. There's been a change in plans," she said sweetly, joining Raissa at her console. "Captain Aubin so enjoyed my, I mean, our performance last evening he invited us to stay. At least until the annual masque. If not longer. I told him I really didn't know how I could manage it, we always have such a tight schedule this time of year, but he insisted. You know how persuasive he can be when he really wants something. I found I just couldn't resist."

Raissa kept her head bent to hide the disappointment that would have been all too evident. Chalandra staying! And until the masque. That was four days away! The Arvadian temptress had arrived at a most inopportune time. Now Aubin and Eirriel would never settle their differences. How could they when the purple-skinned bitch monopolized all of Aubin's free time? It was disgusting watching her hang all over him, listening to her play the ignorant gypsy only when he was around. "I go now, yes?" "You like my dance, no?" Raissa shuddered in revulsion. When would Aubin realize it was all an act?

Behind those slanted, silver eyes was a shrewd mind. Chalandra knew what to do to keep him at her side. Chalandra had never been a problem before because she only stayed a day or two, and Raissa was the first to admit that Aubin did need a little relaxation. But now, she was certain that Aubin would use Chalandra to combat his feelings for Eirriel. Not that Raissa cared one twit for Chalandra's feelings, but she was afraid that Aubin would get a little too involved and they'd never get rid of Chalandra! And what about Eirriel? Raissa thought miserably. If her pride kept her from Aubin now, how would she react to his supposed affection for Chalandra?

"Raissa? Raissa, you're not listening. Raissa!"

Raissa raised her head. "What?"

"You haven't heard a word I've said." Chalandra pouted.

"Sorry, Chalandra. I was too involved in my report."

"Do you think you could put it aside for a few minutes and listen to me?"

Raissa sighed. "All right, Chalandra. What were you saying?"

"I was asking about Balthasar. Is it true that he's dead?"

"Yes."

"Did he really try to kill the Dianthian?"

"Kill? I don't know about kill, but they did seem to have their differences."

"Differences! From what I hear that is hardly the appropriate word."

"Oh?" Raissa arched her eyebrows. "What did you hear?"

"That they were lovers and he was jealous because she gave her favors freely and quite often."

A short choking sound came from Raissa's direction.

"Are you all right?"

Raissa nodded, keeping her laughing eyes from Chalandra's. Lovers! Eirriel and Balthasar! Someone was obviously feeding Chalandra wrong information. Who? Why? She smiled gleefully. This conversation was proving both instructive and amusing.

"Tell me about her," Chalandra demanded.

Ah! Now we come to the real reason behind this little visit. "Who?" Raissa asked, feigning ignorance.

"The Dianthian!" Chalandra cried in exasperation. "Erly."

"Eirriel."

"Oh, yes. Excuse me. Eirriel. Well, what's she like?"

The Melonnian stared down her nose at her. "Why? What's she to you?"

"Why nothing," the Arvadian protested a little too quickly. "It's just that Garreth had nothing but glowing words for her. As for Aubin, all he would say was that she was a new member of the crew who signed on after she was rescued. I tried to ask more, but he refused to discuss it further."

He didn't have to say anything, Chalandra thought bitterly. Last night had said it all! A burning fire raged inside her and it wouldn't be extinguished until quenched by the cooling sweetness of revenge.

Aubin had always been a magnificent lover, one of the few who could evoke any true response from her, and last night he had outdone himself. He had taken her higher and higher with his tender caresses and savage passion only to plunge her instantly into the frigid depths of despair with one word—Eirriel. Even though he was unaware of his cry, the wealth of emotion behind the fevered utterence left Chalandra with no doubts. The woman whose name crossed his lips at the peak of his passion had captured his heart and soul, totally and completely.

Watching the play of emotions on Chalandra's face, Raissa could only surmise that something had come between her and Aubin, and Raissa was willing to stake her life on what, or rather, whom it was. It was obvious that Chalandra was trying to decide whether Eirriel posed a serious threat to her relationship with Aubin.

Oh! This is going to be such fun! Raissa thought, her russet eyes glowing devilishly.

"From what we know, Eirriel's . . . Well, let's just say

she's not your typical Dianthian. Her behavior, at times, is perplexing, but she's extremely intelligent and quick to adapt to any circumstance. She has a . . . pleasant personality. She's not too bad to look at, if you like tall, thin females, and her eyes! They're so very . . . uncommon."

A smug smile tugged at the corners of Chalandra's mouth. So the Dianthian was ugly and ill-mannered! Perhaps she had overreacted, or, better still, maybe she heard wrong. Either way, she'd see to it that Aubin would be too busy to think of anyone. Anyone, but herself, she amended as she rose from the chair.

"The masque isn't too far off. Maybe the poor child will find some enjoyment if she attends. She certainly deserves some kind of fun after all she's been through. I'm sure I can get Tynan to spend some time with her, if I offer him enough. Oh, well, I've taken up enough of your time. See you."

Chalandra left feeling confident that she would recapture Aubin's straying attention.

Raissa's low laugh echoed in the lab. "Chalandra, prepare yourself. You are in for the biggest shock of your life!"

"But I don't want to go," Eirriel protested. "I don't think I can stand watching Aubin with that . . . that . . ."

"Whore?" Raissa supplied, grinning.

"Yes, that does seem to be what I had in mind. But it makes no difference what I call her. I can't face them!"

"You haven't left your cubicle since her performance. The lab doesn't count," Raissa added quickly when Eirriel started to protest. "Are you going to hide in here until she leaves, which may not be for some time, or are you going to submit your transfer request?"

Eirriel gasped. "How did you find out?"

"I found the crumbled up one laying by your restorer." Raissa studied her friend carefully. "Can you stand the thought of him in her arms?"

Eirriel raised pain-shadowed eyes. "No."

"Then fight for him!"

Eirriel laughed, a sharp bitter sound. "Fight! How? I'm no competition for Chalandra. She's beautiful, sensuous, everything I've ever wanted to be and so much more. And she's experienced. She knows how to please him, while I—I know nothing."

"That nothing is what draws Aubin, Eirriel."

At Eirriel's doubtful look, Raissa groaned in exasperation and dragged her friend from the relaxer to stand before the imager.

"Look at yourself. Really look! You're above Chalandra's base beauty. There's an artlessness about you that makes men want to take care of you. Yet at the same time, they sense a dormant passion, hidden deep beneath the innocence that they crave to awaken.

"It's like two scents—one heavy, cloying, the other soft, subtle. The first wears off quickly as you become accustomed to its fragrance, while the second lingers, here and there, making you pause and take a deeper breath of its elusive scent."

"But—"

"But nothing! Do you love him?"

"More than life itself!" came the fierce reply.

"Then fight for him."

"Why do I have to make the first move?" Eirriel demanded. "If he cares for me, as you seem to think he does, why won't he come to me?"

"Because he is a Rhianonian. His heritage is one of war and piracy, of struggle and survival, of fierce loyalties and passionate hatreds. Because Aubin is obstinate, arrogant and too full of pride to admit even to himself that he loves you. That he needs you."

"Pride!" Eirriel spun away from the imager. "What about my pride?"

"Do you love him?"

Eirriel paced in the cubicle, a fierce battle waging silently inside her. Why should she have to sacrifice her pride? She should give Chalandra her blessings, then walk away. They were made for each other—Chalandra, shrewd and manipulating and Aubin, domineering, vain and infuriating!

But could she just walk away? Could she live with herself knowing she let her pride stand in the way of her only chance for happiness? From the deepest depths of her soul came the answer. No! Life without Aubin would not be worth living. They belonged together. She had known that from the beginning.

Eirriel stood once again in front of the imager, staring at her reflection. But how was she to fight? How could she compete with Chalandra? How? Suddenly, she knew. Her eyes glowing wickedly, she turned to Raissa.

"Tell me about this Tynan," she said quietly.

Chapter Fourteen

Standing in front of the imager, Aubin placed the brown-plumed, wide-brimmed hat on his head. Nodding, he smiled, pleased with the transformation.

Tight brown breeches, thigh-length, wide-cuffed boots of dark brown, a sleeveless brown hide vest, a cream-colored, full-sleeved shirt, the neckline open to his waist and the ruffled cuffs falling to his palms, and over his left shoulder hanging to his right hip was his prize possession—his great, great, great, great-grandfather's saber. Exit Aubin, captain of the fleetship, *Celestial*, and enter Aubin, leader of the first pirate band to take to space!

His golden eyes glowed as he thought with relish of that ancient time. An era when might ruled supreme and strength and courage carried the day, not politics. Politics! His smooth brow furrowed as he remembered High Commander Lux. What had Eirriel offered him to convince him to assign her to the *Celestial*? Foolish question, he thought sardonically. One look at the way she had been dressed and it was painfully apparent.

"Such a fierce face. Something is wrong, yes?" Chalandra

said as she swept into his cubicle.

Unaware that he had been scowling, Aubin shook himself. Thrusting all thoughts of Eirriel from his mind, he turned to Chalandra.

"Something is wrong, no," he replied, his warm gaze telling her he was greatly pleased with her costume.

Chalandra had decided to go as High Priestess of Lurline, knowing full well the effect her choice would have on Aubin. She had designed the long, flowing caftan of irridescent silver that swirled like mist around her well-curved form. Underneath, she wore a jumpsuit, dyed to match the shade of her skin to such a precise degree that she created the illusion of only wearing the caftan. Her hair was braided into many thin strands, with small purple beads attached to the ends. Around her neck she wore a multi-faceted neck piece that reached to her shoulders and hung between her breasts. On each wrist dangled several matching bracelets.

"You like?" she purred, reaching out to Aubin.

"I like," he replied huskily, pulling her close. "I like very much."

A tall form swaggered across the floor, dressed in baggy pants that were tucked into his boots at the knees, a full billowing shirt, a long open caftan and a sash around his waist, and another wrapped turban-style around his head. Raissa watched the completely black-clad figure approach, overwhelmed by his rugged handsomeness. Her heart pounded and her palms moistened as she stared into his laughing golden eyes.

"Oh-ho! What have we here?" Garreth questioned, taking in her tight brown pants, her laced, knee-length boots, the full-sleeved orange blouse and brown, wide-brimmed hat under which she had managed to tuck her long hair.

Raissa's breath caught in her throat as his warm gaze raked over her slim form. Smiling broadly, Garreth gave a deep, sweeping bow. "Good evening to you, Archer of the Melonnian Foreguard. I trust you left your weapons in a safe place."

In spite of the emotions that surged inside her, Raissa had to laugh. The arrows used by the Foreguard were two foot stiridium shafts with a double-pronged head. It was common practice for them to be tipped with a fast-acting paralyzing compound.

"Indeed I did, sir. I feared I might frighten the guests. Besides"—her russet eyes twinkled—"I didn't think I could resist the urge to sink it into the hide of a certain purple-skinned bitch."

Garreth roared. "And deprive Eirriel of the honor? Shame on you! Speaking of Eirriel"—he glanced around the cubicle—"where is she?"

"She'll be along shortly. It took some convincing to get her to come though." Raissa smiled smugly, her eyes aglow with hidden amusement. "Prepare yourself, Garreth. There's going to be fireworks tonight."

"Oh?" He raised his brows in question, but Raissa declined to give him the details. "At least tell me what she'll be wearing."

"Something that will meet with your approval."

No matter how he pried, she would say no more.

"Raissa!" Ceara called as she crossed the floor, her arm linked to a tall man who looked vaguely familiar to Raissa. "Where's Eirriel? I've someone here who wants to meet her."

"She had a slight problem with her costume. She'll be here shortly."

"Nothing serious I hope."

Raissa shook her head. "Just some last-minute alterations."

"Good. Chalandra asked me to introduce Tynan to her, but since I'm sure you'll be seeing her before I will, maybe he could wait with you?" Ceara dropped his arm. "Tynan, this is Raissa and Garreth. Tynan is the latest addition to Chalandra's troupe."

Raissa eyed him, her eyes glowing wickedly. Oh, he was perfect! Tall and lean, with brilliant, deep blue eyes, Tynan's tawny hair was cut to his collar and he was dressed as an ancient in a gray caftan over which he wore a long, multicolored, striped vest.

"I'm very glad to meet you, Tynan," Raissa said, her eyes never leaving his face. "Aren't you, Garreth?"

Garreth gritted his teeth. He didn't like the way Raissa was staring at this stranger. Didn't like it one bit.

"Well, aren't you?" Raissa repeated.

"Yeah, real pleased," Garreth muttered.

Tynan's eyes studied Raissa as he remembered his orders to keep the Dianthian away from Aubin. Well, this Raissa wasn't the Dianthian, but he had a feeling if he paid close attention to her, she'd put a good word in with Eirriel and that just might make his job much easier. He reached for Raissa's hand and lifted it to his lips.

"The pleasure's all mine." He held out his arm. "Would you care to dance? Unless, of course, your . . . friend would object?"

Before the tight-lipped Garreth could answer, Raissa slipped her arm through Tynan's.

"Garreth doesn't mind at all," she said sweetly, and allowed Tynan to escort her to the dance floor, leaving behind one very annoyed Rhianonian.

"Excuse me, Ceara, but I feel like a drink."

Without waiting for her reply, Garreth made his way to one of the several tables lined with cruets. Selecting one, he filled his beaker to the top, brought it to his lips, and drank it down in one long swallow, his eyes never leaving the dancing couple.

Damn it all! Why the hell was she dancing with that Arvadian scum? The couple whirled past him and Garreth scowled, then frowned in puzzlement as he watched the two dance. Every time they passed him, Raissa winked and gave him a devilish grin. A nagging suspicion ate at him as he remembered her cryptic remarks. Again they danced past, and again she winked and grinned at him. *She's up to something*, he decided. He'd stake his life on the fact that it had something to do with Eirriel. Strangely reassured, he smiled at Raissa and was rewarded for it by her warm smile that sent shivers down his spine. He took another swallow of the cooling brew. This was going to turn out to be an interesting evening!

"What are you looking so damned pleased about?" Aubin demanded, startling Garreth who had not seen him approach.

"Why shouldn't I look pleased?" Garreth returned. Then, not wanting Aubin to ask questions he wasn't quite sure he could answer, Garreth quickly changed the subject. "Have you seen Eirriel? Do you know what she's coming as?"

Aubin's golden eyes darkened and he muttered, "No, I haven't seen her. As to her costume, I've no idea. It's probably something that will complement her excessively friendly nature."

Garreth frowned, turned on his heels and left Aubin staring after him. Garreth had no intention of letting his captain's foul mood spoil his evening. Passing before one of the portals, he heard his name called. He followed the sound into the passageway and his eyes sparkled with amusement when he saw Eirriel standing in the shadows.

"Of course! I should have guessed!" He threw back his head and roared. "Wait until Aubin sees this!"

There before him stood the perfect consort of Aubin's pirate captain. A long-sleeved, cream-colored shirt was knotted under her full breasts, revealing more than it concealed of her ample cleavage and trim waist. Wide-cuffed, thigh-length, brown boots, while covering most of her long slender legs, drew attention to the brevity of the tight brown breeches which had been hacked off just below her gently rounding buttocks. Strapped to her waist and riding low on her right hip was a wide black belt from which hung a sleek rapier. On her head she wore a wide-brimmed, black hat under which she had managed to conceal all her glorious hair. But it was her eyes that caught and held his attention. Suddenly, he felt reassured. He knew she would be all right. There, burning once again, deep in their depths, was that incandescent spark of life that had been missing these past days.

Garreth bowed and offered her his hand. "Well, Milady Pirate, shall we dance?"

"I'd love to." She laughed.

Garreth led her to the floor. As they swirled around the cubicle in graceful rhythm with the music, he leaned over and whispered in her ear. "I'm the envy of every man here." He grinned. "Especially one gloomy Rhianonian scowling in the corner."

Eirriel turned in the direction of Garreth's nod and saw
Aubin glaring at her over the edge of his beaker, his golden
eyes glittering dangerously. She stopped dancing, took off
her hat and gave him a sweeping bow. As she did, her curls
tumbled in a golden riot to her waist. Giving her head an
impudent toss, she placed the hat back on her head, favored
Aubin with a warm smile and then concentrated on Garreth
and the dancing, well aware of the effectiveness of her ploy
as Aubin's scowl deepened and he emptied his beaker in one
gulp.

"What are you up to, you little minx?" Garreth demanded.

"Why nothing," she protested innocently.

"Nothing my foot! What was that little performance
about? Tell me what's going on!"

"If you must know, I'm just giving your captain a dose of
his own medicine—or will be shortly," she added as she
saw Raissa approaching, leading a very impatient Tynan.

Garreth saw Raissa's pleased smile, the determined glint
in Eirriel's eyes and the expectant look on Tynan's face.
Suddenly everything fell into place. Understanding reflected itself in the Rhianonian's bronzed features and his
deep laugh resounded across the cubicle.

"So that's what the two of you are up to!" Garreth said,
still chuckling. "I hope you know what you're doing." He
sobered as he thought of the trouble Eirriel could get into
with the Arvadian.

"Be careful," he warned. "You're playing with fire."

She raised earnest green eyes to him. "Don't you think
I'm aware of that? This whole thing could very well backfire,
but I'm sick and tired of Aubin's highhanded, overbearing
manner. I won't stand for it any longer! So tonight, one way
or another, I'll see an end to it."

Garreth studied her a few moments, as if deciding the
outcome of the battle yet to be waged. He placed a gentle
kiss on her forehead. "Good luck, pretty lady. And, remember, I'll be here if you need me."

"Thank you, Garreth, but I don't believe I will."

"Why, there you are!" Raissa exclaimed, joining them.
"Eirriel, I have someone I want you to meet. Tynan, this is

Eirriel. Eirriel, Tynan."

Eirriel smiled warmly as she extended her hand to the Arvadian. "I'm very pleased to meet you," she said demurely.

Tynan couldn't believe his luck. When Chalandra had first told him of her plan, he had turned her down. After all, why should he be stuck spending the entire evening catering to an unattractive female? It wasn't until Chalandra had doubled her offer that he had agreed. Now, by Shalane and the Six Virgins, he was glad he did! He took her outstretched hand and brought it to his lips.

"The pleasure's mine, my sweet," he said smoothly.

Eirriel gritted her teeth at the endearment but managed to smile beguilingly. If her ploy was to work, she must appear to be overwhelmed by his good looks and charming manners. As the music started again, she glanced at the dance floor and then back to Tynan.

"I believe this is our dance," she said sweetly, wishing fervently that she had worn something a little less revealing. The feel of his sweaty hands on her bare waist was almost too much to bear.

Garreth chuckled as Tynan led Eirriel away. "It would seem our little Dianthian has made another conquest. Now, to quote our charming innocent, I believe this is our dance."

Raissa's eyes turned a warm inviting brown as Garreth took her arm and guided her onto the dance floor. He held her close and, captured by the soft music, the slow tempo and the haunting melody, they swayed in unison.

Garreth looked down at the woman who had stolen his heart and held it captive the past two years, and pulled her closer. Would tonight be the night? Would she finally give him the answer his soul demanded? He bent his head. In Melonnian, his voice as gentle as a caress, he whispered the declaration. "Raissa, from this night you belong to me as I belong to you."

Raissa looked into the golden eyes of the man who had laid relentless siege to her heart and felt his love reach out and encircle her. The last vestige of her fear was driven from her soul and her final wall of defense crumbled.

"You have my vow," she said softly. "From this night I

belong to you as you belong to me."

Garreth felt his whole being sigh in relief. By Melonnian law they were life-bonded. She was his at last. Now and forever. He placed a gentle kiss on her forehead. When the music ended, he silently led her off the floor, down the passageway, to the secluded corner of the observation window.

"You've pledged to us, Raissa. It means forever."

He pulled her to him. His mouth found hers and as always he was surprised by the warmth that coursed through him at her passionate response. When they finally broke apart, Garreth stared into her russet eyes, his gaze intense.

"You feel it at last, don't you? This rightness. This sense of belonging?"

She nodded. "I feel as if I've waited my whole life for you, for this, and I suppose I have."

"You'll never have cause to regret your trust in me, in us."

"I know."

Garreth wondered why she had at last given him the answer he so desperately craved, but decided not to question it. Raissa, herself, may never even know the answer.

"We should return."

Raissa sighed. "I suppose."

As Garreth led her back to the rec-cubicles, he was heartened to know she was as reluctant as he to join the party.

Chalandra stood off to the side, her lips drawn in a tight line, her silver eyes glinting with rage. Ruined! Her whole evening was ruined! Aubin had done nothing but scowl and drink since they arrived, and Tynan, the traitorous bastard, hadn't left the side of that pale beauty all night. Why wasn't he waiting for the Dianthian to arrive? After all, that's what she'd hired him to do. Wait until he tried to collect! Her eyes scanned the crowd again. Where was the Dianthian bitch?

She spied Raissa and Garreth entering the rec-cubicles hand in hand and shook her head. How could Garreth have fallen for that scrawny Melonnian. Oh, well, she shrugged, some people had the taste of a drexal.

"Garreth, I know this is our evening, but I have one little

matter to attend to," Raissa explained apologetically, her eyes sparkling mischievously. "However, if you care to accompany me, I think you'll find it well worth the interruption."

Garreth gave a quick bow and motioned Raissa forward. "Lead on, Madame Archer. After an invitation like that, how could I resist?"

Chalandra glanced up to see Raissa and Garreth coming toward her. There was something about the way the Melonnian was smiling that aroused her suspicion. Never one to let someone else have the first word, or the last for that matter, Chalandra walked up to Garreth and ran her fingers up his lean chest. She smiled smugly as she saw the grin fade from Raissa's face.

"Well, Garreth," she purred, "you've finally come to claim the dance I promised you." Before he could voice the denial she knew was on his lips, she turned to Raissa. "And who is this? Is the mighty Protectorate so desperate that it must take on untried youths?"

Garreth scowled at Chalandra's obvious slur on Raissa's feminity. He had no doubt that Chalandra was well aware of who she was. Opening his mouth to tell Chalandra where to go, he felt the increased pressure on his arm and clamped his mouth shut. Obviously Raissa had her own reason for subjecting them to the Arvadian's malicious tongue.

Chalandra peered intently into Raissa's face. "Why, Raissa!" she cried in feigned surprise. "I hardly recognized you in that outfit." She stepped back, a bemused frown on her face. "You know, my dear, you really shouldn't hide your hair. After all, it is your best feature. With it hidden, you look just like one of the boys." Chalandra brought her hand up to her mouth. "Oh, dear, I'm sorry. I shouldn't have said that." Her silver eyes glittered unremorsefully.

To Garreth's profound disappointment, Raissa only laughed. "We can't all be lucky enough to look like you, Chalandra."

"Speaking of looks, where is that drab, little cubiclemate of yours? Did the timid thing decide not to come?"

"Why she's been here for quite some time." Now it was Raissa's turn to pretend innocence.

"You promised to introduce me to the child," Chalandra chided her.

"Oh!" Raissa cried in surprise. "I'd forgotten." She glanced at Garreth wickedly. "But then, I've been busy elsewhere. Besides, I just assumed you'd have your hands too full with Aubin to be concerned with Eirriel." She looked around. "By the way, where is our handsome captain?"

Chalandra bristled. That shrewd Melonnian didn't miss a trick! There was no way she was going to admit she'd been deserted.

"Oh, Aubin's such a dear," she lied smoothly. "I just happened to mention I was thirsty and he insisted on getting me a beaker of brew. He should return any minute now."

"I see," Raissa said, her tone letting Chalandra know just how much she did see.

Garreth tired of Chalandra's overbearing company, asked Raissa to dance.

"I'd love to. Talk to you later, Chalandra," she said as she turned to take Garreth's proffered hand.

"Wait! You forgot to tell me. Where's Eirriel hiding?"

Raissa turned to Chalandra. "Hiding? Why, she's not hiding, Chalandra. She's been dancing with Tynan all night."

Dancing with Tynan? But—but he'd been dancing with . . . with. . . . Shocked realization rocked Chalandra's cool control and her jaw dropped. The long-legged female gliding gracefully across the floor was Eirriel! Silver eyes crackled with rage.

"You bitch!" she swore. "Go ahead, laugh while you can. You'll be sorry for this, I promise you! No one makes me look like a fool and gets away with it!"

Chalandra stepped menacingly toward Raissa, but halted as she saw Garreth place a protective arm around Raissa. Chalandra took a deep breath and tried to compose herself.

"You think you've won, don't you? You and your Dianthian friend. Well, we'll see. The evening's far from over. We'll see in whose arms Aubin spends this night!"

"So we shall," Raissa said.

She took Garreth's hand and allowed him to lead her onto the dance floor. They had only taken a few steps when Raissa stopped and turned and faced the smug Arvadian. "I wouldn't be too sure of the outcome, if I were you, Chalandra. You see"—she threw a meaningful glance in Aubin's direction—"he hasn't taken his eyes off her all evening."

Raissa laughed gleefully as Chalandra stormed from the rec-cubicles. His hearty chuckle joining Raissa's, Garreth placed his hands on her waist and swept her around the floor to the lusty rhythm of the Melonnian folk dance.

Aubin took another swallow of the bitter brew. No matter how he tried, he couldn't seem to keep his eyes from following Eirriel. The few times he had successfully forced his attention elsewhere, her tantalizing laugh had drifted across the cubicle and drew him back to her once again. He groaned silently as he pictured her sweeping her hat from her head, her hair cascading down her back. It had taken all his will power not to cross the cubicle and force her to go with him.

He glowered darkly as Tynan ran his hand under Eirriel's rich curls, down her sleek back and then rested it possessively on one nicely rounded buttock. Why the hell didn't she brush the bastard's hand away? he fumed, taking another drink. Or was it just his advances that she spurned? Aubin felt a hot iron stab at his heart as he saw Tynan lean over and press his lips forcefully to hers. He held his breath in blissful anticipation waiting for the answering slap that had always greeted such unwanted liberties and muttered damningly when it did not come. Unwanted! he snorted, his brows meeting in a fierce scowl as he observed her smile up at the Arvadian, obviously pleased by his disgusting show of affection.

His golden eyes dark with fury, he cursed the fates that involved him with a woman who toyed so easily with men's emotions. His thoughts grew blacker as he recalled her supposed injustices at Kedar's hands. Injustices! Hah! She had probably played Kedar for a fool until he had had no choice but to send her away. What of High Commander

Lux? It hadn't taken her long to have him eating out of her treacherous little hands! And now this pathetic fool of an Arvadian! *Well, if he wants her, he can have her and with my blessings!* Aubin snickered to himself. *Make that my condolences. He doesn't know her for the ill-tempered hellion she really is, but give him a few days. . . .* Aubin refilled his beaker and raised it in silent toast to Tynan. *Good luck, my friend. You're going to need it!*

Chalandra, having regained control of her temper, was once again at Aubin's side, watching his darkening mood and his continued consumption of brew. She followed his piercing stare and saw it centered on Tynan's laughing partner. Raissa's biting remark had forced Chalandra to admit that Aubin had indeed spent the entire evening watching Eirriel. But the evening was now drawing to an end, and Chalandra had decided it was time to lure Aubin's wandering attention back to her.

"Do not glower so, my Aubin. It will give you lines." When he appeared not to have heard her, Chalandra ran her hand across his brow. "You worry about your little guest, no? You should not. I tell Tynan to make sure she have a good time. He does his job good, yes?"

This time the odd silkiness of her voice captured Aubin's attention, but not for the reason she had planned. His glance swung to her face. He caught the strange glimmer in her eyes and his own narrowed then flickered to the whirling couple. Was Chalandra responsible for the inordinate amount of attention Tynan was showering on Eirriel? He looked again at Chalandra. This time there was no mistaking her smug look. Chalandra had paid Tynan to take care of Eirriel, he was certain of it. That bitch!

Low laughter reached Aubin's ears. His scowl deepened as he saw Tynan scoop Eirriel up in his arms and spin her around. With her head tilted back and her eyes closed, she appeared, to Aubin's agonizing stare, to be completely enthralled by the man who held her. *Fool!* he berated himself. *You'll look for any excuse rather than admit the truth. Tynan and Eirriel have acted like lovers all evening and nothing you say will make it otherwise!*

Unaware of his turbulent thoughts, Chalandra ran her

hand across Aubin's broad back. "We go now? Chalandra
will make you forget."

She reached up and pulled his head down, capturing his
mouth with hers. But instead of the usual warm, passionate
response, she found his lips cold, unyielding.

You make me forget! Aubin wanted to shout. Not very
likely. But all he said as he pushed her away was, "Not now,
Chalandra." Angry at her manipulations and annoyed that
she took it for granted that they would spend the night
together, he added, "And not later."

Chalandra laughed and placed her hands on his chest.
"You tease, Chalandra? Yes?"

"On the contrary, my dear, I'm quite serious." Irritated
by her cloying touch and blatant lust, he thrust her from
him. "Find someone else to accommodate you," he snapped. "I'm in no mood to service your perverse needs."

"But I want you! I need you!" she cried desperately.

"Really, Chalandra!" he sneered. "Begging?"

"You bastard!" she swore, raising her arm.

Aubin's hand shot up and captured her wrist in its iron
grip. "If I were you, I would think very carefully before I
continued," he warned, his voice edged with steel. "Very
carefully, indeed."

Chalandra wrenched her arm from his grasp and rushed
from the cubicle. What had gone wrong? How had she lost?
She caught a glimpse of brown out of the corner of her eye
and turned to see Aubin striding down the other passageway. So, she thought smugly, Aubin left as well. Alone! She
had not lost completely. Chortling gleefully, she entered her
cubicle, her scheming mind already contemplating a new
way to entrap Aubin.

Eirriel forced another laugh. How she hated the whole
charade. When would it end? She didn't think she could
stand Tynan's mauling much longer. She glanced about the
cubicle, her eyes greedily seeking Aubin. Her spirits lifted as
she spied him standing alone in the corner, then her glance
flickered over the scattered crowd. A smile lit her face as she
saw no sign of Chalandra. Maybe the night had been worth
it, after all. Would Aubin come to her now? Tynan spun her

around, and her eyes drifted back to Aubin. He was no longer there. Frantically, she searched the rec-area. He was nowhere in sight! *Fool!* She fumed to herself. *What did you expect? Chalandra must have left first to prepare herself for him.* Eirriel's eyes registered her defeat.

Tynan brushed his lips against hers. "Why so distraught, lovely one? Are you tired?"

She forced herself to smile. "Yes, I am. I think I'd like to leave if you don't mind."

Tynan's blue eyes grew warm with anticipation. "By all means, let's leave."

"You don't have to go," she protested quickly. "I can find my own way. Really."

"Nonsense. I'll see you safely to your portal. I insist."

Eirriel shrugged her shoulders, too depressed to care. Tynan led her from the cubicle and down the passageway. At her cubicle she turned and gave him a weary smile. "Good night, Tynan. Thank you for your company."

Eirriel started to enter her cubicle, but Tynan yanked her to him and seized her mouth with his. Her arms, trapped between them when he crushed her to him, shoved against his slim chest and pushed him away. Her hand came up and she slapped him soundly on the cheek.

"You take too much for granted, sir!" she snapped indignantly.

She stepped into her cubicle and left a very startled Arvadian gaping at the closed portal. Knowing it would be locked, he tried it anyway. Aside from breaking the portal in, which he doubted was even possible, there was little he could do. Chalandra might not be too pleased when she learned that he did not sleep with the Dianthian, but at least he could say that neither did Aubin. Shrugging, Tynan returned to the masque. He had noticed others eyeing him while he had danced attendance on the icy Dianthian. If Fliimer's luck was riding his shoulder, he could still salvage the promise tonight had held.

"We've stayed long enough," Garreth's voice was rich with promised delights. "It's our bond night, a night to be spent in loving."

They stood once again before the enormous observation windows, staring at the myriad of stars swirling by as the *Celestial* continued on its projected course.

"Come."

Raissa's eyes deepened to a dark brown as Garreth led her to his cubicle.

Aubin stormed into his cubicle. Stripping down to his pants, he threw himself onto the restorer and was quickly overcome by brew-induced sleep. He tossed and turned, as his dreams were plagued with visions of Eirriel—her pale skin glistening in the half-light, her head thrown back in rapture, her arms clinging tightly to the trim back of her brown-haired lover.

With a cry, Aubin woke, his body drenched with sweat and his mind tortured with agonizing doubt. Was she with him now? Was Tynan tasting the sweetness that Aubin so desperately longed to sample? Cursing, he paced about the cubicle. He glanced bitterly at the chronometer. Four more hours until daybreak. Would this accursed night never end!

Eirriel lay in the vitalizer, the warm, swirling water soothing her tension-filled body, but doing little for her overactive mind. She knew she had lost. Aubin was with Chalandra and that was where he wanted to be.

"You won, Chalandra!" she cried in frustration. "He's yours! But I won't stay here and watch!"

She pulled herself from the vitalizer and grabbed the drying cloth. Resolutely, she came to a decision.

She'd follow her original plan and request a transfer. Demand one, if he turned her down! *Ha!* she laughed bitterly to herself. *Your head is still in the clouds. Why would he turn you down?*

She dried off and slipped a long, flowing caftan over her head. Giving her hair a few strokes, she reached for a clasp and fastened it on her head. Dispiritedly, she sat down and quickly wrote the request. She would leave it in Aubin's cubicle while he was still with Chalandra.

"Coward," she mumbled. "You can't even face him." Bleakly, she nodded. She knew if she saw him again she would lose what little determination she had.

Holding the transfer in her trembling hand, Eirriel stealthily walked to Aubin's cubicle. Reaching the portal, she hesitated. Once her plan was set in motion there could be no turning back. Taking a deep breath, she pressed the button and the portal sprang open. She placed her resignation on the floor where he would see it upon entering, then backed out, the portal closing automatically behind her.

Done! She leaned against the portal, the emptiness in her heart leaving her weak. He was free of her and she of him. Tears formed unwillingly. Free of him? Would she ever be free of him? *How do you stop loving?* her soul cried in anguish.

She started as she heard a muffled sound from behind the closed portal. Aubin? Had she miscalculated? Could they have come here instead of going to Chalandra's cubicle? Not wanting to see him, she turned to flee, but wasn't quick enough. Aubin's portal opened and the light from his cubicle bathed the darkened passageway.

She was caught!

Chapter Fifteen

"Eirriel! What's the meaning of this!" Aubin demanded, her request crumpled in his clenched fist.

She straightened her back, but did not turn. "Isn't it obvious?"

"Not one bit! Damn it all! Five days ago you were anxious to stay, now you want to leave. Why?"

"I have my reasons," she said softly.

Aubin placed his hands on her shoulders.

"Don't touch me!" she cried, pulling away from him.

"Tell me why!" he ordered.

She turned quickly to face him, her eyes bright, her cheeks flushed. "Why do you want to know? You don't really care! You have your ship. Your friends. Your mistress. What do you want from me?"

To her dismay, her voice broke. Her hand flew to her mouth and she fled down the passageway toward the welcoming sanctuary of her cubicle. Aubin reached her just as her portal opened. He grasped her shoulder and felt her trembling beneath his touch.

"You're wrong, little one."

She shook her head in silent denial. "Please let me go," she begged, tears that could no longer be held in check, ran down her cheeks.

Aubin turned her to him. "I can't let you go," he said huskily. "You're in my blood, woman. I've been fighting it since the first time we met. I can no longer." He stared down at the woman he could not lose. "I don't know how much I can give you, Eirriel, but I'll give you all I can."

Eirriel raised her eyes to his, seeking some sign of his usual arrogance, but found none. Silently he pulled her to him and brushed her mouth with his. A sob escaped Eirriel. She reached up and slipped her arms around his neck. His mouth found hers again, but this time it was harsh, demanding. She parted her lips under his steady pressure and felt his tongue sampling the soft lushness of her mouth. A shock traveled through her as her tongue met his.

Placing a strong arm beneath her knees, the other behind her back, Aubin lifted her and carried her to his cubicle. Once inside, he lowered her to her feet. His mouth seized hers again. As one hand slowly moved down her back to cup her buttocks and press her against him, the other reached up and snapped open her hair clasp, freeing her riotous curls. Raking his hands through the thick golden strands, he murmured against her mouth. "I've wanted to do that for so long."

His mouth left hers and he stepped away. She lifted her eyes and gasped at the dark passion burning deep in his eyes and the intense desire reflected on his handsome face. Frightened, she lowered her eyes.

"Eirriel, look at me."

Hesitantly, she raised her eyes. Aubin was surprised by the fear and uncertainty he saw in the green depths of her eyes and misread their meaning.

"Don't be afraid, little one. I'll be gentle. I won't hurt you like the others."

"You don't understand," she began.

The protest died on her lips as Aubin's tongue flicked out and teased the corners of her mouth, then ran lightly along the full curves of her lips. His teeth nipped them playfully, sending frissons of warmth through her body until she could stand no more and found herself incapable of thought. She reached up, sank her hands into his hair and drew his tantalizing mouth to hers. Her lips parted and she thrust her tongue deep into the warm moistness of his mouth.

Aubin's hands came up. The loose caftan was pushed from her shoulders and fell to a heap about her ankles. A moan tore itself from his throat as he pressed her close, the throbbing hardness of him searing against her cool skin.

His mouth never leaving hers, Aubin picked her up once again and carried her to his restorer. Leaning on one knee, he lowered her to the silky coverings. He straightened and his smoldering gaze raked down her body.

"Oh, my love, you're so beautiful," he said hoarsely.

His eyes never straying from her face, Aubin stripped off his pants. Eirriel's breath caught in her throat when he finally stood before her. Her eyes blazed like unbanked fires as they followed the trail of golden hair from his muscular chest to his lean waist and then settled on his manhood rising from its bed of golden curls. Her teeth tugged at her lips as the unfamiliar ache that had started in the core of her spread. She raised her arms. With a groan, Aubin lowered himself into her waiting embrace.

Aubin turned on his side, bent his elbow and propped his head on his closed fist. His free hand sought and captured one full breast, then the other, his lean fingers gently rolling the soft, rosy peaks between them until they puckered and grew firm. Eirriel closed her eyes and lost herself to the wondrous sensations caused by his knowing touch. Her breath came in short, shallow gasps as his fingers blazed a fiery path from her breasts, down her smooth stomach, and trailed through the soft springy curls between her legs. She tightened her thighs as his hand ventured to open them.

"Relax, my sweet. Let me."

Not wanting to push her too soon, Aubin withdrew his hand. He dipped his head, his tongue circling the tender skin of her nipple. He rolled the taut peak between his teeth before drawing it into his hot hungry mouth. A groan rose from the depths of her soul and Aubin, feasting on her breasts, felt the last vestiges of her fear flee and her legs relax under his waiting hand. Slowly, he slipped his fingers into the very depths of her womanhood. Instinct controlled Eirriel and she moved her hips beneath his hand. She whimpered when she felt him leave her, but the sound swiftly changed to a gasp of unbelievable pleasure as his mouth and tongue replaced his probing fingers. Her fingers tangled themselves in his hair, pressing him closer as the raging fire that was coursing through her veins consumed her.

A compelling need arose in her to touch him, to please him as he was pleasing her. She ran her small, slender hands across his broad back. Hands, that moments ago drew him closer, now were gently pushing him away. Aubin raised his head, his passion-darkened eyes questioning.

"Lay back."

The blood pounded through Aubin at the sound of her husky voice. She pressed him back to the restorer, her mouth seeking his wantonly. Her hands caressed him, her fingers circling his nipples as he had hers, then creeping lower to twine teasingly in his tight golden curls. A low groan escaped him as she ran her fingers over his bulging hardness with a whisper-soft touch. Her mouth left his and she greedily nipped at his shoulders, ears, and neck. Light feathery kisses played havoc with his senses as she moved languidly downward. Her tongue flicked out and he jerked at its barest touch. The thought that she had been well trained vaporized in the heat she created as she drew his warm velvety length into her seeking mouth.

"Enough."

Needing to brand her his, to erase all others from her memory, Aubin raised Eirriel from him and guided her to lie on the restorer.

"I want you," he moaned as he parted her thighs with his knee. "Now."

Aubin's mouth seized hers again and he lowered himself over her. His manhood nudged her and Eirriel instinctively raised her hips invitingly. Feeling her heat, Aubin thrust forward. Eirriel gasped at the sudden filling pressure. Her nails dug into his side as he tore through the delicate boundary that marked her a maiden.

Aubin froze. "What the hell?"

He raised his head and met her unflinching gaze. Confronted with the truth, he saw her uncompromising passion for what it was—an act of love. And it rocked him to his very core.

"I'm sorry, little one." His deep voice was husky with remorse. "I should have known."

"Yes. You should have," she replied quietly.

Her simple statement of fact said in a tone of voice which held none of the condemnation he had expected gave Aubin hope. He would make it up to her, he vowed. And he would start now.

Tenderly he pressed his lips to her forehead, her eyes, the tip of her nose. His tongue teased the corners of her mouth and when she reached up and laced her fingers in his hair, his lips locked onto hers and their tongues met. Ever so slowly Aubin rolled his hips. Eirriel groaned against his mouth. Leisurely, he withdrew until the tip of his throbbing manhood pressed tantalizingly against her honeyed core. His eyes never leaving hers, Aubin waited until he saw her burning need almost peak, then he deliberately slid into her, drawing out the pleasure with small rotations of his hips.

Again, he withdrew. Again, he waited and watched. Then he slipped into her, again and again.

Eirriel's head rolled from side to side and her lips parted. A fiery ache started deep within her and burned hotter with each motion of Aubin's hips. White-hot need arched Eirriel's hips to meet his penetrating thrusts and she drew her hands from his shoulders, running them down his back to grasp his buttocks and press him closer. Consumed by the raging inferno, Eirriel soared higher and higher. Her eyes flew open and she cried Aubin's name as a wave of exquisite pleasure swept her up and carried her to the ecstatic summit of fulfillment. Her throbbing release proved too much for Aubin's control. He thrust forward one last time, then threw back his head as his body sought and found its own pulsating release.

When his breathing slowed, Aubin rolled off Eirriel and gathered her to him. A contented smile curved her lips and she snuggled against the man who had just transported her to a realm she never knew existed. Her hand caressed his chest, then stopped as she drifted off to sleep.

Listening to her rhythmic breathing, Aubin's arms tightened. He had been her first, he thought with wonder and pride. No, not her first, he corrected possessively, nuzzling her hair. Her only. Ignoring the startling ramifications the unfamiliar feeling brought to his life, his future and the carefully erected wall around his heart, Aubin closed his eyes and slept.

Chalandra stepped quietly into Aubin's darkened cubicle. As the portal swooshed shut, she spied the small beam of light filtering in from the partially closed portal to the vitalizer. She crept stealthily across the cubicle and eased open the portal. A hungry look settled in her eyes as she watched Aubin rise from the swirling waters and wrap a large cloth around his lean waist.

"Good morning, lover," she purred.

A startled look flashed across Aubin's face, then his eyes darkened with anger. "Chalandra! What the hell are you doing here?"

She stepped closer. "You are surprised to see me, yes?"

"Surprised? Yeah, you could say that," he said dryly. "After last night I didn't think even you would have the nerve to come here."

"That's why I come." With one finger she followed a meandering droplet of water down his chest. "I think maybe Aubin not mean what he say."

"I meant what I said, Chalandra," he snapped, grabbing her wrist and flinging it from him. "Now get the hell out of here!"

"Aubin?" Eirriel called softly. "Is something wrong?"

The Rhianonian captain shoved his mistress aside and stepped into the main cubicle.

"It's nothing, my love," he answered tenderly. "Go back to sleep."

"Eirriel!" Chalandra shrieked.

"Chalandra!" Eirriel gasped, bolting up in the restorer, the covers clutched tightly to her breast.

The seething Arvadian swept across the cubicle and flicked on the light. Silver eyes, crystallized with rage, raked

GET YOUR 4 FREE BOOKS
NOW — A $21.96 Value!

Mail the Free Book Certificate Today!

PLEASE RUSH
MY FOUR FREE
BOOKS TO ME
RIGHT AWAY!

Leisure Romance Book Club
P.O. Box 6613
Edison, NJ 08818-6613

▲ Tear Here and Mail Your FREE Book Card Today! ▲

Get Four Books Totally
FREE — A $21.96 Value!

over Eirriel's tousled and obviously naked body.

"My, my, we do like variety, don't we?" Chalandra jeered. "Tell me, wasn't Tynan enough to satisfy you?"

Remembering his recent accusations, Eirriel turned to Aubin and saw him saunter toward her. Planting one knee on the restorer, he leaned over and placed a finger on her lips, silencing her fears. "Shush, little love," he said softly, warmth reflected in his eyes. "There's no need to answer."

He turned to Chalandra, his eyes flat and his voice glacial. "Do you think me such a fool," he demanded, "that I don't know innocence when I see it?" Of course, he had been a fool and he hadn't seen it, but Chalandra needn't know that.

"When you grow tired of her childish gropings, my dear Aubin, you know where to find me," Chalandra sneered, then abruptly left.

Aubin glowered at Chalandra's taunt. "One of these days that bitch will push me too far and I'll—"

Whatever he intended to say was left unspoken as Eirriel dropped the silky covering.

"Could you stand a little more of my 'childish pawings'?" she asked huskily, reaching up and tugging at the knotted cloth.

In answer Aubin ripped the cloth from his waist, tossed it carelessly to the floor and lowered himself into Eirriel's upraised arms.

Tynan glanced up as Chalandra burst into his cubicle. Storming over to the refreshment cabinet, she grabbed the first cruet her hand touched. Furiously she splashed the green liquid into a beaker, raised it to her lips and tossed it down.

Lazily Tynan dragged his tall form from the restorer, as she poured another drink.

"Why, Chalandra, my pet, you do seem to be in a bit of a dither. Whatever could be wrong?" *As if I don't know*, he added silently.

"Ugh!" Chalandra whirled about and hurled the refilled beaker at Tynan.

"Now, now, my dear," he rebuked, calmly sidestepping the carelessly aimed missle. "What would your precious captain say if he could see you now?"

Shrieking curses, Chalandra flung herself at Tynan. With a strength unsuspected in someone with his lanky frame, he caught her and threw her onto the restorer. Blind with rage, Chalandra struggled to her knees. She reached up and raked her nails across his face.

"Vixen!" Tynan roared. "Sheathe those talons of yours before I forget myself!"

Teeth bared, Chalandra slashed her hands defiantly at his hairless chest, raising angry red welts. Bellowing with rage, Tynan seized her by the hair and forced her back onto the restorer. Straddling her, he trapped her wrists in one hand. Aroused by her furious thrashings, he tore the caftan from her. Blue sparks blazed in his eyes as he lowered his mouth savagely to hers, his free hand roaming her lush body.

Closing her eyes, Chalandra ceased her struggles and gave herself up to Tynan's knowing ministrations. She moaned as he glutted himself on the abounding fullness of her well-rounded breasts. She cried out, half in pain, half in pleasure, as he viciously captured her nipple and sank his teeth into her sensitive skin. He spread her legs and ran his hand teasingly over her supple thighs and the aching void between them. She gasped and arched her hips as he thrust his long fingers deep inside her. Again and again, he slowly and skillfully brought her to the very edge of satisfaction. Leaning on one elbow, a smug smile on his thin lips, Tynan watched with mounting amusement Chalandra's frantic writhing and the naked hunger reflected on her sensuous face. Then, a feral gleam lighting his blue eyes, he withdrew his hand.

Her silver eyes shot open. Her mouth agape, she watched Tynan lie back and casually cross his arms behind his head. Burning with frustrated desire, Chalandra quickly surmised his game. Seductively, she rose to her knees. Ever so slowly she ran her hands lightly down his chest. Hooking her fingers in the waistband of his pants, she eased them over his slim hips and tossed them to the floor. Taunting, teasing, but never touching, Chalandra used her hands and her mouth and played with Tynan as he had so callously played with her. Aching for release, Tynan grasped her roughly, threw her onto her back and rolled on top of her.

"Bitch!" he rasped.

"Bastard!" she countered, digging her nails into his back. Tynan captured her mouth with his and drove himself fiercely into her. Wrapping her legs around his waist, Chalandra met his fevered thrusts with wild abandon until, with a final gasp, they collapsed, their violent fires vanquished.

When his breathing slowed, Tynan raised himself on his hands and stared down at her. "Feeling better, my pet?" he demanded smugly.

Chalandra's lips curled wickedly. "You always do seem to know just what I need."

Tynan rolled onto his back, his upper lip twisting sardonically. "And so our partnership continues." He threw her a sidelong glance. "Care to tell me what set you off so early this morning?"

Chalandra hurled herself from the restorer. "It's none of your damned business!" she spat, grabbing Tynan's robe and yanking it on.

"If it concern's the Dianthian maid—"

"Dianthian whore you mean!" Chalandra cut in.

". . . as I believe it does," he continued, ignoring her outburst, "then it is my business."

A disinterested Chalandra crossed to the imager and attempted to run her hands through her tangled curls. "May I?" she asked, reaching for Tynan's brush.

"By all means. You know," he said offhanded, "he expects our help."

Chalandra paused in midstroke. "I'm well aware of what he expects!" she snapped. "I don't need you to remind me."

"But time, my dear. Do we still have time?"

"By his schedule we do."

"And by yours?"

She glowered into the imager, refusing his bait.

Tynan eased himself from the restorer. "I think I'll leave you and your devious little mind alone," he said, stepping through the vitalizer's open portal. "I'm confident that you'll soon devise a plan that will satisfy him and leave the good captain once more free to seek your restorer."

The portal closed just as Chalandra's angry retort slammed against it and reverberated through the cubicle.

Aubin guided Eirriel into the fore conveyor.

"I've got a busy schedule today," he commented as the portal shut. "And I'm already late." His hands behind his back, he studied the ceiling absently. "Can't imagine why, can you?" Chuckling, he kissed his blushing lady lightly on the lips. "Wait for me in my cubicle when your shift is over?"

Eirriel nodded. "But I must warn you," she said, her eyes twinkling, "I extract a heavy penalty if I'm kept waiting too long."

Waving her hand in farewell, she sauntered slowly toward the lab, fully conscious of Aubin's following stare.

"Are you going to stay in there forever?" Chalandra called in to Tynan.

"Until the climate outside improves I am," came the muted reply. "It's safer."

"Suit yourself," she said airily. "I'll just have to find someone else . . ."

The vitalizer portal sprang open and a fully dressed Tynan emerged, his eyes snapping with excitement. "You've a plan then, pet?"

"Oh, yes, my good Tynan. I've a plan. It will take a little time, but"—an evil glow lit her silver eyes and she grinned wickedly—"I think you'll agree it will be well worth the wait."

Chapter Sixteen

For Eirriel the week after the masque passed with incredible speed. Her days were spent in the lab, wading through a seemingly endless influx of data, and her nights in Aubin's arms, experiencing the constant delights of their new-found love.

She had just finished feeding the latest data on the planet, Quorin, into the computer when Aubin's deep voice sounded over the intercom.

"Com-center to lab."

Raissa raised her eyes from the keyboard. "I think it's for you," she said impishly.

"Now why would you think that?" Eirriel retorted saucily as she crossed to the intercom.

Raissa just laughed and returned to her work.

"Lab to com-center."

"Are you almost done?" Aubin asked.

"What I haven't finished can be left for tomorrow. Why?"

"I thought you might like to take our evening nourishment in rec-cubicle three."

"I'd love it!" she exclaimed.

Rec-cubicle three was her favorite because it re-created

the lush tropical landscape of Yiano to such perfection that she could forget she was hurtling through open space on a massive fleetship.

"Good. Can you leave now?"

"Yes."

"Fine. I'll meet you there."

"I'd like to change out of my uniform first, Aubin."

"How long will that take?"

She glanced at the chronometer. "About thirty minutes."

"See you then. Aubin out."

Saying good-bye to Raissa, Eirriel left for their cubicle. Once inside she crossed to the dressing compartment and withdrew an outfit. Laying it on the restorer, she took the clasps from her hair and entered the vitalizer.

Raissa jumped when a pair of warm lips touched the back of her neck. Spinning around in her chair to face the intruder, she exclaimed, "Garreth!"

"You were expecting someone else?"

"Weelll, now that you mention it . . . ."

Scowling, Garreth pulled her to her feet. "If I thought you meant that . . ." he said, capturing her mouth with his.

"There will never be anyone but you, my love," Raissa said softly, staring up at him with warm, loving eyes.

The depth of emotion in her voice sent a warmth burning through him.

"Are you finished here?" he asked hoarsely.

She nodded mutely. His golden eyes dark with love and promised passion, Garreth led her from the lab.

Eirriel placed the brush on the table. Stepping before the imager, a pleased light sprang to her eyes. It was perfect!

The green-and-white-flowered sarong fit snugly against her full breasts and slim hips. Her thick hair, parted in the middle, was fastened behind her right ear and fell over her left shoulder. Strands of crystallized Sealynes adorned her neck, wrists and ankles. Once linked, the casings of the tiny sea creatures absorbed the wearer's body heat and is the phosphorescent glow they cast was uniquely each individual's.

Anxious to see her beloved's reaction to her unusual attire, Eirriel hurried from the cubicle, her bare feet carrying her lightly down the passageway. Entering the rec-cubicle, she called Aubin's name and was disappointed when he didn't appear.

Crossing the warm sand, she sat on a large flat rock and dangled her feet in the water. Enjoying the feel of the warm, fragrant breeze tugging at her hair, she leaned back and waited. Before long, she heard the portals opening. Twisting, she faced not Aubin, but the young ensign, Marn. She stood as he approached.

"Sorry to disturb you, Eirriel, but the captain asked me to convey his apologies. He's tied up in engineering."

"Is it anything serious?"

"No, but it could have been. Luckily Ceara spotted the malfunction right away."

"Did he say how long he'd be?" she asked hopefully.

Marn shook his head.

"Oh," she murmured, unable to keep her disappointment from showing. So much for a quiet evening for two.

"He did say he hoped you'd wait," the young man added quickly.

At his words, a radiant smile lit Eirriel's face. *Whew!* Marn reflected enviously, *the captain sure has himself one hell of a beautiful woman!* His message delivered, he left cursing the fates that had placed the comely young woman so far from his reach.

Alone again, Eirriel settled back on the rock. Lulled by the hot, hazy stillness, her eyes closed and she drifted off to sleep.

"My, my. Don't we look cozy."

Her startled green eyes flew open. Blinking at the bright light, Eirriel sat up, shielding her eyes with one hand. "Who is it?"

"Oh, did I wake you?" Chalandra asked in mock sorrow.

Her eyes now adjusted to the light, Eirriel dropped her hand and sprang lightly to her feet. Ignoring Chalandra's sarcastic remark, she asked coldly, "Did you want something, Chalandra?"

Her silver brows arched in surprise. "What? No polite

pleasantries, Eirriel? Not even a hello?" She shook her head sadly. "It would seem, child, that you've forgotten what little upbringing you've had. I know, dear, it's not your fault. You are awfully young to be away from home."

When Eirriel failed to react to her carefully aimed barbs, Chalandra tried a different tact. Leaning casually against a large boulder, she scathingly ran her eyes up and down Eirriel's tall form. "How quaint you look," she drawled. "So very . . . native."

In a bored voice that gave no hint to the fury boiling inside her, Eirriel sighed. "Is that why you're here, Chalandra? To comment on my wardrobe? I'd have thought you'd have more important things to attend to." She paused. "Choosing veils can be most difficult."

Gritting her teeth, Chalandra ignored Eirriel's baiting. "Now that you mention it, child, I did come for a reason." She dropped to the sand. "Why don't we make ourselves comfortable and have a little talk?"

"I really don't think we have anything to discuss," Eirriel retorted, remaining on her feet.

Chalandra glanced up at the cool Dianthian, wisely concealing her frustration from the mocking green eyes. *How dare she act so damned superior!* she raged silently. *Who the hell does this bitch think she is?* She clenched her fists at her side. How she itched to scratch the haughty look from Eirriel's face, but she knew there was too much at stake to act rashly. *He* wanted her unmarred. *Just a little longer,* she consoled herself, *and then we'll see who is so high and mighty!*

Smiling brightly at Eirriel's bleak, not-too-distant future, Chalandra said, "Oh, but there is, child. Poor Tynan's distraught. He thinks you're avoiding him."

Eirriel's eyes widened increduously. "Avoiding him? I haven't been avoiding him."

"Then you do want to see him!" Chalandra cried. "I just knew the two of you would get along."

"Now wait a minute, Chalandra. I'm not avoiding him, but neither do I want to spend my time with him."

Silver eyes narrowed. "Oh, and who do you want to spend time with?"

Eirriel stared at her, amazed at Chalandra's audacity. After a few moments of silence, she said quietly, "I think you already know the answer."

Chalandra studied her nails distraughtly. "You poor, poor dear," she said ruefully. "Didn't anyone ever explain men to you, child?" She hesitated. "Oh, dear, I don't know quite how to put this."

"I'm sure you'll manage someway," Eirriel remarked dryly.

"I guess the best thing to do in a case like this is to be blunt," Chalandra continued as if Eirriel hadn't spoken. "Child, when pity moves a man to give you a few hours of his time, you'd be foolish to expect it to continue."

"And that's what I'm doing?"

"Yes. Don't you see, child, Aubin—"

"No, Chalandra," Eirriel cut in, her eyes sparking dangerously. "I don't see."

"If you'd let me explain," Chalandra protested.

"No, Chalandra! Let *me* explain!"

Chalandra's head shot up at Eirriel's fierce tone.

"First, you can drop the mother act. It doesn't suit you. Second, I don't need any advice about Aubin. And if I did," she added contemptuously, "you'd be the last person I'd ask."

The Arvadian jumped to her feet, her eyes glittering with rage. "Why you ungrateful little bitch! How dare you talk to me like that!"

Eirriel shrugged indolently. "It's not hard."

"Just because Aubin's sniffing after you, you think you can do as you please. Well, Miss High-and-Mighty, you're wrong!"

Mimicking Aubin's arrogant stance, Eirriel drawled, "Am I?"

"Yes!" she spat. "Aubin's about as reliable as open space during an ion storm! Just look at tonight. He was supposed to be here hours ago, wasn't he?" Her eyes narrowed slyly. "Do you really think it's taken this long to repair a minor malfunction?" She paused, then added conversationally, "I understand Ceara's very helpful."

Eirriel snorted at Chalandra's absurd insinuation, too

disgusted by it even to question how Chalandra knew about the malfunction. Unable to tolerate her any longer, Eirriel said impatiently, "And the point of all this?"

"The point is," Chalandra sneered, "that you're too young and too inexperienced to satisfy Aubin's lusty appetites." Not giving Eirriel time to reply, she continued, "Every man dreams of seducing an innocent, my dear. Aubin is no different. But when the novelty wears off, and it will, he'll be back where he belongs. With me!"

"If you're so confident, Chalandra, why are you here?" Eirriel challenged. She paused, studying the Arvadian. "Could it be that I'm more of a threat than you first thought?"

"You a threat?" Chalandra snickered, amused. "How could you be a threat?"

Serious green eyes stared at the gypsy. "Because, Chalandra, I can touch him in the one place you cannot reach."

"And where, pray tell, is that?"

"His heart," she replied with quiet conviction.

"His heart!" Chalandra laughed, shaking her head sadly. "You poor dear, you really have it bad, don't you?" Dancing silver eyes mocked Eirriel. "Aubin has no heart, child. And if he did, it would be mine as he already is!" she added possessively.

Eirriel shook her head in disgust. It was time to put an end to a discussion that should never have started! As she brushed past Chalandra, the other woman's hand shot out and grabbed Eirriel. With a withering glare at the offending hand, Eirriel jerked her arm away. Not to be put off, Chalandra stepped in front of her, barring her way.

"Let me pass, Chalandra." The softly spoken words had a bite as cold as steel.

"Not until you promise to stay away from Aubin," Chalandra countered, frustrated anger making her voice shrill.

"I can't do that," Eirriel replied simply.

Pushed past caring by Eirriel's cool control, Chalandra lunged at the Dianthian. Caught unaware, Eirriel landed on her back. Before she could move, Chalandra was on her, pinning her shoulders to the sandy ground.

"Bitch! I'll teach you to steal what is mine!" she cried, slapping Eirriel across the face.

Eirriel arched her hips and tossed Chalandra from her. Springing to her feet, she faced the Arvadian, her eyes hard, her lips curled contemptuously. "There is no need to steal what is freely give," Eirriel taunted her.

Snarling, Chalandra threw herself at Eirriel. Anticipating another such attack, Eirriel jumped out of the way. In her haste her heel caught on a rock and she stumbled backwards. Flailing hands found nothing to grab onto and she fell, her head striking the ground with an ominous thud.

"Eirriel!"

Aubin's pained bellow reached her ringing ears. She tried to sit up, but the effort was too great. She closed her eyes against the dizziness.

"Don't move, little one."

Aubin's long strides had carried him quickly to her side. She opened her eyes to see him kneeling beside her, an anxious frown creasing his brow.

"Are you all right?" he asked, his voice deep with concern.

She nodded, then groaned as a pain shot through her head from the sudden movement. Aubin's eyes darkened with rage. Eirriel reached up and touched his cheek. She smiled weakly. "I'm all right, Aubin."

"Can you stand?"

"I think so."

While Aubin was helping Eirriel to her feet, Chalandra decided to take advantage of the diversion and flee. It came as quite a shock to her when she heard Aubin's enraged roar. "Stop!"

Chalandra turned to see Eirriel leaning against a tree and Aubin striding toward her. Panic-stricken, Chalandra could do nothing more than stare into his glittering eyes and wait. Without a word, his large hands closed about her throat. Frantically she clawed at his constricting fingers. Her head started to spin. A numbness began in her toes and spread upward. As if from a distance she felt the sudden release of pressure and she slumped to the ground, gasping for breath.

A bone-crushing grip closed over her wrist and yanked her to her feet.

"Get out of here," Aubin ground out between tightly clenched teeth, "before I change my mind."

Hatred blazing in her eyes, Chalandra jerked her arm from his grasp and swept from the rec-cubicle.

"Aubin?"

Shaking his head to clear it, Aubin turned to see Eirriel standing near him, her arms outstretched. Needing no further encouragement, Aubin swept her to him and lowered his mouth to hers.

Early the next morning, a slow simmering rage burned through him as Aubin entered Chalandra's cubicle. Grabbing the sleeping woman by the shoulders, he dragged her from the restorer. Her heart pounding fiercely from her rude awakening, Chalandra stared up at the seething man with eyes rounded by fear, unable to speak.

"Get dressed!" Aubin roared, shoving her toward the dressing compartment. "I want you off my ship! Now!"

Struggling to maintain her balance after Aubin's abrupt release, Chalandra gasped at his orders. She could not leave! Not yet! As frightened as she was of him in his present mood, there was one who frightened her more.

"I—I can't," she stammered, frantically searching her mind for a plausible excuse.

"What!" Aubin exclaimed, unable to believe she was defying him.

"My ship . . . she's out of range . . . had a delivery." Chalandra prayed Aubin would attribute the hesitation in her voice to fear and not deceit.

With two steps Aubin closed the distance between them. Catching the cold, steely glint in his eyes, Chalandra stepped back. But when his long arms snaked out, she found she had moved neither fast enough nor far enough. Her struggles to free herself proved fruitless as his fingers bit deeply into her shoulders. Callously he ignored her cry of pain.

"In that case, my dear," he began in a deceptively casual tone, "I suggest you call it back. And fast!" he added, his voice growing diamond hard. "Because, my spiteful little bitch, if it's not within range by this time tomorrow, you'll find yourself stranded on the first uninhabited planet we pass!"

"You wouldn't dare!" she hissed.

"Oh, no?"

The softly spoken challenge sent shivers of fear down her spine. He would dare! Horrified, she could do no more than gape at him.

"In the meantime," he continued, "you would be most wise not to leave this cubicle."

Unable to bear her near him any longer, Aubin threw her from him and watched dispassionately as she tumbled backwards, striking her mouth against the restorer's metal frame.

"Remember what I said, Chalandra," Aubin warned as he left her lying there.

Dazed, Chalandra did not move until she felt a warm wetness trickling down her chin. Touching it with her fingers, she realized it was blood. Pressing the back of her hand to her mouth, she stared at the closed portal as one word burned its way through her brain—"tonight!"

Unaware of the explosive confrontation in Chalandra's cubicle, Eirriel slipped into her uniform, grabbed a quick nourishment and joined Raissa in the lab. Midmorning found the two women mixing work with cheerful chatter.

"You know, Rai, if it wasn't for the time we spend working in the lab, we'd never see each other." Ever since Raissa had life-bonded with Garreth and had moved in to his cubicle, the two women hardly saw each other at all.

"That's true," Raissa agreed. She flung a sidelong glance at Eirriel. "I could talk to Aubin."

"And I to Garreth," came the instant reply.

Raissa laughed. "And neither of us would talk to the other. Hand me the last page of Helig's report," she asked, extending her right hand. "I do know what you mean, though. The past few days have brought quite a change to our living habits."

"Nine days," Eirriel mused, sifting through her papers.

"Strange, it seems as though the masque was both yesterday"—she found the page and handed it to Raissa—"and last year."

Raissa scanned the sheet. "Time has been known to play tricks on the unsuspecting mind, my friend." Her fingers flew across the keyboard as she punched the data into the computer. "Now, my good Dianthian, how about a break?"

Without hesitation, Eirriel dropped the papers. "Gladly."

The two women crossed to the small nourishment table. Raissa poured hot spicy liquid into two beakers and handed one to Eirriel.

"To changes." She laughed, raising her beaker in the air.

"To changes," Eirriel replied, touching her beaker to her friend's.

"Well, now, what's this?"

Simultaneously the women turned and found the *Celestial's* captain and its second-in-command leaning casually against the portal frames, their arms crossed in front of their chests. Golden lights danced in Aubin's eyes and an impish smile played about his lips.

"Here we thought you two would be slaving away at your consoles and what do we find?"

"Don't know, Captain." Garreth shook his head. "It doesn't look like slaving to me." He peered at the women intently. "Nope." He shook his head again. "Looks more like shirking."

"Shirking?" Aubin asked in feigned amazement.

"Yup." Garreth nodded. "Most definitely shirking."

Raissa and Eirriel rolled their eyes. Those two were impossible! Eirriel was just about to say as much when she caught sight of the thin, green aura enveloping the two men. Her green eyes narrowed.

"Why have you activated your maral shields?" she asked, referring to the artificial atmosphere contained within the pulsating field of energy.

"After orbiting Zixelux for two days we've finally been given permission to teleport down," Aubin explained.

"And since Zixelux is completely covered by liquid pelfron, we thought the shields just might come in handy," Garreth finished.

"Do you really think you can prevent the Zixeluxians from withdrawing from the Protectorate?"

"I hope so, Raissa," Aubin replied. "They're a vital link in our defense of this sector."

"Main Terminal seems to believe our esteemed captain can force some sense into their sieve-like brains. I, however, have my doubts so I'm going to tag along and keep an eye on him."

Eirriel gave an exaggerated sigh of relief. "Now I don't have to worry."

"On the contrary, my friend," Raissa countered, "now you do have to worry."

Clutching his chest as if mortally wounded, Garreth threw Raissa a crushed look. "You wound me, fair lady. I may never recover."

"Come on, you." Raissa laughed, shaking her head. "I'll walk you to the teleport."

Chuckling at his two friends' antics, Aubin extended his hand to Eirriel.

"How long will you be down there?" Eirriel questioned, slipping her hand into his.

The tall Rhianonian shrugged. "It's hard to say, Eirriel. The Zixeluxian personality is so unpredictable and their rules of state so complex that to set a time limit on it would be senseless. If they're of a mind to cooperate, it won't take long, if not . . ." He left the sentence unfinished then glanced at her. "Why? Will you miss me?"

"Not at all," she replied airily, the soft loving glow in her eyes saying otherwise.

"Liar," Aubin accused, pulling her arm behind his back until she was pressed tightly to his chest.

"Who? Me?" she protested even as she melted against him.

His free hand swung up and caressed her cheek. "What a charming little vixen you are," he said as his mouth closed over hers.

Garreth popped his head back into the lab. "Captain, are you coming or do I have to handle the Zixeluxians all by myself?"

"I'm coming! I'm coming!" he muttered.

Releasing Eirriel, they followed Garreth and Raissa to the teleport. Once their men had departed for Zixelux, Eirriel and Raissa grudgingly returned to their work. The day passed quickly for them. Although the Zixeluxians proved relatively cooperative, it wasn't until late evening that Aubin and Garreth returned to the ship. An hour later Garreth was free to join Raissa, Eirriel and Cian as they finished their evening nourishment.

When Garreth informed Eirriel that the formal reports would keep Aubin occupied well into the early-morning hours, she decided to take advantage of her free time and treat herself to a long soak. Bidding her friends good night, she left.

"Enter," Eirriel called in answer to a gentle rap on the outer portal. "I'll be right out."

Rising from the vitalizer, she reached for her robe and slipped it on. The satiny material clinging to her wet skin, Eirriel entered the main cubicle. Spying the voluptuous form standing in the open portal, she stopped abruptly.

"I'm sorry if I disturbed your vitalizing," Chalandra said, her husky voice sickeningly sweet. "But I need to talk to you. See"—she gestured with a tray she carried in her hands—"I even brought refreshments. Why don't you get dressed while I pour?"

Speechless at the woman's effrontery, Eirriel snatched the green caftan off the restorer and went into the vitalizing cubicle. *How dare she show up here uninvited!* she fumed silently. Talk? She shook her head increduously. With the way last night's talk turned out she had thought Chalandra would've had the good sense to stay away from her.

Dressed, Eirriel gritted her teeth and joined Chalandra, who had made herself very comfortable on the couch.

"Was there something you forgot to mention during our last pleasant conversation?" she asked, dropping into the chair opposite her unwelcome guest.

Chalandra arched an eyebrow at Eirriel's tone but refused to be baited. There was too much at stake to give into anger now.

"I came to apologize," she said quietly. "Please try to understand." She wrung her hands distraughtly. "I love

Aubin. I always knew he never loved me, but that didn't stop me from hoping it could change. That he would learn to love me. Seeing the two of you together, I realized it could never be. It's not easy watching your dreams shatter.

"I really am sorry, Eirriel," she cried, her face the image of a penitent. "Will you forgive me?"

Staring into the almond-shaped, silver eyes, Eirriel was surprised by the sadness she saw there.

"I didn't realize how deeply you loved him," she said softly.

"Then you forgive me?"

"Yes, I forgive you."

"Good." Chalandra brightened. "Perhaps it's not too late to be friends?"

Eirriel studied the Arvadian. Was she to be trusted? She looked sincere enough, but. . . . Eirriel's kind-hearted nature quickly gave Chalandra the benefit of doubt and, after all, no real harm had been done.

"It's never too late, Chalandra," she replied with a warm smile.

Chalandra filled two beakers with a sparkling blue liquid. "I think you'll find this quite a change from your usual drink."

Under Chalandra's watchful eyes Eirriel sampled the brew. "Hmmm. Delicious."

"I'm glad you like it," she replied, setting aside her untouched beaker to refill Eirriel's. "It's an ancient Arvadian recipe that I blended early this morning just for you."

"You shouldn't have gone to all that trouble," Eirriel protested. Feeling a rush of warmth, she took several sips of the unique liquid, welcoming its refreshing iciness.

Covertly watching Eirriel run a hand across her beaded brow, Chalandra assured her that it was no trouble. A strange light sprang to her eyes and she added, "In fact, I was very glad to do it."

Eirriel started to thank Chalandra when a wave of dizziness washed over her. Clutching at the arm of the chair with her free hand, she saw the Arvadian staring at her and was startled by the intensity of the glittering silver eyes. She heard Chalandra's voice, but the garbled sounds made no sense. When she attempted to call out, her mouth refused to form the words. Blinking her eyes and shaking her head, she strained to clear the haze from her eyes.

Her heart pounding violently in her chest, Eirriel could not understand what was happening. Instinctively knowing that Chalandra was somehow responsible, one thought remained clear in her befuddled mind. She must reach Aubin!

The half-filled beaker slipped from her weakened grasp as she struggled to her feet. Gasping for breath, she tried to fight the paralyzing darkness that was sweeping over her but could not. Her knees buckled and she collapsed.

For a moment a raspy, gloating laugh echoed hollowly in Eirriel's head then vanished, replaced by the insulating stillness of oblivion.

Chapter Seventeen

Chalandra crept stealthily into the teleport and activated the beam. Scant moments later the chamber was bathed in a fleeting brilliance and a huge ominous figure appeared. Pressing a finger to her lips, she motioned him to follow. Silently, the pair made their way through the darkened passageway to Eirriel's cubicle.

Once inside, the electronic lock secured against unwanted company, Chalandra greeted her visitor. "May the One-Who-Knows-All smile in your favor."

The dark-skinned giant reached for the heavy chain that hung from his thick neck. Grabbing the large golden symbol, he pressed it reverently to his forehead. "And in yours, Lady."

Her silver eyes glittered gleefully as Chalandra studied her fierce accomplice. Garbed in billowing red pants, long greasy braids hanging in various lengths down his back, a jagged scar running from forehead to cheek, he exuded an air of barely suppressed savagery. A smug smile crossed her full lips. If she had chosen him herself, the choice could not have pleased her more. One look at his fierce countenance would be enough to send the simple-minded bitch into terrified hysterics.

"You know what you are to do?" Chalandra demanded. Tondor nodded.

"Good." She pointed to the partially concealed form sprawled on the floor. "There she is."

Tondor moved toward the drugged girl. Reaching down, he brushed the hair from her face. A light sprang to his small black eyes. Truly, she was a beauty! As always the Master chose well.

"What are you waiting for?" Chalandra snapped, glancing at the chronometer. "The tech will return to his station in less than five minutes. We must hurry."

Grimacing at Chalandra's belligerent tone, Tondor lifted Eirriel into his arms and carefully settled her against his massive chest. He knew the Master would be most displeased should any harm befall the fair-haired maiden before the proper time.

Chalandra opened the portal and glanced down the passageway. Seeing it empty, she beckoned to her huge companion. Quickly they retraced their steps and entered the still-unmanned teleport. Tondor took position in the chamber. Chalandra activated the mechanism, a look of triumph on her face as she watched her hated rival begin her journey to death.

Aubin spied the blinking message unit as soon as he entered his darkened cubicle. He activated the illumination system, then crossed to the table and touched the multicolored knob on the top of the unit. He sat down in the large chair and pulled off his boots as Eirriel's voice filled the cubicle.

"Knowing how weary you would be after the tedious wranglings with your petulant hosts, and how little sleep you would have gotten had I been there to greet you, I decided against it. In my stead I left your favorite nourishment in the warmer, a pitcher of brew chilling nearby and this message: Sleep well, my love, and dream of me. I'll be there when you awaken."

Anxious to see Eirriel, Aubin had pushed the reports off till morning, but since she had circumvented his plan he decided to put tonight to good use and save tomorrow for more pleasurable pursuits. Retrieving the nourishment tray and grabbing the brew, he placed them on the desk near the computer terminal and started punching in the data.

Finishing the report and the food at the same time, Aubin relaxed and poured himself another brew. Sipping the icy liquid, he leaned back, a feeling of contentment surrounding him as he thought of Eirriel's considerate surprise.

Not since Rhianon had anyone seen to his personal needs, and then it had only been because it was expected they should. Kiernan had wanted to send a dresser and server to tend to his son's needs when Aubin had become the captain of the *Celestial*, but Aubin had quickly refused. He hadn't wanted any consideration accorded him because of his rank. It was a decision he had been grateful he had made once he had experienced the hatred and resentment directed at him from some of his colleagues merely because he was a Rhianonian. Had they known his true status on Rhianon, they would have gone much farther to make his time among them unbearable.

Draining the goblet, Aubin let his gaze settle on the restorer. How well she knew him, his little one. Sleep, indeed, would have been his last thought had her luscious body been lying invitingly between the silky covering. His lips turned up in a rueful smile. He couldn't help but wish she hadn't been quite so sensitive to his needs. He sighed. She was right, of course, he was tired. In fact, he realized as he felt the energy draining from him, he was suddenly strangely exhausted.

Aubin dragged himself from the chair and stretched, trying to release the leadened feeling in his arms and legs. He pulled his shirt over his shoulders and let it drop to the floor, then ran a hand across his eyes and shook his head, puzzled at the unusual fatigue he felt. He stumbled across the cubicle and plunked heavily down on the restorer. Struggling out of his pants, Aubin fell back, his eyes closing even before his head touched the pillow.

Warm lips pressed against his. A tongue flicked out and teased the corners of his mouth. Slim fingers ran gently across his lower belly. Full breasts brushed against his reaching hands. Aubin tossed and turned on the restorer, his dreams erotic images of Eirriel in his arms, of her body beneath his, of her hips arching to meet his powerful thrusts. He rolled onto his back and kicked off the covers. By all the gods, he was burning! Burning with an inner fire that threatened to consume him. He saw the shine of moisture on her forehead as he moved over her. Felt the hot gasps of her breath against his ear as she panted with pleasure. Deep within himself he knew he was dreaming, knew Eirriel was asleep in her restorer even as he was asleep in his. But that knowledge did not help, not when the sensation of her hand encircling him was so strong.

Aubin fought against the uncontrollable fire that seared his loins and wrestled with the unnatural lassitude that plagued him and forced his eyes open. He blinked, surprised to see a blurry form leaning over him. Surprise quickly turned to enraged recognition. "Chalandra!" he growled her name.

She raised her head, a pout on her full lips. "No, lover," Chalandra denied, her silver eyes glittering in the darkness. "Not Chalandra. Eirriel."

"Eirriel?" Aubin rasped as he stared into green eyes that moments before he would have sworn were silver.

"Yes. Eirriel," she lied again, reinforcing the image in his mind.

Aubin frowned. It looked like Eirriel, what he could see through his hazy vision, but the voice was wrong. It didn't match the face. He shook his head, desperately trying to clear the fog from his brain, but found it was impossible as the rhythmic stroking of her hand increased.

"Did you think I would leave you alone?" she murmured. "Tonight of all nights?"

Tonight of all nights? What the hell did she mean by that? He opened his mouth to question her but all that came out was a moan of pure pleasure as she lowered her lips to him and drew him deep within the warm moistness of her mouth. All conscious thought fled. Groaning Eirriel's name, Aubin pulled her from him and pushed her into the restorer. Spreading her thighs with his knee, he raised himself above her. Chalandra gasped when his throbbing flesh pressed against her aching center.

"Yes! Now, lover! Now!"

The husky demand pierced the shadows surrounding Aubin's brain and echoed eerily inside his head. He froze. Sweat broke out on his brow as he grappled with the thought-robbing passion she had evoked in him and sought to put a name to the voice. And at last he did! She saw it in his eyes, the moment of reason, and, even as he roared his denial of her, she arched, her motion causing him to enter her. Her legs circled his back and her hands grasped his buttocks. Keeping him close, she continued to thrust against him driving him with her, beyond control, beyond reason, beyond thought. Forcing him to accept what she alone could give him, an end to the maddening fever that raged within him. His soul sick with self-disgust and cursing Chalandra with every breath, Aubin sought what she offered his body, pounding against her with a violence that threatened to tear her asunder. His head thrown back, Aubin drove himself into her one final time as wave after wave of welcoming release washed over him. His body drained of the ungovernable craving that had possessed him, Aubin used what little strength he had left to roll onto his back.

Chalandra lay at his side, breathlessly waiting for the sleep-inducing drug to resume its work. When minutes passed with no sound or movement from Aubin, she reached down and drew the silky covering over the two of them. As she did, her gaze moved to the chronometer and a victorious gleam settled in her silver eyes. Excellent! Enough time had passed to ensure the success of the first step of her plan. Her lips turned up in a pleased smile. More time would go by before the powerful drug released its hold on its unsuspecting victim and by the time Aubin awoke, the Dianthian would be beyond his reach. It would then be Chalandra's task to keep him from searching for his lover until the appointed hour came for the pale-skinned beauty to disappear from his life forever.

Aubin stirred and Chalandra felt a frisson of fear run down her spine. She knew him well enough to realize that his reaction to her trick would be far from pleasant. Just how unpleasant, she thought in panic, she was about to find out. Aubin was awake and hours too soon!

Aubin lay with an arm across his eyes, the other at his side, clenched in a white-knuckled fist. As exhausted as he was, he still couldn't sleep. The scene he had just played was too fresh in his mind. His face twisted with self-loathing and revulsion. How could he have betrayed the woman he loved with so little ease? The fact that he had been unable to master his lust when he realized exactly whom he held in his arms added to his disgust. What, in the name of all the gods, had happened to him? Never in his life had he felt so weak-willed, so out of control. It was a feeling he hoped never to experience again. And what in the hell was happening now? he thought as he felt his energy returning as abruptly as it had drained from him earlier. His eyes shot open and his body went rigid with rage. That deceitful bitch had drugged him! It was the only thing that made any sense.

He moved his arm from his face in time to see a small purple-skinned hand reach for him.

"Don't even think of it," he warned in a voice edged with steel.

Chalandra drew back her hand as quickly as if she had been burnt. She watched with apprehension as Aubin leaped from the restorer, snatched up her clothes and threw them at her.

"Get dressed!" His golden eyes glinted with barely suppressed rage. He grabbed his pants and yanked them on. When he saw that Chalandra had made no attempt to clothe herself, he ground out, "I said get dressed, damn you! Now!"

Never in all their time together had she witnessed the full force of Aubin's explosive temper, and now, not only was she going to see it first hand, it was going to be directed at her! Her mind worked furiously, searching for a way to come through this unscathed. All she had to work with was her body and she gambled that it would be enough.

She sat up and made no attempt to catch the silky covering as it slid down, baring her breasts. Ignoring the caftan he had tossed at her, she met his condemning glare with well-feigned surprise. "Something is wrong, no?"

"You can drop the gypsy act, Chalandra. You don't fool

me. You never have."

"Then why did you lead me to think you liked it?" she demanded.

"How you talked was never what kept my interest," he replied bluntly. "And what did no longer does. It hasn't for quite some time."

She arched her brow. "You expect me to believe the man who made love to me the night of my arrival was disinterested?"

"I don't care what you believe, Chalandra."

"And the past few hours," she continued as if he had not spoken, "that was disinterest?"

No sooner had the words left her mouth when she realized that she had blundered and blundered badly.

"No, it wasn't," he said in a too-quiet voice. "You saw to that didn't you, you cunning bitch?"

By all the gods, he knew! He knew! But how? The drug should have kept him dull-witted for hours yet. Meeting his steely gaze, Chalandra knew she could waste no time on speculation. If she was to escape the deadly promise she read in Aubin's eyes, she had to act quickly.

She scrambled off the restorer and threw herself at Aubin. Wrapping her arms around him, she buried her face in his naked chest and sobbed, "You have to understand, Aubin. The thought that you would never touch me again, never make love to me again was too much to bear. So I waited until you were asleep and I came to you. I hoped that if I offered myself to you you would not turn me away." She raised her head and gave him a watery smile. "And you didn't. You took me in your arms and . . ."

Aubin had reached his limit. Unable to stomach her lies or her touch a moment longer, he wrenched her arms from him and shoved her away, the force sending her sprawling onto the restorer.

"You drugged me!" he roared.

"Yes!" she shrieked. "Yes, I drugged you. And it was easy. Thanks to your skinny child, all I had to do was sprinkle a little on your food and in your drink and you would sleep."

"Sleep!" he cut in. "It did a hell of a lot more than make me sleep!"

"I knew that she had you so bewitched that it would take more than drugged sleep to make you turn to me, so I poured some Cindrax into your brew.

"Obviously not enough," she added under her breath.

Aubin swore. Cindrax! A powerful aphrodisiac combined with a hallucinogen. Chalandra had planned well. If he had been able to fight against the sleep-inducing drug, and the passion-craving properties of Cindrax, to question whom he held in his arms, the hallucinogen would have made him susceptible to the spoken word. In this case, Eirriel's name, her name that paired her face to the voice that did not fit. By the gods, Chalandra would pay for tampering with him!

"I would do it again, Aubin, if it meant I could hold you in my arms one last time. I love you!"

"Love? Love cannot exist in your world, Chalandra. It is smothered by the very duplicity and malevolence you thrive on."

"No! You're wrong. I do love you."

"You come slinking in under the cover of darkness and with the help of a vile drug ply your trade. And you call that love? Pardon me if I disagree." His voice grew hard with mockery. "Last night I'd have taken the lowest, cheapest servicer I found to ease the fire caused by that damned drug." He paused, his cold gaze raking over the Arvadian. With a snort of contempt, he added, "And I did."

"You can't mean that!" Chalandra cried. "You loved me until *she* came into your life. It was to me you came when you needed love. To me!"

"Eirriel has nothing to do with what you and I had. You knew it then and you know it now. I came to you when I needed one thing and one thing only." His lips twisted cruelly. "Love, my beautiful Arvadian servicer, never even entered the picture."

"How can you say these things to me?" Chalandra cried, real tears falling from her eyes because in her own way she did love him, and the hurt caused by his words made her forget that tonight had been done under orders and without love.

Pain distorted Aubin's handsome features and his voice grew harsh with bitterness and self-loathing. "By my actions tonight I betrayed the one person in this whole stinking galaxy who opened her heart and soul to me freely and completely, and never once asked for anything in return. It matters little that your villainous act sapped me of the will to resist."

"You think your Eirriel is so noble, that she wants nothing from you? You think you're better than me?" Chalandra demanded, his continued contempt driving the sadness from her heart and replacing it with hatred and the urge to retaliate. "You're wrong. Your heritage is no better than mine. We're barbarians, both of us."

"Those days are long over for Rhianon."

"The savagery of the past is never gone. One only has to look into the golden eyes of a Rhianonian, any Rhianonian, to see it lurking in the shadows waiting to be unleashed. It's what draws women to your kind. Your Eirriel is no different. She wants to see the beast. To play with the beast. To tame the beast."

Aubin's fists clenched and unclenched as Chalandra's taunts touched his darkest fear. Was it possible Chalandra was right? Did Eirriel. . . . "No!" he said firmly. "Eirriel saw *me*, Chalandra. Not who or what I am, but *me*."

Aubin turned his back on her and walked to the vitalizer, needing desperately to wash Chalandra's foul stench from his body, and the doubts she planted from his mind. In doing so, he missed Chalandra walk toward the portal, her lips curled into a satisfied smile. When the portal opened, she turned to Aubin.

"And you betray her with me. An even exchange, don't you agree, betrayal for love and trust?"

Her words drew Aubin to an abrupt halt, but when he spun around, thinking to choke the life from her, she was gone. If she knew what was good for her, she would get off his ship and stay out of his life forever. But Chalandra rarely did what was appropriate, he smirked mirthlessly and walked to the intercom.

"Aubin to safeguard unit."

"Lebron, here," came the reply from Balthasar's newly assigned replacement.

"I want Chalandra off my ship. Warn her not to return."

"At once, Captain. Out."

That done, Aubin went to the vitalizer to scrub.

A short time later, Aubin was once again lying on the restorer, this time awake and pondering the dilemma of what to tell Eirriel. Lebron had reported that Chalandra hadn't been in her assigned cubicle when he had arrived and that further checking had found her ship gone. Her leaving would make things somewhat easier. Aubin shook his head at the stupidity of that statement. Nothing would make the explanation easier. Still feeling some of the effects of the drug, Aubin drifted off to sleep.

The next morning Aubin was pulling on his uniform when the portal to his cubicle opened. He looked up and was surprised to see a very grim Garreth standing in the portalway.

"What is it?" Aubin asked, an uneasy feeling settling in the pit of his stomach.

"You better come with me, Captain."

Without another word, Garreth led Aubin from his cubicle to Eirriel's.

They arrived quickly. Aubin stopped when he saw Raissa standing beside the restorer, an anxious expression on her face, staring down on the sleeping Eirriel. His heart thudding in his chest, Aubin crossed to the restorer. Raissa stepped out of the way as he reached out a hand and touched Eirriel. His hand passed right through her.

"A hologram, Captain. Raissa discovered it when she stopped by. The women always walk to the lab together."

Lebron, called by Garreth before he went for Aubin, entered in time to hear the explanation. His topaz eyes narrowed as he slowly reconnoitered the area. When his eyes rested on a darkened spot on the couch, he reached behind his back and detached the palm-sized analyzer from his belt and swept it over the stain.

Aubin stared down on Eirriel's image a moment longer then dashed into the passageway to the nearest intercom, two portals away. Slamming his fist on the button, he barked, "Aubin to com-center."

"Shalter here, Captain," replied the night navigator.

"As soon as Theron arrives at his post, I want you to man

the questors. Put a tracer on the Arvadian vessel. I want it found."

"What happened?"

"Just do it!" Aubin snapped. "Out!"

Aubin ran back to Eirriel's cubicle and found Lebron waiting with his report.

"She was drugged, Captain. A fast-acting tranquilizing compound was added to her drink."

"Search the ship, Lebron. Any place large enough to conceal a bod . . . person," Aubin amended quickly, shying away from the word "body" and all it symbolized. Surely Chalandra wouldn't go that far!

"Right away," Lebron said, then turned and left.

"When I returned last night, I stopped by on my way to my cubicle, but she appeared to be sleeping so I just closed the portal and left. I . . . Damn it! Why didn't I think of this before?" Aubin shook his head, disgusted by his stupidity.

Followed by two puzzled companions, Aubin ran to his cubicle. He motioned Garreth to be seated at the computer.

"I want a readout of all authorized teleportations in the last fifteen hours as well as the teleport's actual energy level readings. No," Aubin said as he noticed Raissa pouring them all a drink from the beaker that contained the drugs that had overpowered him the previous night. "Eirriel wasn't the only one to fall victim to Chalandra's knowledge of potions."

Garreth looked up from the console, a look of dismay on his face. "You too?"

A tormented grimace flashed across Aubin's face and he nodded.

"Chalandra has many faults," Garreth remarked, "but I never thought stupidity numbered among them."

"She always placed an exceedingly high value on her life," Raissa said after dumping the contents of the beaker in the wash basin in the cleansing cubicle. She ordered fresh nourishment from the center. "I find it hard to believe she would risk it."

"If you could have seen her, Rai, you'd understand. I wouldn't put anything past her."

Before Raissa could comment, a knock on the portal

drew her attention. She crossed to it and saw a crewman with the order she had placed. Thanking him, she carried it to the table, then poured three mugs of the dark steaming liquid. She handed one to her bonded mate, her captain, and kept one for herself.

"Damn! She wiped out the damned readings!" Garreth swore as he worked the computer. "When I couldn't access the teleport's readings the usual way, I should have suspected something like that."

Aubin stood over Garreth and studied the computer screen. "You couldn't bypass it?"

"That's just it. There's nothing to bypass. She erased the readings. The computer's memory is blank."

"Then how can we trace Eirriel?" Raissa asked.

Garreth looked first at Raissa, then at Aubin before replying grimly, "We can't."

Chapter Eighteen

"No," Aubin ground out between clenched teeth. "I won't believe I've lost her! I'll find that Arvadian vessel if it takes me a lifetime! And, by the gods, I swear if any harm comes to Eirriel I will personally rid this universe of a malevolent, purple-skinned plague!"

It took Theron six hours to locate the *Star Tramp*. "Got her, Captain," the navigator replied excitedly.

"On viewer." Aubin fought the feeling of unease rapidly settling over him. He hadn't expected to locate Chalandra so quickly. It had been too easy, an indication that she had wished to be found. And if that was true, then she most definitely did not have Eirriel.

"Jarce, hail the Arvadian vessel," Aubin ordered. "Garreth, the questors. You know what to do."

Garreth nodded. "If Eirriel is on that ship, the questors will locate her."

"*Star Tramp*, this is the E.P.F.—"

Chalandra's image appeared on the viewer as she cut in, "Yes, yes, Jarce, I know who you are. Well, Aubin, I must say that was certainly quick. I commend your crew."

"You were expecting us?" Aubin asked, already knowing

the answer and dreading it.

"Yes."

"Then I assume last night was a diversion?" Aubin had decided to act cool and unthreatening until he knew the outcome of the scan.

"An enjoyable one, but, yes, a diversion."

"Questor scan negative, Captain," Garreth reported.

His suspicions confirmed, Aubin dropped the mask of nonchalance. His eyes blazing, his voice clipped, he demanded, "Where is she?"

"I really can't tell you. Business ethics. *He* might demand a refund."

"Who might?"

"To learn that, you'll just have to find her." Chalandra paused a moment, then replied with a challenging taunt, "If you can."

Her taunting laugh echoed around the com-center as the screen went blank.

"Communications severed," Jarce reported.

"Captain, she's pulling away. Do you want a tracer?" Theron asked.

"No," Aubin replied. "I'll deal with her in my own way when this is over." He leaned his elbows on the console, and bowed his head while his fingers raked through his hair. He was missing something. What was it? *Think, damn you! Think!*

The com-crew waited as their captain searched for their next move. They knew how deeply their captain was affected by Eirriel's disappearance, but they also had complete faith in their Rhianonian leader. Too many times he had led them out of a seemingly disastrous situation for them to doubt him now.

Aubin's head shot up. "Garreth! The energy levels! They can't be tampered with!"

"Damn! I should have thought . . ." Garreth's hands sped over the buttons on his computer. "Got it! One arrival. Two departures. Using Chalandra's lat-log as a guide, one set was not from the *Star Tramp* or to it."

"Theron, were any other ships within teleport range?"

"When she disappeared? No, Captain, not even using the

Star Tramp as a link. I already checked."

"Then she had to have been taken to one of the planets." Aubin's already low spirits plunged as he looked out at Sector 7-1. He gritted his teeth against his burgeoning frustration. "Garreth, how many?"

"Within teleport range of the *Celestial*, six planets, three satellites. One billion miles of viable land."

"Theron, reverse course. Take us back to our exact location at the time of the departures. Vel 10."

"Aye, Captain."

"Garreth, it's up to the questors now."

"It will take days," Garreth said grimly.

Aubin's golden eyes were raised and Garreth was shocked by the pain so evident within their depths. "I know, Garreth," Aubin said bleakly. "I know."

Twenty hours later a weary Aubin and an equally weary Garreth were in the Deliberation Cubicle, reviewing the questor's data yet again, when Cian and Raissa rushed in.

"Captain, we've located a holograph in the vessel from which we rescued Eirriel. It was made by her mother," Cian explained excitedly. "She was a Kiiryan."

"Kiiryan? Is that another name for Dianthian?" Aubin asked impatiently.

"No. Another race entirely," Cian answered.

"Kiiryans," Garreth scoffed. "The stuff legends are made of."

"Well, this 'legend,'" Raissa said to her bonded mate, "purposely placed a message on that ship headed for Blagden. In fact, it appears the ship was left on Dianthia with the knowledge that it would one day be used by Eirriel."

Aubin sighed wearily. "I've had two days with very little sleep and I cannot absorb riddles. Please explain."

"Kiiryans are a race of mentally advanced scientists, specializing in the galaxywide study of culture," the Drocot explained patiently.

"It seems Dianthia was a study culture for Kiirya," Raissa said excitedly. "I studied about them at the Academy. That's why—"

"This is all very interesting," Aubin cut in impatiently, "but—"

"Kiiryans are parapsychics, Captain," Cian said quickly. "Or mind-touchers, as they call themselves. Extraordinarily powerful ones. Nothing is beyond their ken. Telepathy, telekenesis, prescience are the basic abilities their children are born with."

"Eirriel is only half-Kiiryan." Raissa took up the story. "Her mother was unsure of the end results of Eirriel's mixed blood."

"Hm, could this be what Balthasar was after? The something she denied having?"

"Very likely it was, Garreth," Cian answered. "I believe Eirriel is just coming into whatever talents she may have inherited. She is like a young one taking its first hesitant steps. Wobbly, uncertain of how it is done, of what is done."

Raissa frowned as a thought formed in the back of her mind. "Cian, do you think she was able to see what was to come?"

Cian shook his head. "I don't know what she is or will be capable of. Why?"

"Because," Raissa said quietly, "we all know that Eirriel still believes that Balthasar is alive, despite all our efforts to convince her otherwise."

Aubin, who had been trying to absorb all the information into his overtired mind, sat up and looked at Raissa, then turned to Cian. "That night in the med-unit. She said she wasn't dreaming. If she is part mind-toucher . . ." Aubin ground his teeth in frustration. "There is something in all this, but, by the gods, I don't know what!"

"You are overly tired, Captain, you cannot be expected to have all the answers," Cian soothed, bestowing his calming gaze on Aubin.

Aubin felt the Drocot's special gift reach out and envelope him and some of the tension fled his body.

"I know you are right, Cian, but I cannot rest. Not until I find her." Suddenly, all color fled Aubin's bronzed face and in a ragged whisper he voiced his certainty. "Balthasar. Balthasar has Eirriel."

Raissa gasped. "No, it cannot be." Her eyes sought

Garreth's, but instead of reassurance she found resignation.

"It would explain her fears and her dreams," Cian said gravely.

"We'll find her, Aubin," Garreth said. Then added with a conviction he did not feel, "Alive."

"Will we?" Aubin asked in a voice raw with emotion. "He almost killed her the last time and that was in less than one hour. It's been two days, Garreth. Two days."

Aubin, his face reflecting soul-wrenching pain, slowly rose and left, oblivious to the concerned looks exchanged among his three friends.

Once in his cubicle, Aubin vented his rage. One hand sent the remnants of his last meal clattering to the floor. Balthasar! Balthasar had her! Over and over, the words repeated through his mind like a song's oft-repeated refrain. He snatched up the beaker of Melonnian sweet and sour brew and hurled it violently against the wall.

"Damn you, Balthasar!" Aubin yelled. "Where is she?"

He crossed to the viewer and stared at the stars and planets of Sector 7-1. So many places on which to hide. If they didn't hurry, it would be too late. May already be too late.

"No!" The anguished bellow burst from him. "No! She is not dead!" he screamed as he threw himself on the restorer. Drawing his hand across his forehead, he rested his arm across his eyes.

Eirriel, my love, my life, where are you?

His hand dropped to his side and he stared at the ceiling, unable to fathom life without her. Desperately, he thrust that thought from his mind. He would not live his life without her. He would find her.

Aubin rubbed his eyes as the ceiling dissolved into a white haze. He frowned when the haze did not disappear.

"Please," he heard a muffled voice cry. "The pain. Make it go away."

"Eirriel?" Aubin shook his head. It couldn't be. He was imagining it but a crazed laugh cut off his denial. Balthasar?

The white haze in front of his eyes increased until it obscured his entire vision. Then suddenly, the haze parted to reveal bound hands raised as if warding off a blow.

What the hell? Aubin shook his head, unable to understand what he was seeing. Taking a deep breath, he closed his eyes. When he opened them, the cubicle was as it should be. That was better. The last thing he needed now was an overactive imagination, but as he sat up, the haze returned.

He stared straight ahead, his frown deepening as this time he saw slim hands extended forward, a rope tied around their narrow wrists. A woman's hands. Eirriel's. The surety of that thought rocked him. Before he could question how he knew, a rough yank on the rope caused her to stumble.

"No, please."

This time there was no mistaking the voice he'd grown to love. It *was* Eirriel. Having his suspicions confirmed did little to reassure him. How was he hearing her? Seeing her? Realization of what he was experiencing gave him a start. By all the gods! He was somehow seeing through her eyes! How was it possible? Was this part of her Kiiryan legacy that Cian had spoken of?

Further questions were driven from Aubin's mind as her fear suddenly overwhelmed him. The rope was being held by a green-skinned, hairless priest, his grotesquely obese body clothed only in a breechcloth, and his round eyes glowing orange. His rotund face was painted with red-and-yellow stripes and from enormously large pointed ears dangled huge golden hoops, their center an ornately designed symbol.

Aubin rubbed his eyes, but as much as he might wish it otherwise, the view did not change.

Eirriel was thrown to the ground, and Aubin could feel the breath knocked from her. Silently the priest knelt by her side and painted her face to match his. Aubin felt her fear increase as she turned her head to the right and saw. . . .

"Balthasar!" Aubin's enraged roar broke the connection and the only thing he saw was his cubicle.

Frantically, he lay down and tried to concentrate. He needed to see what was happening to her. As painful as it might be, he had to keep watching. If he were to recognize something, he might be able to find her.

"Why are you doing this?" he heard Eirriel ask.

Then he was back, seeing through her eyes. The light of

madness burning in his eyes, Balthasar stood next to the priest.

"He never fully trusted me. Deep inside, where only I could see, the captain had doubts about me. I knew he would turn against me. It was only a matter of time. Then *you* came along, pretending to be all sweetness and innocence. Fooling everyone, even that old charlatan Cian. But not me! I know what you are, what you can do. And you will at last teach me. With your powers I'll be unstoppable."

Balthasar closed his eyes. Aubin gritted his teeth as he felt the pain Eirriel experienced from Balthasar's probing.

"No more. Please. No more."

Balthasar opened his eyes. "When I have *all* your secrets, Dianthian, the pain will be gone. Forever."

Eirriel squeezed her eyes shut against the pain. Instinctively, as it had happened in her first encounter with Balthasar, she started to rise above her body, but the pain from her effort caused Eirriel to reenter her body and sweat to break out on Aubin's forehead.

"By the gods! Eirriel!" His breathing rapid, Aubin jumped to his feet. "Balthasar, you bastard! I'll kill you for this!"

Aubin paced his cubicle, his fists clenching and unclenching. He stopped when he felt the cool stone against Eirriel's back and the tightness of energy restraints around her wrists, arms and mouth. The priest stepped into her line of vision and Aubin saw that he was standing motionless, his hands at his side and his eyes unfocused. Her gaze swung to Balthasar then to the priest and Aubin heard Balthasar's taunting voice once again.

"You are a fool," Balthasar sneered, his greed and lust for power making his voice shrill. "Your mind is crackling with boundless energy. Feel it . . . Use it . . . Call upon it to save you—if you can!"

Balthasar's triumphant laugh blended with Eirriel's moan of pain as she once again tried to flee her body and once again failed. Aubin threw back his head, willing some of his strength into Eirriel, even though he knew it was impossible.

"That's all you can do, isn't it, you pathetic creature? It's not enough." Balthasar nodded at the priest. "You may begin."

The priest very slowly raised his hand. Aubin felt Eirriel's panic as she stared at the green hand and the thin, curved knife it held.

"That's it!" he exclaimed as he rushed to the computer and began punching in a request. The knife, the earrings, the paint all marks of an outlawed band of Cunarg worshippers. Aubin waited what felt like lifetimes instead of the few micro seconds the computer took to produce the location he needed. A press of a key and the lat-logs were relayed to the teleport.

Aubin snatched the neutralizer from the wall and tore from the cubicle, praying fervently that he would be in time to save the life of the woman he loved.

Stealthily, his neutralizer ready, Aubin entered the misty dark ruin. His gaze sought and found the expected raised circular platform with the golden symbol of Cunarg suspended over it, and the five stone steps leading up to the stone altar. The altar was his destination. There he would find Eirriel.

Eirriel saw the priest's hand finally reach its full extension. Not wanting to watch its descent, she started to close her eyes, then stopped as she felt a new sensation.

It was Aubin! Somehow, she felt him near. How she knew he was, she didn't care. For now all that mattered was that he was here.

Beneath the gag she smiled, which did not go unnoticed by Balthasar.

"Hold!"

The priest's arm froze.

Balthasar closed his eyes and sought the reason for the smile. No! Not now! His eyes shot open and he gnashed his teeth in frustration. He would not be cheated out of seeing her die! He would not!

He snatched the knife from the priest and shoved him roughly out of the way.

"You're too late, Captain."

Aubin, already in motion after Balthasar's order to the

priest, reached the top step and fired. Balthasar grinned as the beam split harmlessly around the altar.

"Cunarg protects all who stand beneath his symbol," Balthasar explained, his eyes glittering with deadly promise as he raised his arm. "All except the chosen."

Aubin tossed aside his useless weapon and lunged forward as the mutant's arm arched downward.

"No!"

Aubin's roar startled Balthasar and the deadly blade fell wide of its mark, embedding itself in Eirriel's shoulder. Balthasar yanked the knife out and whirled to face Aubin as he rounded the altar. Aubin's well-placed kick sent the knife flying from Balthasar's hand and skidding across the stone floor, coming to rest at the priest's feet. Aubin stalked Balthasar who, robbed of his weapon, backed away in fear but not far enough or fast enough. Aubin's hands snaked out and grabbed his safeguard officer by the throat.

"You dare to take what belongs to me!" Aubin ground out between clenched teeth.

As Aubin slowly tightened his fingers, Balthasar desperately tried to unlock the Rhianonian's grasp, but failed.

"You . . . won't . . . kill . . . me . . ." Balthasar rasped. "Your . . . vow . . . to . . . the . . . Protectorate . . ."

"You freed me from my vow when you took her."

Balthasar raked his mind for a way to reach Aubin. He had to do something. Already he was growing weak from lack of air. Another few seconds and the Rhianonian . . . Rhianonian! That was it!

"Break . . . vow . . . expect . . . that . . . from . . . Rhianonian!"

Aubin's head snapped back at the reminder of his heritage. If he killed Balthasar now, he would be no better than his ancestors, those Rhianonians who obeyed the laws when it suited them and changed them when they did not.

With a groan of frustration Aubin released his grip on the mutant. He would have to be satisfied with the justice of the Protectorate. But first . . .

Aubin drew back his hand and Balthasar reeled backward from the force of Aubin's fist against his face. His next punch broke Balthasar's nose, and the next one drove him to his knees. Aubin watched dispassionately as Balthasar attempted to get to his feet then collapsed to the ground.

Thinking he was in no condition to attempt further trouble, Aubin turned his attention to his love. His golden eyes darkened when he spied her pale complexion and her dull, pain-filled green eyes.

"Stay with me, little one. I'll have you to Cian before you know it." He cursed under his breath when he was unable to find the release for the energy restraints.

Balthasar struggled to get up and as he did his hand touched the knife. He glanced at Aubin and smiled mirthlessly as he watched him struggle with Eirriel's bonds. Slowly he got to his feet.

"Hold on, my love. Just a little longer."

Aubin was reaching for his neutralizer, thinking to use it on the shield when his name rang in his mind.

Aubin!

He whirled around.

Balthasar was on his feet, the deadly knife poised for flight, and the priest was lumbering toward him. Aubin looked up and swore as he saw they were both still beneath the symbol that rendered his weapon useless. He moved protectively in front of Eirriel, blocking her with his body and waited.

Balthasar's hand twitched.

It was what Aubin was waiting for. He jumped and sent both his feet into the priest's tremendous abdomen just as Balthasar released the knife. The force of the kick sent the priest directly in the path of the weapon. He cried out in pain and struggled to reach the knife, now embedded in his back. His arms flailing wildly, the priest staggered into Balthasar and the two of them fell backwards, their momentum carrying them to the edge of the platform and beyond. Aubin reacted immediately. The neutralizer's beam struck the two men in mid-air and they vanished.

Aubin turned and ran to Eirriel who was now free, the restraints having disappeared with their creator. Tenderly and carefully, he gathered her into his arms.

"My love, I thought I had lost you," he whispered in a

voice harsh with emotion.

Eirriel's eyes filled with the tears she could at last give into. "I was so afraid you would never find me."

Aubin laughed huskily, unmindful of the unusual moistness in his eyes or the choking sensation in his throat. "That, little one, was impossible. I had inside help."

"How?"

Aubin's eyes darkened as he noted her increasing pallor and the widening stain of blood on her gown.

"I'll explain everything later. Right now I want to get you to Cian." Aubin pressed the conversor. "Aubin to *Celestial*."

"Garreth here, Captain," came the instantaneous, but very surprised, reply.

"Have the teleport tech prepare to activate on my command."

"You have her." It was more a statement than a question.

"Yes. And, Garreth, she needs Cian."

"He'll be waiting."

Aubin felt Eirriel go limp in his arms. His heart thudding in his chest, he croaked, "Get us out of here now!"

Chapter Nineteen

"Damn it, Cian! When will she wake?"

Cian chuckled as he watched the captain storm around his cubicle.

"Two days have passed and still she sleeps."

"She has much to forget," Cian reminded him gravely.

"Forget!" Aubin ground out between clenched teeth. "How can she possible forget? When I think of what that bastard did to her, how he hurt her, I can't see!" He slammed his fist against the wall in frustration. "Forget? By all that's holy, I wish it were possible!"

"It is, my friend," the Drocot said calmly. "Remember, she is part Kiiryan."

Aubin crossed to the small viewer and stared absently at the passing stars. It was some time before his hoarse whisper broke the silence. "I think of all that has happened to her, of all she has been forced to endure and I go cold inside. For the first time in my life, I know what it's like to love someone, to need someone. If she turned from me now . . ."

Cian smiled again. *How similar these two are*, he thought

as he remembered back to his conversation with Eirriel, *how similar their fears*.

Cian had easily repaired Eirriel's knife wound within minutes of her arrival in the med-unit. To get her to relax and rest had taken much convincing. And many answers.

Her voice had been a hoarse whisper brimming with embarrassment and humiliation. "Aubin tells me he heard me. That he saw what was happening to me *as* it was happening to me. How, Cian? How can I do these things? What must he think of the creature I am?"

Her voice had dropped so low that Cian had been forced to strain to hear as she had spoken her worst fear.

"If he should turn from me . . ."

Cian had taken her slim hand in his smaller one and had patted it reassuringly. "You are no different than you were before your ordeal. And he thinks as he always has, that you are the most beguiling creature of all—woman. *His* woman. As for the other"—he had waved his hand in dismissal—"do not worry over it. Much has happened while you were gone. Much was learned. There will be plenty of time to share it with you.

"But first, you must heal your wounds, those both seen and unseen. I will teach you a way, unique to you alone, that will let you sleep a healing sleep. You will awaken refreshed, all harsh memories dimmed to almost nothingness."

His voice had softened then, to a gentle flow of words as he had taught her the healing sleep, the one from which Aubin was so anxiously waiting for her to awaken.

"Breathe slowly, deeply. Allow yourself to relax . . . Feel it happening . . . Your toes . . . your legs . . . your hands . . . your whole body . . . Relax . . . You are floating . . . drifting on air . . . Let it carry you to a place deep within you where only pleasant memories lie . . . Do you see them . . . Reach for them . . . Your father . . . Moriah . . . Onyx . . ."

Cian had watched intently as the tightness had vanished from Eirriel's face and a small contented smile had played on her lips and her breathing had grown shallow and rhythmic. Then and only then had he allowed himself to relax, secure in the knowledge that she would be all right.

It was that knowledge that allowed him the freedom to smile in the face of Aubin's fears.

"She will not turn from you, Captain. Are you not soulmates? She will wake, free from the agony and retain only the dimmest memories. Be patient, my son."

Aubin whirled and faced Cian. "Be patient! That's easy for you to spout. She will wake, you say. Fine. But when, Cian? When?"

"Soon."

The small blue man smiled confidently up at his large companion, bid him a good day's ending, and left Aubin to his thoughts.

Glowering after the departing figure of the Drocot, Aubin threw himself into the nearest chair. Soon! By all the gods, he was sick of that word! An exasperated groan rose from deep inside him and he jumped to his feet. Pacing around the cubicle, he raked his hands through his hair. What if Cian were wrong? What if she wanted nothing to do with him? What if she felt she could only be safe with a Dianthian? He shuddered, unable even to seriously consider that possibility. Especially now. Now when he desperately needed her sweet loving caresses to cleanse away the foul stench that clung to him, had clung to him since that fateful night he had spent in Chalandra's destructive embrace.

Losing his struggle against exhaustion, Aubin shucked his uniform and dragged himself into the restorer. His mind numb and his bones weary from too many days of waiting, he quickly succumbed to the seductive arms of sleep.

Aubin's eyes sprang open at the sound of the portal opening, then widened at the sight that greeted him. Standing in the portalway, her slender form silhouetted by the light from the passageway, was Eirriel.

Silently she closed the portal and crossed to him, her garment whispering as she walked. She stopped by the restorer, reached up and removed the clasp from her hair. Shaking her head, her golden curls tumbled to her waist. She untied the ribbons of her gown and slipped it from her shoulders and let it cascade to the floor.

With a groan, Aubin sprang from the restorer and pulled her to him. Gently his mouth pressed against hers. His tongue flickered across her lips and he was rewarded as they parted under his touch. Fiercely, his tongue delved deeply, searching the warmth of her mouth for the remembered pleasures it delivered.

He reached down, his arm catching her below her knees. Without breaking the kiss, he lifted her and lowered her onto the restorer. Kneeling over her, he gazed lovingly at the woman who had so nearly been lost to him.

Eirriel raised her hands to Aubin's beloved face. She ran her fingers over his eyes, his nose, his mouth. Resting her hands lightly on his lean cheeks, she breathed huskily, "Aubin, my bronze giant, I need you so. Love me, Aubin. Love me."

"I do, my love."

His eyes ablaze, Aubin captured her mouth with his as his hands roamed over her slender body. She moaned when his fingers fluttered teasingly at her inner thighs, then slipped between them to her throbbing core. He groaned against her mouth when he found her hot, wet, and ready to receive him.

"I must have you, Eirriel," he rasped, moving between her parted legs. "I can wait no longer."

Conscious of her recent wound, he held himself in check and entered her slowly. Eirriel, however, would have none of it and arched, taking the full length of him deep inside her. His control snapped when her slim hands came up, grasped his buttocks, and held him close. His mouth crashed down on hers and their tongues met as they soared through a wondrous world of blazing passion that they alone could share.

When his breathing slowed and his strength returned, Aubin rolled to his side and pulled Eirriel next to him. She raised herself on one elbow and stared down on the beautiful face of her lover.

"Aubin?"

"Hmm?" came the sleepy reply.

"Did you mean what you said?"

His eyes opened and the intensity of the fire that burned within gave proof to the words he spoke in a voice raw with emotion. "I love you, Eirriel. More than life."

Her face lit up with a blinding smile. "And I love you, my bronze giant."

Aubin's hand reached up and he drew her head down to his. The kiss they shared was brief and tender. Eirriel rested her head on his chest, a small smile playing on her lips, and slowly drifted off to sleep.

"What do you want to show me?" Eirriel asked excitedly as she eased the uniform pants over her slim hips.

"Finish dressing and you'll see," Aubin replied mysteriously. "Unless"—he eyed her, an impish grin tugging at his mouth—"you don't mind traipsing about the passageway as you are."

Laughing, Eirriel slipped her shirt over her head, then pulled on her boots. Sweeping her hair to the top of her head, she snapped a harkbone clasp in place and let it hang in a thick coil down her back. "There," she said flippantly, tossing her head. "How do I look?"

Aubin drew her close. "Beautiful, as always. Although not as ravishing as last night," he added, golden lights dancing in his eyes.

"You, sir, are a rogue!" she said, trying to wriggle from his grasp.

"And what of you, you little minx?" Aubin demanded, tightening his hold.

"We make quite a pair, don't we?" She giggled, ceasing her struggles. Her green eyes twinkled up at him, then softened. "I love you, Aubin, so very much."

"And I love you," he said huskily, lowering his mouth to hers. A rap on the portal and laughter echoing in the passageway interrupted whatever plans he had been formulating. "Damn!" he swore. Not wanting to release her yet, he kept her clasped tightly to him as he asked, "Yes? What is it?"

"Just us," Raissa replied as she and Garreth strolled hand in hand into the cubicle.

Garreth looked at the entwined couple and winked at Raissa.

"I think we interrupted something. Do you think we should come back later?"

The Melonnian shook her head. "Uh-uh. We've already been waiting close to an hour." She quirked an eyebrow at the pair. "Do you think you two can let go of each other long enough to complete business?"

"Official business, she means," Garreth teased.

Eirriel flushed and Aubin glared at the Rhianonian. Reluctantly, he dropped his arms and Eirriel stepped quickly away.

"Come, little one," Aubin said, capturing her hand in his. "As my crew so conscientiously reminded me, we've work to do." He added softly for her ears alone, "And when the work is done . . ."

Eirriel shivered in delicious anticipation and fervently wished it was finished now.

"Cian's already there," Garreth reported as the foursome left the cubicle. "Raissa and I will meet you there," he added as the two hurriedly walked down the passageway.

"Where are they going?" Eirriel asked.

"You'll see," Aubin replied cryptically.

"It's obvious to everyone but me." She pouted. "As an active member of this crew, I should know too." She stopped in her tracks, pulled her hand from Aubin's and crossed her arms in front of her chest. "I'm not moving until you tell me."

"As an active member of the *Celestial*, are you challenging your captain?" Aubin demanded with mock severity.

Eirriel shook her head.

"Good. Then close that delicious mouth of yours, imp, and come with me. You'll know soon enough, I promise you."

Curiosity spurring her on, Eirriel followed Aubin past engineering and into the docking bays. She was stunned when they stopped in front of her damaged ship.

"What's this doing here?"

"You said you were going to be quiet and follow me," Aubin reminded her.

Without waiting for her reply, Aubin entered the vessel. In bewildered silence, Eirriel followed him to the small cubicle that had been her prison for so many months. There she was greeted by Cian. A quick glance showed her that

Raissa and Garreth were already seated. Slipping into the chair Aubin stood next to, she raised questioning eyes to him.

"I had this vessel brought aboard so that we could study it and hopefully find some clue to Dianthia's location," Aubin explained. "For the longest time our search proved fruitless, but on the day you disappeared, Cian decided to give it one last try and discovered the well-concealed panel. Ironically it was in the very compartment you took shelter in." He shook his head at the hope he read in her eyes. "No, it doesn't lead us to Dianthia. But it reveals the answers to much more sought-after questions."

Aubin opened the double portals. Touching a well-camouflaged knob, he stepped back as a large portion of the rear wall slid back to reveal a hidden screen. He motioned to Cian and the cubicle plunged into darkness. Pressing one last switch, he sat down next to Eirriel and took her hand reassuringly in his.

The screen illuminated. Eirriel was shocked to see the face of a woman with features very similar to her own.

"Welcome. I am Sidra, mate to Alaric and soon-to-be-mother to Eirriel."

Aubin, astonished as everyone that the softly spoken words were in Hakonese, glared disgruntedly over his shoulder and was not at all surprised to see a smug grin on Cian's round face. *Why that sly old man! If he wanted to have a little fun, the least he could have done was let me in on it*, Aubin thought with exasperation. Not wanting to miss any of Sidra's message, he turned his attention back to the screen. He would deal with Cian later.

"My daughter, I know my end will come before I can teach you of your ancestry so I have planted this knowledge in a place you will eventually discover. By the time you hear this, you will be a woman grown and have been sent far from your home. You will not be alone, however, but in the company of close friends, especially one who means much to you and you to him. You will have just endured a great trial, one which has helped you to learn that you possess a unique ability. One that sets you apart from all others.

"My knowledge of these facts is secure. I know with

absolute certainty that what I have said to you will pass.

"I am from Kiirya, a tiny world whose society is based primarily on science. Because we were so highly advanced, our beautiful world became the gathering place for the greatest minds of the universe. To us, they came to relax, to deliberate, to learn. Over the millenia, as a result of this great melding of minds, our knowledge grew to immeasurable proportions. We evolved into a race with extraordinary mental abilities. We learned to read minds, project thoughts, practice prescience, teleport and much, much more. For generations our children have been born with these skills.

"I came to this world, hundreds of years ago, with a cultural survey expedition. We were to study the peaceful Dianthians and record their development. All figures were projected back to Kiirya where they were compared with the growth of other worlds with similar backgrounds. It was all part of a massive universal study for peace.

"It was in my fourth century on Dianthia, close to my group's time of departure, that I first met Alaric. Your father, Eirriel, was a beautiful man. Strong in body and mind. We arranged meetings, sharing our stolen moments while we could. To explain my unique appearance, for it was forbidden to speak of who we really were, I told him I was from a far village. Alaric accepted my story, never questioning it, yet never completely believing it either. His love for me overcame all doubts.

"When the time came for our expedition to depart, I told Alaric I was needed at home and would never be able to return. He asked me to stay and be his mate. Though I loved him more than life itself, I told him I could not stay. Kissing him for the last time, I fled to my people. As I prepared to enter our transport vessel, I realized that if I left him I would be but half a woman. My soul had met its true mate and would be satisfied with no other.

"I went to my superior with my decision. Smiling, she told me that she had known for a long time that I would remain on Dianthia. Leaving me their blessings and a small Kiiryan vessel that would be needed in the future, my people returned to Kiirya.

"Your father and I have been truly happy. I know that my time with him draws rapidly to an end and that were I to leave on this vessel now, I would escape my death, but I cannot. As before, I love your father too much to live without him no matter the cost.

"Eirriel, my beautiful daughter, listen well to what I now say. You are half-Dianthian, half-Kiiryan. Your innate abilities have been weakened by your Dianthian blood. Weakened, but not destroyed. Though you may never be able to read minds, teleport at will or clearly focus on any prescient knowledge, you will develop the ability to project thoughts, to shield your mind from danger, to become mental energy. Perhaps more. The capabilities of your mixed blood even I cannot say. No matter what it brings, remember this. Your legacy is one of peace. Do not misuse it. Be wary of your skills until you are sure of what you are doing. There is one among you who is of a race unto himself. He will school you.

"Before I end, my Eirriel, I say to you be happy, know love, always act with compassion. There are trials in your future which I cannot reveal. You will survive all if you remember to always trust in love.

"To the tall giant at Eirriel's side. My friend, I entrust my daughter's happiness to you. Do not fail me. Before you lies a great blackness. Do not lose faith in my daughter. Her love will never falter. I see also the end of a search and the beginning of a new life. As I said to Eirriel, I now say to you, always trust in love.

"Farewell."

"Mother!" Eirriel cried as the screen went dark. She stared at the blackness overcome by a deep sense of sadness and loss.

Aubin guided Eirriel to her feet. Placing his arm around her shoulder, he led her out of the cubicle and away from the ship. When they arrived in Aubin's cubicle, Eirriel threw herself onto his restorer, unable to control the sobs that wracked her body. Silently Aubin sat beside her, his brow furrowed in concentration and gently ran his hand over her hair.

"Do not lose faith in my daughter, her love will never falter." What did Sidra mean by that? What could possibly happen that would ever make him doubt Eirriel's love?

Chapter Twenty

Ten years ago, the supreme heads of the Empyreal Protectorate ordered the creation of a world to be used only by fleetship crews during their month-long furloughs. Using all the skills at their disposal, the brilliant engineers artificially altered the natural surface of a tiny, uninhabited planet in Sector 1-5 until it was a climatic and geographic blend of the six most popular planets in the galaxies. Thus was born Symarryllyon: Citadel of Pleasure.

This specialized world was the fleetship *Celestial's* destination. Once there the ship would undergo a thorough maintenance check in the orbiting space station while her tense, overworked crew frolicked on Symarryllyon's surface.

"This is Captain Aubin of the E.P.F. *Celestial* requesting permission to approach maintenance station Alpha 6."

"Permission granted, Captain Aubin. We've been expecting you. Have your navigator direct the *Celestial* to compartment three. Enjoy your rest. Alpha 6 out."

"Theron . . ."

"Already done, Captain. We will enter compartment

three in seven minutes."

Aubin laughed. It seemed he wasn't the only one anxious to start furlough.

"Jarce, patch me through to Symarryllyon's communication center."

"Yes, sir." Jarce's hairy fingers pressed several buttons. "Go ahead, Captain."

"This is Captain Aubin of the E.P.F. *Celestial* requesting confirmation of our teleportation schedule."

"Greetings, Captain, and welcome," a soft sultry voice replied. "I am Lena. It is my pleasure to act as liaison during your stay with us. Your T.S. has been confirmed. At this moment the lat-logs are being relayed to the *Celestial's* teleport. Teleportation may commence in twenty minutes. See you then. Lena out."

Aubin activated the intercom. "This is Captain Aubin. Our T.S. has been confirmed. The first group may disembark at 1000 hours. Remember, although on furlough, you are still representatives of the Protectorate. As such I expect your conduct to be impeccable. With that in mind, enjoy your well-deserved rest. Aubin out."

A slight tremor passed through the ship.

"Docking completed," Theron reported, studying his console, "and confirmed."

"Garreth, proceed with shutdown," Aubin ordered. "Jarce, Theron, once your consoles are cleared you may go."

Theron and Jarce completed the necessary procedures with a speed born of anticipation. As one they bid Aubin and Garreth good-bye and entered the conveyor.

A few minutes later Garreth said, "Everything's in order here, Aubin. So if you don't mind, I'd like to see if Rai's ready."

"By all means, Garreth. Eirriel and I will join you shortly."

"See you then," Garreth called as he stepped in the conveyor and the double portals closed in front of him.

With a well-trained eye, Aubin scanned the vacant com-center mentally rerunning shutdown. Pushing himself from his console, he crossed to the small panel on the wall to the right of the conveyor. In rapid sequence his fingers ran across its many buttons. One by one the com-center's brilliant lights went out, leaving only the blue standby lights glowing in the darkness.

Confident that all was in order, Aubin left the com-center to join Eirriel. A surge of elation swept through him as he thought of the month ahead. For the first time since they met he would have her all to himself!

Two weeks passed as planned. Except for an occasional evening nourishment shared with Raissa and Garreth or Cian, the two lovers were left to themselves.

Eirriel proved a constant delight to Aubin. Every experience was new and exciting. Viewed through her virgin eyes, Aubin felt as if he were seeing Symarryllyon for the first time. He took her through the snowy trails of Mendral in a wexal drawn by giant snowsteeds; through the subterranean caverns, sunken gardens and submerged cities of Dolane; and the colorful bazaars, the frenetic festivals of Aflax.

During this time, Aubin came to accept what he had denied for so long. Only with the beautiful spirited Dianthian could he have the fiery exchange of passions, the warm soul-touching tenderness and the soothing inner contentment that had come to mean so much to him.

And so, on the fourteenth day of their furlough Aubin set about making Eirriel his for life.

"What are we doing today, Aubin?" Eirriel asked as she wrapped the large fluffy drying cloth around her, her green eyes filled with excitement.

"Something very special, my love," Aubin replied. "No." He laughed, anticipating her next question. "I won't tell you."

"But how will I know what to wear?"

"That's no problem at all." He pointed to the restorer. "All you need is there. Call me when you're finished." He started for the outer cubicle, then turned. "One last thing, sweet. Leave your hair down."

Before she could ask why, Aubin was gone. Burning with curiosity, she dropped the cloth and reached for her clothes.

Relishing the feel of the soft silky material, she slipped on the loose black pants then drew the knee-length matching tunic over her head. She fastened two golden studs in each cuff of the billowing sleeves and four across the left shoulder to the high collar. Around her waist she knotted the long golden rope so that it rode low on her hips. Slipping on black slippers, she crossed to the imager and brushed her hair. As she placed the brush back on the dressing table, the portal opened.

"I decided not to wait for your call," Aubin said, entering the cubicle.

Eirriel turned to him and his breath caught in his throat. No matter how often he saw her, he never failed to be affected by her beauty. And this morning, garbed in the traditional Rhianonian Syna vestments it was no different. She was stunning!

"Come, love," he said, extending his hand to her. "We've much to do today."

Eirriel's heart swelled as he beckoned to her. Dressed as she was, with only minor alterations, his golden hair and bronze skin were enhanced by the darkness of his clothes. He looked like a young god summoning his virgin bride. Feeling as if perhaps that were true, Eirriel walked slowly to him, mesmerized by the intense emotion revealed in his golden eyes.

Their hands touched. Suddenly, by his doing or hers she didn't know, she found herself in his arms, her mouth greedily tasting his. When their lips finally parted, she opened her eyes and stared into his.

"What is it, Aubin," she asked in a voice filled with wonder, "that makes this day so different from our other days, that makes your touch, your kiss seem so much more? Why do I feel as if something wonderful is about to happen?"

Aubin looked down on the woman more precious to him than life itself and felt a stirring deep in his soul. "Perhaps, my love," he said softly, kissing her tenderly on the forehead, "because it is."

Awed by the change she sensed in him, Eirriel asked no further questions, allowing him to take her hand and lead her from the cubicle. They took the moving walkway down several long passageways to one of the small teleport stations. Within moments they appeared in an open section of grassland surrounded by thick dark woods. Silently Aubin led her through an opening that could not be seen. Gazing in wonder, she realized that the dense outer foliage sheltered the area and created a warm welcoming privacy within it boundaries. As they entered, she gasped at the beauty that greeted her.

The ground was covered with soft needlelike leaves that had fallen from the tallest trees. The branches of these trees thickened near the top and interwove with the others forming a natural roof. Sunlight filtered through, bathing the area in a warm golden haze. Scattered throughout were trees and bushes of all sizes and shapes.

Following a well-worn path that wound its way through the trees, they came to a section free of the smaller shrubs. Spying a tree with low gnarled branches, Aubin stopped. Placing his hands gently on her waist, he lifted Eirriel onto the thickest branch and jumped up beside her. For a moment they sat silently, listening to the peaceful sounds of the woods, then Aubin turned to Eirriel.

"How much do you know of my life before I joined the Protectorate?"

Eirriel frowned, startled by the suddenness of the question and the fact that she knew very little. "Not much," she admitted. "And what I do know I learned from Cian, Garreth or Raissa. You haven't told me anything!"

"I know, sweet, but there's a reason for that. First tell me what you know about Rhianon."

Eirriel told him that Rhianon was a small world with short stretches of plains, an abundance of high mountains and as much water as land. Then she related its history, of how the rapidly increasing population used all available land for housing. Food supplies diminished to such a degree that the Rhiononians were forced to rely heavily on imports from neighboring planets. That, too, was soon exhausted. Left with no other choice, the Rhiononians turned to piracy, stealing food stuffs and anything else they needed from passing supply ships.

After hundreds of years of poverty and violence, a farsighted man named Jumel developed the idea of domed cities. Within two generations the cities were built high in the mountains and on the ocean floor. Once the population was housed in the massive cities, the plains were once again used for agriculture. Now Rhianon was prosperous, technically advanced, and a fierce, powerful, much feared ally of the Protectorate.

"Raissa told me Garreth is from one of the water cities, Cherlon, and that you are from Loridan, the oldest city on Rhianon and the only one still on the flatlands."

Aubin smiled as Eirriel ended her recital. "You learn your lessons well, little one."

"I wanted to know all about your home world. I had hoped it might help me to understand you better."

"And did it?"

She shook her head. "Not really. No one would tell me anything about you."

"They were obeying orders, my sweet. In fact, except for the supreme heads of the Protectorate, Garreth and Cian, no one knows."

Eirriel's lips twisted wryly. "Not even my friend Lux?"

Aubin glowered. Lux was still a sore subject. Although he knew her innocent of his accusations, she never told him how she got the transfer and wisely he never asked again. Refusing to let anything ruin this day, he cleared his mind of Lux and just shook his head.

"But why, Aubin?"

"It was something I promised myself when I left Rhianon. I wanted no favors because of my future." Aubin realized that he had said too much when he saw the perplexed expression on her face. Before she had time to voice her question, he asked, "What do you know about our government?"

"Only that your home city of Loridan hosts the government seat."

A cold feeling started to settle in Eirriel's heart. Deftly she pushed it aside, her thought paralleling Aubin's. Nothing must ruin this day.

"Our present government is a benevolent dictatorship

that extends back to Jumel, our first Lord Director. Until
that time there was no organized government."

Aubin explained that Jumel realized Rhianon was head-
ing toward destruction because her people were barbaric,
self-centered parasites. It took him most of his lifetime, but
finally Jumel convinced the more powerful leaders that it
would take more than domed cities to insure Rhianon's
survival. Before his death, Jumel instituted the offices of
Lord Director, Governor and Sub-Governor. With the new
system a governor was assigned to a district of ten cities,
each city having its own sub-governor. The sub-governor
was responsible to the governor who in turn was responsible
to the Lord Director. The offices of the governor and sub-
governor were appointed by the Lord Director and subject
to removal at any time should he feel they had failed to
fulfill their obligations.

"The Lord Director is not appointed nor elected. The
position is inherited. Jumel passed it on to Rond, his first-
born son, who passed it on to his son, Nexol, and so on
down the line to our present Lord Director, Lord Kiernan."

During his narrative, Aubin had hopped from the branch
and leaned casually against the tree's thick trunk, his arms
crossed behind his head. He paused now and studied
Eirriel, his face set as if weighing a heavy decision.

Watching Aubin, Eirriel knew he was greatly disturbed by
what he was about to say, but she sensed any attempt to
question him would be unwelcomed. Uneasily, she waited
for him to continue. The icy wariness had returned in force
as he walked stiffly away, for she had glimpsed a dark
coldness in his eyes before he had turned away from her.

When Aubin finally spoke, his back to her, it was in a
tension-filled voice which she had not heard for many,
many days.

"Lord Kiernan is my father."

Eirriel sucked in her breath. *No! It can't be!* she cried
silently as his words toppled her carefully built dreams for
the future. A future that included the handsome arrogant
captain of the *Celestial,* not the heir to the powerful Lord
Directorship of Rhianon.

Unable to bear the sight of his rigid back, Eirriel lowered

her eyes to the ground. Now it all made sense. The long walk to a secluded spot. The history lesson he had given her about his great and influential family. The tension in his voice. The coldness in his eyes. It was over, and rather than admit his words of love had all been lies, he chose to reveal his identity knowing she would realize that his station in life put him beyond her reach forever. It all added up, she thought painfully. He wanted her out of his life.

In the stillness of the woods, Eirriel's indrawn breath reached Aubin's ears. An agonizing groan tore from his throat as he felt the loving warmth she had given him driven from his soul by the sound. In its place remained an icy shell.

What made him believe she would be any different? he demanded bitterly of himself as he thought back to his time at the Academy and the girls he had had then.

Though they eagerly sought his restorer, they shied away from any other contact, fearing he would contaminate them with his wicked barbarism. Hurt and bitter from their insensitive treatment, young Aubin grew cold and callous. Women became nothing more than the means to relieve his baser wants. His aloof reputation fired women's passions and they clawed their way to his side, each hoping they would be the one to melt his icy disdain.

Soon he was welcomed everywhere. Taking perverse pleasure in making the women he'd known beg, he took without giving, leaving them satiated but always wanting more. And more he never gave.

Until Eirriel, his beautiful, brave, passionate spitfire.

He had fought his attraction to her, baiting her at every chance, believing it was only a matter of time before she showed her true nature. But it had never happened. Instead, slowly and without apparent calculation, she pierced all his defenses until she had embedded herself so deeply into his soul that he had forgotten his well-learned lessons.

But now he remembered.

He drew himself up to his full height, turned and faced her.

Her heart empty, her soul dead, Eirriel stared at the ground until she heard him turn. Looking up at him, her

hand flew to her mouth. Though she had known his eyes
would be devoid of the warm tenderness she had seen so
often in the past two weeks, she was unprepared for their
cold condemnation. She refused to let him see how deeply
he had wounded her. Before he could attack her, she would
attack him.

She dropped to the ground. "Is it proper to remain
standing before the future Lord Director or must I kneel?"

Aubin clenched his teeth. Of all the reactions he expected,
mockery was certainly not one of them.

"Don't be ridiculous, Eirriel!" he snapped.

"Does that mean I may remain standing?" she pressed.

Not trusting himself to speak, he gave her a curt nod.

"Thank you, my lord." She lowered her eyes meekly. "I
didn't mean to appear ridiculous, my lord, but I'm not sure
how one should behave with a Lord Director."

He stormed to her and grabbed her by the shoulders.
"Damn it! I'm the same man now as I was this morning!
Why should you behave any differently?"

"No!" she denied. "This morning you were Aubin, captain of the *Celestial* and—and. . ." Her voice caught in her
throat.

"And?" he demanded, shaking her.

And the man I love, her heart cried the words she would
not say. Instead, she answered coldly, "And now you are
heir to the powerful Lord Directorship of Rhianon."

"And that makes a difference?"

Again Eirriel had lowered her eyes or else she would have
seen the pained look that flashed across his face. When she
did not answer, he shook her again.

"Answer me!" he shouted.

"Yes," she said slowly, hoping her anguish couldn't be
heard. "That makes a difference. Should it not?"

"No!" came the clipped reply. "A Rhianonian is the same
whether he is a grower or a Lord Director!"

She struggled against him. "Then why did you tell me?"
she cried, unable to make sense of his last words.

The silence that greeted her question hung heavily in the
air. Aubin dropped his hands. "I thought to make you my
consort."

Eirriel cringed at the disappointment in his voice. Drawing upon an inner strength, she sneered at him. "Do you take me for a fool?" she demanded, her eyes blazing with fury. "Consort?" She pushed away from him. "An exile from a backward world, a mixed breed with powers she does not understand and cannot control. This you claim to have considered as your consort!" She laughed in self-derision. "Chalandra warned me. She told me you were no different from other men." Her voice broke. "I should have listened to her," she said softly. Tears sprang to her eyes. "Why, Aubin? Why, after teaching me that life can be so much more, did you take it from me? Better I should never have known."

Sobbing, she turned to run. Caught by her words and the pain in her voice, Aubin reached out and stopped her. Forcing her to him, he raised her face until he could look into her eyes.

"I did not lie, Eirriel," Aubin said softly. "I brought you here to ask you to be my consort. No!" He tightened his hold on her. "You will listen to me." When she stopped her struggles, he continued, "I had hoped that the love we shared would overcome who I was. When I heard your reaction, I thought you were rejecting me."

"Why did you think that?"

"Because of lessons I learned when I was young. Rhianonians are respected, it's true. But they are also feared. And, above all, they are never, never loved. And I am no ordinary Rhianonian," he added grimly.

To his complete amazement, Eirriel smiled. "You are no ordinary man, my bronze giant. Why would you be an ordinary Rhianonian?" She reached up and ran her hand tenderly down his face. "It was not my rejection of you that caused my gasp, but my belief that you were rejecting me."

Now it was Aubin's turn to smile. Rejecting her? How could he? She was his life. His love. His eyes darkened as he saw her love for him clearly reflected in her brilliant eyes. In a voice husky with emotion, he said, "I could no sooner reject you than I could my soul, little one. Without you, the sweetness leaves the air, the warmth flees the sun. You have brought such happiness to my life with your radiant smile, your haunting eyes, your compelling innocence." He drew her to him. "In you, I have found spirit, intelligence and passion. All that I want, all that I need. In you, I have found love."

His mouth crashed down on hers in a kiss filled with a love so intense that it threatened to tear him apart. And Eirriel reveled in it, murmuring protests when he dragged his mouth away. She watched without speaking as he reached up and drew from around his neck the thick chain he was never without. Once unfastened, it parted into two thin strands of gold.

"I would take you as my consort now, my love, but that can only be done on Rhianon and in the presence of my father. I cannot wait until then to make you mine. These are Syna Circlets. They have been in my family for generations. They are given to the first-born son at his birth. When he finds the woman he would make his consort, he gives one to her and keeps one for himself until the time they stand before the Lord Director for the binding ceremony and the bestowing of the double Life Circlets. Then the Syna Circlets are rejoined and returned to the case to wait through the years for their firstborn son."

Placing one of the circlets on Eirriel's head, he gently pulled her hair over the chain arranging it so it fell in place across her forehead.

"Traditionally they symbolize the rejoining of two souls, and over the years we have learned that they create a link between the couple. As long as their love for each other exists, the bond can never be broken."

"Then it will never be, for I will love you forever."

Aubin handed the other circlet to Eirriel. "Now you must set mine in place."

As she did, Aubin saw a brilliant radiance burning deep in her eyes. Awed, he felt his heart swell with love. When Eirriel finished, she stepped back and took his hands in hers. In a voice as tender as a caress, she said, "What I have, I give to you. My heart, my life, my soul I place in your hands freely and with trust. My love is yours now and throughout eternity."

Aubin lowered his mouth to hers. Slowly and with great tenderness they made love. Afterwards, lost in the glory of their oneness, they slept.

Chapter Twenty-one

Several hours passed before the chill of the late-afternoon air woke the lovers. Dressing quickly, they followed the winding trail through the woods and made their way back to their cubicles. Alerted by the grumbling of their stomachs that they had missed midday nourishment, Aubin proceeded to order food. Within moments a huge tray, laden with various fruits, vegetables, and meats, arrived. Eirriel placed it on the table while Aubin poured them some sholaine. No sooner had they begun eating, when they heard a sharp rap on the portal.

"Come in," Aubin called out, his eyes narrowing in speculation when he saw their visitor.

"Special envoy Zale," the young woman introduced herself in a clipped formal voice.

Aubin motioned her to be seated, but she refused.

"I'm sorry to disturb your furlough, Captain Aubin, but Supreme Commander Shand ordered me to you with all due haste. I was to give you this." She handed him a small cylinder. Looking pointedly at Eirriel, she said, "It concerns a matter of high security, sir."

Before Aubin could reply with Eirriel's security clearance, Eirriel rose. "If you excuse me, love, I really could use a long, hot soak."

"This shouldn't take too long, my sweet." Aubin's warm gaze swept over her. "I'll join you shortly."

Eirriel felt her blood tingle in anticipation. Throwing him a daring look, she sauntered into the vitalizer. It wasn't until the portal closed that Aubin turned his attention back to the envoy and her special message. Crossing to the small viewer, he placed the cylinder in the slot, sat down and listened.

"Damn!" he muttered when the recording was over.

"What did you say, sir?"

Aubin turned to Zale, a look of consternation on his face. "Tell Supreme Commander Shand that I will accept this mission with the condition that my crew gets two weeks added onto their next furlough."

"That's already been done, Captain," the envoy said coldly.

Aubin arched his brow. "Oh?"

"Supreme Commander Shand said something to the effect that I was to tell Captain Aubin that his crew would be well rewarded for this inconvenience and that the reward would also include an extended furlough."

The Rhianonian captain noticed the envoy's unease and couldn't resist pushing her. "Knowing Shand the way I do, I doubt very much he called me Captain Aubin."

Zale looked at him in obvious distaste. "Actually the words he used were 'Tell the young whippersnapper, of course, the damned furlough would be extended.'"

Aubin roared. Whippersnapper indeed! Who else but Shand still used that archaic word? "Did he say anything else?"

"Only that he knew you would take the assignment without asking about financial recompense."

This brought another shout of laughter from the Rhianonian before he grew serious. "Tell Shand I'll leave as soon as my crew is assembled."

"Very good, sir." Zale quickly left.

Aubin sat down at the viewer and reran Shand's message

before destroying it. As always Shand expected the impossible, only this time it didn't look like Aubin had a chance in hell of delivering it.

Annan was in the throes of a civil war. A new leader had recently appeared and was pushing for an alliance with Blagden, which neither the Protectorate nor most Annanites desired. The information was sketchy, delivered through a muddled web of sources from Segar, one of the Annanites' rebel leaders.

Under the guise of a rendezvous with a Special Envoy carrier, the *Celestial* would pass close enough to the restricted Annanite air space for Aubin to teleport down to the planet's surface. Since the extent of the Blagdenian involvement was not known, Aubin would be disguised. He would meet with Segar, who would take him to his meeting with the present, but ailing, leader, Tiala. Any other information, like the name of the new leader, would have to wait until Aubin met with Segar.

Tired of waiting, Eirriel stepped from the vitalizer, drew on her robe and joined Aubin. The teasing glint faded from her eyes when she saw his solemn face.

"What's wrong?" she asked as she sat down next to him.

He took her hand in his. "We've been ordered back to duty."

Her eyes widened. "But why?"

Aubin hated deceiving her, but he had no choice. "There's a Special Envoy carrier stranded without escort. We've been nominated as their escort."

"It's not fair," Eirriel pouted.

"Whether it's fair or not," Aubin chided gently, "those are our orders." He smiled at her obvious disappointment. "I know, sweet, I hate to leave here, too. Now, be a good girl and start packing. We've got to move fast."

In spite of Aubin's desire for speed, it wasn't until later that evening that the *Celestial's* disgruntled, but obedient, crew reported to their stations. Once again at his console, Aubin gave orders to get underway.

"Shalter, proceed at vel 10."

The night navigator slowly raised the control bar. "Proceeding at vel 10, Captain."

"Garreth, how long before we reach the rendezvous point?"

Pressing a few buttons, Garreth glanced over his shoulder. "If we maintain this speed, twenty-five hours."

"Very good. Vanux, notify all unit heads the briefing will begin in fifteen minutes."

"Yes, Captain."

"Garreth, come with me."

Bidding the night crew a good day's end, Aubin and Garreth walked silently to the Deliberation Cubicle. Seated at the oval table, Aubin turned to Garreth. "How long before we reach Annan?"

The ship's second-in-command had been fully briefed by the captain and was prepared with the information. "Twenty-four hours."

"And you'll reach the intercept point one hour later?"

Garreth nodded.

"Good. Once you do that you'll have to reduce speed to vel 5. I don't think the carrier can handle anything higher."

Garreth did some quick calculations. "Thirty-two hours to Zyrol, sixteen hours back at vel 10. Forty-eight hours total." He frowned. "Is it safe for you to be down there that long?"

"I'll be disguised and that should help. But it doesn't really matter, I'll need at least that long to ensure my meeting with Tiala even with Segar's help."

Garreth shook his head, not liking Aubin's planned meeting with the Annanite leader without backup. "I don't like you going by yourself."

"I'm not too fond of it either," Aubin admitted grimly. "But my orders were very specific on that point. I wish they were half as helpful in other ways," he added dryly.

"You still don't know who's working with the Blagdenians?"

Aubin raked his hand through his hair. "No. I just know someone is pressuring them to form a trading alliance with Blagden. If they do, they break the treaty with the Protectorate. Once that happens, we lose not only our major supplier of yral ore, but one of our scarce holds in that sector."

"Is this Segar reliable?"

The Rhianonian captain shrugged. "Shand seems to think so. Now, before the others join us, I want to finalize the details. We can't afford an error."

Garreth was tempted to try and pressure Aubin into letting him go along, but seeing his friend's set expression, he knew it would be useless. Just as they finished reviewing their plans, the unit heads started arriving. When they were all seated, Aubin addressed them.

"In approximately twenty-three hours our trajectory will carry us through the Rama VII star system close to Annan. As we pass over the mining colony, I will teleport down to the city of Sumal to attend a conference with the Annanite leader. The *Celestial* will continue on to the rendezvous point, escort the Special Envoy carrier to Zyrolian air space, then return for me."

"It's for this routine mission that our furlough was cut short?" Theron asked.

Aubin nodded.

"All other fleetships were too distant to intercept the carrier before it reached the unallied sectors of Rama VII. Any other questions?" His eyes scanned the group. "Fine. One last thing, please inform your units that their next furlough will be extended to make up for this one being cut short and that they should see a substantial bonus within the next few weeks. That's all for now. I'll see you tomorrow."

Garreth hung back when the others left and walked with Aubin to the conveyor.

"What have you decided to tell Eirriel?"

"Just what I told the others."

"Nothing about Blagden?"

Aubin shook his head. "I see no reason to mention their proximity to us. It would only frighten her."

"I guess you're right."

As Aubin entered the conveyor, Garreth waved good night and left to find Raissa.

Eirriel waited anxiously for Aubin to arrive. Ever since the envoy had arrived on Symarryllyon, a feeling of doom had settled over her. When the portal opened and she saw him, the feeling increased.

"Aubin what's wrong?" she asked as she went to him.

"Nothing," he replied easily. Taking her hand, he led her to the couch and pulled her onto his lap. "Tell me, do you like living with me instead of Raissa?"

In spite of her worries, Eirriel had to laugh. "How would I know? I just got all my belongings moved in."

"Then you're all settled in?"

She nodded.

"Good. At least I'll know where to find you when I get back."

She frowned. "Get back? From where?"

"From Annan," he replied casually. Hoping Sidra was right and her daughter could not read minds, Aubin repeated the story he had told the unit heads.

All her senses screamed at her. There was more to his trip than he was saying. What was he hiding? And why? She wanted to question him, but she seemed to know her inquiries would remain unanswered. Instead, she asked how long he would be away and was totally unprepared for the answer.

"Forty-eight hours!" she exclaimed. "By yourself!" She tilted her head and studied him through eyes that were narrowed and intense. "You've never teleported anywhere by yourself and certainly not for two days." Fear, fed by her uneasiness, made her voice harsh. "What is it you're not telling me?"

Touching the tip of her nose with one finger, he shook his head. "What a suspicious little mind you have, my sweet." He chuckled, then chided her gently. "There have been occasions in the past that I have managed, by myself, to carry out certain assignments."

Eirriel blushed at the subtle reminder that he was more than capable of handling anything that came up. She threw her arms around his neck and held him close. "I'm sorry, Aubin. It's just that I have this feeling that something terrible is about to happen." She looked at him, her eyes dark with worry. "You will be careful, won't you?"

"Knowing I have you waiting for me," he murmured huskily, "how could I be otherwise?"

Giving a small cry, Eirriel's mouth seized his with a passion that left Aubin shaken. Lifting herself from his lap, she stood facing him. Her eyes burning into his, she slipped the caftan slowly from her shoulders and let it drift to the ground around her feet. Without a word, she turned on her toes and walked to the restorer.

With a groan, Aubin stood and stripped off his clothes. He knelt over Eirriel and his breath caught in his throat as her hand reached out and encircled him, drawing him to her.

Eirriel's fear and Aubin's foreboding gave their lovemaking a desperation that heightened their senses and drew from them an outpouring of love that words could never have conveyed, until all rational thought fled and they soared together to the heady summits of ecstasy.

Twenty-two hours later, Aubin was in the com-center, Garreth at his side.

"We reach Annan in thirty minutes."

Grimly, Aubin nodded and left for his cubicle.

Shucking his uniform, he slipped his arms into the full sleeves of the white shirt. Leaving it open to the waist, he pulled on the baggy black pants and tucked them into the knee-high red boots. He drew a long red sash around his waist and knotted it over his left hip.

Aubin's mouth twisted in a grimace when he saw how ridiculous he looked, but as a hawker of goods he would have free access to the bustling open air market of Inner Sumal without fear of discovery.

He grabbed the red bandanna and spun it. Just as he was about to tie it around his forehead, he remembered the circlet. Smiling as Eirriel came to mind, he drew it from his head, fastened it about his neck, then tied the twisted cloth in place.

He glanced at the chronometer. Fifteen minutes. Debating briefly over a quick trip to the lab, he decided against it. They had said their good-byes that morning and seeing him dressed as he was, Eirriel would only start asking questions that, until now, he had managed to avoid.

"Aubin to lab."

"Lab here."

Was it his imagination or was Eirriel's voice unusually soft? "I just called to say good-bye, sweet."

"You're leaving now?"

"In a few minutes."

"Oh . . . You'll be careful?"

He could hear her voice wavering. For a moment he resented her limited abilities. If only she could tell him what she feared! Quickly, he pushed aside the thought. She deserved better from him.

"I'll be careful, my love. Keep our restorer warm. I'll be back before you have time to miss me," he said with an assurance he hardly felt.

"Good-bye, my bronze giant."

"Good-bye, little one."

"Aubin! I love you!"

Eirriel's ragged cry tore at his heart long after the intercom went silent. He fought against the need to rush to her side, to hold her close and kiss away her fears and his sudden unshakable belief that the lovemaking they had shared just a short time ago would have to last him a lifetime.

Resolutely, Aubin forced the unsettling notion from his mind and strode from the cubicle.

Garreth was already in the teleport when Aubin entered.

"Do you have it with you?" Aubin asked, his concern making his voice harsh.

The tall Rhianonian nodded and extended his hand. Aubin took the golden hoop that held the tiny transmitter and clipped it to his left ear.

"Be careful, my friend," Garreth warned, as he clasped Aubin's hand firmly. "I still don't like the feel of this."

"Neither do I, Garreth," Aubin replied solemnly. "Neither do I."

Walking to the teleport's inner chamber, Aubin reminded Garreth of the sensitivity of their position and the strength of his orders. "Remember, the true extent of the Blagdenian involvement is still uncertain. If you should encounter them, a confrontation is to be avoided at all cost. Until it is official, we cannot risk giving Tozgor the excuse he is seeking to attack."

Aubin paused and Garreth raised his eyes expectantly.

"Watch out for Eirriel," Aubin said, his voice husky with emotion. "Keep her safe for me."

Garreth touched his hand to his forehead, acknowledging the request, then activated the controls, unable to shake the disquieting premonition that his friend and captain was walking blindly into danger.

Chapter Twenty-two

Twenty-four hours after the *Celestial* returned to Annan air space, Aubin's failure to report as planned caused a concerned Garreth to call an emergency meeting of the unit heads.

Pacing about the Deliberation Cubicle, his voice and expression grave, he explained Aubin's excursion to the mining colony.

"Due to the treaty's stipulation prohibiting the approach of armed fleetships, the *Celestial* could not orbit while the investigation was being carried out. Therefore, using the Zyrolian Mission as cover, we were able to pass within teleportation range of Annan. Our return course again gave us the excuse to transverse Annan air space and be within range for the captain's return."

Garreth paused. Placing his hands on the table, he leaned forward, his intense gaze sweeping the attentive faces of the men and women seated around him.

"Captain Aubin," he said slowly, "is twenty-four hours late."

Before the startled group could do more than gasp, a raging Eirriel burst into the cubicle. Her eyes flashing dangerously, she faced Garreth. "Why wasn't I asked to attend this little gathering?" she demanded.

Garreth swore under his breath. He knew Eirriel. If she learned of his plans, she would insist on being included, taking matters into her own hands if he refused. That he could not risk. Aubin's parting words fresh in his mind, Garreth gestured to the group.

"As you can see, only the unit heads have been invited." Noting her accusing glare focus on Raissa, he added, "Unit heads or their proxys. Since you are neither, I must ask you to leave."

Her lips curled contemptuously. "Do you actually expect me to believe that?"

"Believe whatever you wish, Eirriel," he replied coldly. "But the fact remains, you were not invited. Now, please leave."

She thrust her jaw forward in defiance. "I'm not going anywhere until you tell me about Aubin."

"You've already been told all you need to know," he said firmly as he sat down, his back to her.

"I want to know why he hasn't returned!"

Garreth closed his eyes against the pain in her voice. "Eirriel, I'm ordering you to leave! Now!"

"No!"

"Then you leave me no choice." Hating what he had to do, Garreth nodded at the safeguard officer. "Please escort Eirriel to her cubicle, Lebron."

Reluctantly, Lebron rose and crossed to Eirriel. When he placed his hand on her shoulder, she pulled away and stepped toward Garreth.

"Three days, Garreth. Three days with no word of Aubin." Her hands were clenched tightly at her side. "I want to know where he is, Garreth and I want to know *now*!"

Garreth slammed his hands on the table and jumped to his feet.

"Enough!" he roared, his eyes dark with rage. "Either you leave right this instant or I'm charging you with insubordination and confining you to your cubicle to await a formal hearing!"

A few minutes of heavy silence greeted Garreth's enraged bellow. In that all-too-brief time, he watched with grim resignation as the fiery, green orbs of fury soldified into glittering crystals of hatred.

"Tell me, Lebron," Eirriel said softly, "is it true only crew members can be charged with insubordination?"

Puzzled, the safeguard officer, nodded.

"So be it."

With her right hand she tore the blue emblem from her uniform.

"Eirriel!" Raissa got to her feet. "Don't!"

She tossed it at Garreth. It hit him in the face and slid to the floor. "I hereby give formal notice." Her voice bit at him with the glacial sting of sub-zero temperatures. "I quit!"

Garreth groaned. Damn her! Why must she be so damned stubborn? He stooped to retrieve the torn badge, a rueful smile on his lips. At least she had given him an indisputable reason for sending her away. Straightening his tall frame, he turned icy, golden eyes on her.

"If this is what you want . . ." He paused briefly, giving her time to revoke her decision, but as he expected she did not.

"As you wish," he said sardonically, with an ever-so-brief bow. "Safeguard Officer Lebron will escort you to your cubicle. The lower level of this ship is no place for a civilian."

Eirriel could have screamed in frustration. Her anger had, once again, gotten the best of her. Knowing she had trapped herself, she hung her head. "I'm sorry. I only wanted to know where he was."

She followed Lebron across the cubicle to the portal. As it opened, he stepped aside to let her pass. When she did, she turned and placed a restraining hand on his chest. "I give you my word," she said quietly. "I'll go straight to my cubicle and remain there. Stay," her voice broke, "stay and find him." She raised luminous, green eyes to Garreth. "It's been three days, Garreth." Her voice lowered until he could barely hear it. "Three days. He could be dead."

Tears she had so valiantly held in check, now fell from her eyes. Eirriel rushed to her cubicle and threw herself on the restorer. Tears spent, she lay on the restorer, her eyes clenched tightly against intrusion, her mind careening through an ebony abyss that echoed the desolute void of her soul.

A faint muffled noise that sounded like, "Is there anyway to reach him?" nudged the corners of her consciousness. Then, "I don't know. My only contact is long overdue." Slowly, becoming louder, the words, "When did you last hear anything?" became more distinct until at last she recognized Garreth's deep, resonant tones. "Ten hours ago."

With a start, she realized that in her despair her inborn ability instinctively surfaced once again. Her mind had expanded, penetrating the metal walls of the *Celestial* as if they were composed of nothing more than mist, and was aware of all that took place in the Deliberation Cubicle.

She saw Garreth, his brow heavily creased with worry, anxiously drumming his fingers on the table as he listened to Lebron.

"Garreth, I think I speak for the entire group when I say I understand the gravity of the situation on Annan. What I don't understand is why we were kept so completely in the dark? Surely our security clearance was high enough to have allowed our involvement in this mission?"

His statement was followed by an angry murmur of agreement and the nodding of heads.

"The captain wanted to brief all of you but Main Terminal insisted he reveal it only to me. They felt that if something were to go wrong—"

"Which it did," Raissa commented dryly.

"The fewer who knew about it the better," Garreth finished after throwing Raissa a glaring look, "Discovery would bring serious diplomatic ramifications. Our treaty states no interference."

Cian snorted. "Of course, Blagden is not interfering."

Garreth turned to the Drocot. "Not in any way we can prove, Cian. That's why Aubin's down there."

"Why Aubin?" Ceara asked. "Why not a specially trained agent?"

"Because several years ago Aubin rescued Tiala's son

from a damaged spacecraft. Since that day, the Annanite leader has held a warm regard for him. Tiala's a powerful force on Annan. Main Terminal hoped the captain's connection with him would allow a more open communication."

Jarce, who had been doing some furious computing, leaned over to Theron, pointed to the figures and whispered a question.

When Theron nodded in agreement, Jarce addressed Garreth. "You said you haven't had any contact from the captain since he left?"

Garreth nodded.

"I don't find anything strange in that. According to my calculations, there is no way his conversor could have reached us at our present location."

Jarce's statement brought startled looks to the faces of the unit heads.

"Then if we move within conversor range, he might call!" Raissa exclaimed.

The Rhianonian shook his head grimly. "I'm afraid not, Raissa. Because of the distance we are forced to maintain from Annan, the captain carried a specialized unit which would have no difficulty in spanning that distance. I have the receiving unit here." He pointed to a tiny, square box attached to his belt. "Aubin could have reported in any time within the last twenty-four hours."

"And nothing from Segar?" This from Jarce.

"Not within the past ten hours. He made contact shortly after the *Celestial* moved into surveillance position. He reported that Aubin had been escorted from the marketplace by two men wearing the Annanite Leader Lamd's colors just three hours after Aubin arrived on Annan. Segar has spent the past thirty-six hours trying to arrange a conference with Leader Tiala to request his aid in locating Aubin. Segar's progress reports were sent every two hours without fail. That's what causes me such concern now."

"You think something may have happened to Segar?"

"Yes, Theron, I'm afraid I do."

"Then how are we going to find the captain?"

"That, my good Ceara, is why I called this meeting." He

searched the solemn faces of his comrades. "Any suggestions?"

"What about a questor search?" Raissa volunteered.

Jarce shook his head. "To scan the entire colony with any kind of accuracy would take too much time at too close a range."

"A mini-cruiser would never be able to land undetected," commented Theron.

"It seems to me," Cian said slowly, "that the only clues to Aubin's whereabouts would be found on the planet's surface."

The Rhianonian stared into Cian's wise, blue eyes. "I know, Cian, but the captain's orders specifically stated that no one, under any circumstance, was to teleport down to Annan with the exception of Aubin himself. My orders were even more unconditional. Keep the *Celestial* out of Annan air space at all cost."

Raissa jumped to her feet. "Then I say to hell with orders!"

"So do I!"

"And I!"

"And I!"

Blue eyes twinkled and the corners of a small mouth turned up. "Well, Garreth," Cian remarked, tugging at his beard, "I think you have the answer you were waiting for."

For the first time since Symarryllyon, Garreth laughed. "You are right there, Cian. It seemed to me, the only way to find Aubin was with direct disregard for Protectorate orders. I was willing to risk it, but I could not do it alone." He smiled at the men and women willing to sacrifice their careers to save the life of their captain. "Well, my friends, if you'll all be seated we have work—"

Garreth stopped in midsentence as a crackling rent the air. Grabbing the receiver, he turned the knobs, desperately trying to eliminate some of the static. Jarce quickly interceded, but with no more luck than Garreth. Segar's frantic transmission continued to fade in and out. ". . . reth . . . read me? Men waiting . . . Aubin cap . . . landed . . . be execu . . . hours. Caught . . . weapon . . . pathic scan . . . cover . . . beware . . . amd." His scratchy voice rose shrilly. ". . . portal! ARRRUGHHH!"

"Segar? Do you read me?" Garreth's concerned inquiry was greeted by static, then silence. "Segar!"

After a few moments of continued silence, Garreth looked at the unit heads. "It's no use. Whoever found him must have destroyed the transmittor as well. Raissa, did you get it all?"

Raissa nodded and switched on the portcorder. Listening intently, they tried to piece together Segar's broken message. As they feared, Aubin was captured and facing execution. As to when they had no idea. After much discussion, they decided that Segar had named Lamd as the one behind the treachery.

Garreth frowned. How was it possible for Aubin to have been caught so soon after his arrival? How had Lamd discovered Segar's carefully concealed location? Gruffly, he asked Raissa to replay the recording. Placing his head in his hands, he concentrated on Segar's words.

"Stop!" Garreth ordered. "Rai, go back to the word *caught.*"

The Melonnian did as he bid.

". . . caught . . . weapon . . . pathic scan . . . cover . . ."

"That's enough." Garreth shook his head in frustration. "What the hell does he mean?" he ground out fiercely.

"He means," a soft voice said quietly, "that I am Aubin's only hope."

Garreth's head shot up and he whirled around. Eirriel was standing in the portalway, a stubborn set to her stance. Before he could voice the annoyance she read in his eyes, she continued, "Don't you see, Garreth? Segar was telling us how Aubin was caught."

"We know that, Eirriel!" Garreth snapped. "What we can't decipher is the methods they used!" His eyes narrowed in suspicion. "What do you mean you're his only hope?"

Her calm, cool gaze met his irate one. "Aubin was caught by a telepathic scanner."

The unit heads exchanged puzzled glances. Segar? Aubin caught? Telepathic scanner? Slowly, all faces, but one, registered shock as the realization rapidly filtered through them. Eirriel knew everything that had taken place since she was ordered from the cubicle!

In contrast to the astounded stares of his comrades, Cian smiled smugly. Again her enigmatic ability had surfaced spontaneously when the need arose. He could only hope it wasn't too late!

"Telepathic scanner. Hmm." Cian stroked his beard. "It makes sense, Garreth. There's no other way the captain could have been discovered so soon."

"Then you agree, Cian?" Eirriel pressed eagerly. "I'm the only one who can save him."

The Drocot nodded and looked at his companions. One by one they nodded their agreement.

Eirriel turned to Garreth and said quietly, "Will you listen to my plan?"

Realizing there was no other way to save his friend's life, the grim Rhianonian reluctantly withdrew his promise to Aubin and motioned Eirriel forward.

Chapter Twenty-three

Concealed by the murky light of predawn, Eirriel crouched behind one of the large boulders that bordered the only entrance into Inner Sumal. The rapid pounding of her heart seemed to echo loudly in the stillness as she watched the sleepy group of hawkers trudge past. Slipping cautiously between the jagged rocks, she followed them through the massive stone gates, down the narrow, twisting pathways to the edge of the marketplace. Spying a darkened alleyway, she stepped inside and waited.

While she did, she thought back to her last conversation with Garreth and the look on his face when she refused to let Lebron accompany her. Swearing violently, Garreth had argued that Aubin might not be facing execution if someone had been with him. Calmly Eirriel had reminded him that though she could easily shield her own mind, she had yet to learn if it was possible to shield another. If she could not, the unshielded mind would endanger them both. Trapped by the validity of her reasoning, Garreth had grudgingly agreed and had sent her off to the dispensary.

With Raissa's help, Eirriel had chosen high-heeled, knee-high, red boots, a full, black, calf-length skirt to be worn over six white underskirts with the left side tucked into the waistband, a white blouse with short, puffy sleeves and intricate red designs embroidered around the low, off-the-shoulder neckline. To complete her costume, she had selected five golden bracelets for each wrist, four necklaces of varying lengths and the circlet which, like Aubin, she had refused to part with and had fastened around her neck.

Outfitted and anxious to begin her search, Eirriel had met Garreth at the teleport. In his outstretched hand he had held a pair of large, golden hoop earrings. As with Aubin, one was the powerful transmittor. Reminding her to check in every two hours and agreeing not to speak unless she directly mentioned his name, Garreth and Raissa had said their good-byes and she had teleported down to Annan.

A high-pitched squeal followed by a deep shout of laughter jarred Eirriel back to the present. She was startled to see the once empty marketplace alive with brightly clad men, women and children, all working at a frantic pace to prepare their stalls for the day's business. Over the cacophony of sounds, she could hear the deep richness of a baritone singing a lusty ballad of days gone by.

Eirriel drew a deep breath. It was time. Straightening her skirts, she tied the red bandanna around the back of her head and sauntered from the alleyway.

"Mother of the Universe!" Boruk exclaimed as she passed in front of his stall. The multicolored floor covering dropped from his hands and he jabbed his large companion roughly in the ribs. His blue eyes wide with wonder, he said excitedly, "Look, brother, did you ever see such beauty?"

Koltrax, his broad back to the bustling square, grinned in amusement. This was Boruk's first hawking and everything that greeted his young eyes drew some breathless comment.

"No, little brother," he replied fondly, ruffling Boruk's hair. "I'm sure I never did."

"You didn't even look," Boruk accused. Tearing his eyes from the golden-haired vision, he glanced up in time to catch the teasing lights that were still dancing in Koltrax's green eyes. *So, that's the way of things this morning*, Boruk thought, grinning. *Well, now it's my turn!*

"So it's true, what Aaran told me," Boruk said, shaking

his head sadly. "When a man reaches your great age, his interest in women passes." He raised his eyes to the sky. "Father of All, may I never get that old!"

"My great age!" The bearded hawker roared with laughter. "Why you young cub! I'll have to remind you of the immenseness of age ten years from now." He placed his hands on his hips and quirked his brow. "As for the other, have you yourself not warned me that a woman would cause my early death? But enough of this." He turned to face the marketplace. "Where is your beauty?"

Before Boruk could reply, an exasperated shriek drew Koltrax's attention. His eyes widened, then narrowed in appreciation. A young woman stood before an empty stall, her hands on her hips and green fire flashing across her eyes.

"Aubin, damn you! Where are you?"

Koltrax vaulted over the front of his stall and crossed silently toward her.

"Something is wrong, pretty lady?"

Startled, Eirriel whirled around.

"Perhaps I can be of some assistance," he continued smoothly. He jerked his head toward the empty stall. "You appear to have misplaced someone."

"Misplaced someone!" Eirriel cried, quickly recovering her wits and falling into her role. "Me!" She tossed her head. "Bah! Men!" she spat, throwing up her hands in disgust. "You're all alike! He leaves me three days ago. I've lost him!"

"You misunderstand," Koltrax said quickly, giving her a blinding smile. "Of course *you* did not lose *him*. But come, green eyes, tell me, if he left you three days ago why do you look for him now?"

"Why do you care?" she demanded.

He brought his hand to his heart. "Because it pains me to see such beauty so distressed."

In spite of herself, Eirriel had to smile at the picture the ruggedly handsome man presented.

"Ah, a smile more radiant than the Sun Queen herself. Permit me to introduce myself," he said, reaching for her hand. Bringing it to his lips, he gave her a short bow. "Koltrax, hawker extraordinaire, at your service. And you?"

"Eirriel."

"Eirriel," he repeated. "An unusual name. And your . . . I don't suppose he was your brother?"

She shook her head.

"I thought not. Well, what did you call him?"

"Aubin."

"Aubin. Hmm, another unusual name. Tell me, green eyes, has he ever done this before? Come to a hawking and failed to set up?"

She shrugged. "I don't know. I've never come before. He wouldn't let me." She pouted. "And he said no this time, too, but I refused to stay at home again. So I waited. Why are you laughing?"

"Did it ever occur to you that he might be visiting a . . . a friend? After all, it does not take three days to set up a stall."

She shook her head. "No, his friend's too sick to visit." Her eyes narrowed as his laughter increased. Suddenly she realized what he was alluding to. Flinging her head back, she said proudly, "Aubin needs no one else!"

Seeing her standing there, her firm breasts thrust forward, her head thrown back, her green eyes boldly challenging him, Koltrax could only agree with her statement. She would be enough for any man!

"What about his sick friend?" Koltrax demanded, desire making his voice gruff.

"No. I'm certain he wouldn't risk visiting him. Segar's . . ."

"Segar!"

Koltrax's hand shot out and closed around Eirriel's wrist.

"Let go of me!" she ordered, gasping when his grip tightened.

Struggling to free herself, the blood drained from her face as she caught sight of his fierce expression. Lips that so recently curved in an easy smile, now formed a tight grim line, and his arresting eyes were devoid of all emotion.

"Who are you?" he demanded harshly. "Why are you here?"

"I already told you! My name is Eirriel and I came to find my lover!"

Muttering under his breath, the brown-haired hawker

dragged Eirriel across the open square toward the very alley that had concealed her presence a short time earlier. Her face burning from the other hawkers' lewd comments and Koltrax's lusty replies as he pulled her along, she balled her fist and swung it with all her might against his upper arm. Koltrax reeled and Eirriel found herself free. Spinning around, she tore off in the opposite direction only to be wrenched backwards by a savage yank on her hair.

Before she could regain her balance, Koltrax snatched her up and tossed her over his shoulder. Ignoring both the cheers of the crowd and the pounding of fists on his back, he continued toward the alleyway. Once there, he set her roughly on her feet. Her wrists held firmly in one hand, the other resting lightly in her hair, he stared down at her with murderous green eyes.

"What do you know of Segar?" he demanded, his voice edged with steel.

"Nothing!"

"Liar!" he growled, his fingers knotting in her blond curls.

"No! I know nothing!"

"Lying bitch!" he roared, twisting Eirriel's hair so viciously that tears sprang to her eyes. "Why are you here?"

"To find Aubin!" she gasped.

"Koltrax!"

Boruk's voice failed to cut through the red haze that had clouded Koltrax's mind since Eirriel had mentioned Segar's name. Segar, lifelong friend. Segar, the only connection between Koltrax's armed resisters and the unknown power that offered aid against Lamd. Segar, missing twenty-four hours, found destroyed in his home. Was this woman's hand the one that murdered him?

Koltrax raised his hand to strike her but found his arm stopped.

"Koltrax! No!"

"Boruk?" He turned puzzled eyes to his brother.

"She tells the truth," Boruk said quietly.

"You are sure."

Boruk nodded.

"So be it." The hawker released Eirriel who quickly stepped out of his reach. "It seems I owe you an apology.

Boruk has always been able to tell truth from lies."

Her eyes flickered from the clear, innocent eyes of Boruk to his brother's and saw that all hate and rage had vanished replaced by a deep, painful sadness. She placed her hand on his shoulder.

"Segar was your friend?" she asked softly.

"You say his name as if you know him," Koltrax accused his voice harsh. "Perhaps, for once, Boruk is wrong."

"Not wrong, brother. Just untruthful," he admitted solemnly.

"What!" Koltrax exclaimed, his eyes darkening with rage. "Why did you do this?"

"There is a reason. Listen to me!" Boruk grabbed his brother's arm as he started to move away. "Think!" The young man's voice was intense. "What was it about her besides the obvious, that caused your notice?"

Koltrax met his brother's gaze, awed by the wisdom older than Boruk's years that burned deep within his clear, blue eyes. Hesitantly his gaze swung to Eirriel. Boruk watched with relief as he saw realization light Koltrax's eyes.

"She does not belong here," Boruk continued. "She knows of Segar, it's true, and she knows of his death. Even before us, I think. But . . . but"—again Boruk was forced to raise his voice to cut through the older man's blinding pain— "but she had no part in it. Lamd, alone, did that."

"Is this true?"

Eirriel nodded.

"You knew long ago that he was dead?"

Again, she nodded.

"How? Tell me how!"

She shook her head sadly. "I'm afraid I can't."

Koltrax nodded his acceptance. "Then I think we must talk, but not here. Come."

He reached for her hand and led her to the entrance to the marketplace. Casually, he glanced around the open square and was not at all surprised by what he saw.

"We must make this look good for the watchers," he murmured, then pulled her close and captured her mouth with his.

Caught offguard, Eirriel responded to the thrill that shot

through her and returned his passionate kiss. She reached up to encircle his neck and her hand tangled in his shoulder-length hair. Her head jerked away as her mind told her what her body had momentarily forgotten. This was not Aubin! A strangled cry tore from her throat and she stepped back, staring at him with agony in her eyes. Her trembling fingers pressed against her lips and she lowered her head in shame.

For Koltrax, Eirriel's eyes had reflected her thoughts all too clearly and he consigned the missing Aubin to the slimy depths of the Atra marsh before resigning himself to the knowledge that he stood no chance of winning her affections.

"Don't be ashamed, green eyes," he said softly. "You didn't betray him. It was your longing for your Aubin that responded to me. Not you. Now come," he continued, his voice once again cheerful. "Act as if I'm the greatest man in the universe. We're being watched. No! Don't look. I'll explain later."

Hand in hand, they joined Boruk, who had already returned to the stall. Between mouthfuls of the food the youth had quickly prepared, Koltrax briefly told Eirriel of his small band of rebels and Segar's dual role.

"You're from his allies, aren't you?"

Eirriel nodded.

"Are you here to help?"

"Not officially," she replied. "Aubin was sent to learn how much of a real threat this leader is."

"Oh, Lamd's real enough," Koltrax snarled. "In the short time he's been here, life on Annan . . ."

He broke off when he saw Eirriel's grim look. "But you don't want to hear about that, do you?" he accused harshly. "It doesn't matter that he's executed fifty innocent people in two months! That he's increased his daily tithe until what little remains barely feeds the children! So what if we starve as long as you and your kind aren't affected." He slammed his fist on the counter and his eyes blazed with frustrated rage. "What kind of power are you that lets this happen?"

"The Protectorate is a power that affects the lives of many," Eirriel said quietly. "Too many to interfere indiscriminantly."

"Indiscriminantly!" Koltrax roared.

"Brother," Boruk's calm voice cut through Koltrax's rage, "Lamd is our problem. We have no right to demand assistance. Neither do we need it."

Koltrax's condemning stare swung from Eirriel to Boruk. "Just what do you know about what we do or do not need?" he snapped.

"A lot more than you realize," came the quiet reply.

The tall hawker frowned. "How?"

Boruk shook his head. "Later. First we must find Eirriel's Aubin."

Koltrax stared at his young brother, puzzled by the change that had come over him. Again, he questioned not seeing it until now. But Boruk was right, now was not the time. Later there would be time to understand.

"As before, brother, you are right." He turned to Eirriel. "Perhaps it would help if you were to describe your Aubin."

Eirriel proceeded to give a complete description of the man who had become her life. Her concern knew no bounds when the frown marring Koltrax's handsome face deepened.

"It seems I know of your lost Aubin," he said grimly. "He was escorted from the square by two of Lamd's men shortly after daybreak two days ago."

Eirriel touched her right earring, activating the transmittor. Garreth would want to hear this, she thought, confident that he would keep to the plan and listen silently.

"You haven't seen him since?" she asked, her eyes flickering between the two brothers.

Both shook their heads.

"Segar mentioned the possibility that he faced . . . faced . . ." Her voice trailed off and she lowered her eyes. When she raised them a brief time later, they glistened with unshed tears. "Execution," she finished in a voice barely above a whisper.

"Save your tears, green eyes," Koltrax said tenderly. "There's been no execution. Not yet, anyway."

"You're sure?"

Koltrax nodded. "Lamd likes to do things in a big way. If he planned to execute Aubin, we'd all know about it. In fact, our presence at the 'ceremony' "—his lips curled in disgust as he said the word—"would be mandatory. It has been in the past."

After a few moments of silence, Koltrax started from the stall. "You stay with Boruk, Eirriel. I'll be back."

"Koltrax! Wait!"

Eirriel called after him, but Koltrax merely turned, threw her a kiss and continued on his way.

Angrily she faced Boruk. "Where's he going?"

"I can't tell you."

"You have to!" she insisted.

Boruk shook his head.

Eirriel stared at him, torn between the order to keep silent about the monitor and the need to warn Koltrax. Was there a way to do both? She touched the earring, breaking contact with the *Celestial*.

"Boruk," she began, her voice a desperate whisper. "You must tell me! Koltrax is in great danger!"

Again, Boruk shook his head. Eirriel could have screamed in frustration. There was no way around it. She had to tell him. "You don't understand! Lamd has a weapon that's unlike anything used before. It's . . . it's . . ."

As she groped for words to explain, Boruk stepped closer. He placed a hand on her shoulder. "What you don't understand, Eirriel, is that I do."

Eirriel blinked in bewilderment. "You know?"

"Yes. As long as he stays out of Lamd's sanctuary, I can shield him."

Eirriel's eyes rounded in awe as she realized what he was saying. Boruk was a telepath! And a powerful one at that. Certainly his skills were greater than hers.

"Not necessarily greater, Eirriel. Just more developed."

"You can read my mind?"

"Now that you've dropped your barrier, I can. It's not something I can do all the time and not always clearly. Sometimes I only receive vague impressions." He gave a rueful smile. "I wish it was more, then I'd *know* what Lamd was plotting."

"Can't you do anything to stop him?"

He shook his head. "Not yet, anyway. Each year my skill

becomes greater and my range broader. Right now I can do nothing more than shield Koltrax and determine those who are truly against Lamd."

"How much does Koltrax know?"

"Not much. I felt it better this way. Koltrax is not one who would like being protected, especially by his younger brother. Besides, I must not be involved. At least not yet," he added, his voice burdened by future knowledge.

Eirriel gazed into his intense blue eyes saddened by his forefeited youth and at the same time reassured by his inner strength. Koltrax was safe. Now all she had to do was wait for his return to learn if her beloved was safe as well.

Across the square, hidden from view by a deserted carrier, two men in red and gold watched Koltrax's departure with interest. The taller of the two pressed one of the jewels on his wristband.

"Leader Lamd?"

"Yes, Tondl, what is it?" came the immediate reply.

"The hawker, Koltrax, has left."

"And the woman?"

"She is alone with the boy."

"Good. Remain as you are. I'll be there as soon as I've seen to the prisoner. Lamd out."

"Boruk, shouldn't Koltrax be back by now?" Eirriel asked, a worried expression on her face.

The youth shrugged. "He'll be back when he has the information he seeks. There's no need to worry."

"I can't help it!"

Another few minutes passed, then Eirriel slammed her hands on the counter. "I'm not waiting any longer, Boruk. I'm going to find him!"

Before Boruk could stop her, Eirriel ran out of the stall.

"Eirriel! Come back!" he called, running after her.

"Not until I find Koltrax!" she yelled over her shoulder.

"Eirriel!"

A deep shout from behind her made her spin around. Koltrax stood next to Boruk, his hands on his hips and a fierce scowl on his face. Frightened of his anger, Eirriel paled and grabbed the nearby stall for support. Realizing instantly what she was thinking, Koltrax forced himself to smile and strode to her, his mouth forming the words, "He's alive." With a cry of relief, Eirriel flung herself into his arms and smothered his face with kisses.

"Enough, green eyes." Koltrax laughed, gently putting her aside.

"Is he all right? Can I see him? Does he know I'm here?" she asked excitedly as they walked back to the stall.

"Not so fast, pretty lady. I only learned that he's still alive and where he's been quartered."

"But you're sure he's unharmed?"

"I didn't say that," he corrected gently. "I'm afraid a few days in Lamd's untender care does not insure good health."

"Is it possible to free him?"

"I believe so."

"When can we—"

"*We* are not doing anything," Koltrax said firmly. "I am."

"I'm coming with you!"

"No, you are not!"

Eirriel's eyes flashed with rage. "You can't stop me!"

"Listen, green eyes," Koltrax said, taking her hands in his, "we can sit here and argue the rest of the day away or . . . Or"—he raised his voice when she started to speak—"I can go through with my plans. It's your choice." He paused, then added in a voice that forbade defiance, "But either way, you are staying here."

"But—"

"Eirriel, I know you're anxious to see him, but if you would just think for a minute you'd realize that I'm right. If he's going to be rescued, it has to be done fast. My men and I are familiar with the pits of Lamd's Sanctuary."

"Lamd's Sanctuary!"

"Of course. Where else would someone as valuable as your Aubin be kept," he replied dryly.

Eirriel grabbed Koltrax's arm. "You can't go in there. There's got to be another way. Aubin would not want you to risk your life for him!"

He raised haunted green eyes to her. "It's no longer just for Aubin, Eirriel. Lamd took two of my men yesterday for questioning. One is already dead, the other barely alive. I have to go."

"Can't you send somebody else? Boruk, make him see . . ."

"He's doing what he has to do."

Boruk's grave voice silenced her protests, but it was the look of grim resignation in his piercing blue eyes that sliced her heart in two. She lowered her eyes in defeat.

"When will you leave?"

"Right now."

"Now!" Her head jerked up and she stared at him as if he had suddenly gone crazy. "But it's still light! Don't you think it would be safer after dark?"

Koltrax shook his head and said grimly, "With Lamd darkness doesn't always bring safety. Often it's just the opposite. No, our advantage is surprise and speed. I don't think Lamd expects anyone to care enough about Aubin to risk their life for him and he doesn't know who I am or that I know he has my man."

"You will be careful?" she whispered, her fear for him reflected in her luminous green eyes.

The hawker's intense gaze studied her upturned face. When he returned, she would take her lover and walk out of his life forever. Knowing he shouldn't, but knowing it would be easier to stop himself from breathing, Koltrax pulled her to him and lowered his mouth to hers for an all-too-brief, bittersweet taste of what he could never have. Reluctantly, he raised his head.

"Oh, green eyes," he said, his deep voice husky with emotion, "why couldn't I have met you first?"

Eirriel said nothing. Koltrax would always be special to her, but her very soul belonged to Aubin. It could never be otherwise. And Koltrax knew it. He stepped away from her.

"Boruk?"

"Yes, brother?"

"Keep her safe. If she tries to leave, knock her out. Understand?"

"Yes," he said quietly. "I understand."

"Koltrax? Thank you."

"Don't thank me, Eirriel," he said, his need to take her

back in his arms and the knowledge that he couldn't made his voice gruff. "As I told you, I'd be going anyway. Besides"—he gave them both a lopsided grin—"I'd do anything to cause trouble for Lamd."

The rebel leader gave them a cheerful wave and left.

Since Boruk already knew about the transmittor, Eirriel turned her back from any other prying eyes and reported to Garreth, as Boruk stood off to the side, greedily drinking in what he knew to be his last sight of his much-loved brother.

The young hawker was not the only one observing Koltrax's departure with emotion. Across the square, Lamd had joined his men just as the angry hawker had roared Eirriel's name and had watched their warm reunion and tender leave-taking with a slow, seething rage.

"Tondl," Lamd said, his voice deceptively calm, "I want that rebel and I want him now."

The officer nodded to two of his men and they silently melted into the crowd.

"As for the woman," Lamd continued, "bring her to me."

"And the other?"

"The child?" Lamd shrugged. "Leave him. Unless, of course, he gets in the way."

"And then?"

"Kill him."

Chapter Twenty-four

Eirriel looked up and saw two men in red-and-gold uniforms standing in front of the stall.

"Yes, may I help you?"

"Indeed you can," said the younger man. "You're to come with us."

Eirriel frowned. "Me? Why?"

"You'll find out in good time, little lady. Now let's go."

"Who are you?" Eirriel demanded, beginning to worry.

"Strange that you don't know," the older man commented as he stepped inside the stall. "Don't you think so, Karal?"

Karal nodded. "That it is, Manyx."

"You seek something?" Eirriel gave a sigh of relief as Boruk entered from the back. "Perhaps I can help you."

"We don't need any help, child," Manyx snickered. "We have what we seek right here."

With that, he grabbed Eirriel roughly by the arm.

"Get your hands off me!" she ordered through clenched teeth.

"Let go of her!" Boruk demanded. "Or I'll—"

Arrogantly Manyx stared down at the youth. "Or you'll

what?" he challenged.

In answer, Boruk threw himself fiercely at Manyx forcing him to release Eirriel. But the young hawker was no match for Lamd's well-trained officer and he quickly found himself on the ground, a deadly-looking weapon pointed at his chest.

"No!" Eirriel cried, throwing herself in front of Boruk.

"Get out of my way, woman!" Manyx roared.

She glared at him defiantly. Karal jumped over the counter and dragged her away. Caught in his iron grip, Eirriel knew her struggles to be useless.

"Don't hurt him," she begged. "He's only a child."

Boruk rose slowly to his feet. "Child I may be," he said quietly, his eyes dark with rage, "but I won't let them take you."

Eirriel met his blazing eyes with her pleading ones. "Yes, you will, Boruk," she said urgently. "You must!"

Boruk ground his teeth in frustration. As much as he ached to feel Manyx's face under his fist, he knew Eirriel was right. Hating himself, he stepped back.

With a smug grin, Manyx lowered his weapon. "Let's go," he barked, "before I decide I've been too easy."

His face burning with humiliation, Boruk watched helplessly as they led Eirriel away.

Eirriel stared at the transmittor laying in her open palm and fought the urge to fling it across the chamber and watch it smash against the wall. Putting it back in her ear, she crossed to the window. Standing with her back to the portal, she stared up at the stars clearly visible now that Annan's sun had set. Somewhere out there was the *Celestial* and Garreth.

Why hadn't he answered her? Was it possible the transmittor was damaged? Her lips twisted grimly. More likely it was being blocked just as Segar's had been. Well, whatever the reason, she was on her own—unless by some miracle Aubin had been freed and, with Koltrax's aid, was able to find his way to her side. Her fingers toyed with the circlet as her mind pictured Aubin strolling toward her, free and unharmed.

She shook her head. There would be time for that later.

Now she had to concentrate on Lamd and the story she would tell him when he arrived. No matter what, she couldn't let him learn of her true connection with the Protectorate.

Deep in thought, Eirriel did not hear the portal open. Neither did she hear the sound of heavy footsteps as they crossed the floor and stopped just behind her. Instead, it was the sense of being watched that forced awareness on her and made her skin crawl. Whirling around, her eyes grew wide with fright as she saw him. She clutched the nearby chair for support, her dry throat refusing to give voice to her soundless cry. The harsh, evil laugh she knew so well echoed loudly in her ears. She closed her eyes against him and pressed her palms to her ears, but he stepped closer and forced her hands to her side.

"Surprised to see me, my dear?" Kedar asked, his voice sending an icy numbness through her veins.

Too stunned to do more than stare, Eirriel allowed him to guide her to a chair. Almost gratefully, she accepted the drink he pushed into her hand. She raised it to her lips and emptied it. Without taking her eyes from him, she placed the goblet on the table.

"How . . . how did you find me?" she stammered as the burning liquid began to revive her deadened senses.

"Believe it or not, quite by accident. I had no idea you were the woman in the marketplace." He lowered his lean frame into the chair facing hers, an amused smirk on his face. "Then why am I here?"

Eirriel nodded.

"That, my sweet, is easy. I got bored with the spineless creatures on your wretched world. When Tozgor requested my presence on Annan, I eagerly complied. And you? I seem to recall putting you on a ship bound for Blagden."

"It crashed. I was pulled from the burning wreckage by the miner, Chal."

"Burning wreckage?" He raised his brows. "You seem to have escaped remarkably fit."

"Yes, it seems I was lucky, although it wasn't until recently that my memory returned. And not fully," she added. "There are still things I can't remember."

"Yet you remembered me."

"You!" she spat. "No matter how badly someone is hurt, they never forget the slime that caused their hurt!"

"I see your tongue is still as sharp as ever," he growled. "Tell me, if you were rescued by miners, why are you in Sumal and not one of the mining camps?"

She tossed her head. "I was bored. Sumal promised excitement."

"How did you live?"

"There are ways," she said brazenly.

Watching her with his piercing black eyes, he demanded suddenly, "Is that how you met Koltrax?"

She met his gaze coolly. "Among others."

He arched his brow. "Who?"

"Oh, come now." She laughed coyly. "Do you really want to know?"

He nodded.

"Well, let me see." She started naming any name she could think of, ticking them off on her fingers as she did. "There was Chal, of course, his brother Stef, Toxman, Maln, Theron, Jarce, Kaye, Koltrax, whom you've already mentioned. Hmm. I think I've forgotten some one. Oh, yes. Yvel and . . ."

"Aubin perhaps?"

Kedar had supplied his name so quickly that she couldn't help the small catch in her voice when she said, "Aubin? No, no Aubin?"

Kedar's fist slammed on the table. "Liar! Don't you think I know that you came searching for him!"

Eirriel felt a sinking sensation in her chest. "But I wasn't."

"Oh, come now," he said wearily. "My men reported your charming little scene to me shortly after it happened. They've been watching you all along. Waiting until you were alone to bring you to me."

"Bring me here?" she repeated, frowning. "Your men? But it was Lamd's men . . ." Her eyes shot open and her hand flew to her mouth. "Lamd! You're Lamd!"

Kedar chuckled. "How clever you are, my sweet. Yes, I'm Lamd. It suited my purpose to use another name." He sat back casually, and rested his elbows on the chair side. His hands locked together, one finger on either side of his nose, he studied her from under his hooded eyes. "I suppose you know what that purpose is?"

Her heart pounded fiercely in her chest. Not trusting her voice to stay steady, she shook her head. He flung himself from the chair and yanked her to her feet.

"I've had enough of this game." His eyes glittered like black crystals. "You'll tell me what I want to know and you'll tell me now!"

"I don't know what you're talking about!"

"I think you do." He threw her back into the chair. "My dear, we are about to make the first of two bargains."

Eirriel's lips twisted in contempt. "Bargain with you?" she sneered. "I'd sooner bargain with the black god himself!"

Placing his hand on the arm of her chair, Kedar leaned forward, his face inches from hers. "I think, my lovely Eirriel, that if you are not careful you just might find yourself in that position."

"Compared to yours, his company would be refreshing!"

"And the captain? Would you see him there as well?"

Eirriel paled.

"I thought not."

Kedar straightened and turned from her. It was in that moment that she made her move. With lightening speed she snatched up the goblet and smashed it on the table's edge. Armed with the jagged glass, she lunged at Kedar. Warned by the sound of shattering crystal, Kedar stepped easily out of her way. Eirriel whirled and faced him. Keeping her arm fully extended, she made wide sweeping motions with her impromptu weapon. An amused smirk on his lips, Kedar remained immobile, his dark eyes following Eirriel as she backed slowly toward the portal.

"That won't do you any good, my dear," Kedar taunted. "The portal is secured."

Finding that to be true, Eirriel shrieked with frustration. Frantically her eyes scanned the chamber. There had to be another way out. As if he could read her mind, Kedar gave a sadistic laugh.

"There is no escape," he said deliberately. "I lost you once, Eirriel. I will not again."

Eirriel sucked in her breath. She could not, would not be his plaything! Preferring death, she charged Kedar, but he had anticipated her move. Throwing himself to the floor, he curled into a ball and knocked her over with his rolling body. With the skill of a warrior, he was on his feet before she regained her balance. Grabbing her wrist, he twisted her arm behind her back.

Gasping with pain, she fought desperately to free herself, but to no avail. Her strength deserted her and she sagged against him. Kedar felt her surrender and released her, his triumphant laugh harsh in her ears as she slumped weakly to the floor. She raised her tear-stained face to him.

"Why . . . didn't . . . you . . . kill . . . me?" she asked between sobs.

"Because, my little warrior, is not death the greatest escape of all?"

Exhausted, her head hanging in defeat, Eirriel did not even protest when he picked her up and sat her in the chair.

"Now then," he said, backing away from her. "Where were we? Oh, yes. You were telling me about Aubin and how you met."

"He—he rescued me," she said in a small voice. "The ship was damaged by a meteor storm."

"And when did this happen?"

"Four—four months ago."

"And your position on the *Celestial*?"

Her voice dropped to a whisper. "His woman."

Kedar arched his brow in disbelief. "His woman?"

"Yes."

"His woman!" Kedar snickered, greatly pleased by her lowered status. "How did you get here?"

Pulling herself together, Eirriel took a deep breath. "With Aubin. I was bored, seeing nothing but the walls of his cubicle all day long. I promised to make it well worth his trouble if he took me along."

"Why did he come here?"

She shrugged. "I don't know."

"You expect me to believe that," he drawled.

"Believe whatever you want!" she snapped. "Why would the captain of a powerful fleetship confide in me—a mere woman?"

"If that's true, then why did you search for him? Surely someone else could have easily taken his place."

"I thought of that. But unfortunately Captain Aubin is my only way off this barren piece of rock."

Kedar did not believe Eirriel, but he knew he would get no other answer from her this way. Slyly he decided to try another route. "Would you like to see your captain?" he asked suddenly.

Eirriel couldn't help the light that sprang to her eyes and Kedar couldn't help but notice. *And she would have me believe the captain means nothing more to her than a way off this world,* Kedar smirked. *Well, she will pay for her little deception.* But first there were other matters to attend to. He crossed to the wardrobe and pulled out a long, hooded cape.

"Put this on," he ordered, flinging it at her. "You'll need it where we're going."

He led her from the cubicle into a long corridor, down a winding narrow stairway, through another twisting corridor to the rear of the sanctuary and into the courtyard. They crossed to a large stone building. Stepping aside, Kedar pulled the massive door open.

"After you." As she brushed past him, he grabbed her wrist. "Do not make a sound. It's not my plan that he should see you . . . yet. That will come later. But be warned"—he shook her arm—"any sound from you will cause him great harm."

He yanked the hood forward so that her face was well concealed.

Eirriel entered the stone building, her stomach heaving at the stench of the stale air. Walking down another corridor, they stopped abruptly at the rounded entrance of a larger chamber. Kedar reached for a small unit attached to his belt and aimed it at the flickering portal.

"That's close enough," he warned as he stepped through the now-darkened threshold. Again, he aimed the unit and the chamber was illuminated, the dull glow casting eerie shadows on the stone walls.

Eirriel bit her lip in an attempt to quelch the cry of dismay that sprang to her throat at the sight that greeted her eyes. The vault was small, damp and at least two centuries old. Aubin stood across from her, his arms shackled by a glowing energy field so high above his head that he was forced to remain on his feet. His pants were torn in several spots, a large bloodied tear over his right thigh evidence of some deep, grievous wound.

"Captain," Kedar called cheerfully, stepping closer, "how are you this lovely evening?"

Aubin raised his head and glared at Kedar, golden sparks of defiance flashing across his hard, mocking eyes, eyes, though almost swollen shut from numerous beatings, silent testimony to the strong will and determination of the Rhianonian. The small gasp that escaped Eirriel's tightly clenched lips at the sight of her beloved's bruised and battered face drew Aubin's attention. Afraid that he might recognize her, she drew further back into the shadows.

"Don't concern yourself with my lady, Captain," Kedar said glibly. "I tried to convince her that the sights down here would exceed even her perverted appetites, but she wouldn't listen. Had to see you for herself. Didn't you, my sweet?"

In answer, Eirriel mimicked Chalandra's low, lusty laugh. Kedar ran his hand lightly down her back and pulled her to him, aware that her face remained hidden.

"What did I tell you, Captain?" Kedar said silkily. "Lusty wench she is. Quite a comfort at the end of the day as well."

Kedar's gloating chortle echoed off the hollow walls. His inference might fall on unconcerned ears now, but when the lady's identity was revealed, Aubin was sure to remember the subtle hints he heard today.

The possessive arm about her waist and Kedar's lewd remarks that she feared were prophetic proved too much for her. Her careful control slipped and her mind cried out. *Aubin, my love*!

Aubin's head jerked up. "Eirriel?"

Aubin's hoarse cry made Eirriel aware of her blunder. She paled. Anxious green eyes studied the darkly handsome face of her captor. What was he thinking? How would he make

Aubin pay for her mistake? All too soon the answer came.

"So, Captain, the mere sight of a woman, even one whose face and shape you cannot see, teases your senses and brings a name to your lips." His lips twisted into an evil smirk. "Your reputation is well known. That you remember her name proves to me that she means a great deal to you. I must say it pleases me greatly. What was her name? Ah, yes. Eirriel. A beauty I am sure. All your women are. Tall, slender with gleaming tresses, and sparkling eyes. Tell me, Captain, could it be that she warms your heart even as she warms your restorer? Eirriel. Does the name evoke memories of soft, silky skin? Of firm breasts that quicken under your touch? Of a voice that turns husky with passion as you thrust yourself deep inside of her? I hope so, Captain. Because memories are all you will ever have of her again. I will find your Eirriel and I will make her mine!"

"No!" Aubin roared, pulling at his restraints.

"Yes. And I have ways of making a woman mindless with passion. By the time I finish with her, your Eirriel will be mine. In every way."

"Never, you bastard!" Aubin bellowed, his enraged struggles increasing as Kedar's confident laugh rang out. "You'll never have her! *Never!*"

"We will see, my good Captain," Kedar said softly. "We will see."

Kedar's taunts and Aubin's words ripped through Eirriel's soul. How could Aubin know that Kedar's words were no empty threat? Silent tears streamed from her eyes as she listened to the man she loved deny what had already happened. By all the gods, if he should learn who the woman in the shadows really was. . . . She gasped as Kedar grabbed her arm and led her from the chamber.

Kedar's taunting snickers bore into Aubin's brain as the vault plunged into darkness and he was once again alone with his thoughts.

"I warned you," Kedar railed through gritted teeth, his grip tightening painfully about her arm.

Kedar couldn't know! "I did nothing," she protested frantically. "Nothing!"

"That may be, my sweet, but somehow he sensed your

presence." The Blagdenian commodore's black eyes lit with an evil glow as he recalled the sudden look of shocked hope that had flickered across his prisoner's face. So the Rhianonian had tender feelings for the lovely Dianthian. He had not counted on that bit of good fortune. He licked his lips in anticipation. How much better for his plans. He shivered as the damp chill penetrated the heavy fabric of his uniform.

"Come, my pet. We have much to discuss."

Eirriel yanked her arm from him. "There is nothing I wish to discuss with you, Commodore!" *Nothing that I dare give voice to*, she amended silently.

Kedar arched his brow in surprise. "Pardon me, my lady," he replied smoothly, giving her a short, cursory bow. "I was under the impression the fate of the good captain would interest you. I must have erred."

Eirriel blanched, a look of anguish marring her lovely features.

"Judging from your waning complexion, I would venture that my first conjecture was correct." He paused waiting for a reply, when none was in the offing, he demanded, "Well, was it?"

Not trusting her voice, Eirriel nodded.

"Then I suggest you mind your manners, my dear," he said icily. "The future of Captain Aubin lies solely in my fickle hands. You would do wise to remember that. Now come along." He grabbed her arm again. "This place is as cold as the dead."

Once back in Kedar's lavish lodgings, Eirriel wrenched her arm from Kedar's grasp and crossed to the opposite side of the chamber, the distance giving her a false sense of security. Kedar ignored her minor display of defiance and poured two beakers of a sparkling orange liquid.

"There is no need for the cloak, my sweet. These chambers are sufficiently warmed."

Eirriel favored him with a withering look. It wasn't the chill of the chamber that made her keep the cloak wrapped so tightly around her, but the warmth of his regard.

When she made no attempt to obey him, Kedar bristled. The bitch was as haughty as ever! He stormed across the chamber and, with one quick motion, tore the offensive garment from her shoulders and dropped it to the floor.

"Ah, much better." He waved his hand in the direction of the sumptuous couch. "Please make yourself comfortable." Again, she made no move to obey his wishes. Scowling, he grabbed her arm, dragged her across the chamber, and threw her onto the couch. Her green eyes blazing with fury, Eirriel started to rise but the icy blackness in Kedar's eyes warned her against it. "You have much to learn, my sweet Eirriel," Kedar growled. "I will tolerate only so much defiance." He handed her a beaker. "Now, what shall we toast to, sweet lady? Life or death?"

The color drained from her face as his allusion pierced her angry mind, but, as before, she refused to answer.

"Come, no answer?" he chided. "Well, then, shall we try new beginnings?" He looked at her over the edge of his beaker. "Drink!"

Mechanically she emptied the beaker. The fiery liquid seared her throat, bringing tears to her eyes and she gasped for breath. Kedar allowed himself a moment to savor her discomfort, then moved to the table. Standing with his back to her, he slowly refilled his beaker.

"Since it is obvious that you place great value on the life of my Rhianonian guest, I think now is the time for our remaining bargain. However, unlike our earlier one, I won't press you for an answer right this moment." He paused, then added, "You have until tomorrow morning." He turned and faced her.

Eirriel's fingers tightened around the stem of the beaker as she saw his look of unbridled lust.

"I want you," he stated, the deadly calm in his voice reinforcing her fears. "I have since that morning you burst into your father's chamber. But I want you willing and loving."

Eirriel rose, her eyes ablaze. "Never!"

A sneer twisted his thin lips. "Never, my dear Eirriel, is a long time. Now do be so good as to sit down. You have not yet heard my proposal."

Knowing she had no choice, she stiffly did as he bid.

"You *are* learning," he observed dryly, then continued in

a light tone that belied the seriousness of his words. "Here's the bargain. You will return with me to Dianthia where you will be my loving, obedient consort. In return, I will grant your captain his life. If, however, you choose to turn down my generous offer, you will accompany me anyway, as my slave, but only after you have witnessed the slow, tortuous death of your former protector, as well as the destruction of the *Celestial*. Oh, yes," he added at her shocked stare, "I know she's well within range. How else would the captain get here except by his own ship? I will take my leave now, but be warned. I expect an answer by morning." He started toward the portal, then turned to her. "Oh, I almost forgot. Should any harm come to you by your own hand I will be forced to take my sorrow out on Captain Aubin, the *Celestial*, and," he paused dramatically, "your people."

Eirriel gasped. "But you can't! Of any of us they are innocent!"

Crossing the chamber, he pulled her to him. "Oh, but I can and I will," he promised, lowering his mouth to hers.

Seeing his face coming closer, Eirriel struggled to free herself but failed. His mouth took hers savagely and he kissed her long and passionately.

"Just a sample of what is to come," he whispered in her ear.

Without thinking, Eirriel's hand shot out and she slapped him across the face.

"Bitch!" Kedar struck her, the force of the blow driving her to her knees. His eyes became black orbs of burning coal and his lips drew back, revealing tightly clenched teeth as he raised his hand to strike her again. She cringed against the impact, but Kedar halted. "No, I won't hit you again. I wouldn't want to risk damaging your lovely face. There are better ways to punish you." He stormed across the chamber and yanked the portal open. "If you'll excuse me, my dear, I think I'll pay another visit to my other guest."

"No! Please!" Eirriel threw herself at Kedar. "I'm sorry! It won't happen again!"

"No, I'm sure it won't," he rasped, flinging her from him.

Kedar's depraved laughter resounded through her head as she watched the portal close and heard the metallic click of the lock. "No!" Her fists pounded frantically against the portal. "AUBIN!" Tears running from her eyes, she leaned weakly against the portal. "Aubin!" She slumped to the floor, her head in her hands. "What have I done? What have I done?"

Across the darkened courtyard, in a cold, dank vault, an exhausted fleetship captain cried out in his sleep. "Eirriel."

Chapter Twenty-five

"Lady Eirriel, my Lord Lamd asks that you prepare yourself for him," the young Annanite said meekly.

Eirriel stood with her back to the girl, staring at a large, stone building that housed a captive dear to her heart.

"He wants you to wear this."

"Place it on the restorer, girl, then leave," Eirriel said wearily.

"I cannot! Lord Lamd has commanded that I help you dress. I dare not disobey him!"

The fear and youth in the girl's voice forced its way through Eirriel's morose thoughts. She turned, her red-rimmed eyes registering surprise. "Why, you're just a child!"

"I'm sixteen, my lady!" she said proudly.

"Sixteen!" She looked no more than twelve. "What are you called?"

"Edrea."

"Well, Edrea, I suppose I have little choice. I can't have Ked . . . Lamd punishing you because of me. Prepare my vitalizer, please."

Edrea raised her large, violet eyes. "Vitalizer?"

Eirriel sighed. She'd forgotten that most of this world's inhabitants only spoke a smathering of Hakonese. "I wish to wash, child."

"Oh, yes, milady. Right away."

As Edrea scurried off to the smaller chamber, Eirriel again turned her eyes and thoughts to Aubin. *My love, will you know what I do this day? If only I could see you, even for a moment, and explain.*

Eirriel shuddered. Explain what? she thought bitterly. Explain that she must give herself to the most vile serpent that ever slithered from the slimy ooze of Blagden! That she must do so willingly, in exchange for Aubin's life even though she knew he would rather die than see her do this. Her mind flooded with pain. As for herself, she would rather do it than not, for the consequences if she refused were too great. At least Aubin would live even though he would be lost to her forever. Her only consolation was the knowledge that he would never learn that she was with Kedar and why.

"Milady," Edrea called from the inner chamber. "All is ready."

Eirriel cast one last mournful look in the direction of Aubin's prison, then turned to begin her preparations for Kedar.

Attaching the billowing, diaphanous, silver cape to the shoulders of her gown, Eirriel stood in front of the reflector and surveyed herself.

Made of soft, free-flowing, black material, the gown was cut so that the long, narrow sleeves, full skirt, tight bodice and low neckline greatly accentuated her tall, slender frame. She had chosen to wear no jewelry except for the Syna Circlet, gambling that Kedar would not know its significance. Edrea had drawn her hair back in a knot, carefully combing it over the circlet so all that showed was a slim, golden band across her forehead.

Kedar had chosen well, she observed bitterly. The garment's design gave her a regal beauty, while the color set off the paleness of her skin and the golden color of her hair. Her glance drifted upward and eyes that glittered like green ice stared back at her.

"Hail, Eirriel, Ice Queen," she jeered, mocking the glacial void that was now her soul.

A sound from behind drew her attention. She whirled, her gown twisting around her from the sudden moment and saw Kedar standing at the open portal, his black eyes glistening with anticipation.

"So you chose to come with me after all. I am glad."

"Chose to come with you!" she replied disdainfully, her back straight, her head high. "Surely even you can see that's not the case. Choice!" Her sharp, bitter laugh sliced the air. "There was no choice."

Kedar grimaced. *Still the proud bitch! Well, we shall see how long she remains such. We shall see indeed!* He offered Eirriel his arm.

"Come, precious one. We've two places to stop before we depart from this wretched, little world."

As he did the previous night, he led her through the long, winding passageway, down the stairway and out the rear portal. Instead of turning toward the stone building, they crossed the grassy courtyard to a large, cobblestone archway. Unlocking the heavy metal gate, he shoved her forward and stepped inside.

Eirriel turned puzzled eyes to Kedar. His lips were twisted into a cruel sneer and his eyes gleamed. Without a word he inclined his head toward the rear of the courtyard. Her frown deepened as she swung her head around and saw two men, one tied to a post, the other standing with his back to them, aiming a weapon at the bound man. Tightening his hand around her elbow, Kedar guided her closer to the prisoner.

"Koltrax!" she shrieked, recognizing the immobilized captive.

The brown-haired head was raised. "Eirriel!"

Eirriel snatched her arm from Kedar. Breaking into a run, she almost reached Kotrax when Kedar caught up with her. His arm shot out. Grabbing her roughly, he jerked her to a halt. Fighting to free herself from his powerful grip, she screamed Koltrax's name once more.

"You bastard!" Koltrax roared as he strained furiously against his bindings. "Take your filthy hands off her!"

Kedar watched the hawker's futile struggles with such obvious delight that Eirriel felt an icy terror grip her heart. What was Kedar planning to do?

As if he knew what she was thinking, he turned to her. "Did you ever see a sonulator before, my sweet?" he asked, pointing to the weapon held by the wyman.

A new wave of fear rushed over her. Her eyes grew round with horror and her throat closed around any denial she would have voiced.

Easily reading her, he smiled pleasantly. "Ah! I thought not. It's a simple, but deadly, weapon. The hybrid wave it emits resonates an object at such a rapid rate that it literally . . . How shall I put this? Oh, yes. Bursts into atoms. Observe."

Kedar nodded. The wyman aimed his weapon at his prisoner's heart. Then, Kedar raised his arm. In his hand was a smaller version of the sonulator.

"Cashor."

The Blagdenian turned to his commodore. His dark face paled and he stepped back, but it was too late. His screams of agony echoed throughout the courtyard long after he had vanished.

Kedar swung his hand toward Koltrax. "You have vexed me for the last time, hawker."

"No!" Eirriel threw herself in front of Koltrax.

Kedar grabbed her and yanked her away from the Annanite with such force that she staggered and fell to the ground. Her hair, long since fallen from its knot, spilled across her face. She whipped her head up, the curls tumbling riotously around her shoulders, and raised her face to the Blagdenian commodore.

"Please don't do this."

"Don't beg him, Eirriel," Koltrax growled.

"But—"

"No! My destiny has finally caught up with me. Nothing you can do will make it otherwise." His piercing gaze swung to his captor's dark face. "Are you ready, you bastard, to see how a man dies?"

"Oh, Koltrax."

There was a wealth of emotion in Eirriel's softly spoken

words and the perceptive hawker missed none of them. Green eyes locked with green and in doing so missed seeing Kedar, once again, raise his arm.

"I love you, green ey—"

"Noo!" Eirriel screamed as her horrified eyes watched the courageous rebel leader soundlessly disappear in a fatal burst of blue light. She dropped her head to her hands. Tears spilled from behind closed eyes and the ache in her heart made it difficult to breathe. What had she done? What had she done?

A hand on her shoulder commanded her attention. She forced all thoughts of Koltrax's violent death from her mind and focused on the loathsome beast who stood so smugly before her.

"Enough grieving. Get up."

Ignoring his proffered hand, Eirriel got to her feet.

"I'm sorry I put you through that, my dear," he said in a voice that implied otherwise. "But I felt it would make things easier if you knew where I stand."

Her glittering green eyes met his cold black ones. "I know only too well where you stand, Kedar. What puzzles me is how. Most of your kind slither on their bellies!"

Kedar sucked in his breath. "For your good and the good of those whose lives you hold in your hands, I will let your remark pass, coming as it did after such a disturbing sight. I will not again. Next time you will learn what I do to those who displease me. Now then, we've one last matter to see to. After that, we can devote our time to getting to know one another better. Much, much better. Follow me, please."

He led her through a passageway to the building that housed Aubin. He stopped and turned to her. Slowly he drew a small pouch from his pocket. "Give me your hand."

Eirriel raised her slim hand and was shocked when he dropped a solitary ear ornament into her palm.

"Ah, I see by your expression that you recognize it."

"But why shouldn't I recognize my own jewelry, Kedar?" She was about to ask for the mate, but she glimpsed the amused smirk on his face and knew her bluff had failed. She closed her mouth.

"That's better, my sweet. I'm glad you finally realize

there's no longer a need for pretense between us." He stared into her eyes. "You saw the sonulator. You saw what it can do. If you should displease me, or if you should even attempt to take your own life, I will not hesitate to turn it on your people. When they are destroyed, I will hunt down your captain and he will fare no better." His voice grew steely. "You, however, will not have the good fortune to die as they. Not right away, that is. First I will give you to my men. Do you understand?"

"Yes."

"I'm glad we understand each other. Now listen and listen carefully. You will use this transmittor to contact the *Celestial.* Giving them the co-ordinates 2-5-5 West, 4-6-9 North, you will tell them to give you fifteen minutes and then they are to activate the teleport."

Eirriel felt a wave of relief wash over her. Kedar was actually going to keep his word and free Aubin. Suddenly, her face fell. "It won't work, Kedar. The transmittor is damaged. I couldn't raise the ship when I tried yesterday and I know she was well within range."

Kedar snickered. "Oh, it works . . . now." Without giving her time to comment, he continued, "A word of warning. A lot can happen in fifteen minutes. Should you not follow my orders precisely, it will be a team of protectors, each armed with a sonulator, who will be teleported up to the *Celestial* instead of your captain, who, I'm sorry to add, would no longer exist."

"I'll do whatever you say."

"You remember the coordinates."

"Yes."

Kedar nodded to the transmittor. "Begin."

"Eirriel to the *Celestial.* Eirriel to the *Celestial.* Garreth, are you there?"

"Eirriel!"

Garreth's relieved cry brought tears to her eyes as she realized she would never see him again.

"Where the hell have you been? Why haven't you reported in sooner?"

She froze. For some ridiculous reason she hadn't expected any questions.

"Eirriel? Are you still there?"

Garreth's concerned voice and Kedar's sharp jab snapped Eirriel into action. "Yes, Garreth. I'm here. I ran into trouble yesterday. I had to hide. I couldn't risk contacting you, but everything's clear now."

"Did you locate Aubin?"

"Yes . . . yes, I did. It's . . . as we expected. He's been . . . captured."

"Eirriel, are you all right? You sound as if something is wrong."

"No!" Her reply was too quick. "No, Garreth, I'm all right. Just a little anxious to get Aubin safely aboard that's all."

"How do you plan to reach him?"

"I'm outside the building where he's being held. It'll take me about fifteen minutes to reach him."

"Is it safe? Can't you just give me his lat-logs and let me teleport you up now?"

Eirriel looked frantically at Kedar. She shut the transmittor down.

"What do I say to that?"

Kedar smirked. "You better think of something."

She reactivated the transmittor. "Garreth, are you still there?"

"Yes. What happened?" came the anxious reply.

"A protector passed. I couldn't chance being overheard. Now listen carefully. I've got to go in and isolate Aubin from the other prisoners. Are you ready for the lat-logs?"

"Why do you have to isolate Aubin? Can't we just teleport all of them up?"

"No! You can't do that!"

"Why?"

"You'll realize why after you've talked with Aubin."

"But—"

"Garreth, please! There isn't time to argue! The protector will pass again shortly. Here are the lat-logs. 2-5-5 West, 4-6-9 North."

Garreth repeated the numbers.

"Right."

"What about Segar? Is he dead?"

Segar's name brought Koltrax forcefully to Eirriel's mind and her face contorted with pain. Deliberately she turned her thoughts from him. There would be time to mourn later. Her lips twisted bitterly. Too much time.

"Yes, Garreth. I'm afraid Segar's dead. Now remember fifteen minutes. And, Garreth, have Cian at the teleport. Aubin's very seriously injured."

"He'll be there. Are you sure fifteen minutes will give you enough time?"

Eirriel glanced at Kedar who nodded. "Yes, I'm sure."

"Okay. Be careful. See you fifteen minutes from now."

"Good-bye, Garreth." Eirriel's voice choked as she deactivated the transmittor and handed it to Kedar.

"That was excellent, my dear," Kedar said silkily. "Now one more job." He threw her a sidelong glance. "It might require a little more acting. *He* must be convinced."

Eirriel's felt a sinking feeling deep in the pit of her stomach and her voice was little more than a whisper of dread as she asked, "He?"

"Why, Aubin, of course. I can't have him searching for you when he recovers, now can I?"

She knew then that he was going to make her pay for causing him to send her away from Dianthia. Make her pay by destroying forever the love Aubin had for her. Her heart contracted and she wanted to scream her anguish. "You want him to believe I betrayed him!"

"How quick you are. That is precisely what I want you to do."

"Please," she pleaded, "he doesn't know where Dianthia is. He won't be able to come after me."

"He'll come."

The certainty in his voice told Eirriel Kedar would not be swayed. Frantically, she sought any reason to prevent her from having to face Aubin and make their love a lie. "What if we let him think I died saving him. Yes," she cried desperately, "if he thinks I'm dead, he won't have to look for me."

Kedar merely smiled again and ignored her words. "Come," he said as he took her arm and led her inside. "Time is wasting and unless you want my men to teleport up to the *Celestial* in Aubin's place, we'd best hurry."

Aubin, now unshackled, was lying in a crumpled heap on the floor, the wound on his right thigh and a fresh one on his head both bleeding profusely. Tears in her eyes, Eirriel whirled on Kedar.

"You bastard! What have you done to him!"

"Be careful, my dear, he'll hear you. We wouldn't want him to think you hated me, now would we? As for his wounds, you needn't concern yourself. I believe the *Celestial* has a Drocot on board. It's rumored they can heal anything. I guess we'll put that to a test. Now dry your eyes and go to him. Time is running out."

It was a very pale Eirriel who entered Aubin's cell. She sank to the floor and gathered him in her arms.

"Aubin. Aubin, beloved, can you hear me?" For what she knew would be the last time, she let all the love and caring she had for this man pour into her voice. "It's me, Eirriel. Aubin, wake up."

"Eirriel? Is it really you?" His voice was a hoarse croak.

"Yes, it's really me."

"Knew you were near . . . felt you last night." He turned his aching head slowly toward the portal. "Garreth?"

"He's waiting for you on the *Celestial*."

Anger flickered across his eyes. "Shouldn't have let you come alone!"

"It was the only way."

"Had no right!" he ground out. "Promised!"

"Aubin, listen to me!" She lowered her voice to a whisper. "I'm the only one who could get past the monitor. No!" She pressed her finger against his cracked lips, stopping his questions. "Garreth will explain when he sees you."

He reached up and gently caressed her face. Eirriel leaned into his touch, knowing it would have to last her a lifetime.

"Can't believe you're here."

Unbearable agony ripped through her soul at the love she saw burning between his swollen lids.

"We had so little time," she whispered raggedly.

"Can't . . . hear . . . you," he rasped, finding it increasingly difficult to force words out of his parched throat.

"I said we're almost out of time. We must hurry. Do you

think you can stand?"

"Yes," he muttered, not at all sure he could.

Aubin gritted his teeth against the unbelievable pain that seared through him as Eirriel helped him to his feet. Leaning heavily on her, he limped to the stone bench. Gasping for breath, he sat down. Eirriel knelt at his feet, her deep concern for him evident in her pale face and dull eyes. In spite of the agony screaming at him from every part of his body, Aubin felt his heart swell with joy.

"Never . . . thought . . . I'd . . . see . . . you . . . again," he gasped. "So . . . beautiful."

Eirriel lowered her head, hiding eyes that were bright with tears.

Aubin grimaced as a fresh wave of pain washed over him. "Love . . . you . . . always . . . have."

A sob caught in her throat. Unable to bear his touch without returning it, she rose and slowly moved toward the portal.

"Where . . . are . . . you . . . going?"

With her back to him, she said, "Garreth will activate the teleport in a few minutes."

"Then . . . come . . . here."

She shook her head. "No."

"Too . . . far . . . miss . . . beam." His hoarse voice hinted at his confusion.

"I know," she said weakly. "I'm not going."

"Not . . . going!" Aubin staggered to his feet. "Can't . . . mean . . . that!" Ignoring the throbbing in his head and the spreading fire in his thigh, he stepped toward her. "You . . . can't . . . stay . . . here!" he ground out through teeth clenched tightly against the pain. His iron will fought the blackness that threatened to overcome him. "Won't . . . let . . . you!"

Eirriel shuddered at his words and the course they forced her to take. Her heart rebelled, her mind countered, her soul sobbed, her mind consoled. Drawing on an inner strength she didn't know she possessed, she straightened her back, turned and faced him. Nowhere in her icy, green eyes or cool, poised demeanor was there a glimpse of her tortured soul as the flame that burned within her flickered and died.

"Yet you remembered me."

"You!" she spat. "No matter how badly someone is hurt, they never forget the slime that caused their hurt!"

"I see your tongue is still as sharp as ever," he growled. "Tell me, if you were rescued by miners, why are you in Sumal and not one of the mining camps?"

She tossed her head. "I was bored. Sumal promised excitement."

"How did you live?"

"There are ways," she said brazenly.

Watching her with his piercing black eyes, he demanded suddenly, "Is that how you met Koltrax?"

She met his gaze coolly. "Among others."

He arched his brow. "Who?"

"Oh, come now." She laughed coyly. "Do you really want to know?"

He nodded.

"Well, let me see." She started naming any name she could think of, ticking them off on her fingers as she did. "There was Chal, of course, his brother Stef, Toxman, Maln, Theron, Jarce, Kaye, Koltrax, whom you've already mentioned. Hmm. I think I've forgotten some one. Oh, yes. Yvel and . . ."

"Aubin perhaps?"

Kedar had supplied his name so quickly that she couldn't help the small catch in her voice when she said, "Aubin? No, no Aubin?"

Kedar's fist slammed on the table. "Liar! Don't you think I know that you came searching for him!"

Eirriel felt a sinking sensation in her chest. "But I wasn't."

"Oh, come now," he said wearily. "My men reported your charming little scene to me shortly after it happened. They've been watching you all along. Waiting until you were alone to bring you to me."

"Bring me here?" she repeated, frowning. "Your men? But it was Lamd's men . . ." Her eyes shot open and her hand flew to her mouth. "Lamd! You're Lamd!"

Kedar chuckled. "How clever you are, my sweet. Yes, I'm Lamd. It suited my purpose to use another name." He sat

"Kedar?" Aubin stared at her in shocked disbelief. "Kedar?"

Eirriel gasped. He hadn't known! He had believed his captor to be Lamd. By all the gods, from her own lips had come the name that would condemn her for all eternity!

"No! Please!" she whispered brokenly. All strength left her and she would have crumpled to the stone floor if not for Kedar's arm clamped securely around her waist.

"Kedar!" Aubin growled the name that had haunted him for so long.

Golden eyes locked with black ones as Aubin saw his tormentor clearly for the first time, saw him and knew him for who he really was—his sister's murderer. He watched, momentarily stunned, as Kedar ran his hand possessively across Eirriel's hips, up her abdomen and slipped it inside her low neckline to fondle her breast.

back casually, and rested his elbows on the chair side. His hands locked together, one finger on either side of his nose, he studied her from under his hooded eyes. "I suppose you know what that purpose is?"

Her heart pounded fiercely in her chest. Not trusting her voice to stay steady, she shook her head. He flung himself from the chair and yanked her to her feet.

"I've had enough of this game." His eyes glittered like black crystals. "You'll tell me what I want to know and you'll tell me now!"

"I don't know what you're talking about!"

"I think you do." He threw her back into the chair. "My dear, we are about to make the first of two bargains."

Eirriel's lips twisted in contempt. "Bargain with you?" she sneered. "I'd sooner bargain with the black god himself!"

Eirriel forced herself not to pull away from his touch, but when he pressed his lips to her neck, she could not prevent the shiver of revulsion that swept through her.

Aubin's pain-wracked mind saw the shudder not as one of disgust but as one of enjoyment and he snapped. A venomous red mist descended, obscuring everything but the need to reach Kedar. With a snarl, he lunged forward.

At that very instant, a brilliant flash illuminated the cell and Aubin landed with a loud thud on the deck of the *Celestial's* teleport. Unable to believe he had been snatched away just when his lifelong enemy was finally within reach, Aubin roared with frustrated rage.

Rushing to his friend's side, an anxious Garreth bellowed for Cian. A few frantic moments passed before Garreth realized that Aubin had arrived alone.

"Eirriel?" Garreth cried, grasping Aubin's shoulder. "Where's Eirriel?"

Aubin closed his eyes against the agony that seared his soul. "Gone," he said bitterly, then sank into the welcoming arms of oblivion.

Chapter Twenty-six

Cian bent over the unconscious Aubin, angered by the sight of his bruised and battered body. Scowling, he passed the portable diagnostic unit over him.

"Mostly contusions and abrasions, with a fractured right radius, and an extensive laceration on his left thigh that will require immediate repair. He's already lost a lot of blood." He raised his head and glared at Garreth. "What in blazes happened down there? And where is Eirriel?"

Garreth shook his head. "I don't know. All he said before he passed out was that she was gone. Can you rouse him long enough for me to get some answers?"

The Drocot placed a thin, tubular device over Aubin's right temple. "This should do the trick for a while anyway. Talk to him and I'll arrange for the transporter."

Cian crossed to the intercom as Garreth knelt beside Aubin.

"Aubin," he called gently. Aubin's eyes flickered. "Aubin, wake up."

Swollen eyelids parted to reveal pain-dulled golden eyes. He touched his good hand to his face. "Hurts," he rasped.

"Yeah, I know." Garreth's voice was husky with emotion. "Lie still. Cian's calling for a transporter. No!" he cried as Aubin's eyes closed. "You've got to fight it!"

"Tired."

"I know, my friend, but I need some answers. Just stay awake a little longer and then you can sleep all you want. Okay?"

Aubin nodded.

Garreth placed his head close to Aubin's mouth. "Where's Eirriel?"

Aubin's face contorted with hatred. "Gone!"

"Where?"

"Don't know . . . don't care."

"With whom?"

Aubin spat out Kedar's name.

Garreth recoiled in surprise. "You've got to be mistaken! She wouldn't go with him. She hates him."

Aubin grabbed Garreth's arm, his grasp stronger than Garreth thought possible. "Believe what you want . . . told me herself."

"All right. I believe you," Garreth said quickly.

Aubin became increasingly agitated. Garreth tried to calm him, unsuccessfully.

"Too late . . . I was too late . . . Told her I loved her . . . laughed . . . told me . . . wouldn't amount to anything . . . wanted him . . . lovers . . ."

Garreth frowned. Something was terribly wrong. Eirriel loved Aubin more than life itself and hated Kedar just as passionately. As for Aubin never amounting to anything. . . . The very statement was absurd! She had told Raissa how much she was looking forward to being the consort of the future Lord Director. He thought back to his recent conversation with Eirriel. She had been vague and upset, had lied about it being too risky to use the transmittor, but at the time he had attributed it to her concern for Aubin. Now he wasn't sure. The only thing he knew was that he wouldn't get any clear answers from Aubin. At least not now.

"Like all the rest . . . should have kno . . ." Aubin's voice faded and his eyes closed as the drug-induced consciousness dissipated.

"Cian! He's out again!" Garreth called anxiously.

The Drocot laid a reassuring hand on his friend's shoulder. "That's as it should be, Garreth. His mind needs time to heal its wounds. Did you find the answers you sought?"

"Not all, I'm afraid. But I did learn where Eirriel is. She's with Kedar."

"Kedar!" Now it was Cian's turn to voice his shock. "Where's the safeguard team? We must—"

"No, Cian," Garreth cut in. "According to Aubin, she went willingly. Apparently she loves him."

"Of all the idiotic things I have ever heard," Cian huffed. "And, of course, the young fool believed her."

Garreth nodded grimly. "If you could have seen the mixture of torment and anger in his eyes, heard the hatred and confusion. She's either a consummate player or she really loves Kedar."

"She loves Aubin," Cian stated firmly.

Garreth sighed wearily. "Either way, I can't teleport down and bring her back." He stood up. "Take Aubin to the med-unit and do what you can. Call me at the com-center when he's stabilized."

Cian pressed a button on the hovering transporter and it lowered to the ground. With the help of Cian's two assistants, Aubin was carefully placed on the long, rectangular litter. As soon as he was settled, Cian punched another button and activated the air jets. Slowly the transporter rose to waist level.

"Direct it to the repair cubicle and be quick about it!" he ordered his assistants. "I'll be ready in five minutes."

Cian turned on his heels, his short legs carrying him quickly to the med-unit.

Garreth entered the com-center and immediately began issuing orders. "Theron, place the ship on caution watch. Jarce, get Raissa here now."

"Caution watch activated, sir."

"Raissa's on her way."

"Jarce, send the following message to Main Terminal on Hakon: Chronicle 179X14: D15-10M. Captain Aubin rescued and secured in the med-unit. Due to abusive treatment, he cannot be subjected to in-depth questioning.

However, he did report that culturist mate, Eirriel of Dianthia, was detained on Annan. He also has determined that Commodore Kedar of the Blagdenian Invasion Force is behind the political unrest there. The situation is highly unstable and I am requesting that you proceed with a diplomatic inquiry at once. We're remaining out of known Blagdenian tracking range while awaiting your orders. Garreth, Second-in-Command, E.P.F. *Celestial*. Relay that as a code six."

"Code six. Yes, sir."

Garreth activated the intercom and addressed the crew. "May I have your attention please. Captain Aubin has returned but is in need of rest. During his brief period of incapacitation, I am retaining command. All personnel are to remain at their watch stations until further notice. Garreth out."

"You wanted to see me, Garreth?" Raissa asked as she entered the com-center.

"Yes. I want you to tend the questors. You're to monitor Annan constantly, keeping alert for any signal that resembles the sonic pattern of Eirriel's transmittor. If it comes, it will be a brief, rapid signal. Unless you watch for it, it will be missed."

Raissa, sensitive as always to her life-bond's moods, set aside her questions until later and bent over the questor controls.

"Theron, set the viewing screen at maximum magnification. I want to be able to see anything that might be leaving Annan's orbit."

"Viewing screen on max."

Garreth depressed a switch on the console. "Ceara?"

"Ceara here, Garreth," the chief engineer promptly replied.

"Can you rig a tracer probe that will pass through a Blagdenian shield undetected?"

"Of course."

"It must also be able to lock onto the frequency of the TR-98 transmittor and relay a sporadic signal that our questors can monitor."

"How much distance will it have to cover?"

"That's up to you. In order to follow the warship, we'll need to be outside their tracking range. That will put us just inside ours and a quick move on their part would almost certainly cause us to lose them. I don't want to chance that. With a probe midway between our two ships we shouldn't have a problem tracking the movement of the warship. Can you do it?"

"I'll need time."

"How long?"

The intercom was silent as Ceara did some quick calculations. "About two hours," she said finally.

"That's too long, Ceara. I figure we've got little more than one hour—if that long," Garreth added grimly.

"It can't be done! I've got to completely rewire one of the ship's probes—"

"You can do it, Ceara," Garreth cut in earnestly. "You've got to!"

"I'm glad you think so," she muttered. "Ceara out."

The next hour was perhaps the longest hour of Garreth's life. He had always hated waiting, and now he found himself waiting for everyone. For Cian to report that Aubin would be all right. For Ceara to complete the probe. But more than anything, for Eirriel to make a move. He would never believe she stayed with Kedar freely. Never!

"Med-unit to com-center." Cian's voice broke into Garreth's thoughts.

"Yes, Cian?"

"Can you come to the med-unit?"

"I'm on my way," he replied, jumping to his feet. "Theron, Raissa, you know what to do. Call me when you have something to report."

"In here," Cian called when he heard the portals to the med-unit open.

Garreth's taut nerves relaxed as he gazed down on Aubin. Except for the discoloration on his face, all his wounds were healed.

"Then he's out of danger?" Garreth asked, his relief evident in his voice.

Cian nodded. "Physically. I've repaired all that was

needed, but he must be observed carefully for the next twenty-four hours just as a precaution." He pursed his lips and shook his head. "It's his spirit I'm concerned about. Sedated as he is, he keeps calling for Eirriel, alternately pleading with her to come back and damning her to a lifetime of misery." The small, blue man turned and left the cubicle. Garreth followed. "I don't buy it, Garreth," he said, absently stroking his beard. "She wouldn't leave him now that he's finally taken her for his. And for Kedar? Never!"

"More happened down there than we're aware of."

"So you think she's in danger?"

Garreth looked down at the medic, his grim expression far from reassuring. "I think she's in way over her head. It's my opinion—"

"Com-center to Garreth!"

Garreth flew to the wall unit. "Yes, Rai?"

"I've got the readout, Garreth. It was just long enough for me to get the lat-logs."

"On my way."

Garreth bolted from the med-unit and tore down the passageway, arriving at the com-center a little out of breath. He slammed his fist on the intercom. "Ceara! The tracer?"

"Almost done."

"Let me know the minute it's completed." He turned to Theron. "Anything on the screen yet?"

The Straton shook his head. "Nothing yet, Garreth."

"Raissa, those lat-logs, were they near the planet's surface?"

She looked at him with surprise. "Just above. But how—"

"I'll explain later. Feed those lat-logs into the navacomputer. Theron, alter our course so that we have a direct line of vision with those co-ordinates."

"Altering our course now."

"Rai, keep monitoring the questors. There's a possibility the transmittor may be activated again." Garreth hit the intercom. "Ceara, progress report!"

"We've run into faulty sensor panels, Garreth. It will take longer than I expected."

"How much longer, damn it?"

"About ten minutes."

"Ten minutes! That's too long."

"That may well be!" Ceara snapped. "But with three panels to be rewired and rerouted it can't be done any sooner!"

"Do the best you can, Ceara. Garreth out."

"Garreth, this just in from Main Terminal. Maintain position Two. Other fleetships are on the way. Should arrive within ten hours. Do not attempt to engage Blagdenian warships alone. You are to continue surveillance of planet until reinforcements arrive. I repeat. Do not engage Blagdenian warships alone. Shand, High Commander, Main Terminal, Hakon."

"Garreth!" Theron exclaimed, pointing to the viewing screen. "Look!"

Just moving into view, from behind the planet, was a Blagdenian warship!

"Theron, battle watch! Raissa, does the approximate position of that warship coincide with the signal's lat-logs if you take increasing velocity into account?"

Raissa's hands flew over the console. "Yes."

Garreth punched the intercom. "Ceara, is it ready yet?"

"No!"

"How much longer?"

"Five minutes."

The Rhianonian thought for a moment, his brow creased in concentration. "All right. You've got the five minutes. As soon as the tracer is completed place it in expulsion tube four, then notify me. Garreth, out. Theron, plot a course that will keep us in direct line with the warship, but just out of its range."

The chief navigator quickly punched the required data into his computer. "Course plotted."

Garreth's intense eyes flickered over Raissa, Theron and Jarce. In view of the latest message from Main Terminal he felt compelled to ask, "Does your stand on orders still hold?"

"Yes, sir!" the three declared simultaneously and emphatically.

"Then, Theron, proceed." As the Straton raised the control bar, Garreth turned to Raissa. "Rai, keep a watch on those questors. Let me know the instant you pick up that transmittor."

"Garreth!" Raissa cried. "They're firing at us!"

"Defense field on full!"

"Defense field on full," Theron reported rapidly.

The com-crew grabbed their consoles for support as the *Celestial* was rocked by a near miss of the sonulator.

"Ceara!" Garreth bellowed into the intercom.

"Ready!"

"Theron, you know where I want it. Relay those lat-logs to tube four."

Theron's hands flew over his console. "Lat-logs relayed."

"Ceara, discharge the tracer!"

"Tracer discharged!"

"There's the signal again!" Raissa cried.

"Jarce, patch it through audio."

The Xerthian activated the temporary relay and the air of the com-center crackled with static.

"Can't you clear—" Garreth began, but halted as Eirriel's frantic whisper became crystal clear.

". . . back! Please! It's a trap! You'll be destroyed! Go back!"

"Do you want to reply?" Jarce asked.

"No! We can't risk alerting Kedar to her transmission."

"You've got to get out of there!" Eirriel's voice grew louder, more insistent. "I didn't save Aubin's life for you to kill him now! Move! Damn you! Mo . . ."

"Jarce?" Garreth whirled to face his communications officer as Eirriel's voice was cut off.

His furry fingers checking and rechecking, Jarce's brown eyes met Garreth's. "Sorry, Garreth. Unless you want me to try and contact her, there's nothing I can do. She shut it off."

Before Garreth could reply, Raissa's startled exclamation followed directly by Theron's drew his attention. Jerking his head toward the viewing screen his face drained of color. Kedar's ship was no longer alone! Three other warships had appeared and now joined him in attack position. It was a trap just as Eirriel had said!

"They've destroyed the tracer!" Raissa reported. "Now they're firing—"

Garreth didn't give her time to finish. "Theron! Hard port, vel-ll! Get us the hell out of here!"

Chapter Twenty-seven

Eirriel was oblivious to her surroundings. She glanced neither to the right nor to the left, but stumbled along, responding automatically to the intermittent pressure on her right elbow, conscious only of the ever-increasing ache in her heart and the all-consuming emptiness in her soul.

Kedar led Eirriel through the narrow corridors of the warship, *Malin*, chafing at her halting step and dazed expression. What was wrong with the female? Had her senses flown? He gave her elbow a sharp jerk.

"Damn it, woman! Walk! I want you safely secured in my quarters before we break orbit."

Eirriel continued as before, in no way affected by Kedar' threatening tone if, in fact, she even heard it.

By the black god himself, she tries my patience! Kedar swore silently. *She might as well be dead for all the life she has shown since that interfering Rhianonian was returned to his ship. You'd think I had him exterminated rather than rescued!*

A smug smile curled his thin lips and an evil glint gleamed brightly in his black eyes. Captain Aubin was destroyed! Not in fact, perhaps, but in a way that was so much more satisfying. For the rest of his life he would have to live with the knowledge that the woman he loved preferred someone else's arms to his. Kedar frowned as he remembered the burning hatred that had darkened the piercing golden eyes when Eirriel had mentioned his name. It was as if it held some special meaning for the Rhiannonian. For a brief moment Kedar wondered when their paths had crossed, then shrugged it aside. Whatever the reason, above his possession of the woman Aubin loved, it only added to his satisfaction. The only regret Kedar had was that he had been unable to watch the Rhiannonian's face when he realized that vengeance, so close to assuagement, would have to wait until a further meeting.

Kedar drew Eirriel to a halt when they reached his quarters. He opened the threshold with a wave of his hand across the small, glowing box attached to the wall, then shoved her inside.

"If she gives you any trouble, call me at once," Kedar said, after ordering a protector to stand guard. "I'll be in the mastery."

"Yes, Commodore," the protector said, saluting. His massive legs apart, his large arms crossed in front of his barrel-shaped chest, Zod took his place before the threshold.

Kedar entered the mastery and assumed the seat of command. "Radnor, what's the most direct route back to Dianthia?"

The Blagdenian navigator studied his charts. Punching several buttons on the unit before him, he answered, "Twenty-seven, six NW."

"Keep us concealed behind the planet until the other warships are prepared, then move us out at A6 following the usual course. Once the last warship has departed and is out of tracking range veer to 27-6 NW and proceed at A12."

"Commodore, such a course will carry us directly across Protectorate territory," Lieutenant Harlan pointed out. "We could run into a fleetship or two which just might take offense to our being there."

"That's their problem, isn't it?" Kedar sneered. He turned and addressed Radnor. "When will we arrive in Dianthia?"

"Will we continue as part of the formation?"

Kedar laughed smugly. "We were never a part of that formation. I merely used their appearance to force the *Celestial* away."

"Then why were they here?" Radnor asked.

"The *Brangal's* commodore informs me they are on their way to quad 324 in division seventy-six. He wouldn't tell me the details of his mission, I can only hope it will further annoy the Protectorate. Since our path lies in their route, we'll use them to continue to deter the *Celestial*. Let them think we are part of a large force, and when we reach our turn point, the *Brangal* and *their* escort will continue on to their destination."

Radnor pointed to the star chart. "The *Brangal* will depart here?"

Kedar nodded.

"At our current speed we will reach the breakaway point in thirty-six hours. From there we will reach Dianthia in fifteen days, Commodore."

"Commodore Kedar." The *Malin's* first lieutenant strode over to him. "I would be remiss in my duties if I did not remind you that we will be in direct violation of numerous treaties once we enter Quad 51. Not to mention deceiving another commodore of your true motives. We cannot—"

The young man jumped when Kedar bellowed, "Cannot! There is nothing I *cannot* do, Lieutenant. Nothing! The *Brangal's* commodore would not be dismayed by my use of his escort, instead he would be jealous of my ability to use what is available to my best interest. As for the treaties you keep referring to, they are worthless pieces of diplomacy Tozgor agreed to only as a means to an end. It is his plan to lull the Protectorate into a false sense of security, then attack. Annan is just the first of many planets we will conquer."

Harlan arched his brows in disbelief and scoffed, "I can hardly forsee the Protectorate being foolish enough to recall all their fleetships from patrol because of one planet."

"I see it is now my turn to remind you, my sister's son," Kedar chided softly. "You are young and new to your position." His eyes darkened and his voice grew steely. "It is not your place to foresee anything! Now unless you have some hidden knowledge you'd care to impart, I suggest you go back to your post!"

"But the fleetship," Harlan continued weakly.

Kedar grinned at Harlan but it was a smile that lacked warmth.

"Should we encounter a fleetship or two, a few short bursts from the sonulator should rid them of any thought of attack. If, however, they should attack, then, regrettably, I shall have no recourse but to destroy them."

His tone left the young Blagdenian with the distinct impression that any further voicing of objections would not be healthy. Gritting his teeth, Harlan saluted and returned to his post at the scanner.

"Dagan, send a message to Blagden informing Tozgor of our success on Annan. Tell him we are returning to Dianthia until he again has need of our services. Give him our arrival time."

"And the girl?"

"She's of no concern to Tozgor, therefore I can see no point in mentioning her."

No concern, thought Harlan angrily. *Of course she's no concern! Tozgor isn't even aware she exists. An oversight, my mother's brother, that will soon be rectified, I promise you,* he vowed, bitter at having borne the brunt of Kedar's ill will.

The commodore glanced at the interim gauge. One hour had passed since he left Eirriel in his quarters. She should be well settled by now. He rose to his feet.

"Lieutenant Harlan, take command. I'll return shortly."

"Yes, Commodore," he replied, his better judgment keeping his voice cool and unemotional even as his heart plotted revenge.

Kedar's usual slow, even stride was hurried because of his anticipation to reach his quarters. Nodding briefly in answer to the protector's salute, he waved his hand in front of the light and stepped inside.

Eirriel jumped to her feet with Aubin's name on her lips. As she saw Kedar, the spark that had been in her eyes died, leaving them blank and lifeless once again. Her brief reaction did not go unnoticed. Furiously Kedar stormed across the chamber. With an oath his hand swung back and he struck her across the face.

"You would be wise, my dear," he said, his voice soft, but deadly, "to forget he ever existed." He paused, his brow creased in concentration. "Yes," he said as if coming to a decision, "I think it's time to rectify that."

Eirriel sucked in her breath as she grasped his intent. Desperate to prevent the confrontation, she said coolly, "They won't fight, you know. Garreth has orders not—" Her hands flew to her mouth as she realized what she had said to Kedar.

The Blagdenian commodore chortled triumphantly. Bowing at the waist, he said, "Thank you, my sweet. You've just given me my answer."

Eirriel watched in horror as Kedar drew her transmittor from the pouch in his pocket. Crossing to the wall, he pressed a button and a small screen was illuminated. Familiar with the workings of the *Celestial*, she knew that it projected the same view as seen from the mastery of Kedar's ship. Extending his arm so that Eirriel could follow his movements without difficulty, Kedar activated the transmittor.

"No!" she cried, grabbing for Kedar, who easily stepped out of her reach.

"Yes," he replied, his black eyes glinting with pleasure. He nodded toward the screen. "Observe."

After a few agonizing minutes that seemed like hours, Eirriel saw the *Celestial* move into view. At the same time the intercom sounded.

"Commodore, a Protectorate fleetship has just come into view," Harlan reported.

"Yes, Lieutenant, I see that. Plot a course that will bring us within firing range of the *Celestial*. I'll be right there. Kedar out."

"You bastard!" Eirriel spat. "You promised!"

Kedar raised his brow in mock surprise. "I did?"

"You know damn well you did," she countered. Her green eyes flashed dangerously, but her voice grew calm as she shrugged and said, "Go ahead. Your puny ship is no match for the *Celestial*."

"We'll see won't we, my dear?"

"I hope so." She yawned lazily. "I do so love a good, uneven battle."

"Bitch!" Kedar gritted through clenched teeth. He tossed the transmittor on the table and took a few menacing steps toward her. He was stopped before he reached her by the intercom.

"In firing range, Commodore."

"Very good, Lieutenant Harlan. I'm on my way. Kedar out." He faced Eirriel. "We'll continue this later, I promise you."

Arriving at the mastery, Kedar threw himself into his chair.

"Radnor, prepare to fire on the fleetship."

"Sonulators ready, Commodore."

"The other warships, Lieutenant? How long before they're in position?"

"Less than five minutes."

"Very good. Radnor, fire at will."

"Firing . . . now!"

Kedar's thin lips curled with pleasure as the *Celestial* was buffeted by the sonulators' powerful forces.

"Commodore!" Harlan cried out. "Something's being dispatched from the *Celestial*!"

Kedar leaned forward. "A weapon?"

"No," Harlan said slowly, studying the scanner. "It's a probe of some—"

"Commodore!" Dagan cut in. "There's a signal being sent from inside our ship!"

"Damn!" Kedar's fist slammed the intercom. "Zod!"

"Yes, Commodore," the protector replied instantly.

"The girl! She's sending a signal! See to it!"

Eirriel quickly stood as the threshold opened and the protector burst in. She backed away until she was pressed against the wall. Her voice grew louder, more insistent.

"I didn't save Aubin's life for you to kill him now!" she shouted as the protector reached her. "Move! Damn you! Move!"

With one wide sweep of his hand Zod knocked the

transmittor from her hand. Eirriel bent to retrieve it, then jerked her hand away just as a heavy foot smashed down on it. Grabbing her by the shoulders, the large man easily lifted her from the ground.

"Put me down, you bastard!" she swore, kicking her feet wildly. "Put me down!"

A deep rumble began in his massive chest and he laughed. "With pleasure."

She hit the floor with a thud, the force knocking the breath from her. Staggering to her feet, she caught the brilliant flash of the explosion that lit up the screen. Her warning had come too late!

"Commodore, the other warships are in position," Harlan reported.

"We have them now!" Kedar's exultant laugh echoed through the mastery. "Radnor, the sonulators?"

"Ready, sir!"

"The probe first, then the fleetship!"

"Understood."

"Fire!"

"Firing!"

The smirk that had settled on his face when he saw the probe destroyed vanished as Kedar watched the *Celestial* veer sharply to the right.

"We missed her, Commodore," Harlan took great pleasure in reporting.

"I can see that for myself, you fool!" Kedar snapped.

"Do we pursue?" Radnor queried.

"No," Kedar said after a moment's thought. "The next time we meet the *Celestial* it will be one on one. Resume our previous course."

"Very good, sir."

"Harlan, there's nothing more to be done here. I'll be in my quarters."

Harlan's knowing smirk followed Kedar from the mastery. What he wouldn't trade to be able to see through walls!

"You did well, Zod," Kedar said, saluting the protector. "Remain here and see to it that we are undisturbed."

The protector snickered and returned to his position as the threshold closed behind him.

It was a triumphant Eirriel who greeted Kedar as he entered his quarters.

"I knew you were no match for the *Celestial*," she chortled gleefully. "It's only too bad they refused to return your fire."

"If they had, my dear, you would have risked the same fate as you seem to desire for us. Do you value yourself so little that you seek death instead of life?"

"Instead of life, Commodore?" Her cool gaze met his. "There is no life inside of me, only death."

His eyes darkened ominously. He pulled her to him. "Then I think you better resurrect yourself, because what I want from you most certainly requires life!" He caught the glimmer of defiance in her eyes and said, "However, since you obviously prefer death, I think it only fair that you have company."

Releasing her, Kedar went to the intercom. "Lieutenant!"

"Yes, sir?"

"Is the *Celestial* out of firing range yet?"

There was a slight pause. "Not quite, Commodore."

Kedar looked at Eirriel.

"No! Please! I'll do whatever you want!"

"Thank you, Lieutenant Harlan. Continue as you were. Kedar out."

The Blagdenian leisurely crossed to a sumptuous chair in the far corner of the chamber.

"I'm glad we agree," he drawled as he turned and faced her. "It makes life so much easier."

Eirriel glared at him, refusing to answer. Choosing to let her silence pass, he sat down. He raised steely black eyes to her.

"Undress!"

A look of triumph settled on his face as Eirriel slowly drew off her gown.

Chapter Twenty-eight

Kedar's groin tightened painfully as Eirriel stood before him as he had pictured her for so long. Naked and waiting to be taken.

He had planned to take her slowly, to make her beg him for the pleasure he would give her, but he found that he could not wait. He had to have her now!

Eagerly, he crossed to her. "You're mine at last!"

He reached out and pulled her to him. His mouth swooped down on hers. When his probing tongue was refused entrance, Kedar brought his hand slowly up her side to cup her breast a moment before roughly kneading it. He quickly took advantage of her gasp of pain and his tongue at last drank of the sweetness he had long desired. Groaning, he rubbed his swollen manhood against her belly as his other hand came down and pressed her against him.

It was too much for Eirriel. She had thought he would just take her. She had prepared herself for that, if that were possible. But never had she thought he would kiss her, touch her.

She yanked her head away. "No, please. I cannot!"

Kedar merely laughed and forced her head back to his

waiting mouth. Frantically, she pounded on his back, then wedged her hands between them and shoved hard against his chest, forcing him to release her. She stumbled backwards a few steps, her fingers scrubbing at her lips, trying to erase the feel of his mouth on hers.

He lunged for her, and Eirriel managed to avoid his grasp. Her eyes frantically sought an escape, but found none.

"I'll fight you, Kedar!" she ground out. "I won't make this easy for you."

Kedar watched her, his breath coming in ragged gasps. "Yes! Yes! Fight me!"

Eirriel stopped.

"Run from me."

She looked at him stunned by his unfocused gaze and by the tautness of his body as he rasped again, "Fight me!"

Suddenly, she knew what he needed from her and with that knowledge came her salvation.

"You *need* me to fight you!" Eirriel laughed, a soft challenging laugh. "Well, Kedar. Enjoy this!"

Eirriel closed her eyes and for the first time since the episode with Balthasar, she deliberately sought to leave her body. And it worked.

Kedar kissed Eirriel—or tried to. Even in the heat of passion, he knew something was not right. She was too still, too unaffected by the disgust she had previously shown him. He ground his teeth in frustration as he felt himself softening. No! He would have her! He would not be denied after all this time! He brought both hands to her breasts, and again there was no response from her.

"Fight me, damn you! Fight me!"

She stood there, motionless. Kedar felt all heat drain from him. He willed his manhood to swell, but it was now as cold and as lifeless as the woman he held in his arms.

From a distance Eirriel watched as Kedar kissed her vacant, unresisting body. She laughed to herself as she realized that no matter what he did to her body, the essence of who she was remained untainted. *So this is what it is to be a Kiiryan*, she thought with wonder. *Thank you, Mother.*

When she saw him turn away in anger, she knew she had won.

With no more than a thought, she was back in her body.

"I will not fight you."

Kedar jumped when she spoke. He turned to her and saw her green eyes sparkling defiance when they should have been clouded with fear.

"This is not over between us, Eirriel," Kedar promised. "I will have you."

Eirriel's lips curled up in a secret smile. "You may try, Kedar. You may try."

Enraged, Kedar left his quarters. He would make her pay for this little fiasco, he vowed. He would take her until she begged him to stop and then he would take her one more time!

But it was not to be. To Kedar's continued frustration, no matter how he sought to provoke her, Eirriel refused to fight him. And his manhood refused to swell.

By the time they arrived on Dianthia, Kedar had decided on the form of punishment he would inflict on Eirriel.

A tense crowd of Dianthians gathered in front of Eirriel's home, waiting. They had been summoned to meet the returning invader. He had a surprise for them, they were told.

Kedar, accompanied by Lieutenant Harlan, stepped out onto the front steps of the house.

The crowd fell silent. Now they would learn of what further demands he would make on them.

"My people." Kedar's voice was strong and vibrant, fed by the hatred directed at him from the crowd. "One that was lost is found." He turned and extended his hand.

The crowd gasped as a very pale and very subdued Eirriel slowly walked out of her house. Their shouts of pleasure were cut off in their throats as they saw her place her hand in his.

Kedar smiled. Now she would pay. "I present to you my consort."

The Dianthians stirred as the full impact of Kedar's words hit them. Slowly, one by one, they turned their backs to her.

Their actions made Kedar's smile widened. *How predictable these fools are*, he thought, as he mentally rubbed his hands together in anticipation. He nodded to Lieutenant Harlan.

Harlan stepped forward, raised his weapon and fired once, twice into the crowd. Two Dianthians vanished, screaming in agony.

"Noo!"

Eirriel launched herself at Harlan, but Kedar's arm snaked out and he yanked her to him.

"Harlan." Kedar motioned to the crowd. To Eirriel, he said coldly, "The price of defiance, my dear."

Eirriel slumped against him as Harlan fired once more into the crowd and another Dianthian vanished.

When the moons rose, Eirriel paced about her old chamber, waiting for Kedar to enter and demand his right of conquest. It no longer mattered to her whether he took her or not, he had successfully crushed her spirit by murdering three of her people just to teach her a lesson. She would fight him, if that was what he wanted, what he needed. And she knew she would fight him with every portion of strength she could dredge up. She would try to hurt him as he hurt her by killing her people. She would. . . .

She froze when the door opened and turned slowly to face Kedar.

"You are not waiting for me in your sleeper?"

"No! I have learned my lesson well. I will fight you."

Kedar laughed. "That is very nice, my dear, but it is no longer necessary. I have found your females to be very attractive and they fight most satisfactorily."

Eirriel blanched. "No, please. It's me you want. I'm here. Don't hurt them."

"I'll try, but sometimes I forget my strength. As for you, perhaps when I tire of these women, I may turn to you. Then again, perhaps I won't." Kedar paused. "Sleep well, my sweet. And do try to ignore any screa—moans you might hear." With that parting shot, Kedar left.

Eirriel stared after Kedar. What had she done? Her people were suffering and it was because of her. They would hate her now. Hopelessness more overwhelming than the dark loneliness she had felt on the ship headed to Blagden all those months ago, crashed down on her and she sank to the floor and sobbed.

A pair of warm gentle hands reached her and pulled her close. Even in her despair, she remembered her vow to fight and pushed away.

"Shh, my child, my poor sweet child."

Eirriel's head shot up. "Moriah!" Her tears flowed even fiercer, if that were possible, as she saw the woman who had raised her. "Oh, Moriah, what have I done?"

Moriah pulled Eirriel to her comforting bosom as she used to when Eirriel was a child.

"There, there, love. Cry. If anyone deserves it, you do." Moriah's voice was warm and gentle, belying the glittering hatred in her round brown eyes, hatred for the monster who had returned to wreak further pain on them. Even having her little Eirriel in her arms again did little to ease the blackness in her heart. *Look what he has done to her*, she thought bitterly. *Making it so that she is a pariah among the very people who use to adore her.*

Finally, Eirriel's sobs subsided and she sat up. She took a deep breath and raised her eyes. "I've made such a mess of my life, Moriah." Her voice was a bleak whisper. "I thought I could do it. Thought I could offer myself to Kedar but I couldn't. How was I supposed to let him touch me as Aubin had? How? What have I done?"

"Aubin? Who is Aubin?"

Eirriel's mouth curled up into a smile and her watery eyes glowed with a love so deep that Moriah felt her breath catch when she saw it. Eirriel's hand came up and she ran a finger across the Syna Circlet.

At first she had feared to wear it, but when she realized that Kedar had no inkling of the significance of the thin golden chain, she kept it with her always. A link to the bronze giant who had captured her heart and soul. And whom she had been forced to betray.

Her hand dropped and her smile faded.

"This Aubin means much to you?" Moriah prodded gently, curious about the man who had brought such love to her little charge.

"Everything."

Moriah smiled. Perhaps there was hope. Perhaps this Aubin would come for Eirriel. She stood up and led Eirriel to the sleeper. "Come, lay back and tell me all about your Aubin."

"He's not my Aubin anymore, Moriah. I . . . I . . . He hates me now."

"Because of Kedar?"

"Yes."

"Tell me."

And Eirriel did. She told Moriah all that had happened since she was sent from Dianthia so long ago and as she poured out her story, she realized that somehow, someway Kedar would be made to pay for all he had done.

"I have a little surprise for you, my dear," Kedar said softly.

His lips curled in a sly smile, he led Eirriel to the stable. She glanced up and saw the suns high in the pink sky, a sight that had always made her smile but not today. Her smiles were stolen from her as was the joy she should have felt by being home at last.

With the exception of Moriah, who saw firsthand the truth of her relationship with the Blagdenian, none of the Dianthians could understand why the daughter of their Primary Olden had returned from her travels as consort to the hated conqueror.

She shivered, chilled by the fear of her people's fate should they learn she was Kedar's prisoner and not his willing lover, and from the harsh hand clamped around her wrist.

As she walked across the open yard to the stables, she could feel her people's hatred directed at her. Eirriel forced her head high and greeted their sneers with a haughty disdain. She had only been home twenty-four hours, she reasoned. They could only judge her by what they saw and heard. Perhaps in time. . . . She laughed a silent bitter laugh. If Kedar had his way, her people would be wishing her in the domain of the black god. Of course, how could they know she was there already.

A rough tug on her arm dragged her from her thoughts.

She looked up and saw Kedar watching her expectantly.

Then she heard him. "Onyx!"

Not caring that Kedar's eyes glittered with dark promise, Eirriel ran to her much-loved steed and threw her arms around his powerful neck.

"So, I take it you like my surprise."

Eirriel straightened. "And the price? Will you murder more of my people so that I might have him?"

Kedar smiled, a smile that did not reach his eyes. "No, there will be no killing for the privilege of riding your estalon."

Eirriel looked at him warily.

"No, my dear." Kedar continued, "I think of him as insurance. If you disappoint me . . ."

There was no need for him to finish the threat. Eirriel understood. Onyx would be destroyed.

"Enjoy your ride, my dear. I'll expect you for nourishment. Don't keep me waiting."

Eirriel nodded. She waited until Kedar was out of sight before she again buried her head in Onyx's shoulder. Tears of happiness streaming from her eyes, she raised her head.

"Take me away, Onyx. At least for a while."

And he did. Until it was time to return for the evening nourishment she was ordered to share with Kedar.

She waited for him till the food grew cold and the brew warm. And then she waited some more.

He never appeared.

It was a pattern that would be repeated continually during the following months.

At the rising of the suns, Kedar would stop by her chamber on the way to his. He would smile with satisfaction as he stretched and yawned. Some young girl or woman had fought him well he would always tell Eirriel before he apologized for ignoring her. Perhaps tonight he would make up for his inattention. As he left, he would remind her that her presence was demanded at the midday nourishment. She would be there, he would not.

He would next appear, without fail, just as she was about to take her daily ride on Onyx. He would remind her of his gift of Onyx, warning her with a look that it was a gift easily taken away and would again insist she appear for nourishment, which she did and he did not.

Kedar's continual assault on her nerves had a profound effect on Eirriel. Her appetite decreased and the result was obvious with one look at her pale, drawn face, and her dull lifeless eyes. She was edgy and the slightest noise would make her jerk in fearful anticipation.

Her only respite came when she flew Onyx. On his back she could forget how truly desperate her life had become.

Two months later Moriah brought Eirriel wonderful news. Kedar had been summoned back to Blagden, a summons that had left little time for anything but immediate obedience. He had departed leaving Eirriel and a limited staff behind. Grateful for the peace Kedar's absence had brought, Moriah's step was light as she entered Eirriel's chamber.

"I think you've had enough rest, my lady," Moriah said, yanking back the casement coverings and letting the warm pink glow of the suns fill the chamber. "You've already slept the morning away."

Eirriel turned from the bright sunlight and pulled the silky coverings over her head. "Go away," she mumbled sleepily.

Chuckling, Moriah stood with her hands on her hips and stared fondly at her charge's covered form. Shaking her head, she reached out and firmly, but lovingly, smacked what she judged to be Eirriel's buttocks.

"Get up, you lazy wench! Do you plan to waste the whole day?" Her cheerful voice hardened. "You might as well enjoy your freedom while that—that monster is away."

Eirriel pushed back the covers and slipped from the sleeper. She sighed wearily. "Please don't start, Moriah. I want to forget he even exists, let alone controls my life! That was the first peaceful night's sleep I've had since . . ."

Since Symmarryllon, she finished silently. Icy fingers of loss clutched at her heart as they always did when she thought of Aubin and their oh-so-very brief time together. She felt her eyes grow moist and forced the tears away. It was too painful to dwell on. She must keep her memories of

him locked deep within her soul or they would destroy her.
He was out of her life forever, and she must learn to accept
that.

"Well, in a long time," Eirriel finished with a forced
cheerfulness that did not fool the astute Moriah, who
merely shook her head sadly.

Moriah left to prepare her charge a nice hot cleanser and
Eirriel spent, for the first time in weeks, a few frivolous
moments deciding what to wear. A shiver shot through her
spine as she remembered her previous appearance garbed as
a Dianthian.

It had been during one of the few times Kedar had
actually appeared for nourishment. Unmindful of his lieutenant or the few other Blagdenians who had joined them,
Kedar had railed at her for embarrassing him with the
simple, unsophisticated and common Dianthian design.
With one violent motion, he had ripped the offending
garment from her. From that moment on, everything she
had worn was first approved by him.

But now she was free of him and his dictates, at least until
he returned, and now she would wear whatever she liked.

Reaching into the back of her wardrobe, she pulled out
what she laughingly called her pre-Kedar outfits. The lovely
pale green blouse laced from the waist to a low rounded
neckline. Its long full sleeves opened down the top seam and
were joined at the wrists by a delicate dark green ribbon that
matched the ankle-length billowing skirt. To complete the
ensemble, she chose soft slippers of dark green.

Eirriel's lilting laughter filled the chamber. "Oh, Moriah,
it feels so good to be free once again."

Moriah watched the young woman dancing around the
chamber. It did her old heart good to see Eirriel contented,
laughing and singing. It had been months since Eirriel
raised her beautiful voice in song. Moriah's soft brown eyes
darkened with worry. How long would it be before Kedar's
oppressive behavior broke Eirriel's spirit forever? She
cursed the Blagdenian, damning him for all eternity.

"I'll have someone prepare Onyx for you, sweeting. You
enjoy your cleansing while I fetch your nourishment."

Eirriel lowered herself into the warm relaxing waters of

the cleanser. Umm, she thought. Not as nice as the vitalizers on the *Celestial*, but nice just the same. Her eyes clouded as memories of Aubin, triggered by thoughts of the *Celestial*, crept unbiddingly into her mind.

How she missed him! Her arms ached to hold him, her hands to caress him. Her body yearned for his fiery touch, a touch at once rough but gentle, demanding but yielding, passionate but tender. Did he miss her? She shuddered painfully. With the wounds between them so newly healed, she could well imagine his thoughts as he had listened to her vicious taunts. He would have felt tricked, deceived. All the old fears and mistrust she had finally managed to quell in him would have resurfaced with soul-shattering force. Her heart protested but her mind knew he would hate her now. Hate her as passionately as he had loved her.

"Maybe I'll be free to see you again, my love. Then I'll be able to explain my words and try to convince you I never stopped loving you. That everything I've done has been out of fear for you." Even as she spoke, her head rocked back and forth hopelessly. He wouldn't believe her. She had lied too well. No, what they once had was lost forever.

She laid her head back, closed her eyes and let her mind drift into the past as Cian had so carefully taught her. A short time later she rose from the cleaner, her mind as refreshed as her body. She dressed quickly and by the time Moriah entered, she was seated on the sleeper, patiently awaiting her nourishment.

"I expected you to still be in the cleanser," Moriah said cheerfully.

Eirriel raised her eyes to Moriah and whatever she was going to say was lost in the clatter of dishes as the nourishment tray slid from Moriah's hands.

"By all the gods!"

"What is it?" Eirriel rose quickly to her feet.

Moriah crossed to Eirriel and grabbed her firmly by the shoulders. "Tell me truly, Eirriel. Have you been with him? With Kedar?"

"You know he has never touched me," Eirriel replied quickly. "Moriah, please. You're frightening me. What is it?"

Moriah smiled, a brilliant smile that would rival the suns, and pointed to the reflector. Reassured by Moriah's smile, but still confused, Eirriel crossed to the reflector.

And as she stared at her image with eyes that once were green but now were amber, she smiled.

"I bear Aubin's child!"

Moriah nodded. "The change has come upon you late as it did with your mother. I had forgotten that Sidra's eyes did not change in the first month but in her third. You can also expect to carry the seedling long past the expected time. If you follow your mother's pattern, your child will be delivered alert and healthy and without need of the usual incubation period."

Eirriel threw herself into Moriah's arms. "Aubin's child! A part of him to have with me always."

As Moriah held the happy young woman close, she couldn't help but remember Kedar and a coldness settled in her heart. What would he do when he learned of the child?

An eager Eirriel left for her daily ride on Onyx once Moriah convinced her it would not harm the child.

She slipped from Onyx's back to the soft ground of a tiny dale some distance from her home. Laughing and hugging herself, she kicked off her shoes and dangled her feet in the gently flowing stream. Leaning back on her hands, she closed her eyes and listened to the haunting melodies of the killiard birds.

She was so absorbed in their haunting sound she failed to hear the steady thud of approaching footsteps.

"Hello, Eirriel."

Her startled amber eyes flew open. Her hand shot to her mouth. It couldn't be! She tried to speak but the words caught in her throat.

"Well, aren't you even going to say hello?" Timos asked, hoping his voice sounded normal. Moriah had told him she carried another man's child, but he was unprepared for the devastating ache that tore at his soul when he saw her beautiful amber eyes. It should have been his child that caused the change in her eyes and her body.

"I feared you were dead," she said when she finally found her voice.

Timos laughed a short bittersweet sound that seemed to hang in the air. "And I thought you were dead." He sat down next to her. "It's been hell, not knowing if you were alive. Knowing only that if I had kept my feelings to myself you would never have been alone. Never have been captured."

He took her hands in his, the pain in his voice reflected in his eyes. "I'm sorry, Eirriel. I let you down."

"It's I who should be sorry. I never meant for you to believe—"

"Shh, I know you didn't lead me on. I've had time to think, to see the truth of your feelings for me." He paused "As for you're not knowing I was alive, it was safer that way."

"Safer?" Her voice reflected her confusion and her hurt. "You . . . you think that I will hurt you?"

"You came back with Kedar. What else was I to think?"

Eirriel shook her head sadly, her eyes shadowed by deep despair, and her voice a pained whisper. "You too? My people all hate me now. Oh, they're careful not to show it. Kedar saw to that. But I can see it in their eyes, hear it in their voices, feel it in my mind. Do they . . . Do you truly believe I would be with him if I had any other choice?"

"You have to understand. He's destroying their world and their lives little by little. He kills randomly, without reason or warning. He takes what he wants, not caring how little he leaves behind." Blue fire flared in his eyes and his lips grew taut with rage. "And now he takes our women."

Eirriel felt the weight of his accusation and lowered her head in shame. "He does that to punish me. I should not have refused him."

"Then he has not . . ." Moriah had told him Kedar had not touched her, but still Timos needed to hear it from her.

She shook her head. "I stopped him. I was wrong. The next time . . ."

Timos took her hand in his. "There needn't be a next time. Come away with me. There is a place of safety."

"Don't offer me a freedom I cannot take. Too many lives depend on my staying with Kedar."

"You love him that much, this captain of yours?"

"Beyond all else," she answered fiercely, then frowned. "How do you know about Aubin?"

"I have been in contact with Moriah since the day you returned."

"That was months ago. Why are you only coming to me now?"

"I had to see for myself that Kedar held no place in your affections."

"How could you think I loved him?"

"You are much changed from the Eirriel I once knew. And as you said, many lives depend on me. I had to know I could trust you. I have not been idle. When Kedar returns, it will not be to the idyllic existence he had before. Our people are at last ready to fight."

"You mustn't!" Eirriel cried out. "I have seen what he is capable of. We have nothing to fight him with."

"But fight him we will," Timos ground out fiercely. "And if some of us must die, so be it. At least our deaths will no longer be in vain."

"Oh, Timos. You must be careful." She lowered her eyes. "I—I don't think I could bear it if something happened to you."

Timos's heart swelled at her concern, but as she looked at him again with eyes that announced her condition he knew that as long as she carried Aubin's child she would never be his.

"I promised Moriah I would not keep you long. You need your rest." As he helped her to her feet, he couldn't help the question that burst out of him. "Will your captain come for you?"

"His love has turned to hate," she said with quiet conviction. "He will not come."

Timos helped Eirriel onto Onyx's back. "He will *no* come." Her words reverberated in his mind and Timos held back the smile that reached his soul. He will not come. Perhaps, after all, he still had a chance.

"Moriah!"

The older woman looked up as Eirriel rushed in. "You saw Timos?"

"You knew I would?"

"Yes. I told him he had waited too long. You needed to know that he was all right."

Eirriel frowned. "We talked about much, but he didn't say how he came to be free when so many are captive."

"He arrived in Edlyn several days after you were sent away. I had been released by then and saw him approaching. I was able to convince him that it would do no good to be captured along with the other men. Reluctantly he agreed to remain in hiding. Young Tamal acted as a liaison and ran messages back and forth between Timos and me. He has organized a resistance, Eirriel. It has been hard convincing our people to fight, but slowly they are coming around. He is much changed, our Timos."

Chapter Twenty-nine

During the next few weeks, Eirriel lived each day with the passionate desperation of the doomed. She enjoyed her precious freedom to the utmost, knowing it could be wrenched from her at any moment.

A month after Kedar had been gone, Timos and Morial had finally convinced her she had nothing to fear. The people were ready. When Kedar returned, it would be to his death.

It was in this untroubled mood that she was disturbed in her dreams one night by the quick gentle touch of warm lips. Still asleep, Eirriel reached up, her arms encircling his neck and pulled him toward her.

"Aubin, my love," she murmured.

"Bitch!" the mouth she had so tenderly been kissing hissed. "I told you never to mention his name again!"

Eirriel gasped. "Kedar!"

"I warned you what would happen."

Fear pierced Eirriel's heart, chilling her as she remembered his threat to kill Aubin. Her eyes downcast, she stammered, "I . . . I was asleep. You startled me."

"That's even worse!" He grabbed her roughly by the

shoulders and lifted her head off the pillows. Eirriel closed her eyes against the pain of his ever-tightening grasp as he growled, "For the first time you responded to my kisses. I thought you missed me. My heart thrilled at the knowledge that you might be glad to have me back. Then you murmur that accursed name and I know all the passion I craved and finally tasted was for him!"

Throwing her from him, he marched across the chamber. His black eyes glinting with hate and fury, he paused at the door. He stood with his back to her, his voice calm, deadly. "I know, *beloved*, that you will hate to see me leave so soon after my arrival, but I suddenly remembered a certain matter that needs my attention. It seems I've already delayed too long."

"Wait! Please!" Eirriel cried, her voice shrill with fright.

Desperation driving her, she threw back the covers and ran to Kedar. Suppressing a shudder, she pressed her body against his back. Reaching around him, she caressed his chest.

"Don't leave yet," she whispered in his ear. "Let me prove to you that I did miss you."

Brushing her lips lightly across the back of his neck, she reached over and flicked on the light switch. Striving desperately to make her voice husky, she said, "Come, my lord, let me show you how much I missed you."

Her eyes blank, her face pale, the only clue to her disgust and terror was her tightly drawn lips. Eirriel turned from him. Mimicking Chalandra's slow, sensual walk, she crossed to the sleeper, untying the silky ribbons of her robe as she did.

His blood still ablaze from her teasing touches, Kedar swore under his breath. Was she so desperate to save her lover that she would willingly bear his touch to save him? Yes, he answered bitterly, she would. But what a performance it would be! She would put her heart and soul, as well as her body into it. Though it galled him to know it was love for another man that guided her actions, Kedar was no fool. He would accept the feast she laid before him and enjoy it to the fullest. But afterward, he vowed silently, his face fierce with hatred, afterward she and her lover would both pay dearly for her deception!

He whirled just as Eirriel's gown floated to the floor. She stood before him, her pale skin naked to his hungry gaze. His breath caught in his throat as she turned to him, her arms outstretched, beckoning, her long golden hair tumbling forward, giving teasing glimpses of her full breasts as she moved. She raised her face to him, her moist lips inviting, her round eyes beseeching.

His breath coming unevenly, he took two steps forward then stopped as he saw her eyes clearly for the first time. Amber! His jaw dropped in surprise. Her eyes were amber! All desire fled him and sweat beaded on his brow as the riddled legend from his past came back to haunt him.

Many generations ago, even Kedar had forgotten how many, Zyria, the only female offspring of the wyzard, Kathos, fell in love with Keda, the handsome heir to the house of Kedaria. Never one to let an opportunity pass, Keda talked to the beautiful, golden-haired Zyria of love and of a bond that would hold them together forever. Believing his words, Zyria willingly gave herself to him. True to his black-hearted nature, Keda soon grew bored with her. His loving caresses grew harsh and abusive. Humiliated and disillusioned, Zyria threw herself into a fiery fissure. Crushed and demented by the death of his beloved Zyria, the wizened Kathos cursed Keda and his heirs.

"When the House of Kedaria is all powerful, the male heir will fall deeply in love with a pale-skinned female of incomparable beauty. When it seems that nothing can go wrong, when the heir has all the riches, all the power he desires and the comely maid, beware! For as Keda changed, so will the beauty. And as Zyria died, so will the last male heir of Kedaria!"

In a fit of outrage Keda slew the wyzard, but his ominous last words hung over the House of Kedaria to this very day.

His heart pounded fiercely in his ears. Could it be the time of the prophecy for the House of Kedaria? Was his death at hand? Kedar rushed to Eirriel and grasped her shoulders.

"Look at me!" he roared.

Eirriel raised her face to him, with fear in her eyes. What was wrong? Had Kedar seen through her? Her heart sank as she realized that had to be the answer. Why else would he be so angry? The gods help her, she had failed!

Kedar frowned in confusion as he stared into her eyes. Where were the beautiful green eyes that had haunted his every waking moment, plagued his every dream? Eyes that shone like the green suns of Chol?

"How did this happen?" he demanded, shaking her roughly. "Why? What does it mean?"

Eirriel looked at him totally confused. What, in the name of all the gods, was he talking about? Seeing her blank expression, Kedar snarled and flung her from him. Was she stupid or just stalling?

"Your eyes! Why aren't they green anymore?"

Her hand automatically flew to her face. She had grown so accustomed to her eyes' amber color that she had forgotten he had not seen them since the change. How was she to explain? He would kill her, Aubin, and her people.

"It's no concern of yours," she said haughtily, as she reached for her discarded robe.

"No concern!" he bellowed. "Have you forgotten that you are my property or do you need to be reminded?"

Heedless of his threatening tone, or the deadly black look in his eyes, Eirriel turned her back to him and slipped on her robe. She gasped when he grabbed her arm and whirled her around.

"Do I take your silence as defiance?" he asked in a deceptively soft voice.

Sparks of anger flashed in her eyes. Her jaw thrust forward rebelliously, she wrenched her arm from his grasp and stepped back.

Kedar struck quickly, slapping her fiercely across the face. "That should remind you who is your master!"

Suddenly they heard an outcry from the courtyard, followed instantly by a rush of sounds. The Blagdenian commodore flew to the casement and was startled by the sight that greeted him. The Dianthians were attacking! Caught offguard, the Blagdenian wymen were struggling to overcome their attackers.

Kedar cursed under his breath. So she was to be the means of his destruction! Never expecting the cowardly Dianthians to attack, he had left most of his invasion force home, leaving only a handful behind for effect. His mood changed quickly to one of confidence as he saw Harlan appear shouting orders. His lips twisted in a pleased smirk. The rebels would soon be captured. He was alive and in no danger. So much for legends, he scoffed.

A noise from behind him drew his attention back to Eirriel. His eyes still on the battle, his voice held a hint of amusement as he said, "It seems that someone has managed to rouse your people."

Eirriel's face lit up. "Timos!"

"Ah, I have heard of him. He has evaded my men for some time and now he walks right into our hands." Kedar turned away from the casement. "It's a surprisingly brave, but predictably futile, attempt.

"I wouldn't try that," he warned as he saw Eirriel sneaking toward the door. "Come here!"

She stopped but did not turn. Her voice rang with confidence as she said, "I no longer belong to you. Timos will be victorious."

"Don't be foolish. He hasn't a chance."

She turned and looked directly into his black eyes, her face a vision of serenity. "I know Timos. He will win."

Understanding seared through his mind. Timos! How gullible he had been. He had thought Aubin was her only lover, but now he remembered her pained cry as he carried her to her chamber that day so long ago. Timos!

"So it's Timos, is it? Was Aubin just a ruse to keep me from the truth? Well, I hope you enjoyed your lover while I was away because you'll never see him alive again!" Kedar promised, his voice lethal, his eyes glittering with fury.

Eirriel's mind reached out. All too clearly she saw Kedar's agony at the thought of her in Timos's arms and beneath that, she read his fear of the legend about his family and his reason for the trip to Blagden.

She smiled as she realized what she had to do. "I have no fear for Timos, Kedar. You will not harm him. You will not harm anyone. You have been stripped of your command.

That is why you were called home." Her laugh was victorious, her voice tantalizingly sensuous. "Yes, I did enjoy my lover while you were away. Night after night we loved, laughed, tasted of each other. Here, in this very chamber. And after we loved, we planned your defeat."

She stood and faced him. "You noticed my 'change' and asked about it. It's nothing really. The 'change' comes upon all Dianthian women when they are bearing." She paused, waiting until the light of realization blazed in Kedar's eyes. "Yes, I'm bearing and it's—"

"Arugh!" Kedar roared in anguish, hate and fury. "You gave him what you denied me! Now you will give it to me!"

"No!"

Eirriel's quiet denial stopped Kedar.

"You may try to take it, but I will not give it to you. But before you do, remember well the 'change' that came upon Keda. You have lost position and power. Would you lose your life as well?"

Eirriel turned her back to Kedar and in doing so missed him raising his weapon.

"You should leave now, Timos will—"

The beam from the sonulator struck Eirriel in her back and carried her across the room to crash into the wall.

Kedar laughed as Eirriel slowly picked herself up. No sooner had she gotten to her feet then she doubled over in agony as a searing spasm tore through her lower abdomen.

Kedar raised his weapon again.

"No!" Eirriel screamed just before the sonulator struck her one more time.

Kedar crossed the chamber and stood over her as she struggled to stand. "Where is he? This Timos who would save you?"

He reached down and yanked her to her feet. Ignoring her cry, he shoved her toward the sleeper. Tears coursing down her face, Eirriel's lips formed a soundless cry of denial as warm fluid gushed from between her legs.

Without warning, Kedar was hoisted into the air and thrown against the wall.

Eirriel looked down on the stunned form of Kedar. Black hatred reared in her eyes for a brief moment then vanished, replaced by a serene expression and calm eyes that gave no evidence to the hurt and rage that rampaged through her mind.

"What the—" Kedar sat up, shaking his head. A quick glance around the chamber showed it to be empty save for Eirriel and himself.

You will die for what you have done!

Feeling the words more than hearing them, Kedar shuddered, chilled to the marrow by the hatred of the words.

You are burning. Blistering. Your lifeblood is no more. In its place is rock. Flowing molten rock.

Kedar's screams echoed throughout the dwelling as he writhed on the floor.

Scalding. Scorching. Molten rock.

His hands tore at his skin, frantically trying to destroy the source of his pain.

A life for a life.

Abruptly all sounds ceased. The very silence more ominous than the screams.

Chapter Thirty

"Eirriel, please hear me," Moriah pleaded, her brown eyes brimming with tears. "Wake up, young one. You've got to wake up."

A voice heavy with sad resignation drifted from the darkened corner of the chamber. "It's no use, Moriah. I'm afraid she's lost to us." Timos slumped in a chair, his bright blue eyes dull with pain, his face grim. "The healer could find no physical reason for Eirriel's continued unconsciousness. It must be as he said. Whatever she experienced was so ugly, so horrifying that she chose to retreat from reality rather than face it. She's closed her mind to it and to us."

Two weeks had passed since he and his fellow Dianthians had finally revolted against their Blagdenian conquerors. Knowing that Kedar would quickly turn his anger on Eirriel, Timos had rushed to her side. He had been halfway to her chamber when the agonizing screams had begun. Despair had momentarily overcome him until he had realized that the cries had come from no female throat. Then the despair had resurfaced within him in greater force at the sudden silence.

He would never forget the unnerving sight that had greeted him as he had burst into Eirriel's chamber.

She stood unmoving and naked, her gaze unfocused, while her life blood ran down her legs and formed a pool around her feet. A short distance from her was the torn and bloody shell of what was once the merciless conqueror of their people. Both were mute testimony to the terrifying and unimaginable events that had taken place in a mind-bafflingly brief space of time.

Timos placed his head in his hands, his handsome face twisted by the crushing guilt that weighed heavily on his heart.

"If only I had acted sooner, before Kedar had returned, I might have saved Eirriel from the horror she was unable to endure."

"Don't blame yourself, my friend. It could not have been easy convincing our people to fight."

"Eirriel!" Timos got up from his chair, his expression rapidly changing from disbelief to relief.

"My lady!" Moriah cried.

"How long have I been asleep?"

"Two weeks have passed since I carried you from your chamber," Timos answered. "We'd just about given up hope. The healer could not explain your strange state." His voice choked. "I thought I'd lost you again, my love."

Eirriel sat up. Taking his hand in hers, she met his intense gaze with sad eyes that once again shone green.

"Please, Timos, do not expect what I cannot give."

Timos dropped her hand and walked away.

"You were delirious for the first six days," Moriah explained. "You called for Aubin constantly. On the seventh day the healer pronounced you physically sound, but that day and each day since, you slipped deeper and deeper into yourself until the last two days you were so deep that you made not a sound."

Eirriel turned to Timos. "Please, my friend, come and sit by me. There is much I need to say to you. Much I need you to understand." She turned to Moriah and motioned to the other chair. "You know some of my story, but not all."

For Timos's sake, Eirriel started at the beginning and

repeated much of what Moriah already knew. She told him of how she was rescued by Aubin, of her experience aboard the *Celestial,* of Chalandra and Balthasar, of the Syna Ceremony and finally of her flight from Annan with Kedar.

"Kedar threatened to kill Aubin if I didn't go with him and that was something I could not allow. My life would have been meaningless if Aubin were to die. I don't have him now, nor will I again, but he is alive and that is enough.

"You know what my life here has been so I need not tell you of that. But before I tell you what happened that morning, I must tell you of myself and my heritage. Things that must be carried no further than these chambers. Things I never knew until I met Raissa and Cian.

I am not the pure-blooded offspring of a Dianthian Olden and his Dianthian mate, but the mixed blooded offspring of a Dianthian Olden and his Kiiryan mate."

Slowly she spoke of her mother and how she learned who and what she really was. "Cian told me that my ability was far greater than I could ever fathom and that one day I would utilize it to its fullest. When it came, the realization would be overwhelming and devastating, the usage swift and natural.

"I won't burden you with a detailed description of the events that took place two weeks ago. Let it suffice when I say that I, not a weapon, destroyed Kedar and that I would do it again without a moment's hesitation."

Moriah gasped for though she had not seen Kedar's mutilated body, she had seen Timos as he came staggering out of Eirriel's chamber, his face white, his eyes blank and his mind numb, mumbling soundlessly, the words unrecognizable save the name of Kedar. After a silent prayer of thanks for Eirriel's deliverance, Moriah had thrust aside all thoughts of Kedar and had focused her attention on the needs of her charge. Now to learn that her sweet Eirriel was responsible for Kedar's death and that a mere thought had brought it about was unbelievable!

A burst of pride struck her at the strength and ability of the young woman she had raised. How proud Alaric would have been. He had often hinted that Eirriel might be different, but, a sly grin appeared on her face, had he suspected just how different?

Timos's reaction was hardly one of pride as he sat listening to Eirriel's tale. He had suspected that she had somehow destroyed Kedar, but to actually hear how it was done! Incredible!

Oblivious to the thoughts of her two companions, Eirriel continued telling them of the lessons she had learned from Cian that had enabled her to heal herself in both mind and body.

"That is my story. I know it will take time for you to fully grasp all that I have said. Time for you to lose your fear of me."

"We don't fear you, Eirriel," Timos stated emphatically. "But I want to know why you waited so long to destroy Kedar."

"In spite of what Cian said, I never really believed my power was so great. I've always reacted automatically, when I was in great danger and there was no one else to protect me. Until now, it has always been a means of protection, nothing more. I believe Kedar's actions were the catalyst I needed to complete the circle of my powers. Now that I know how to control them I will never be forced or controlled by anyone again!"

"Eirriel, is there any way for you to reach Aubin? If your power is half as great as your love, can't you command him to come to you?" Moriah's brown eyes sparkled with excitement. With Kedar dead and the Dianthians once again in control, all that was needed to insure Eirriel's happiness was the return of her lover.

Timos was stunned. Bring Aubin here? No! He wanted to shout. Eirriel belonged to him. One day she would admit it, but first he had to help her forget the dashing fleetship captain and that could only happen if he was not around. His blue eyes studied the face of the woman he loved as he anxiously awaited her answer. Would she bring him here? Could she?

Eirriel shook her head sadly. "Even if I could reach him, which I doubt, I could never command his love. Love is something that must be given freely or it is meaningless. He will hate me now for betraying him with Kedar and I love him too much to force him to come to me."

"I understand. It was just a thought. Now you must rest."

Moriah and a very relieved Timos left and Eirriel fell quickly to sleep.

By the time Moriah arrived with the morning nourishment, Eirriel was dressed and ready to start the day.

"Moriah, please have Timos and the Oldens meet me in my father's conference chamber within the hour. There is much we need to discuss."

Moriah opened her mouth to speak, but then thought better of it. She nodded her head and left.

Eirriel was standing by the open casement, her back to the door when Timos arrived. The pink glow of the dual suns filtered in, creating a hazy, dreamlike aura around her. The long green gown with its rounded neckline and full billowing sleeves enhanced the shapeliness of her figure. Her long hair was interwoven with a matching green ribbon and hung down her back in a long braid.

"Good morning, Eirriel."

She turned at the sound, her eyes registering surprise at his solitary arrival. "Where are the others?"

How beautiful she looked, Timos thought. How young. How vulnerable. His heart quailed at the news he brought. Would it cause a relapse? Startling realization penetrated his mind as he stared into her striking green eyes. No, it wouldn't. This was not the carefree innocent of his youth whose greatest concern was the choice of her wardrobe. This was a responsible, determined woman whose strength had been sorely tried and who had survived. Survived to become more stable, more capable and in complete control. Timos felt a momentary twinge of regret at not having had a hand in the shaping of her new-found maturity.

"They will not be here, Eirriel," he said flatly. "They're all dead."

She gasped. Her knees buckled and she grasped the desk for support. Dead! All dead! Fifteen innocent men and she never even knew!

For a moment Timos thought he had misjudged her then he saw her compose herself. Her back straightened, her head lifted, and her eyes blazed. Again, he marveled at the growth of the woman before him.

"How did it happen?" she asked quietly. "When?"

"Before your return to Dianthia. They refused to support Kedar so he had them massacred." His blue eyes darkened with hatred as the memory returned.

All Dianthians had been called to bear witness to the destruction of the Oldens as warning of what would happen to those who would not cower before the conquerors. The Oldens had stood lined up in the yard, their heads high, their expressions proud. When the Blagdenians turned their weapons on the old men, no cry of pain had been uttered, no testimony to the agony of their death had shown on their faces. Of all the people there, only Timos knew the pain that was wrought by the deadly weapons, having seen it turned upon one of the common people whose dignity and upbringing did not include stoic acceptance. The man's tortured screams had echoed through Timos's mind until he had thought himself the victim.

"We must try to restore peace and prosperity to our land, our people," Eirriel said, her soft voice breaking into Timos's memories. "Try to make them forget." Her eyes narrowed and her voice grew hard. "No! Never forget! It's painful memory that can prevent this from happening again." She waved at a chair. "Sit, Timos. There is much to discuss."

Awed by the authority in her voice, Timos sat and listened, his surprise increasing as she laid out her plans.

They would set up a temporary sovereignty with the two of them in command. There would be none who would show umbrage at their venture because the common people were in great need of leadership. It was only natural that Timos, who was trained to be an Olden when the time came, and Eirriel, daughter of their Primary Olden and a favorite of the people, would be the ones to take charge.

Timos would teach them the ways of the Oldens so that the people would have the ability and knowledge to govern themselves. Eirriel would instruct them on the methods of progress she had learned from Aubin and his comrades. Both knew they would first have to combat the fears and superstitions planted in the people by the Oldens before anything could be learned. They gave themselves one year to accomplish this. At that time they would step down and the people themselves would choose who would govern them.

"Of course you must move in here so that we may discuss any problem we encounter," Eirriel said spontaneously. Catching Timos's look of pained reluctance, she added quickly, "It will only be for a year at most. If it's your ryland . . ."

"No! No, it's not that. My ryland can easily operate without me." He paused groaning inwardly. How could he tell her? To be close, but not to touch her. To talk, but to say no words of love to her. It would be unbearable. "I'll stay, Eirriel."

Yes, he would stay and he would be here when she needed aid, when she needed companionship, when she needed comfort. And by all the gods, he swore that by the end of the year it would be him she would need, him she would desire, him she would cry out for when she slept. *Him!*

There was a brief rap on the door and then Moriah entered. "I thought you might be a bit hungry," she said cheerfully, placing a large nourishment platter on the desk. "You've been closeted in here all day. The suns have long since set."

Eirriel smiled apologetically. "Timos, I'm sorry. You must be starving."

"A little," he grinned sheepishly.

"A little!" Moriah's hearty chuckle echoed through the chamber. "A little he says. Knowing him, I'm sure that right about now he could eat enough for three men."

"When you're finished with your teasing, Moriah, please prepare the guest chamber."

Moriah arched her brows questioningly.

"We have much to do. Timos has agreed to stay here until we see it through."

The old woman's brown eyes lit up at the answer to her prayers. Eirriel needed someone in her life. With Timos around constantly, she was bound to grow more than a little fond of him. It was what Alaric had always planned—her future linked with Timos's.

"I'll be about it then, my lady," she said, closing the door quietly behind her. Her cheerful voice could be heard in the far end of the dwelling as she bustled about issuing orders and seeing them promptly carried out.

So ended the first of many late nights and the beginning of a daily pattern for Eirriel and Timos. They rose at the first hint of daylight, attacking their duties with fierce determination, and worked well into the night. Both drove themselves like demons in an effort to reconstruct their world. The work proved as hard as they expected, but both agreed the reward would be well worth their efforts.

Each day was divided into three time periods: the two smaller devoted to learning, the larger spent tending the rylands.

During the first part of every day, Timos taught the ideals of Kyberan, his name for the new government, in which he combined his ideals and beliefs with the preachings and traditions of the Oldens. Contrary to the ways of old, both men and women were given an equal say in this new system.

Five men and five women would be elected by all the people to the Concilium of Taihum for a period of ten years, unless a concile died or was found unworthy at which time a new vote would be taken. Each concile would be given a certain dominion for which and to which he or she was responsible. The Concilium of Taihum would meet every day for six months with the exception of every sixth day, which would be devoted to the people.

On that day, each concile would hold a day-long session with the people he represented. All complaints, recommendations, or questions would first be recorded then discussed. If the concile could solve it by himself and if it did not involve people outside his dominion, he would do so. If not, it was presented before the full Concilium.

The Concilium of Taihum would choose from amongst themselves the Chief Concile. He or she would have the final say in times of indecision, would hear and act on any complaints of action or inaction by any of the other conciles.

The large middle period of the day was spent in the rylands. Eirriel, with Timos's aid, would explain the new methods she had learned while with Aubin. No longer would her people slave from dawn to dusk with little progress. The new skills and aids she devised would triple their efficiency, thereby tripling their production.

It was the final part of the day that Eirriel enjoyed the most. This was the time she spoke of what lay beyond their small planet. It was hard to explain the vastness of space to people who, until now, had never even left the protections of their tiny hamlets, to people who thought the vile Kedar and his men were from some remote section of their own world.

Timos would sit in on these sessions for he, too, had much to learn. But it was the teacher not the teachings that drew his interest. Although Eirriel seemed content with her role and the progress they were making, it wasn't until these times that Timos saw her come to life. Her brilliant green eyes would sparkle, her cheeks would flush, her voice would grow animated. Each person, place and event was described with an exuberance that made the listeners feel that they were there seeing the strange people and sights for themselves.

Timos found the transformation in her at once astounding and worrisome. He knew Eirriel too well to believe her denials. It was a person far from Dianthia who still held her thoughts and, more importantly, her soul.

Time moved rapidly, the only blemish on Timos's happiness his continued concern for Eirriel. She drove herself relentlessly from first light till dark, very often falling asleep in the middle of a sentence, her body so tired that she would not even wake when he carried her to her chambers and left Moriah to tuck her in.

By the time six months had passed, Eirriel and Timos had completely changed the Dianthians' way of life. The lessons had all been learned and an eager people waited to reap the benefits of their tedious labor.

The day before the election of the ten people to the Concilium of Taihum arrived it was decided that instead of making the long journey to their homes after they voted and then returning the next morning for the result of the vote, all the Dianthians would be given overnight provisions and temporary shelters. Eirriel and Timos supervised the preparations for their people. Huge tents were erected as protection from the weather, one tent allotted to each hamlet. Moriah and a group of women would use one tent for the preparing and dispensing of food.

Eirriel and Timos looked around and surveyed the progress. All was readied. The time was right. Tomorrow would be the vote.

Chapter Thirty-one

By first light on the day of the election all the men and women of Dianthia were lined up and the vote was under way. As previously planned, the votes would be counted by one member of each hamlet and the announcement made the next morning.

The votes counted, the results locked away, and the people settled, Eirriel and Timos sat down and relaxed, with pleased smiles on both their faces.

"Well, my friend," Eirriel said softly, "it was a long hard task but it's finally over. Tomorrow is the dawn of a new era for our people. One of peace, prosperity and happiness. I wish them all well." She rose and walked to the door. "Tomorrow you return to your dwelling. Thank you for your companionship and aid." A sob caught in her throat as she murmured, "I shall miss you," before fleeing to her chambers, leaving a very puzzled Dianthian staring after her.

A short time later, Timos, too, retired. Unable to sleep, he paced in his chamber. He knew what he wanted, but was hesitant to reach for it. During the past six months he had kept himself from her, not giving her any clue to the torment in his heart, of the fire that seared his body whenever he saw her.

He groaned, throwing himself on the sleeper. Didn't she know how she affected him? How he lay awake night after night, knowing she was asleep in the next chamber and knowing he could never go to her? Wanting to hold her, to touch her, to love her and knowing that he could not? His mind was a jumble of confused thoughts. Why was she so upset about him leaving if she felt nothing for him? Yet if she wanted him to stay, why did she remind him that he had to leave? He slammed his fists down in frustration. Leave be damned! He would go to her now, beg her if need be, to let him stay. For if he was to have any peace at all, he knew he must at least try.

His blue eyes blazing with determination, his jaw set, he hoisted himself from the sleeper and strode quickly from his chamber. At her door he hesitated. If she turned him away now, he would destroy any chance for the future. But in his soul he knew he had to try, for if he did not, it would be himself who was destroyed.

He pushed the door open. His breath caught in his throat. Eirriel stood before the reflector, brushing her long golden tresses. The hazy lavender glow of the chamber lights filtered through the translucent material of her short white sleeping gown, silhouetting the perfect curves that lay underneath. The floor-length reflector gave Timos an ample view of what otherwise would have been hidden. The garment, open to the waist, was held loosely closed by a solitary ribbon which prevented her full breasts from spilling completely into the opening with each stroke of her brush.

His gaze reached her face and he was startled to see the circlet, a constant reminder of her link with Aubin. Did she never take the damned thing off? Well, no matter. If she came to him now, it would be enough. He would worry about the circlet later.

Something alerted Eirriel to Timos's presence and she spun around. Searching his eyes for a clue to his appearance, she saw the all-too-familiar gleam of desire.

He pulled her against him. Almost against her will, her

hands came up and dug into his hair as she gave herself up to his demanding kiss. It was not the savage searing sensation that raged through her at Aubin's touch, but a gentle, pleasant tingling that felt undeniably good. Suddenly, she moved away from him. Timos looked at her, hurt and confused.

"I cannot! I must not!" she choked in an effort to dismiss the need that was rising in her. The need for arms to hold her, for hands to caress her, and for lips to murmur tender words of love in her ear.

Timos walked to her. He ran his hand slowly down her hair. Placing his hands gently on her shoulders, he turned her to him. His eyes studied the face of the woman he loved.

"I love you, Eirriel, enough for both of us, if need be. I won't press you for words of love, but won't you open your heart and give me a chance?"

Eirriel shook her head sadly. "It seems I am forever destined to cause you pain."

Timos released her as if her touch burnt his hands. "Why? Why did you let me kiss you if it didn't mean anything to you? I thought . . . Never mind what I thought."

Timos walked to the casement and stared out at the early-morning activity. Soon it would be time for the ceremony and he no longer felt like celebrating, the ache in his soul was too strong.

"You deserve a woman who can give herself wholly to you. I cannot. For good or evil, it is Aubin I love beyond all else. Maybe in time my love will change, but I doubt it. For each night, while I sleep, my soul cries out for want of him. Without him I am not whole."

Eirriel crossed to Timos and placed a hand on his slim shoulder. He shied away from her touch, and she laughed wistfully. "I seem to remember this happening once before. That time you sent me away. This time I'll go of my own accord."

Timos did not want to hear about the time by the pond. The memories and recriminations it brought to him were too painful and as a result he sought to hurt her in the only way he knew. "Go, then. I won't try to stop you." He laughed sardonically. "Not that I could."

Eirriel cringed at his reference to her power, but accepted

it for what it was, a way of striking back.

Timos took one last look at the woman he would always love, but could never have, as Eirriel turned and walked silently from the chamber.

A month had passed since Eirriel had left her dwelling and she was no closer to an answer now than she had been then. Why, after all the changes she had brought to Dianthia, was she unable to change herself? *Into what?* she wondered wearily. *Into someone who is content with life as it is,* she answered back, *and not someone who wastes time wishing for things that can never be again.*

She climbed from the water to a flat rock just above the pool's edge. Grabbing the large cloth she had warming in the suns, she absently dried herself.

All must be well in Edlyn, she mused, since she had heard nothing since her arrival at her secret cove. As always, Moriah was following her orders perfectly. And Eirriel knew Moriah would continue to see that no one discovered her whereabouts, especially Timos.

But if they should need her. . . . No, they wouldn't. Timos was Chief Concile now. He was the one they needed.

A pained look flashed across her face as she thought of her old friend. He would have his work to keep him busy until his pain lessened. *And what do I have?* she thought bitterly. *Nothing but time to think.* She ran her fingers through her curls and shook her head. *That is what you wanted,* she reminded herself sternly. True, she admitted reluctantly, but, by the gods, it was so damned lonely.

Removing the towel, she lay back and spread her hair about her. The hot suns beat down on her, warming her on the outside, but having no effect on the aching chill that had long since settled in her heart.

What was wrong with her? Why was she suddenly wishing for company? Her fingers ran lightly across the ever-present circlet. No, it wasn't just company she wanted. Her brilliant green eyes looked skyward and her mind cried out for her lost love. *Aubin, my bronze giant, where are you? Are you happy? Do you think of me with other than hate in your heart?*

She closed her eyes and pressed her fingers tightly to them as she found herself besieged by unwanted images of Chalandra.

"I will make you forget," Chalandra murmured huskily. She ran her hands up her long legs, passed the softness of her womanhood, over her smooth abdomen, to her full, voluptuous breasts. Her hips writhed seductively. Her tongue darted out, flicking across her parted, sensuous mouth. Her eyes glassy with desire, she beckoned again to the tall shape hidden in the shadows. Her deep throaty laugh filled the air. "She has left you for another. Come to me, my wild rutting stallion. Chalandra will make you forget."

With a groan, the man fell on her. Eirriel gasped as the light reflected off his broad, bronzed shoulders and curly, golden hair. Chalandra laughed again. This time it was a laugh of victory as she wrapped her arms and legs about him. Her hips moved upward to meet and match each penetrating thrust of her lover.

Eirriel watched in horror. *No!* she cried silently. *It can't be Aubin. It must be some other Rhianonian! Please, don't let it be Aubin!*

The couple's rhythm became faster and faster. Reaching the summit of their ecstacy, they collapsed and lay motionless. Chalandra looked into the face of her lover and asked in her low throaty voice, "Who is your love now, my magnificent lover? Eirriel?"

The golden head raised itself higher and matched her stare. "Eirriel?" Aubin replied, his voice still husky with passion. "I know no one by that name."

"No!" Eirriel screamed in anguish, her cry echoing in the stillness, setting the various birdlife to frantic flight. "Do you forget me so soon, my love?"

She jumped up and tore through the lush undergrowth. Tears poured from her eyes. *Aubin, my love, my life, I am nothing without you!* She ran up the rocky ledge to the small cave behind the waterfall that served as her shelter and threw herself onto the small sleeper. She cried for Aubin, for Timos, and, for the first time since she left her dwelling, she cried for herself and her wasted life.

After a while, her tears spent, she fell into a deep slumber, her slim shoulders still shuddering with silent sobs. A short time later she woke suddenly, startled by an overwhelming feeling of being watched.

"Who's there?" she asked fearfully, sitting up.

Her eyes searched the darkness and she shivered as the chilling dampness reached her bones. Deciding it was the cold that had roused her, she pulled a covering over her nakedness and lay back down. Still sleepy, her eyes closed. Soon the cave was filled with her soft rhythmic breathing.

A tall shape rose from the shadows and knelt over Eirriel. Hard lips touched hers, gently at first, then with increasing pressure.

Eirriel's eyes opened and she struggled, pushing against her attacker's broad shoulders. Yet, even in her panicked state, the feel of his lean muscular back felt somehow familiar. As did the touch of his closed mind.

Aubin!

She ran her hands up his back to his hair and her struggles ceased. She pulled him down to her, returning his kiss with all the passion of a reunited lover. Her tongue met his hungrily.

Abruptly, he pulled away. "Well met, my love."

In her joy, Eirriel missed the underlying edge of steel in those softly spoken words.

"If I didn't know better, I would believe you actually missed me."

Eirriel watched as Aubin rose to his feet and her happiness fled. Something wasn't right. He seemed angry. But if he had not forgiven her, why was he here? She cursed her mixed blood. If she were a pure Kiiryan, she would know the answer. Immediately she was sorry for the thought. Her father had been a wonderful part of her life and she had loved him dearly.

In spite of her foreboding, she watched greedily as Aubin crossed to the niche at the opposite side of the cave and knelt to light the fire.

Aubin's short sardonic laugh echoed off the stone walls. "I'd forgotten what a passionate wench you are, my sweet."

His words confused her. Why couldn't she get a sense of
[h]im? Why was she nervous when she should have been
[e]cstatic?

"How did you find me?"

"It was suddenly very important that I locate you. I had
[h]elp."

"Why was it important now, after all this time?" *Please
[te]ll me it's because you missed me. That you understand and
[h]ave forgiven me.*

But he didn't say what she so desperately craved. Instead,
[in] the same cold precise voice, he said, "My father is ill, and
[I] am needed at home."

"Oh." Such a bland little word when her heart was
[b]reaking. Perhaps he was waiting for her to make the first
[m]ove. After all, he was a Rhianonian with all their pride
[an]d arrogance and she had left him.

She moved toward him. "I'm sorry about your father. I
[k]now how dearly you love him." She reached up and put
[h]er arms around him. "I have missed you—"

She stopped as eyes of glittering golden ice bore down on
[h]er. Reaching up, Aubin grabbed her wrists and pushed
[th]em away from him.

Eirriel stepped back and stared at him as waves of
[lo]athing assailed her. She backed away until she felt the cold
[w]alls of the cave against her skin.

"Please. What's wrong? What have I done?" Her trem-
[bl]ing voice reflected her fear of the man who used to love
[h]er.

"What have you done?" he repeated increduously. He
[la]ughed, a hard, mocking laugh. "You played the game well,
[m]y lovely Dianthian," he said, his voice dangerously soft.
"[I] actually thought you loved me. What's worse, I let my
[d]efenses down. I fell in love with you." He snorted with
[se]lf-contempt. "Fool that I was, I trusted you as I had never
[tr]usted another woman. I should have realized you were
[m]erely killing time." His lips twisted in a cruel sneer.
"[W]hy, as you so sweetly put it, should you be content with a
[m]ere fleetship captain who also happened to be a
[R]hianonian?"

"You can't believe I meant those words!" she cried, her
[fa]ce pale.

"What would you have me believe?" he demanded, his eyes growing dark with rage. "Why else would you run away with my enemy? You had me convinced you hated Kedar, that he tried to force himself on you. Yet you called him your old lover. Old lover! Hah! How you two must have laughed at the poor gullible fool."

"No! We didn't! He wasn't my lover!"

"You deny he took you to his restorer?"

She lowered her eyes in shame. Her voice a pained whisper, she said the words she knew would condemn her. "No, I can't deny that." With a sob of despair, she went to him. "Please, listen to me!" she cried desperately. "It's not what you think! I had no choice! He would have killed you! Destroyed my people, my world! I couldn't let that happen!"

"Always the noble martyr," he jeered.

"If that's what you believe, then why are you here?"

"To get my revenge. Only it seems someone beat me to it. At least half of it," he added menancingly. "Kedar may be out of my reach, but you're not."

He grabbed her and pulled her to him. His mouth swooped down on hers and Eirriel pushed him away.

"Please! Not like this. Not in hate!"

His eyes glittered in the firelight. "Why not? That's all there can ever be between us now. You saw to that."

"Please, you must listen . . ."

"Aubin?"

Eirriel's head shot up as Chalandra's voice reached her. "Aubin, where are you?"

"Go back and wait, Chalandra," Aubin called over his shoulder. "What I have to do won't take much longer."

Chalandra's throaty laughter echoed in the cove. "Do hurry, lover. I grow bored."

Eirriel felt her soul wither and die. He had brought Chalandra. He never meant to stay. She raised her luminous green eyes to him. "Why, Aubin? Why did you bring her here?"

"Why not? For all her faults, at least she's never betrayed me."

"And what she did to me doesn't matter?"

"Should it?"

She laughed bitterly. "Apparently not. Since your mind is set against me, there's no reason for you to stay. Go, your lover awaits."

"There's every reason to stay," Aubin countered. His hand shot out and captured her wrists. With a savage yank he tossed her onto the sleeper.

"That's where you belong, my sweet! Lying naked, with your legs spread, waiting patiently for the next man who comes along."

Eirriel attempted to get up from the sleeper, but Aubin, anticipating her action, was on her even before her feet touched the ground. Pinning her beneath him, he easily imprisoned her thrashing arms with one large hand. With the other, he caressed her breasts, his achingly familiar touch evoking a response she desperately sought to deny. Twisting frantically, she tried to free herself. Oblivious to her tears of rage and hurt, she opened her mouth to hurl protests at him, but Aubin seized the moment and slammed his mouth down on hers, his tongue plundering what it once had savored. Unable to let him take what, until now, had been freely given, and hating herself for what she had to do, Eirriel closed her eyes.

Aubin shook his head and lifted himself from the cold, damp floor of the cave. He glared at her with a mixture of hate and awe.

"So you've finally come into your own," he sneered. Nodding his head slightly, he added, "Congratulations, my dear."

He watched Eirriel rise from the sleeper. His eyes narrowed and he frowned as a niggling suspicion formed and took life.

"Kedar! *You* killed him!"

Alerted by her visible start, Aubin knew he had inadvertently stumbled upon the incredible truth behind Kedar's demise. To mask his astonishment, he demanded snidely, "What happened, my sweet? Did you tire of him in your restorer?"

But Eirriel had neither seen the flicker of amazement in his golden eyes nor had she heard his sneering question. His abusive taunts and despicable actions had already strained her tautly leashed control to the breaking point, and the mere mention of her tormentor's name, even after so long, proved too much. Her fragile rein snapped and loosened within her a violent maelstrom of conflicting emotions.

Hate, love, pride, passion, self-pity, sorrow, remorse and shame all warred for supremacy. Her eyes closed against the ache that tore at her soul, and heedless of her long nails biting into her tender palms, she clenched her fists tighter and tighter as she fought against them all—and lost. Helplessly she tumbled into the bottomless abyss of despondency. As she plunged through the chilling blackness, she unknowingly reached out.

Aubin's head was jolted back by the force of Eirriel's thoughts. Blood thundered in his ears and his breath came in ragged gasps as he "watched" Kedar's savage attack on the woman he had once loved. His blinding rage demanded satisfaction and was far from assuaged when he "witnessed" his longtime enemy's brutal demise. An agony the like of which he had never dreamed possible pierced his heart and rent his soul in two as he "saw" the costly consequence of Kedar's frenzied attack. His anguished cry of denial shattered the silence.

"By all the gods, no!"

His eyes dark with grief for the child he would never have, Aubin shook his head. "I didn't know. I'm sorry."

But it was too late. His earlier words formed by the cancerous hatred that had ravaged his body since that fateful day on Annan had done irreparable damage.

She laughed bitterly. "Are you?"

"Of course." He moved toward her.

"Don't come any closer," she warned. "I don't think I could bear your touch." She laughed again, a sharp bitter sound so unlike the lilting one that had delighted him so long ago. "There was a time when I craved your touch, ached for it, but no longer."

"I loved you," she said, her voice hoarse with emotion. "I loved you enough to condemn myself to a life of debauchery, to offer myself to a man whose mere presence made my skin crawl. I went with him freely, knowing you would hate me, but knowing I had no choice." Her eyes blank, her voice empty, her spirit gone, she spoke as if he wasn't there. "The things he wanted from me and the brutal abuse he inflicted on me I suffered. But I survived because I knew the man I loved with all my heart, my soul, with every breath of my body was alive and free and would continue to be so as long as I behaved myself. But I did have one small victory. Kedar never had me. Never made love to me. I made sure of that."

Drawn by a need he could neither deny nor understand, a need to take her in his arms and kiss away all the pain that had been forced on her because of him, a need that broke through the shell of hate that had surrounded his heart for so long, Aubin moved forward.

"Don't!" she cried. "Haven't you done enough already?"

The truth of her words stopped him and he lowered the arms that had begun to reach out for her. His grim eyes followed Eirriel as she snatched up a caftan and slipped it on.

"I don't want to hurt you, Aubin, but neither do I want to see you again." She walked passed him to the mouth of the cave. Without turning, she said, "Please be gone when I return."

Eirriel ran down the stone stairs, yanking off the circlet as she did. She stopped when she saw Chalandra and threw it at her feet. "I believe this belongs to you now."

Chalandra stared after her in disbelief as Eirriel ran into the brush and disappeared. As if she thought it might disappear, Chalandra snatched up the circlet and placed it on her head, then left to find Aubin.

Aubin stared after Eirriel, torn between his heart and his pride, until Chalandra entered and embraced him, until he felt the chill of metal across her forehead as he pressed her face against his neck.

He shoved her away. "Where did you get that?" he demanded.

"What? Oh, this?" She laughed as she touched the circlet, then tossed her head in the direction she had just come from. "*She* gave it to me. Said you would want me to have it now." She studied his face. "Does it mean she's out of your life forever?"

Aubin's eyes darkened with pain and he nodded. Pushing the emblem on his shirt, he ordered the teleport to transport them back to the ship.

Chapter Thirty-two

"Did you see Eirriel?" Garreth asked anxiously, entering Aubin's cubicle. "Will she come back?"

"She won't be back."

Garreth stopped in mid-stride, so taken aback that Chalandra was still on the *Celestial*, let alone in Aubin's cubicle and lying on his restorer, that her words did not penetrate his stunned mind. He watched in mounting fury as she rose seductively from the restorer and crossed to Aubin, placing her hands possessively on his chest. She turned and faced Garreth, a smug smile of triumph curling her full lips.

Then he saw the circlet and her words slammed home. His eyes darkened and he clenched his fists at his side. "You, Captain, are a fool," he snapped, then turned and left the cubicle.

Muttering under his breath, Garreth strode into his cubicle and directly to the table across from the portal where he snatched up a cruet of brew and splashed some into a beaker. He raised it to his lips, but found himself too choked with anger to drink it. Instead, he used it to vent his rage and hurled it against the wall.

The sound of the shattering crystal woke the napping Raissa.

"What the—" She stopped as her startled gaze flew from the dripping golden liquid to the stormy golden eyes of her life-bonded mate and the furious set of his jaw. "What's wrong?"

"He's a damned fool, that's what!" he shouted as he paced about the cubicle. "Do you know what that bastard's done? He's sent Eirriel away and kept that lying, deceitful whore! Not only that, but that bitch now wears the Syna Circlet!"

"What!" Riassa shrieked. Her cheeks flushed and her eyes turned a dark brown. "She's wearing what?"

"You heard me!" he snapped.

"This has gone far enough!" Raissa stalked toward the portal.

"Where are you going?"

"To settle this mess once and for all! Are you coming?"

Garreth grinned. "I wouldn't miss it!"

"Wait!" Raissa re-entered their cubicle and crossed to the intercom. "Raissa to safeguard unit."

"Lebron here."

"Lebron, I think the time has come for our purple-skinned "visitor" to depart."

"Does the captain know?"

"Not yet."

"I'll be right there." Raissa could hear the delight in the officer's voice. "Lebron out."

Garreth shook his head. "I hope you know what you're doing, my love."

A flicker of doubt passed through Raissa's eyes, and she sighed. "I hope so." Her voice then grew firm with conviction. "But Eirriel's my friend as is Aubin, and I can't stand by and watch him destroy himself any longer."

Garreth and Raissa burst into Aubin's cubicle unannounced. Raissa's eyes glittered dangerously as she saw the partially clad couple entwined on the restorer. She walked to it and yanked Chalandra out of Aubin's arms. Snatching up the Arvadian's tunic, she threw it at her.

"Get dressed and get out!" Raissa ordered in a voice that brooked no defiance.

Chalandra tossed her head arrogantly. "Does your staff give orders now, my captain?"

"Not staff, friends!" Raissa retorted.

Chalandra started to protest but Aubin interrupted. "Sit down, Chalandra," Aubin snapped. "Go on, Raissa. You obviously want to talk with me."

"I prefer to do it in private." Her lips curled contemptuously. "What I have to say is not meant for the ears of the coniving, deceitful, underhanded, daughter of a Blagdenian whore who has tricked herself into your life again!"

"Why you bitch!"

Chalandra flung herself from the chair and lunged at Raissa. Momentarily stunned by the suddeness of the fierce attack, the Melonnian found herself on the floor with a one hundred five-pound gypsy on her chest.

"I'll scratch your eyes out, you—" Chalandra let out a string of Arvadian curses.

A smug smile tugged at the corner of Raissa's mouth as she said softly, "I doubt that."

Arching her back, Raissa tossed her assailant off. Springing to her feet, she turned to see that Chalandra had managed to land upright and was ready to continue the fight. Before she could, Aubin threw himself between the two spitting females.

"Enough!" he bellowed. "Chalandra, wait for me outside. I will hear what Raissa has to say."

Chalandra's silver eyes flashed angrily as she stalked from the cubicle. The moment the portal closed behind her, she found herself in Lebron's tight grip.

"You're to come with me," the safeguard officer growled. Without further ado, he escorted her to the teleport where her belongings waited. "You're to leave the ship now, Chalandra. Don't try to contact the captain because you won't succeed. And neither will you be allowed to return, so don't even bother to try."

"You can't do this!"

"Oh, no?" Lebron asked softly.

"I'll be back," she vowed. "And when I do—"

Lebron's amused chuckle cut into her angry tirade. "Don't count on it."

"Teleport's ready," the tech reported.

"Thank you, Kan." He motioned to the inner chamber. "Shall we, my dear?"

Realizing she had no choice, she started to push past Lebron but was stopped by a restraining hand on her shoulder.

"A moment. I believe you have something that belongs to the captain?"

A few seconds passed before the light of realization lit her silver eyes. Ripping the circlet from her forehead, she flung it at him. Without a word, she tossed her head, snatched up her belongings, and entered the teleport. A pleased grin settled on Lebron's face as she disappeared in a brilliant flash of light.

Aubin drew on a shirt, then stiffly walked to the table and poured himself a drink.

"Well, Raissa, what is so important that you had to disturb my period of relaxation?"

Raissa whirled and faced him. "You are! Have you looked at yourself lately? I mean really looked? Your face is creased in a permanent frown. You never smile, never laugh anymore. You're moody and angry. You snap at the crew for no reason. Always demanding, never asking. When you're off duty, you spend your time locked in your cubicle either drinking or whoring!"

"What I do is of no concern of yours, Raissa. My time and my reasons are my own." His eyes glinted menacingly. "Unless, of course, you and Garreth think I'm neglecting my duties."

"You know we don't, Aubin," Garreth said gravely. "That's the only facet of your life that has remained untainted."

"Aubin, you're our friend. It tears us apart to see you like this. Chalandra will destroy you."

For one brief moment, Raissa and Garreth were given a glimpse of the torment and confusion that warred within Aubin as he said softly, "Chalandra isn't the one who betrayed me, Rai. Now, if you don't mind, I'm really not in the mood for lectures so unless you've something else to say,

I want you to leave."

Garreth decided to try a different approach to reach hi
friend. Helping himself to a beaker of brew, he sat dowr
"All right, Aubin. No more lectures. Perhaps you'd b
interested in hearing what we learned on Dianthia?"

Aubin arched his brow in surprise. "You went t
Dianthia?"

"Yes," Raissa answered, quickly understanding her lov
er's ploy. "Once Lebron reported that there were no signs c
the Blagdenians, I went down to study their culture firs
hand. Garreth accompanied me. Since you were ther
already looking for Eirriel, I didn't think you'd object."

"No, of course not."

"We teleported to Edlyn and talked with the new ruler.

"The Chief Concile wasn't too friendly until we told hir
we were Eirriel's friends and I convinced him I wasn't you.
Garreth's lips twisted wryly. "Apparently he has no grea
love for you, Aubin. But that's Rai's story, mine is Keda
and the changes on Dianthia since his death."

"I know he's dead, and I know who killed him," Aubi
said harshly. At their obvious curiosity, he explained curtly
"I was sure the Blagdenian bastard would have made Edly
his base so I teleported directly there. When I found n
signs of him or his company of murderers, I began to as
questions. All the Dianthians would tell me was that he wa
dead and that Eirriel had suddenly gone into seclusion si
months after his death. When no one would tell me where,
returned to the *Celestial* and used the questors to loca
her."

"The link between the circlets?" Garreth asked.

Aubin nodded.

Raissa's eyes narrowed and she said slyly, "You *knew* sh
still had it."

Yes, he knew. He had fought against his desire to handl
his circlet and had won, until a month ago. With a will o
their own, his hands had searched for it among his cloth
and he had been surprised by its blazing warmth. A warmt
that could only mean one thing—that the other circlet wa
still being worn by the woman he had once loved. Had sh
destroyed hers, his would have been destroyed as well. Ha

she cast hers aside, his would have felt as any other metal. And if hers was worn by another, his would have the bite of the deepest winter. His hate had been too strong, to question why she still had worn her circlet and he had dropped his as if it had burned his fingers and had never touched it since. But, yes, he knew.

Unwilling to explain all that to his misguided, but well-meaning, friends, Aubin merely shrugged. "It was a chance."

Firm in her belief that it had been anything but chance, Raissa let the subject drop as did Garreth. Instead he asked, "Did she tell you Kedar brought her to Dianthia directly from Annan?"

"We had more to discuss than her leisurely romp through space," Aubin snapped.

Ignoring his caustic remark, Garreth repeated what he had learned from Timos of Eirriel's return and her life with Kedar, little knowing that Aubin was all to aware of what Eirriel's fate had been or that locked deep in his heart was the bitter ache for the child he would never hold.

"After his death, Timos and Eirriel completely restored their world. They reorganized the government, modernized their growing system and re-educated their people. All in six months, Aubin! Incredible! And from what Timos said Eirriel was the compelling force."

"He's a very bitter man where you are concerned," Raissa said. "It appears he loved her since before the invasion. He thought her dead only to see her return as his enemy's consort. He saw Kedar dead and thought her his at last only to learn she wanted you and no other.

"She gave up everything because of you! The people had elected her Chief Concile but she declined. She left her home and her friends to try and get you out of her system. Timos hasn't heard from her since she left a month ago so all he can do is assume she still loves you. And you come back without her, tied to a woman I wouldn't wish on a Blagdenian! I hope you're happy!"

Raissa turned and left, Garreth following silently behind her.

"Do you think he listened?"

"I don't know, Garreth. Since Chalandra's no longer around to distract him maybe he'll finally do a little soul-searching. I only hope it's not too late."

Long after his friends had departed, Aubin sat staring into space. Slowly he sipped another throat-searing blend of marnax, as his mind remembered a green-eyed temptress and the love they had once shared.

What a mess his life had become since Annan!

By the time the ruin Kedar and his Blagdenians had made of Annan and several other Protectorate holdings had been corrected and the *Celestial* was once again free to continue her usual patrol, nearly six months had passed. Two and a half months later, Aubin had received word that his father had been seriously injured in a riding accident and he was needed at home.

He had immediately checked the state of affairs with his father's chief advisor and had learned that his father was recovering, albeit very slowly, and that he had several months leeway before conditions on Rhianon became critical.

He had been relieved. There would be enough time to fulfill his vow of vengeance.

His offer of a large reward for information on Kedar and a small world known as Dianthia had quickly reached Chalandra's ears. Pulling from her many sources, the Arvadian had soon learned the exact location of the Blagdenian commodore. Armed with the desired information and a convincing tale of woe, Chalandra had come to Aubin. His heart filled with hate and his mind set on a course of revenge, Aubin had readily believed the cunning accusations of Balthasar's control over her and had welcomed Chalandra against the advice of his close friends. Shortly after her arrival, the crew of the *Celestial* had found themselves on the way to the little known star system of Zimmeron IV.

During the weeks it had taken them to reach the distant Dianthia, Raissa, Garreth and Cian had all tried to convince Aubin of Eirriel's faithfulness. Each had argued of the love that had made her risk the mission to Annan and had insisted that she had given several clues to her plight in her brief conversations with both Garreth and Aubin. Shying away from the painful memories of his last encounter with Eirriel, Aubin had closed his mind to everything except Chalandra's carefully worded insinuations. Under her careful tutelage, his hate had grown until it became a festering wound that ate endlessly at his soul, obliterating all else.

Aubin dragged himself to his feet and crossed to the table. Automatically he refilled his beaker, downed the fiery liquid and again replenished the empty container. He paced about the cubicle as he remembered the sweet taste of Eirriel's lips and the happiness in her eyes when she had seen him again. After a few cutting remarks from him, the sparkling green eyes that had haunted his dreams for so long had grown dull and lifeless. Her soft lilting voice had changed to a pained whisper and her proud regal bearing had wilted. He shook his head in disgust as he heard Cian chiding him about his ability to break her spirit.

"Tells you something if you care to hear it," he'd said.

Did it still tell him something? Did it mean, as Raissa and Garreth claimed, that she still loved him? Had never stopped loving him? But she had left him for the arms of another! his heart cried out. Or had she? She told him she and Kedar had never made love, that she had kept him from having her. He shuddered though as, once again, he saw and felt what she felt when Kedar just touched her. She had not felt love. Love had filled her belly with his son. A son he could never hold, never love, he thought bitterly. She did that. And Kedar. If she had stayed with Aubin, their child would be alive.

Aubin hurled the beaker into a darkened corner as he roared his frustration, his anger, his confusion. Trapped by the divergent memories that besieged him from every direction, he left the cubicle, following whatever path his feet decreed.

In the passageway he encountered Lebron. Wordlessly the safeguard officer placed the retrieved circlet in Aubin's hand. Aubin glanced at it and nodded his thanks. So, Chalandra was gone, he mused, then sighed with relief. At least he didn't have to deal with sending her away. His lips curled in a slight smile as he realized he had been planning on sending her packing. That should tell him something, shouldn't it?

Holding the circlet in his fist, he continued his wanderings, all images of Chalandra banished forever from his mind. It came as quite a surprise to him to find himself standing in front of the tiny Kiiryan vessel that had carried Eirriel into his life—and into his heart.

Compelled by a force he could not control, he entered it and made his way to the cubicle he had rescued Eirriel from those many months ago.

Memories assaulted him from every side. He pressed the hidden button. As he dropped into a chair, Sidra's voice began to speak.

"To the tall giant at Eirriel's side."

Aubin stared at the screen, visibly shaken. What quirk of fate made the recording begin at the very point that pertained to him? Realizing he would never know, he forced the question aside and concentrated on the Kiiryan's message.

"My friend, I entrust my daughter's happiness to you. Before you there lies a great blackness. Do not lose faith in my daughter, her love will never falter. I see in front of you the end of a search and the beginning of a new life. As I said to Eirriel, I now say to you, always trust in love.

"Farewell."

Absently Aubin fingered the circlet. Suddenly aware of what he held, he raised the golden chain up before his eyes. As clearly as if she stood before him, Eirriel's voice, filled with all the tenderness, love and promise it had held, came back to him.

"What I have I give to you. My heart, my life, my soul I place in your hands willingly and with trust. My love is yours now and throughout eternity."

Aubin sprang to his feet, a light burning deep within his eyes, and, for the first time in agonizing months, his heart was free from the festering hatred that had torn at it. He knew what he had to do. Slipping the circlet into his pocket, he bolted from the cubicle, fervently praying that he wasn't too late.

* * *

Her heart heavy with loss, Eirriel lay for a while, not moving, not thinking, until she heard Onyx neighing. She got up from the sleeper and quickly dressed in her red riding skirt and white blouse. Grabbing the brush, she gave her hair a few short strokes, tied it back with a red ribbon, then hurried from the cave. She would be able to think more clearly after a ride, she always could.

Excited by the prospect of flying Onyx, she ran hastily down the rocky ledge without paying attention to where her feet landed. She never saw the small uprooted tree that had blown across the steps until it was too late. Frantically she jumped over the obstacle. Her skirt was snagged by one of the branches and she lost her balance. Her screams echoing through the cove, she fell. The last thing she felt was the searing pain that shot through her head as it struck the stone stairway. Blackness overcame her. She tumbled down the incline, the jagged edges of the rocks cutting her arms and legs. At the bottom of the steep slope her rolling motion was halted by the prickly thick branches of the candrax.

"Where is she?"

Timos looked up to see a tall, bronze stranger storming into his receiving chamber. Timos's calm, blue eyes searched the blazing golden ones in front of him and he knew at once that the man was none other than Aubin. Anger and hatred coursed through him at the sight of the man who had stolen Eirriel from him.

"Well, where is she?" Aubin demanded again.

"Where is who?" Timos asked, painfully aware of whom Aubin was seeking.

"Eirriel!"

"I should think you of all people should know where to find her," Timos spat bitterly.

"She's not at the cave," Aubin snapped. "I want to know where she is!"

"Don't worry. She'll return. That's where she lives now. Away from those of us who love her. Alone. With her dreams. She'll return."

Aubin shook his head grimly. "I don't think so."

"Why not?"

"Just a hunch."

Timos caught the look of uncertainty that flickered i
Aubin's eyes before he concealed it.

"What's wrong? There's something you're not saying
Didn't you see her earlier while your two friends kept m
busy?"

"Yeah, I saw her. We had a slight misunderstanding.
came back to clear it up."

"Slight misunderstanding!" Timos abruptly got out of th
chair. "Don't you realize that where you are concerne
there can be no slight misunderstandings? Moriah!" Timo
shouted, walking to the door.

"Timos? What's wrong?" Moriah asked as she hurrie
into the chamber.

"Has Eirriel been here?"

Moriah frowned. "Not since she left. Why?"

"Because she's not at the cave where *he* left her." H
threw a look of disgust at Aubin.

The older woman stepped back, startled. She hadn
noticed the stranger when she arrived. Her eyes narrowe
"You're Aubin, aren't you?"

Aubin nodded. "Moriah, where would she go if she wer
upset?"

"When she's upset, she usually rides Onyx. But why d
you ask? If you've come back for her, she had no reason t
be upset."

"I didn't come back for Eirriel," Aubin said bitterly. "
came back to kill Kedar. I had no intention of ever seein
her again."

"Did you tell her that?" Timos asked through clenche
teeth.

Aubin nodded curtly.

"You bastard!"

Timos hurled himself at Aubin, and both men tumbled t
the floor. Timos punched Aubin in the stomach.

"She loves you! How could you hurt her?"

Aubin's right hand caught Timos in the ribs and sent hir
flying across the chamber. Staggering to his feet, Timo
railed at Aubin. "I would have given her anything, but a
she ever wanted was you!"

The Dianthian brought his left fist up and it connected soundly with Aubin's jaw. He swung with his right, but Aubin blocked it and delivered a solid blow to Timos's midsection.

"I don't give a damn what you offered her, you bastard!" Aubin roared, his voice cold with rage. "All I want to know is where the hell she is!"

The two men circled each other. Aubin was taller, broader than Timos, but Timos's hatred fed his strength. They were so wrapped up in their fight that they didn't hear the commotion outside. It wasn't until a very pale Moriah stepped between them, begging them to listen that they stopped.

"It's Onyx. He's outside! Riderless!" The old woman twisted her hands in worry. "Something's happened to Eirriel!"

The two men rushed outside. Onyx was rearing high on his hind legs, his powerful forelegs wildly thrashing the air.

"Cadan, fetch the other estalon," Timos ordered. "And hurry!"

Aubin, however, had other ideas. Grabbing Onyx's mane, he threw himself on the rearing stallion's back. Onyx bucked, protesting the unwanted, unfamiliar burden. Clutching the long mane in both hands, Aubin spoke gently, but urgently. "Easy, boy. Easy. We both want the same thing. Easy now. Take me to your mistress. Take me to Eirriel!"

At the mention of Eirriel's name, Onyx lunged forward. His hoofs tore at the ground as he built up speed. Spreading his massive wings, he took a mighty leap and climbed into the sky. Aubin looked over his shoulder and cursed aloud. Timos was below him on his own estalon. Soon he would be directly behind them.

"Faster, Onyx! Faster!" he said desperately.

He had to reach Eirriel before Timos did or he knew he would never see her again. Timos would hide her and she'd never know that he came back.

He had teleported to Eirriel's hideaway, determined to take her with him. He had hoped that once he had her alone he could convince her that he still loved her. That, in truth,

he had never stopped loving her. That Chalandra mean
nothing to him, never had.

He refused to believe she could not forgive him or tha
she would not take him back. His mind refused to deal witl
the possibility of living his life without her.

When he had arrived at the cave and found it empty, he'
been frantic, fearful that he'd driven her back to the waitin
arms of the Dianthian ruler. Raging, ready to kill to get he
back, he had teleported to Edlyn to fight.

His heart had pounded violently when he saw the massiv
estalon riderless because he knew Onyx would never hav
left Eirriel unless she were badly in need of help.

Sweat beaded on his brow at the thought of his green-eye
vixen being hurt—again. *Oh, my love*, he silently promise
Eirriel, *I vow by all that is holy, you will never know sadnes
and pain again.*

Onyx whinnied, the sound drawing Aubin from hi
thoughts. They were over the cove, and he searched th
ground for some signs of the woman he loved. His hear
twisted as he spied her crumpled form partially hidden b
the dense foliage.

By the gods! What had happened? Why was she so still
His mind shouted denials at the horrifying thought tha
crept unbidden into his mind. *No! She can't be dead! I won
lose her just when I've found her again!*

Onyx landed near his motionless mistress and Aubi
leaped from his back and knelt before her. Cringing at th
cuts and scrapes on her face and arms, he searched franti
cally for a pulse. Yes! There it was. Weak, but at least sh
was alive! Running his hand over her, he checked for broke
bones. He sighed in relief. There were none. He pressed th
conversor.

"Aubin to the *Celestial*."

"Garreth here."

"Garreth, tell Cian to meet me in the teleport right now,"
Aubin's voice was gruff with concern.

"Where are you? What's wrong?"

"Dianthia," he replied brusquely. "Eirriel's been hurt."

"How?"

"I'll explain later, Garreth. Right now the importan

ing is that she receive treatment."

He was so intent on the conversation that he had failed to
e the smaller estalon land behind him. Nor had he seen
imos hurl himself from his mount nor heard the sharp
ntake of breath as the younger man heard Aubin order the
eleport to stand by.

Aubin placed his hands gently under Eirriel and lifted her
s easily as if she were a child. As he settled her in his arms,
er head rolled toward his chest. The blood drained from
is face at the sight of her bloody, matted hair.

"Aubin to *Celestial,*" he said hoarsely. "Activate the—"

"You're not taking her anywhere!" Timos said through
eth clenched in rage. Stepping toward Aubin, he grabbed
is shoulder and spun him around. His blue eyes widened
ith shock. "Give her to me!"

"What?"

"You heard me! Eirriel's coming back to Edlyn with me.
oriah and I will care for her."

"Are you crazy? Can't you see how badly she's been
urt?"

"Yes, I can see!" Timos snapped. "But you're not taking
er anywhere. You lost that right when you walked away
om her." His lips drew back in rage as he said, "You did
is to her as surely as if you pushed her yourself! Now give
er to me!"

Aubin stared at the man before him, wishing desperately
at his hands were free. His golden eyes glittered with fury.
a voice as quiet as death, he said, "She's mine and what's
ine I keep!"

"I challenge your right to keep her!" Timos roared.

Aubin shook his head in disgust. "I know your pride is
jured because I have what you want, but I won't waste any
ore precious time fighting with you. Eirriel needs help.
elp that is only available on my ship."

Timos's mind whirled, his thoughts unknowingly travel-
g the same path as his rival's had minutes before. He knew
e would never see Eirriel again once she was on Aubin's
ip. His intense blue eyes studied the limp form of the
oman he loved. It was obvious that she was critically
jured. As much as it galled Timos to admit it, the

Rhianonian was right. There was nothing he or Moria
could do for her. He hung his head in defeat. He would ne
stand in her way.

"Au–Aubin?" Eirriel's voice was a ragged whisper. "Is
really you?"

"Yes, my love," he replied tenderly, his voice and eye
filled with love. "It's really me."

She grimaced and her eyes closed as a sharp pain seare
through her head.

"Eirriel!" Aubin called frantically. "Eirriel, you've got t
stay awake!"

She forced her pain-dulled eyes open. "You . . . you cam
back."

"Yes, little one. I came back. Did you think I'd let yo
walk out of my life now that I'd found you again? I love you
Eirriel," he said, his voice hoarse with raw emotion. "
always have. I always will. We were meant to be, you and I.

"But what . . ."

"Sh. Don't talk. There's no hurry now, my love. We hav
all the time in the world."

Eirriel brought her hand up and tenderly caressed th
face of the man she never thought to see again.

"That we have, my love," she replied huskily. "That w
have."

Timos closed his eyes as a brilliant flash of light illum
nated the cove. When he opened them again, Aubin an
Eirriel had vanished. Bidding Onyx to follow, Timo
mounted his estalon, and, raising his hand in silent farewe
to his lost love, started back to Edlyn.